GENTLENESS
AT THE DISMAL RIVER

LLOYD WARNER

THE COZY BOOK CLUB

One of the first ladies to read the unpublished manuscript of my first book, Faith at the Dismal River, defined it as being 'cozy.' And so, it has been my intention that each book in the Fruit of the Spirit series be considered as such. If you are considering reading this book, but have not read the first in the series, which is Faith at the Dismal River, I strongly urge you to read that book first, as it holds the key to the early life of Miss Laura Martin throughout the rest of the series.

The Dismal River Series is available for purchase at
www.lloydwarner.com

The Fruit of the Spirit series consist of the following books:

Book I   Faith at the Dismal River (Published June, 2011)
Book II   Joy at the Dismal River (Published March, 2012)
Book III   Peace at the Dismal River (Published October, 2012)
Book IV   Goodness at the Dismal River (Published March, 2013)
Book V   Love at the Dismal River (Published July, 2013)
Book VI   Gentleness at the Dismal River (Published October 2013)
Book VII   Meekness at the Dismal River (Pending February, 2014)

Gentleness at the Dismal River

ISBN: 978-0-865459-28-1

Copyright © 2013 by Author Lloyd Warner
840 Northridge Drive   Rapid City, South Dakota, 57701
605-430-1877 • www.lloydwarner.com

CHAPTER 1
THE LITTLE BLACK BOOK

Katie Taggat opened the back door of her ranch home, not expecting to hear a muffled cry, followed by a loud crash of furniture breaking. A child screamed. Suddenly, a small puff of pink whipped by her and was out the door. Still carrying her five month old daughter, she rushed into the kitchen and into the wide hallway. There was Martin, her six year old stepson sitting on the floor, amid what was once a small secretary. He was staring at his right arm where a shard of glass was sticking out of the flesh near the elbow. With his other hand, he gripped his right wrist. He watched the blood starting to well up around the wound. Looking up, he saw his mother. It was a welcome sight, despite his pain and fear.

Martin's first were words were, "I'm sorry, Momma, but I was trying to catch Pinkie." Looking down, he asked, "Am I going to die?" Blood was now beginning to drop on the hardwood floor of the hallway.

Seeing that this frightened boy needed some assurance, she said, "No, Martin, I'm not going to let you die. Remember, I was a nurse. I will take care of you. Don't move just yet." Marie, Martin's twin sister came into the house. She was now looking at the blood. An ashen faced Martin sat among the pieces of the broken desk. "Marie, stay with him, while I put Kylee in her crib. When I get back, go ring the bell outside of the door. Keep ringing it until someone shows up. It is my prayer that one of the men will hear it and will come to the house."

After she put Kylee in her crib, Katie gathered what she might need from the medicine cabinet. By the time that she had laid out the bandages, she could hear the bell ringing in the backyard. She knelt by Martin, telling him,

3

"I'll pull the glass out of your arm. Keep it real steady. If you don't want to look, either close your eyes, or look away. Then I will put some gauze on it to help stop the flow of blood. I will want you to hold it in place while I put a tourniquet on your arm. Do you understand?" He nodded his head. Katie could still hear the bell ringing. *Why isn't Ty here when I need him? She remembered when Tag, Ty's father lay on the living room floor as she tried to stop the flow of his blood. He had been shot by his wife, Laura. Ty wasn't there either!*

Katie pulled the shard of glass from his arm. Martin gave a short gasp, but then looked to his mother and smiled, impervious of the blood that now spurted from the wound with each heartbeat. When Katie pulled the glass from his arm, she got a brief glimpse of her reflection. The glass was a part of the mirror that had been secured atop of the small desk. She remembered that oftentimes when there was a knock at the front door, she would stop to look in the mirror before greeting her guests. Then too, there were occasions when sitting at the desk, she would look up at herself in the mirror. She sensed a touch of vanity in seeing one's image.

Suddenly, she returned to the reality of the situation. She heard the hoof beats of a horse, coupled with the continued ringing of the bell. It stopped when she heard Ty's voice, questioning Marie. Entering the hallway, he looked down at the broken furniture. This, coupled with the blood on his wife and son, brought him to comment, "Wow! That was some wreck! Who is the winner in this fracas?"

In her fury, she screamed out to him, "Ty Taggat, it is easy for you to say after we have repaired the damage." Scolding her husband, she asked, "Why was Martin in the house by himself? When we went to the cemetery, he was with you. Had we not been hot and thirsty, we would have

4

not come for another hour." She was trying to control her emotions as well as her tears. Drying her eyes with a piece of gauze, she continued to rail against her husband. "No telling what might have happened to him. He might have bled to death."

Tylor reached out to his wife when he saw how upset she was with him. "But, he didn't. Don't you think that God was looking after him? He sent you here at the time that he needed help. Things don't just happen, Katie. Now let's get him to Summit City to let the doctor have a look at him."

Realizing that she had over reacted, she tried to calm down. "You're right. You are so like your mother, praising and planning. If she wasn't doing the one, she was doing the other. Marie is a lot that way." Returning his hug, she said, "Look, she has a cloth and some water to clean up the floor. Good thinking. I'll get Kylee, and we'll get this boy fixed up."

Tylor started to leave. He said, "I will take my horse to the barn and be right back."

Arriving at the clinic, the family went in and took a seat. Katie began to take charge of the situation. She took Martin to the nurse-receptionist. "Hello Darcy, is Dr. Mockett available? Martin cut his arm and will probably need stitches."

"No, but Dr. Jessup is filling in for him today. I will tell him that you are here." She pushed her chair back. "I will get Martin's file. Come with me and we can get started."

Tylor remained in the waiting room, holding Kylee. Marie had found a children's book to read. When he heard the outer door open, he looked up. Becca Kurtz came in and seeing Tylor, she came to sit beside him. Seeing that he was having difficulty holding Kylee with his club fist, she held out her arms and asked, "May I hold this precious little girl? My goodness, you are growing." She took Kylee from Tylor. She whispered, "Have you heard? After all these years, we are going to have a baby at our house. After having a boy, we are hoping to have a girl this time."

Somewhat embarrassed by the news, Tylor blushed a bit. Most disturbing was the fragrance of her perfume. It never ceased to bring back memories, which started at the time they began dating in college. "Congratulations! What does Harry think about this?"

"He is elated. Growing up with two older brothers, he would welcome a daughter." Looking around, she asked, "Where's Katie?"

"She's back with Martin. He cut his arm and I imagine he is getting stitches in it about now. However, I don't hear him putting up a fuss." Trying to think of a distraction to the fragrance of her perfume, he asked, "Is Harry busy with his fence contract? If he has some time, I need about a mile of fence to be built. It seems as if we never have enough time for the extra construction."

Thrilled at the news that Harry will get more work, she answered, "He might have some time before we start the haying. It seems as if everyone starts after the fourth of July." Reaching into her purse, while still holding the baby, she continued. "I will make a note to have him get in touch with you. He does enjoy building fence. With this pregnancy, I am so forgetful that I need to make a note of everything." Reaching out, she touched Ty's arm. "Your suggestion that he find additional employment has made all the difference in our lives. I have you to thank for saving our marriage. When I see you and Katie with your family now, I think how greatly you have been blessed." Looking up, she said, "Here she is now. Tell her my good news." Handing Kylee back to Tylor, she got up and went back to one of the examining rooms.

Dr. Jessup came out with Katie and Martin. When he saw Tylor, he said, "This boy of yours is tough. There was no whimpering, only a gritting of the teeth." He put his hand on Martin's shoulder. Martin beamed at the doctor's praise. "Son, keep it clean and dry. I will see you in about a week to take the stitches out." Turning to Tylor, he shook his head. He continued. "You know, it has been a number of years since your mother's passing, but of all the patients that I have seen, I believe that I miss her the most. She was a true lady, a lady of integrity." He turned and went back to his next patient.

Handing Kylee to Katie, Tylor said, "It is getting near noon, so why don't we stop at Nick's for dinner. Then you won't have to hurry around to fix something for us when we get home. Maybe Martin would like to show Grandma Darla his bandage."

"It would be a big help," said Katie, "but, I hate to think that with the doctor bill today and the added cost of eating out are you sure that is a good idea?" Tylor smiled, thinking that Katie had adopted the philosophy toward money that his mother had embraced.

Tylor smiled. He knew what she desired, but was reluctant to part with a dollar. "If you think it would be big help, then it is one of my better ideas. You need a break once in a while." Tylor drove to Main Street and parked in front of Nick's Café. Marie and Martin rushed in, causing the familiar bell at the door to ring. Martin was showing Grandma Darla his bandage and Marie was trying to tell about how much blood that he had shed.

Looking down at his hands, Ty said, "Go ahead and order. I need to go wash up. In all of the rush, I didn't take time to wash the cowboy off of me."

When Tylor returned, a plate of spaghetti and

7

meatballs was setting at the table for him. Sitting down, he remarked, "Wow! That was fast!"

"We have asked the blessing on the food," Katie said, straightening out her napkin at the side of her plate. "You go ahead. The children were hungry, so we started without you."

Nick laughed. "Monday is spaghetti day, or at least, that was what I was informed of by Maude when I bought the restaurant. When Maude broke her leg and your mother came to help out, your mother came up with five menus for the noon meal for the five days of the week. Saturday was the exception. They said that your mother and a lady named Vera could feed all of the customers that came through the door without a bit of trouble. It works so well, that we have continued the same menu. We do deviate on special occasions, but it is easy for Darla and me. Don't you remember all this? They said that you were in a sort of a playpen, so that they could keep an eye on you? You must have been about six months old."

Looking down at his plate, he laughed, "Yeah, I do faintly remember being on exhibition."

Nick looked out the window, as if he was expecting Laura Taggat to walk through the door. He said, "Tylor, you were blessed with a mother that sincerely cared about people. She often talked about being touched by God. I do think that a lot of people were touched by God through her."

Tylor paid for their meals and remarked, "Nick, the recipe for the spaghetti and meatballs is just like I remember it at home. Thanks for what you said about my mother. She always spoke highly about you. When she came to the ranch as the cook, she would tell how you would thank her after each meal."

Arriving at home the family entered the house.

Katie began to weep. "Oh, look at my precious little desk. It is nothing more than a pile of firewood!" She knelt down, beginning to pick up the pieces of the broken mirror.

Martin began to cry when he saw his mother was in tears. "I'm sorry, Mom. I didn't mean it to happen this way."

Tylor put his hand on Martin's shoulder. "Son, what happened here to cause so much damage and hurt you as well?"

He rubbed his eyes, trying to dry the tears. He said, "I came for some milk and cookies like I said I would. When I opened the screen door to go back outside, Pinkie rushed in and I tried to catch him. I know that Momma doesn't want him in the house. He ran one way, like it was a game with him and we both ran into the desk." Shrugging his shoulders, he sobbed, "It just fell apart. I'm sorry, Momma."

Tylor sorted through the mix of paper, pencils and stamps. He began to search out the legs of the oak desk. "Look, Katie, I don't see that any of the wood is broken or splintered. Except for the mirror, I can't find much wrong with it, other than it is certainly disassembled."

Relieved at his words, she said, "Oh, Ty, do you think you can fix it? It was one of the items that Viola Teasdale gave your mother."

Tylor was looking at what appeared to be the back of the desk. When he brought it closer, he got up and took it over to the sunlight that was streaming through the living room window. "There is something here, but I can't make it out." Rubbing his thumb over it, he said, "It looks like a name; 'L Eiklan—1898.' Evidently that is who made it."

Katie gasped. "Oh, Ty, when Marie and I were at the Teasdale Cemetery this morning, Marie was asking about the people that are buried there. Of course, she went

9

to her mother's grave first and we talked about her. We stopped and prayed, thanking God for the years that she was with the children. It was then that she said, 'Momma, could we pray at the other graves?' I remember the name on one of them was Luther Eiklan." With tears clouding her eyes, she continued. "The Teasdales must have been an amazing family. Evidently, they saw that eventually, each person had a granite headstone. I was going to look in the cemetery journal, but usually, there is nothing more than a record of their burial."

Tylor tipped his hat back. He remarked, "It is interesting that here was a man that evidently had spent some time on the ranch, how much we don't know." He went back to look over the rest of the pieces of the desk. He continued while he picked up some more of the wood. "Evidently, Luther was a craftsman, as witnessed by how he had fitted the pieces together." Once again, Tylor rummaged through the tablets and writing instruments, when he pulled out a crudely bound black journal. "What's this?" he exclaimed.

Katie took it, and opening it up, she whispered, "I can't believe it. This is printed, as a child would print. It is faded somewhat, but the first line reads, 'MY NAME IS TIMOTHY CONAN MORAN.' There is a date, but it looks like Octobre 13, 1857. Is that how they spelled October a hundred years ago, or it might be an old English way of spelling. Ty, what does this mean? Here is a book dated 1857, in a desk made in 1898. I don't understand."

Ty had been studying the desk, when he asked, "What did you say? You know, I think that I can put this back together. I believe that the mirror was added later, because it is fastened with screws. The rest of the desk may have had some glue to hold it, but it is fitted together without any nails or screws. Martin, go to the kitchen and find a screwdriver and we will remove the frame of the mirror." Turning his attention back to Katie, he asked, "What were you saying?"

Katie continued thumbing through the book. Looking up, she smiled. She answered him, "This appears to be sort of a crude diary, but I don't understand why we haven't run on to it until just now." Setting it aside, she said, "I need to let Kylee nurse and put her down for her nap. Do what you can, Ty, but it would make me happy to have it restored."

Removing the mirror frame, he exclaimed, "Look, Martin! Here is a small dowel that apparently works as a locking mechanism for a hidden compartment in the desk. That is where the journal was hidden. Had you not run into it, we may never have found it. I sense that the ledger will reveal much of the history of this ranch." Standing up, he said, "C'mon, let's gather up every scrap of wood and take it out to the garage. We can put it together out there. See, something good has come out of all this, despite you ending up at the doctor. Look what you and that pink dog have created! Incidentally, where is Pinkie?"

Martin grinned. He realized that his father was trying to make him feel good about the accident. "I don't know, Dad, but as soon as I help with the wood, I will try to find him. He was scared as much as I was. Maybe, he will quit trying to sneak into the house after what happened."

After putting the wood in the garage, Tylor came back into the kitchen. Katie was at the kitchen table, studying the new-found ledger. Looking up, she said, "Ty, you look like a man that could use a cup of coffee and a piece of pie. Let me warm the coffee and I will tell you what we have found. And, what I am going to do with the hidden treasure." Getting up, she started the coffee to warming and placed two pieces of cherry pie on the small plates.

Tylor started to eat his pie. He laughed and said, "I know it was a serious situation, but it was rather comical to see the two of you sitting amongst the rubble. Other than six stitches in Martin's arm and a broken mirror, I think the two of you came out of it pretty well. We are still not sure about Pinkie, but Martin went out to find him. He is hoping that this will cure him of wanting to sneak into the house." Taking a sip of coffee, he continued. "Speaking of Pinkie, do you remember how it was when we went to find a pup for Martin? Pinkie was the smallest, most timid pup of the litter. With the blending of the white hair among the red hair of his coat, he did have a pink tinge to his coloring." Shaking his head, he said, "I tried to discourage Martin from choosing him, but he felt sorry for him. He thought that he was the one that needed the most attention." Laughing he said, "Naming him Pinkie should have been enough to give the pup a complex. However, he is aggressive and anxious to bring the milk cows to the barn. Not only has Martin been good for Pinkie, but Pinkie has been good for Martin,"

Getting up to refill his coffee mug, he said, "Katie, you have been letting me do all of the talking. Earlier, you mentioned something about what you were going to do with this treasure. I'm not sure that it is all that valuable, but I reckon that by now, your plan has been perfected."

"I am rather reluctant to bring this up," replied Katie, while she was thumbing through the black journal, "but I have had a yearning to write, to write a book. Secretly, I have written some of my memoirs, but many of them are a bit sad. However, if I were to write a book, I was uncertain to know what I would write about. This morning, when Marie and I were praying for those buried in the Teasdale Cemetery, I felt so empty. For most of them, they were only a name and two dates on a piece of granite. I had no idea in what manner they contributed to this ranch, to be found worthy of being buried there." Caressing the crude black journal, she remarked, "I believe that I will find the answers in this book. Not all, but enough that I can reconstruct it into a historical novel. I have an overwhelming sense that Timothy Conan Moran is buried in the Teasdale Cemetery, even though his name is not on one of the headstones. I just know it!"

Her husband noticed the tears well up in her eyes. He stood up and went to her, and placed his hands on her shoulders, while she sat at the table. He kissed the top of her head. He saw the black hair with the ringlets here and there. "Go for it, Katie, go for it. Are you far enough along in your planning to arrive at a title?"

She nodded, "The Ghosts of the Teasdale Cemetery!" She stood up and hugged her husband. "Thank you for your words of encouragement. I was a bit reluctant to mention my dreams of writing, but I saw that your mother found such joy in her painting of portraits. I promise to not neglect you or the children, but I am excited to get started."

Ty released Katie and reached for his hat that was on the counter. He started to put it on, when she rebuked him. "Couldn't you have held me a bit longer? Surely the ranch won't fall apart if you hug your wife a few minutes longer."

Giving her one last hug, he chuckled, "I'm sorry, Mrs. Taggat, but I have a piece of furniture to put together. Should you see Martin, send him to the garage. We have a wooden puzzle to solve, while the author is formulating the first chapter as we talk. You will need to look for a replacement for the mirror. Also, if I hurry and replace the mirror frame, I may be able to negate the seven years of bad luck." He was laughing, as he went out the kitchen door on his way to the garage.

Hid in a nook
Was a little black book
With scarcely a look
In the well worn book
An idea comes to mind
So Katie must now find
The Ghosts of the Teasdale Cemetery

CHAPTER 2
MEAGAN FARLEY

With black hair and dark eyes, Meagan Farley was a comely lass. That is, if you ignored the red spots that covered her face and body. Measles are usually not that serious, but often times, it is the simplest of things that alter one's life so drastically. When she heard the door close, Meagan wept. She was being left behind. It wasn't as if her being left behind was temporal, but she sensed that she may never see her family again. The potato blight that caused the famine of 1847 in Ireland was not short lived as everyone believed it might be. The Farley family was no exception. They worked the fields of Sir John Bellingham near the city of New Bridges. Sir John and his wife Mary were benevolent people and it grieved them to see their tenants suffer from starvation. With no food for the winter, or money to buy food, they had arranged passage for the Farley family to migrate to the land of opportunity, the United States of America.

It was planned for the family to leave their thatched cottage, to board the sailing ship, *The Spirit of Spring*, in Dublin on November 2, 1848. They understood the dire circumstances that had affected so many in Ireland had also reached their home as well. What was particularly difficult for them to understand, Meagan was unable to go with them. Her sister, Tully wanted to stay behind with her. It was she that had contracted the measles earlier, exposing Meagan to the measles that now covered her body. The older brothers, Sean and Dolan, had the measles previously, even before the girls were born. Conan and his wife Rachael knew that at twelve years of age, Tully would have a difficult time remaining in Ireland. Meagan, now fifteen

15

had been assured employment by the Bellinghams. Rachael understood that it would not be an easy life for Meagan, but it would be better than starving on the streets of Dublin. She was aware that Meagan would not be allowed on board ship, and it was unwise for her to travel, or bring risk to others in the crowded hold of the ship.

A servant girl from the Bellingham estate was to stop in each day to bring food and check on Meagan's welfare. As soon as Meagan was well, she would begin employment, probably as a scullery maid. This was a position that afforded only board and room, until such time that she should marry.

It wasn't many days after Meagan moved to the Bellingham Estate, that Mary Bellingham had second thoughts about such an attractive girl being a part of the household. She was extremely capable and was promoted to serving the family during meal time. It was there that Meagan caught the fancy of the two sons, Eric and Clayton, eighteen and seventeen years of age. The Bellinghams were of English royalty. Mary was not about to allow her sons to fraternize with the likes of the daughter of an Irish tenant farmer!

With bated breath, and several months of correspondence, Mary had arranged for Meagan to go to England. She had enjoyed the trip across the Irish Sea and arrived at the Bellingham estate at Cotswold; the home of Lord William Bellingham and his wife Virginia. William was the older brother of John. However, his wife was much younger than Mary. Once again, Meagan was relegated to the duties of a scullery maid. She sensed that perhaps Mary Bellingham had not been kind in her correspondence to Lord Bellingham. One thing that Meagan had learned under the rule of Mary was to be gracious, prompt and never look her employer in the eye. Once again, Meagan, in her gracious manner found favor in her mistress' eye. She had been given the responsibility as an upstairs maid, while looking after the three year old daughter, Grace.

There were times that Meagan yearned for her family, but realized that God had blessed her in this fine home and the gentleness of Virginia Bellingham. Rarely was she in the company of Lord Bellingham. He often spent his time in Parliament while he was in London. Meagan thought him to be rather aloof, even in the presence of his wife and daughter. One thing that she noticed was that he wore fine white gloves constantly, even at the dining table. He always wore dark clothing, which complemented his black hair and overpowering demeanor. She felt uncomfortable in his presence, even though he rarely spoke to her. Because of the graciousness of his wife, she could tolerate his cold mannerism. She also cherished the loving nature of Grace, with her blue eyes and blonde hair.

Just when Meagan was at peace with her situation and not having any thought of her future, Virginia Bellingham became ill. The doctors didn't have any idea of the cause of her illness, or a remedy for what ailed her. Despite their efforts, Lady Virginia Bellingham died the morning of December 3, 1850. Sensing her impending death, she had called Meagan to her bedside the previous evening. She quietly said, "Meagan, I am dying. I'm sorry, but I can no longer see to my daughter, Grace. I commit her into your hands. See to her in the coming days. I love you." Meagan was at a loss for words, but she nodded. Her eyes were clouded with tears. She clutched Virginia's hands in her own. The tears began to stream down her cheeks. Their parting was interrupted when Lord Bellingham came into the room.

Seeing Meagan at her bedside, he grabbed her arm,

pulling her to her feet. "Get out!" he shouted. "Get out!" Meagan ran from the room, looking over her shoulder for one last glimpse of her mistress.

Two days later, Lady Bellingham was buried in the family cemetery.

The next day, Lord Bellingham left the estate. No one knew where he had gone, or when he would be back. Everyone continued their duties. Grace missed her mother, but Meagan was with her each moment of the day, taking her meals in the nursery. After a time, Grace no longer asked about her mother.

A month after Lady Bellingham's death, Lord Bellingham returned to the estate. Meagan learned of his arrival when the downstairs maid brought her the evening meal. All evening, she expected him to come see his daughter, but he never showed up as expected.

That evening, Meagan was preparing for bed. She was in her flannel nightgown, and was sitting on the edge of the bed, brushing her hair, when the door suddenly opened. Lord Bellingham stepped in and slammed the door shut. He gazed down at her, but said nothing. She stopped brushing her hair and looking up at him, she calmly said, "Lord Bellingham, I am getting ready for bed and Grace is asleep. I could have her ready for your visit first thing in the morning."

"It isn't Grace that I came to see," he haughtily replied, as he started towards her.

Meagan's heart began to pound wildly. She said, "Lord Bellingham, it is rather late. I don't know why you have come into my room, but would you please leave."

He began to remove his jacket. He sneered, "I think that you know why I am here. You are not so naïve that you don't understand that your allurement has brought me to your bed."

Meagan leaped up from the edge of the bed and ran toward the door. He grabbed her by the arm and slapped her. She fell back on the bed. Releasing her, he continued, "Let me put it another way. Your options are few. Take me to your bed, or by this time tomorrow night, you will be on the streets of London. Being a penniless Irish wench on the streets of London is not a pleasant thought. Once you were no longer under the protection of your family, your fate was sealed."

Meagan understood what he was talking about. She had heard of the life of the hapless girls on the streets of Dublin. London would be no different. And too, there was the welfare of Grace to consider. She knew that what he demanded was not what she wanted, or looked forward to, but she knew of no other option at the present. I need to bide my time for a solution, unfortunately, now is not the time. Regardless of what option I choose, I will not be leaving this room with my honor intact. Getting up from the bed, she went to Lord Bellingham and began to unbutton his shirt. At no time, did he ever remove his white gloves from his hands.

Despite her tears, that which seemed as an eternity to Meagan finally came to an end. Lord Bellingham was leaving the room when he grabbed her arm. "Take a bath in the morning to wash off that Irish scum. I will be back tomorrow night. In the meantime, don't do anything stupid. Remember what I said about your options while you are filling your stomach with my food." Meagan recalled all too well, the pangs and effects of starvation.

She snuffed out the candle and returned to her bed. Despite her tears and exhaustion, she found time to pray to God. Her plea was, "Oh God, show me your way, show me your way."

Troubled sleep came to Meagan. She dreamt that

she had been taken to London in the two wheeled cart and dumped at the outskirts of the city.

Early the next morning, she rang the bell for the downstairs maid to bring her bath water. After the scullery maid and the downstairs maid had brought the bath water, she began to remove, not the Irish scum, but the scum of Lord Bellingham from her body. While she was soaking, she began to formulate a plan. It would be a plan to completely take the Lord by surprise. After drying herself, she found some lotion that had belonged to Lady Bellingham. She began to lotion her skin. This was a luxury that she had been denied up until now. After her bath, she went for Grace. She dressed her in her finest and they ate breakfast together. With each morsel she put into her mouth, she rehearsed the words of Lord Bellingham when he told her, 'remember what I said about your options while you are filling your stomach with my food.' Later, she and Grace went for a walk among the grounds. During this time, she would point out to her, certain flowers and animals that would be in this park-like setting. She was a very attentive and intelligent little girl. Meagan would often tell her stories about the animals and butterflies that fluttered about. Lady Bellingham had been unaware that Meagan was illiterate. Consequently, Meagan had become an excellent story teller. Grace would beg for more and more of her stories.

After lunch, while Grace was taking her nap, Meagan began to prepare for the promised visit from Lord Bellingham. She worked with her hair that it might have more body and curl. She took great care while she filed and shaped her fingernails. She went into Lady Bellingham's room and found one of her nightgowns, as well as a vial of her perfume. She altered the gown by adding colored ribbons and making little bows. Lord Bellingham must not recognize the gown! Going to the pantry, she found a bit of vanilla to add to the perfume, so that as he came close to her, there would be nothing to remind him of his late wife!

At the time of the evening meal, Meagan had dressed in her best dress and took Grace with her. She was surprised and disappointed when Lord Bellingham did not eat with them in the dining hall. However, that would not alter her plans for the evening. Putting Grace to bed for the night, Meagan returned to her bedroom. Act one of her plan was about to begin.

Hearing footsteps in the hall, Meagan stood up, with her back to the door. As the door opened, she slowly turned to greet her guest. However, it was not Meagan clad in the nightgown! In her plan, she knew that she, Meagan Farley could not abide the continued humiliation and abuse at the hands of Lord Bellingham. She must become someone else. She was not real, but only an actress. She would become Charlotte, the French courtesan! There had been enough talk among the servants in the kitchen for her to get an insight of the actions of a French courtesan. If I am to survive, I must make this work. She had lit additional candles, compared to the single candle the prior night. Going to Lord Bellingham, she took his face in her hands and gave him a kiss. She walked behind him and began to remove his jacket. She noticed, all the time that she continued in her role of the courtesan, he began to shake as if he was frightened. Having second thoughts of her own, she chided herself. I must continue to have control of the events of the evening. After removing his shoes, she stood up. He became quite aggressive. She became frightened, but calmed herself. She remembered the role that she was playing. As Charlotte, she took a deep breath, vowing to remain in control of the situation, knowing that the abuse would soon begin. Later, she marveled that the abuse lasted

21

much less than the previous evening. When he left the room, she was amazed that he had never removed the white gloves from his hands, nor said anything about her bathing to remove the Irish scum from her body.

She heard the door close. It was as if the curtain had come down on the first act of a play. Charlotte once again became Meagan. Removing the nightgown with the ribbon and bows, she put on her flannel nightgown. She washed her face and neck to rid her body of the aroma of the perfume. Snuffing out the candles, she crawled into her bed. Before dropping off to sleep, she quietly prayed, "Forgive me Father, forgive me. I have survived another day!"

And so, the late night visits continued. Each night, her quiet prayer was the same, "Forgive me Father, forgive me. I have survived another day!" There were times that she discouraged his nightly visits, but when they resumed, it seemed to her that the abuse lessened a little bit each day, until one night he never showed up at all. After three nights of his absence, Meagan questioned the butler as to Lord Bellingham's absence. She learned that Parliament was in session and he would be gone for a period of time, the butler was not sure how long.

Meagan was now feeling more secure with her presence at the manor, but the conditions of her security was unsettling. Had the allurement of Meagan through the charms of Charlotte, the French courtesan waned such that she no longer held the interest of Lord Bellingham? After a month long absence, he suddenly appeared at her bedside. It was quite late. She thought that it was after midnight. She was frightened. The stage was not set as in previous visits. Getting out of bed, she begged, "It is quite late, could you give me time to make myself ready?"

"I have been gone a month. Why weren't you

expecting me? I have traveled most of the night to come to you." She sensed that his absence had made him irritable and angry.

She said, "I see that you are tired. Here, let me take your jacket and shirt. Why don't you sit on the edge of the bed and I will remove your shoes." She then began to massage his shoulders and neck. He stood up and removed his trousers, clad only in his undergarments. "Lie here on the bed and I will help remove some of the tension in your body while I massage you." He was lying face down, so she straddled his body. She began to massage him from his neck to his feet, all the time humming an Irish lullaby. He was soon fast asleep.

Giving him some time to enter into a deep sleep, she continued to hum the Irish lullaby. *Now is the opportunity to determine the reason of the white gloves.* She took his right hand and carefully removed the glove. Close examination revealed no reason for continual wearing of the glove. She returned it to his hand. When she was removing the glove on the left hand, it seemed to be snug, to such an extent that she tugged at it to remove the glove. Lord Bellingham stirred and moved the hand to his side. It was then that she saw the purpose of the gloves. The middle finger and the finger nearest to the little finger were swollen and a fiery red. At first glance, they appeared to have been burnt, but on closer examination, Meagan saw that the fingers were swollen as a result of excess scar tissue. The middle finger was missing most of the finger nail as well. It was a gruesome sight. More frightening, *would I be able to get the glove back on his hand?* Being careful to start the glove over the injured fingers first, she soon had the glove on the hand. Only then did she cease the humming of the lullaby.

She covered him with a blanket and took the candle

and quietly closed the door. She gave a sigh, leaning against the door. After a moment, she went to the extra bed in Grace's room. She did not want to be in her room when he awakened.

The Irish lass with the coal black hair
To her delight, thought it only fair
Acted as a French courtesan
To deceive the noble Englishman
An idea comes to mind
So Katie must now find
The Ghosts of the Teasdale Cemetery

CHAPTER 3
'BIG' TIM MORAN

The next morning Meagan went to her bedroom, only to find that Lord Bellingham was gone. Later in the morning, he came to tell Grace goodbye. He approached Meagan. He reached out and grasping her cheek between thumb and forefinger, he said, "I will be back on Saturday. I will see you then. Do you understand what I mean?" He waited for her to reply before releasing her check.

"Yes, my Lord. I understand fully what you mean." She gave no indication of how severely his pinch to the cheek pained her.

Meagan had a premonition that Saturday was a day to be feared. Grace was not feeling well this morning. She feared that she too was suffering from the same symptoms. She definitely wanted to be feeling her best. By Saturday, Grace had recovered, and she thought that she herself was feeling better. She continued to have the feeling of impending doom.

Saturday night, Lord Bellingham came to her, but things did not go well. He was demanding and difficult to please. It was if the actress Charlotte failed to appear for the opening curtain, and her understudy, Meagan Farley had to replace her on the set.

He started to leave her bedroom, when he said, "I will be gone for a month. I will leave in the morning. I will be traveling to Trolong. Virginia's sister Anne and I will be married on Tuesday. We will then travel the continent for a month. Look after Grace during my absence."

"But, what will happen to me?"

"Anne will probably bring her own staff to see to her needs as well as looking about Grace." Looking at her with a smirk on his face, he continued, "I'm not sure that I want you in the household. The Irish maids always seem to cause trouble. When I get back, I will see to you. Perhaps some of the gentry of Parliament may be willing to find something for a talented girl like you." Meagan was shocked at his remark and impending marriage. She thought, I fear that I will be cast out like a worn out shoe. Also, upon the return from the honeymoon, there would be someone from the manor to inform Anne's staff about the Lord's visit to my bedroom. There are no secrets in the manor! I will confront him now with the uncertainty of my status in the manor.

"Are you sure that any of the gentry would want me, if they were aware that I am carrying your child? Lord Bellingham, I will give birth to a man child the first part of October." Meagan smiled. She saw the transformation of his demeanor. The earlier smirk had been replaced by a look of unbelief.

After hearing the news, his face turned ashen. It was now flush, as he denied the paternity of the child. "You are a liar. You've played the harlot with every man on the estate. I should have dumped you in the streets of London the first day that you came here. My sister-in-law knew that you were trouble. Enjoy your stay, because as soon as I return from my honeymoon, you will be gone."

Meagan remained calm. "Do you hate me so? Have you no compassion for your own flesh and blood? In your heart you know that I have been with no other man. I have no intent to do you harm. I have not revealed any of this to others, nor will I? This was brought upon me because I am a woman. I am poor and I am Irish in the land of England. Because of these three things, I was an easy prey. I will survive, but I fear for the child that I am carrying. I beg of you, that you might show mercy to your son." She turned from him, that he might not see her tears. She then heard the door close and he was gone.

Meagan's days were filled with tending Grace, but her nights were filled even more. It seemed that she slept very little because of the uncertainty of her remaining at the manor. And yet, she continued to be faithful in ministering to Grace. It was Grace that she would miss the most. She had been somewhat isolated from the rest of the staff, so had no friends.

Lord Bellingham and his wife Anne arrived at the estate on a day that Meagan hoped was not indicative of what was to come. The sun did not shine all day. The rain came in torrents. The wind pushed it along, encouraging it with each gust.

The butler informed Meagan to have Grace ready to greet her father and meet her stepmother, in reality, her aunt. Grace was happy to see her father, but was timid in the presence of Lady Anne. After a time, Lord Bellingham said, "Meagan, take Grace to her room and have the upstairs maid watch her while you meet with us in about one hour. We will have our afternoon tea prior to meeting with you. I will have someone call you when we are ready." Meagan and Grace returned to the upstairs.

While Meagan was waiting, she took the opportunity to pray. She bowed down before the hearth, and she began to quietly pray. "Father, I know that I have not sought your guidance, but today, I submit to your will. Show me your plan in my life, and I shall submit to it. If it is to be the streets of London, I will seek your will in my life." She could pray no more, the tears flowing down her cheeks. She could utter only one more word. "Amen."

Meagan was still on her knees when she was summoned to the downstairs study. When she closed the door behind her, she saw that Lady Anne was not present.

"Lady Anne was a bit exhausted, so she asked that she be excused. She and I had discussed you earlier, so I will tell you what decision has been reached." Lord Bellingham was seated behind a desk. He had not offered Meagan a chair. She remained standing. He continued, "She will bring her own staff, so tomorrow you will be relieved of your duties. I expect you to say your goodbyes to Grace at that time. I had said previously that I did not care to have Irish maids in the manor, so I have two options for you to consider."

Meagan brought her hands forward, clasping them one within the other, waiting to hear the options. He continued, "I will pay you what wages that you have earned, plus fifty shillings. I will provide transportation to whatever city in England that you choose. Once you have stepped down from the coach, I never want to see or hear from you again."

"And the other option?" she asked.

"I have a man in my employment that is seeking a wife. His wife died four years ago, and he is desirous of remarrying to a woman that will give him children. He is about fifty years of age, and a responsible man."

"Tell me, Lord Bellingham, is he a gentle man?" She continued, not waiting for his reply. "Also, is he aware that I am with child?"

"I would say that he is a kind man. He is my stable master, and as he is gentle with the horses, I would say that he would be gentle with his wife. He is aware that you are with child, but that is all. Even I am unsure of the paternity of this child. He has seen you on the grounds when you have taken Grace outside. Keep in mind, the same conditions are required as in the first option. I never want to see or hear from you again."

Fearing of being alone in the city, Meagan said, "I will accept the last offer. When may I meet this man?"

28

Lord Bellingham smiled, "He will be here tomorrow, right after the noon meal to claim you and your baggage. He requested to go to the village near Cotswold to have the vicar conduct the marriage ceremony. I am not surprised by your decision. I see that you fear the city. Say your goodbyes to Grace tomorrow morning."

Lord Bellingham stood, his gloved hands spread before him on the desk. Flashing through her mind, Meagan saw the white gloves and the two hideous fiery red and swollen fingers. Dismissing the thoughts that flashed through her mind, Meagan saw that she was being dismissed. She turned to go. She asked one last question, "And, the name of the man that I am to marry?"

"Timothy Moran, but some call him, Big Tim." Meagan smiled. *Moran, yes I believe that Moran is an Irish name. That is good!*

Big Tim was to be at her side
Standing close to his Irish bride
Saying their vows before God and man
Leaving behind the noble Englishman
An idea comes to mind
So Katie must now find
The Ghosts of the Teasdale Cemetery

CHAPTER 4
THE BRIDAL COTTAGE

The morning of her departure, Meagan took Grace downstairs for breakfast. They ate alone. Afterwards they prepared to leave and Meagan went into the kitchen. She asked the cook to prepare a light lunch for Grace and her to take with them. They planned to walk the grounds of the estate.

They entered Grace's bedroom and Meagan said, "Grace, this morning we will take a walk in the park. I have asked the cook to pack us a lunch, so that we might enjoy each other this fine day."

Grace clapped her hands together. She said, "Will we see any animals in the park?"

She replied, "I would certainly hope so. Has there ever been a time that we have gone that we didn't see at least one animal?"

Grace nodded her head. "Yes, there was the time that we only saw a squirrel. Miss Farley, will you tell me a story? I like your stories. You are a good story teller."

She smiled, even though her heart was heavy at the thought of leaving this delightful girl. "Yes, yes I will. Today I will tell you a special story. It will be so special that you will remember it the rest of your life. Do you remember the last story that I told you?"

Grace looked rather quizzical. "Miss Farley, I do believe that I forgot. Do you remember the story?"

"Of course I do! It was about the kitten that had nine whiskers."

"That was a good story, but how can you be sure

that I will remember the story today?"

Meagan laughed. "Grace, I fear that you ask too many questions. However, after we have eaten our lunch, I will tell you the story that you will never forget. Now let's go. Remember, this will be a special day. You are now five years old. And, five year old girls are like elephants, they never forget anything."

Grace tugged on Meagan's arm. She asked, "Is the story about an elephant?"

Placing her hand on the child's shoulder, she said, "You will just have to wait and see if the story is about an elephant. Come on, let's get the day started."

They walked some distance from the manor before Meagan found a stump to sit upon. Grace enjoyed being free, so she ran from tree to tree. A gray squirrel came to watch her antics, and would run if she came too close.

Meagan sat upon the stump, and her thoughts went to Timothy Moran. I wonder if he asked the Master if I am a gentle woman? *Oh, Momma, Momma, how I need you to hold me, and to give me wise counsel. My fears so encompass me, that perhaps I am not making a wise decision.* She continued to sit there quietly, staring off into space, but seeing nothing. Will I give birth to a girl, or will it be a man child as I told Lord Bellingham? A gentle tug on her arm indicated that a little girl was ready for her lunch.

After lunch, of which Meagan ate very little, Grace begged for her story.

Meagan began, "In a beautiful garden, there was a big fat toad. He told every animal that came along that he was the king of the garden. One fine day, he was sitting in the sun, warming himself. He began to doze and his chin began to fall lower and lower and lower to the ground. A furry caterpillar was crawling through the garden. She was pretty, despite having to creep along the path in the dirt. She had two bands of fur that were red, and one was brown."

Grace interrupted her, and asked, "How long was she, and how do you know that she was a girl?"

Meagan answered, "Well, she was about as long as your middle finger, and she was so pretty with her colorful bands, that I knew that she must be a girl." Grace nodded, and looking down at her fingers, she held up her middle finger.

Meagan continued, "The furry caterpillar crawled under the chin of the big fat toad. As she went by, she tickled the toad's chin and he awakened. He croaked, 'Who is the one that awakened me?' In her tiny little voice, the caterpillar said, 'It is me. I have come to tell you goodbye. I have enjoyed staying in your garden, but the time is near for me to leave.' The toad asked, 'Will you come back to see me?' Once again the tiny little voice said, 'Oh yes, but you won't recognize me. I will have a different body. But I will come to see you.'

Once again, Grace spoke up. "Did the big fat toad tell you this story? Will he tell me the story if I forget it?"

"Grace, I will finish the story and you can tell me if you think that you will forget." She nodded, expecting Meagan to continue with the story.

She began again, "The toad asked, 'What kind of body will you have? If it is different, how will I recognize you?' The caterpillar said, 'I will come back as a butterfly, and I will fly back to this garden to see you.' The toad laughed, 'Impossible! There are a lot of butterflies in the garden, and many of them look alike. I won't ever see you again.' The caterpillar said, 'But you will, you will! Look for the butterfly that lands on your head. That will be me, and only me! I promise that I will come back. That will be my sign to you that I have returned. I will leave now, and you look for the butterfly on your head.' The caterpillar crawled off, while the big fat toad returned to his nap. That is the story that you will never forget."

Grace laughed as she stood up. "Miss Farley, I like that story. That is the best story that you have told me." She thought a moment, and then asked, "Why did you wait until today to tell me that story?"

Meagan was amazed at the discernment of this young child. "Grace, I told you the story because I am leaving today. I am getting married, but I never want to forget you. Therefore, whenever a butterfly lights on your head, you will know that your very special friend, Miss Farley, has come to you."

"Me too, Miss Farley, me too! When a butterfly lights on your head, you will know that I have come to see you." She took Meagan's hand. "But couldn't I come to live with you, and be your little girl?"

"I am sorry, but that is not possible. You belong here. Your father and Aunt Virginia are here, and I will go to be with my husband. Let's return to the manor, and you can help me pack. I will be leaving as soon as my husband comes for me." Taking her hand, they returned to the manor.

Grace helped her pack her few belongings. Earlier, Meagan had knotted in a handkerchief the money that Lord Bellingham had given her as promised. Grace had wanted to go with her, but Meagan insisted that she remain in her room. "You may watch from your window. When my husband comes for me, I will wave goodbye to my friend. Goodbye, Grace."

Meagan walked down the long driveway and waited at the road. She waited about five minutes before seeing a horse pulling a two-wheeled cart coming over the small hill to the west. After the driver halted the horse, he stepped down. Meagan turned toward the manor, and seeing Grace at the window, she waved goodbye. Looking over to the window that had been her bedroom, she thought she saw a familiar figure. She waved goodbye to Charlotte, the French courtesan.

Turning to the man, he took her hand to help her into the cart. She said, "Mister Moran, I presume?"

"Yes, Miss Farley."

She sat down and said, "You may call me Meagan, but I prefer to address you as Mr. Moran."

"That will be fine, Meagan. We will go to the village to have the vicar perform the marriage ceremony." She nodded.

They rode in silence during the two mile trip to the village. However, Meagan was making a mental assessment of her intended spouse. She noted that the horse pulling the cart was not the best of animals, but Mister Moran did show great patience with the animal. Evidently, even though he was the stable master, Lord Bellingham didn't let him have his choice of horses.

Arriving at the manse, Tim Moran helped Meagan out of the cart. They approached the door, where they were greeted by a tall, white haired man. He was rather thin, but his clear blue eyes were such that they made a quick evaluation of the young lady that accompanied Tim Moran. Before Tim could make the introductions, he introduced himself. "Miss Farley, greetings, greetings to our home. I am Thomas Bentley, the vicar of the church." Turning to a plump gray haired lady, he said, "This is my wife, Marta. We have delayed our afternoon tea that we might share it with both of you before the ceremony. Miss Farley, while Marta is preparing our refreshments, may I visit with you briefly in my study?" She nodded, and began to follow him. She looked at Tim, and he gave a nod of approval. He made himself comfortable in a straight backed chair.

They entered the study, and she took note of the expanse of books on the shelves that lined the walls of the study. Only the one window and the door broke the continuity of the dark shelving. Closing the door, he motioned to a chair, indicating that Meagan might be seated. He sat in an oak chair with arms, and a leather seat. After they were seated, he began to speak. "Miss Farley, needless to say, I am a bit troubled by this marriage. Tim Moran is a member of this congregation. He is a kind man, a devout man, but he is also a lonely man, or he normally would not enter into marriage under these circumstances. I don't fully understand your circumstances, but I don't want to see Tim hurt. I understand that after being abandoned by your family, you came here from Ireland. Are you familiar with our Protestant faith?"

Looking into the eyes of the vicar, she began. "I was not abandoned by my family, but was forced to remain in Ireland when they migrated to America. I had contracted the measles and was unable to accompany them. I am not familiar with your Protestant faith, but I do believe in God. It was He that I sought council of in regard to my marriage to Mr. Moran. After learning of my pregnancy, my employer gave me two options. I could go to any city in England to seek to survive, or marry Mr. Moran. Before making a choice, I asked my employer if Mr. Moran was a gentle man. He assured me that he was, so I chose to marry him. I would hope that Mr. Moran might have asked the same question regarding me. The father of my child has chosen to reject acknowledgment of paternity, so my options were few."

The vicar nodded his head. "Miss Farley, I have two requests of you. One is that you learn to love Tim, kind man that he is. The other is that you accompany him the times that he comes to worship and learn to love the Savior that Tim loves as well."

The tears trickled down her cheeks. She nodded her head. She whispered, "I promise."

After the four adults drank of their tea and ate the scones, the vicar married the couple in a simple ceremony. They prepared to leave in the two-wheeled cart. Mrs. Bentley brought a basket of fresh baked bread and scones and gave to Meagan.

In their silence, after a time they came to a thatched cottage. Once again, helping Meagan to the ground, Tim said, "I will take the horse to the stable, and be back to help you get the house in order." She went to the door thinking, those were the most words he had spoken all afternoon.

The evening shadows were announcing the close of this late winter day. Meagan pushed the door open and peered into the darkened interior. She heard a voice, asking, "Who's there, who's there? Timmy, is that you?"

She answered, "I am Meagan, Mr. Moran's wife. I'm sorry, but I wasn't expecting anyone to be home. Who are you?" Her eyes became adjusted to the darkened interior, when she saw a small gray haired lady in the middle of the room, moving her head from side to side. In her right hand she held a cane, and with the left hand she was reaching out as if she was searching for something.

The woman replied after a moment. "Is that you, Lila? I thought that you had died. Where is Timmy?"

Meagan replied, "Mr. Moran went to put the horse away. He will return in a while." Her eyes became adjusted to the darkness of the room. She sensed that the old woman that stood before her was blind. She asked, "Are you Mr. Moran's mother?"

She nodded, and clutching the shawl about her shoulders, she gave a shiver. "It is cold in here. Sometimes,

Timmy forgets to put wood on the fire. Can you start up the fire? I don't feel any heat? Where did you say that Timmy went? I can tell that it is getting late, and he needs to be here."

Meagan went to the fireplace, and stirring the coals with a poker, she brought hot embers to the surface. Finding wood nearby, she had the fire going. She went to the lady, and said, "Here, give me your hand, and I will take you to this rocker near the fire." Sitting her down, she continued to talk with her. "This is your chair, isn't it?" Once again the woman nodded, and feeling the heat from the fire, she began to rock, ignoring her guest.

Meagan added water to the pot that hung over the fire. Looking around, she found tea, and after a time, she handed a cup of tea to the lady, while she continued to rock. She took the opportunity to look around the cottage. She noted a small room that served as a bedroom. Looking further, there was also a bed in a loft at the far end, away from the fireplace. It reminded her of her home in Ireland.

Lighting a candle, she heard Mr. Moran enter the room. He greeted his mother, and then turned to Meagan, he said, "Come, and I will show you the things in the pantry and what I expect as far as meal preparation. Did Mother cause you any problems? Most of the time she is rather docile, but there are times that she becomes confused."

In about thirty minutes, Meagan had the supper prepared. It wasn't as sumptuous as the meals that she had at the manor, but it was certainly better than the last meals she had shared with her family in Ireland. Mr. Moran asked the blessing on the food and they ate in silence. At the close of the meal, Tim pulled up a large rocker near the fire and began to silently read from his Bible. Megan did learn that his mother's name was Francine; however, Meagan addressed her as Mrs. Moran. Francine got up from the table. She said, "I am going to bed now. Goodnight Timmy, goodnight Lila."

Tim never corrected her. He bid his mother goodnight.

Meagan said, "My name is Meagan. Do you want me to help you get into bed?"

Haughtily she replied, "No, no, I have put myself to bed for seventy-two years and I don't need any help tonight." After a few minutes, she called from the bedroom, "Lila, Lila, you forgot to set my water on the nightstand. Also, this is the third night in a row that you didn't turn down my bed. You are the most forgetful woman I have ever met."

Meagan went for a small mug of water. She walked by Tim, and she gave him a look. In return, he shrugged his shoulders and returned to his reading.

When she returned, she sat in a chair across from Tim. She said, "Mr. Moran, we cannot continue like this. We need to communicate with one another, like talk to each other. I need to know what you expect from me. First of all, who is Lila? Your mother seems to think that I am she?"

"She was my first wife, but she is gone now."

"When you say gone, is she dead, or did she leave?"

Tim had the strangest look on his face, as if he had been found out. Meagan's first thought was, did he kill her? Am I living in the house of a murderer? He does act rather strange!

"I said she is gone! You don't need any more information than that." He returned to reading his Bible. She was not so easily convinced, but would not pursue the issue any further at the time.

After a time, Tim got up from his chair and setting his Bible aside, he remarked, "I am going to bed now. I will awaken you in the morning and we can go over how I like my breakfast prepared."

While Tim was taking care of the fire, Meagan went into the bedroom and changed into her nightgown. She had put slippers on her feet, so that she might climb the ladder to the loft. When she came out of the room, Tim asked in a surly manner, "Where are you going?"

"I was going to the loft," she replied. She turned to him. "Isn't that where you are sleeping?"

"Yes, but you can sleep with my mother. I am not ready to take you to my bed at this time." Carrying a candle with him, he began to climb the ladder. "Good night, Meagan."

She shrugged her shoulders at his remark. "Good night, Mr. Moran."

She entered the bedroom and saw that Mrs. Moran had established her portion of the bed was to be the middle. Neither did she have a good night sleep. Mrs. Moran talked in her sleep as she tossed and turned. Morning came all too soon, but the night wasn't without tears. She wept for the arms of her mother that she might be consoled. And, already she was missing the laughter of Grace, for there was no laughter in the Moran household. That must change!

Early the next morning, Meagan was awakened by Tim. He instructed her on the making of his breakfast. He said, "Now that you are here to look after mother, I will not need to come back at noon. Therefore, you can pack something for me to eat. While mother takes her afternoon nap, it would be well that you go into the nearby woods and pick up some of the downfall for us to burn. There are carrying straps in the woodshed."

When he left the cottage, Meagan could not help but shed a few tears. What, no kiss for the bride! I fear that my husband has no romantic interest in me at all. When it is nap time for mother, I will find out the fate of Lila!

Meagan put Francine down for her nap. She said, "While you are taking your nap, I will gather some sticks in the woods, so that we might have it warm for you."

Mrs. Moran nodded, and then asked, "Are you going to leave like you did the last time? Lila, I am glad that you came back. I think it was good for you to be gone for a while. You are nicer to me than you were before."

"Don't worry. I will be here in time to fix your supper." She gave her a smile, and patted her arm before leaving the room.

Meagan went to the wood shed and found the straps for binding the wood. However, she did not go into the woods, but started for the village of Loxnard. She didn't run, but kept at a swift walk. She needed to talk with the vicar. Arriving in the village, she saw that he was on his way from the manse to the church. She ran the last way so that she might arrive at the door about the same time that he did.

Somewhat out of breath, she gasped, "Vicar Bentley, I need to speak with you."

"Good heavens, girl. Is it that important that you have run here?"

She nodded, and he began to open the door. She said, "Yes, yes it is."

"Come in and we will sit here at one of the pews." After he sat down, he said, "Now, tell me, is there a problem?"

Meagan blurted right out, "Who is Lila? Francine Moran thinks that I am Lila. When I asked Mr. Moran about her, he only said that she is gone. When I asked what he meant that she was gone, he said that I didn't need to know anything more than that she is gone."

He stood up and began walking toward the door.

Turning to her, he said, "Come with me and I will show you Lila. You need to know about her." They stepped outside and he opened the gate to the cemetery that was along the pathway to the church. They walked among the headstones and he stopped at one. It was a small white stone that had been discolored from the weathering. "Here is where she is buried. Now you need to know why she is here."

Megan peered at the name; it read, 'Lila Moran, beloved wife of Tim Moran.' Underneath were two dates; 1820-1846. She asked, "How did she die?"

The Vicar motioned to a stone bench. "Let us sit here, and I will tell you about her. Tim's father was the stable master at the Bellingham estate, even as Tim is now. The stable is all that Tim has ever known, as he followed in his father's footsteps. Before he became the stable master, he was the primary driver of the estate. There were occasions that he would drive to London when it was necessary for William Bellingham to serve in parliament. He met Lila at a wayside inn near Cotswold. Because he is a handsome fellow, he had swept her off her feet and they were soon married. After about a year, Tim's father died and his mother moved in with them, as her eyesight had gone bad. Lila couldn't handle Francine and her constant complaining, so she ran off, returning to the inn where Tim had met her. Tim waited for her to return, but she did not. After a time, Tim went to the inn and brought her back. She would stay a month, and then she would leave. This went back and forth about three times, but you could see that she was not happy. Tim had gone to London to bring Lord Bellingham back to the estate. A couple of farm boys found Lila's body in a pond. She had apparently drowned herself in about three feet of water. Now you know about Lila." He said nothing more, slowly shaking his head from side to side.

"Was he abusive to her to cause her to take her own life?" asked Meagan.

Shaking his head, the vicar answered. "I don't think so. There was no evidence of him being physical. I think that she knew that Tim was going to bring her back each time. I don't think you need to be concerned that he is violent. What do you think?"

Meagan looked down at her hands before answering. "He doesn't say much, but I don't think that he wanted a woman to bear him children. He wanted someone to care for his mother. Last night I expected that he would take me to the marriage bed, but he sent me to sleep with his mother."

"Give it some time, Mrs. Moran, give it some time," said the vicar. "Tim does want children, but he and Lila had no children during their short marriage. Perhaps your being with child is an indication that he wants to be a father. Also, with a more stable marriage, other children will come along. He is a good man, you know."

Almost shouting, she exclaimed, "No, I don't know. He is so quiet. He scarcely speaks, even if I ask him a question. It is more likely to be a shrug of the shoulders. You tell me he is a good man and a kind man, but I don't know. Things aren't right in that household, things aren't right!"

The old vicar reached out and patted her hand. "Give it time, Mrs. Moran, give it time." He got up from the stone bench and went into the church, leaving Meagan to ponder his parting words.

After she left the churchyard, her thoughts turned to the words on the headstone; 'Beloved wife of Tim Moran.' Would a man put those words on his wife's headstone, if he had killed her? The vicar did say that Tim was in London at the time of her death. I sense there is more to her death than the vicar and Tim are telling, or maybe even they do not know. Meagan came to the edge of the woods, and began to gather sticks of wood that she might bundle up to carry back to the cottage. All the time that she was picking up the sticks, she was praying to God, seeking counsel of Him. Was she to remain with Mr. Moran, or take her chances in the city? She still had the coins tied in her handkerchief to give her a start. By the time that she reached the cottage, she had peace that she wouldn't make the move to the city. At least for now!

The die is cast
But will it last?
At the hand of her mate
What shall be her fate?
An idea comes to mind
So Katie must now find
The Ghosts of the Teasdale Cemetery

CHAPTER 5
A CHILD IS BORN

Spring came to the English countryside. With the coming of spring, came the yearning to plant a garden. Meagan remembered how she enjoyed digging in the rich soil of Ireland. She sensed that the dirt here was not so rich, but she began by stirring up the soil. When the women of the congregation of the tiny church at Loxnard learned of her endeavor, they were anxious to share their supply of seeds, so that she might get started. Since the weather was warming, she didn't have to spend so much time in the woods to gather the downfall for the fire. She did have to gather enough to provide fuel for the preparing of the food for the family. She tried to encourage Francine to spend some time each day to sit in the sunlight, but Francine was content to sit in her rocker and expect Meagan to wait on her.

No matter how many times Meagan corrected Francine, she continued to call her Lila. Her ramblings were often incoherent, but from time to time, Meagan could understand a reference to the pond where Lila had died. She seems harmless enough, but I must remain cautious when we are alone. As frail as she appears, there are times that she is rather rebellious. She seems to possess an unusual amount of strength. On occasions, Mr. Moran had trouble controlling her.

Meagan looked forward to the meetings at the village church each Sunday. It was her only opportunity to be around other people. Mr. Moran continued to be a bit aloof. She was never sure if she was pleasing him, or not.

Of course, Meagan thought, the further along I get in this pregnancy, the less attractive I appear to be. After the baby arrives, will he be desirous of my affections?

Early in June, Meagan had left the house after Mr. Moran had gone to work. Francine was still sleeping, so she thought that it would be a good time to gather wood. She had hurried to gather enough sticks for the day. She sat on the trunk of a tree that had been uprooted by the wind. She began to pray silently, seeking solace for her soul. 'Oh God, give me peace, as my soul is so weary this day. I understand how Lila must have felt, but I fear that I am too cowardly to take my own life. Perhaps, you could help me out by striking me dead.' She began to weep, when she considered what she asked of God. 'I am sorry God for being selfish. I am your servant. I look forward to bringing this man child into the world.' Drying her tears, she looked up. A brown and white butterfly flitted before her face. She could feel it as it lit on her head along the hairline of her forehead. She cried out, "Thank you, God. You have sent Grace to lift my soul!"

It seemed that the bundle of twigs was lighter after her commune with God. The visit from the butterfly was reminiscent of her last days at the manor when she had told Grace the butterfly story. Perhaps Grace has had a butterfly visit today as well, now that she has come to mind. I pray that she is happy and content with those that care for her.

Before going into the cottage, Meagan stopped at the garden to admire the plants. They had eaten some early peas, as well as a number of radishes. She was constantly thinning the radishes as each one seemed to clamor for its own place in the row. She had planted potatoes, a reminder of her days in Ireland. The squash, yes, the squash. She had been determined to plant each seed that had been given to her by the women of Loxnard. It seemed that each woman had an abundance of squash seeds. They were just beginning to put forth their yellow blossoms. She noted the bees were beginning their pollination process. There were a few butterflies as well. I wonder if my Grace butterfly will visit my garden, now that she has found me.

Going to the cottage to check on Francine, Meagan turned at the door and looked out over the garden with its blossoms and vegetation, seeing the insect world being busy about their tasks. She prayed, God, it is my prayer that I come to know you better. And, that I might know your son, Jesus, in a closer way. The vicar speaks so highly of Him. Some things I do not understand. If only I could read, perhaps I could study the Bible as Mr. Moran does each evening. Would it be too presumptuous of me to ask him to read to me while I knit? He is such a quiet man. I will ask! It will do one of two things, either he will tell me to be quiet, or he will begin to open up to me.

While Meagan was praying, several miles away, a young girl and her nanny were walking among the trees on the Bellingham estate. The young girl, Grace said to her nanny, "Miss Carlyle, would you please tell me a story?"

"Grace," she replied, "I am not very good at telling stories. Unfortunately, I didn't bring a story book to read to you today."

"But, Miss Carlyle, can't you make up a story. That is what Miss Farley would do."

"Oh, all right. Let me see. Once upon a time, there was a kitten."

Grace interrupted. "Is this about the kitten with nine whiskers?" Miss Carlyle nodded, thinking that maybe she could weave a story about a kitten with nine whiskers. "Yes, yes it is."

Once again Grace interrupted, "Miss Farley told that one to me before she left. Tell me a different one."

"Very well, but, but I did say that I wasn't very good at telling stories. Let me think. In the garden, there was a big fat toad, sitting in the sun." Grace ran around a tree, and picking up a stick, she began to hit the tree. Displaying a bit of exasperation, the nanny said, "Don't you want to hear about the toad?"

Grace shook her head and said, "No, Miss Farley told me about the toad the day she left. I miss her. She was a good story teller. I wonder if she misses me." Tossing her stick aside, she ran out into the meadow where the wild flowers were blooming. Disgusted, the nanny leaned against a tree, thinking about the young man she had left behind when she accompanied Mrs. Bellingham at the time of her marriage. *I wonder if he misses me, as much as I miss him.*

Suddenly her thoughts were interrupted. Grace came running to her. "Miss Carlyle," she shouted with glee. "I saw her, I saw her!" Gasping, she said, "I saw Miss Farley. She touched my ear, and then my shoulder. I know that it was Miss Farley that came to see me, just like she said she would!"

"I didn't see anyone in the meadow," she said. "Are you sure that it was she?" Grace nodded. Fear came into her heart. Lord Bellingham had instructed her that Meagan Farley was not to have any contact with anyone on the estate. Taking Grace by the hand, she said, "Come, let's return to the manor. It is almost time for our lunch." They made their way back to the manor and the nanny said, "Grace, this can be our little secret about seeing Miss Farley. Maybe the next time I will be able to meet her. Then she can tell me a story as well."

Grace softly laughed. She put her hand to her mouth. *Doesn't Miss Carlyle know? Butterflies can't talk!*

Meagan Moran was elated that she had planted a

garden. The days of summer warmed the countryside and the garden flourished. As the garden flourished, so did the bond between Tim and Meagan. He saw how much time that Meagan put into the weeding and harvesting of the vegetables. He also took note that as the time of her delivering drew closer, it was more of struggle for her to accomplish the tasks of the household, as well as the garden. Oftentimes, after the supper hour, he would take up the hoe to help with the weeding. At those times, Meagan would have tea or a fruit drink along with a scone as a reward for his labors. They would sit together and she would purposely touch his hand, arm or shoulder. At first, he would shrink back, but after a time, he seemed to relish the caress. With the caresses, he became more verbal with her. Sometimes, she would accompany him into the woods when they gathered the sticks for the fire. She was no longer able to carry the firewood.

The days of October began to appear on the crude calendar. Meagan was uncertain how Francine would react to the baby in the household. She was content to remain in the rocking chair by the fire, mumbling most of the day, or demanding that Meagan wait on her with her unusual demands. Tim had fashioned a cradle for the baby, but Meagan was uncertain of the sleeping arrangements for her and Francine after the baby was born. Even now it was difficult for the two of them. Meagan sensed that there would be times that she would take the baby with her to bed to nurse when the nights became cooler.

The thirteenth day of October dawned a day that Meagan would remember as long as she lived. She had spent the prior day, harvesting her squash. She had a restless night, and when Tim awakened her in the morning, she said, "It is time. I know that it is time. You need to go for Mrs. Cooke. I will get up and fix your breakfast and get

49

your mother settled in her rocker."

Tim said, "Forget the breakfast. I will go to the stable and get the cart to bring the midwife here. See that Mother is in her rocker, as you will need the bed." He brushed his hand across her brow and said, "I will hurry. I love you, Meagan." He went out the door, and was gone. She stared after him in unbelief. Those were the first words of endearment to come from his lips in their marriage!

The birth pangs began to come closer and closer, Meagan cried out, "Tim, Tim, where are you?" She realized that was the first time she had failed to address him as Mr. Moran. Despite her crying out, Francine was impervious to Meagan's suffering.

Hearing the approach of a horse, Meagan relaxed. She turned her head to the side on the pillow. Looking up, it was not Tim that came through the doorway, but Lord Bellingham! Seeing Meagan, he demanded, "Where is Big Tim? He was to take Miss Carlyle and Grace to the circus in Cotswold this morning."

She replied, "I'm sorry, Sir, but he left before breakfast to go to Loxnard to get Mrs. Cooke to help me."

"When he gets back, tell him that I need him at the stables. You lazy Irish wench, why should you need any help!"

He started to turn back to the door when Meagan answered him. "She is the midwife. I am about to give birth to your son this morning. Surely you have others that could drive Grace and her nanny to Cotswold." She cried out, as the pain started up again.

"My son! Hah! You just don't give up, do you? I did you a favor by finding a husband for you. Don't expect anything more!" After a time, she heard his horse galloping away from the cottage.

A short time later, Tim and Mrs. Cooke arrived.

Meagan said nothing to Tim about her visit from Lord Bellingham. Mrs. Cooke was skilled in serving as a midwife, and Meagan gave birth. Mrs. Cooke said, "Oh, Meagan, you have a fine baby boy. He has black hair, and his eyes are so dark that they are almost black. I will get him cleaned up, and you can hold him while he nurses."

Meagan was sitting up, ready to receive her son. Mrs. Cooke brought him to her. Meagan said, "I will call him Timothy Conan Moran." She cradled him in her left arm and she exposed her left breast for him to suckle. Caressing his thick black hair, she said, "I will call him Conan, but others may call him 'Little Tim.' Oh, what beautiful dark eyes. Conan, you are a charmer." When he started to suckle, he brought his left hand up to lay on her breast. It was then that she saw a thin membrane of skin joining the middle finger and the finger next to the little finger. Now I know the secret of Lord Bellingham and the wearing of the white gloves! He was born with his fingers joined as well, but a botched surgery left him with his hand and fingers deformed. Someday, this information might well be to Conan's advantage. Thank you God, for you have given me a sign.

What child is this?
To bring such bliss;
Nine fingers, ten toes
Two dark eyes, one button nose.
An idea comes to mind
So Katie must now find
The Ghosts of the Teasdale Cemetery

CHAPTER 6
AUTUMN AT THE 99 RANCH

After dinner, Ty went to the stable and saddled the bay horse that he called Bayou. He wasn't particularly a good horse, but he was one that would cover a lot of territory in a short time. Ty wanted to get away from the hub bub of the custom feedlot and look over the ranch operation. Late September brought forth a day of warmth. Therefore, there was no need of additional outer wear. Also, there were no threatening rain storms to worry about as well. The summer haying was finished, so there was a bit of a loll in the ranch activities. Ty remembered that his father Tag had also enjoyed riding among the cows and calves. The calves were mature enough to exhibit if it was to be a good calf crop or not. Except for the times that they had encountered a severe drought; Tag would always brag that this year's set of calves were the best that he had ever raised. It had become somewhat of a family joke.

Satisfied, that unless something happened within the next six weeks; he determined that this set of calves could well be the best group that this ranch had ever produced. Touching spurs to his horse, he headed back to the ranch. I may get back to the house before Martin and Marie return home from school. I might even get Katie to warm up some coffee and pie for me.

Removing the saddle from Bayou, he returned him to the small pasture nearby. After he left the stable, he saw that Katie was in among the cottonwood trees that grew near the Dismal River. He saw the wagon that she used to haul Kylee around the ranch. He remembered that he encouraged her to buy a stroller for Kylee, but she had said that the ground was too rough for a stroller. She had reminded him that his mother had transported him around in a feed cart that she had found in the feed room shortly after coming to the ranch as a new bride.

Ty neared the river, and he thought that Katie was praying while she was sitting on the large stump. He drew nearer, he saw that she had her face in her hands, sobbing, and crying out, "Oh, God, why, why! I don't understand why you have let this happen! It is more than I can understand!" He stood nearby, not wanting to interrupt her communion with God. After a few moments, she rubbed her eyes, trying to dry them. She then arose from the stump. Looking in at Kylee in the wagon, she saw Ty standing nearby. Rushing to him, she cried out, "Hold me, Ty, hold me. It is more than I can endure." She began sobbing again while Ty held her close to his chest.

Reaching down to caress her head, he said, "It's alright, Katie, it's alright. Let it all out, and then you can tell me what has upset you."

Giving one last sob, she freed herself from his arms. "It's the book, Ty, it's the book! I should have never started to write that book!"

Grabbing her by the shoulders, he questioned, "What do you mean, Katie, what do you mean? I thought that is what you wanted. I see you writing from time to time, but you never let me see what you have written. Momma would never let us look at the portraits she was painting until they were finished. I presumed that you have taken the same stance with your writing."

She nodded, and said, "But this is different. This book has taken on a life of its own. Meagan is so real, that it is as if she has taken over my body." She stopped then, and looked over the Dismal River. Ty looked at her, unsure if it was his own wife!

Turning back, she said to him, "As I research

the time in which Meagan lived and endured the 'potato famine' in Ireland, I find that millions of people starved to death. She was separated from her family. As an illiterate orphan, she was subject to the whims of those superior to her. Unfortunately, she was also beautiful and naive, which made her more at risk."

"Do you think being beautiful is bad?" asked her husband.

"Yes, yes I do," she replied. "Because of all these things, she was desirable and was taken advantage of, being forced into immorality. Perhaps the saddest part was when she was cast out because she was no longer needed. It is a case of used, abused and refused."

Ty was puzzled, as he asked, "Well, is there a happy ending to this story? How much does the journal reveal?"

She answered, "I don't know. I have determined not to read ahead, so that I don't cloud the present with what happened in her future. That may seem strange to you, but I want it to be as accurate as possible. Unfortunately, I'm limited to the details, so that I must fill in the blanks. Perhaps, I am taking this too personal. It has been good to talk to you about the life of Meagan." She turned to pick up her daughter. She said, "Thanks for listening to me."

Ty touched her arm, as he challenged her. "Katie, I know you well enough, that you are brushing this aside. What is it?"

She had not yet picked up her daughter, but she lashed out at her husband, flailing at him, beating on his shoulders. He grabbed for her, bringing her close to his chest. "I hate you, Ty Taggat! I hate you! How could you do this to me?" She continued to struggle, trying to hit at him, sobbing all the time as she was shouting at him.

"What is the matter with you? Stop it! Have you gone mad?"

"I know about you and Becca Kurtz! Your mother once said that Katie knows everything! Well, I do! I know that Becca is going to have your baby! It took a while, but, now I know. Let me go! You have never stopped loving her! Well, you may no longer love me, but I'm not going to let her have you. I hate you for what you did, but I still love you. I have loved you since that first day that I met you in the hospital in San Francisco. Let me go!" The anger and accusations dried up the tears, but she continued to struggle.

Ty said, "Katie, I will let you go as soon as you calm down. Now let's sit down on this big stump and determine just how much you know and how much you don't know." He sat down on a large stump, big enough for both of them, but she chose a stump close by. He continued, "Yes, Becca is going to have a baby, but let--."

"See, then I was right. Why did you wait until now to tell me? You knew it as long ago as when Martin cut his arm. Am I right?" She folded her arms in defiance.

"Yes, yes, that is when she told me, there in the waiting room."

Katie almost shouted in her next statement. "She didn't just tell you, she whispered to you, that she was going to have a baby. She did whisper to you, didn't she?"

"I guess she may have, but tell me, where did you get all this information?"

"Marie told me. She was in the waiting room when Becca came in and sat down beside you. I remember your mother telling me about a saying that her Grandma Martin would say, 'only a fool, a drunk, or a child will tell the truth.' Go ahead and take your pick."

Ty chuckled, "That was over two months ago when she told me." He paused, while he corrected himself. "Excuse me, whispered to me. Have you been holding this in all this time?"

"Marie told me this morning before they left for school. It seems that Trevor Kurtz made the announcement on the school bus yesterday. Then she told me that she had overheard Becca tell you in the waiting room earlier, and that she had thanked you. Evidently, you were the first to know and the only one. Keep in mind another of Grandma Martin's sayings was that 'little pitchers have big ears.' Marie was there, you know." Katie folded her arms as an evidence of smugness.

Ty started laughing, when he considered all that Katie had told him. She interrupted his laughter. She haughtily said, "I see nothing funny about all this. You said nothing about Becca being pregnant. What am I to think?"

"You should think that your husband is a man that minds his own business. It was not my place to make the announcement that was given to me in a whispered manner. I was relying on the Summit City 'grapevine' to spread the news. Apparently it is not working. Do you have any more questions for me?"

"No."

"Then I have a question for you. Did you ever consider that maybe a six year old girl might not have understood the whole conversation? Becca did thank me for saving her marriage when I had suggested that Harry find work off the ranch where he could be his own boss. This had taken place when I was still a deputy sheriff. It helped to establish his self esteem. Carl and also Becca were second guessing his ability to be a cowboy. He is an excellent fence builder. In fact, it was there in the waiting room that I told her to let me know when he could build a mile of fence for us on the ranch. And, I didn't whisper it either." Ty got up from the tree stump. Looking down at Katie, he said, "Katie, have a little confidence in me.

I thought that our marriage was stronger than that, but I guess I was wrong. At one time, I did love Becca, but that is gone. A few misplaced words should not jeopardize our trust in one another. I know that Marie didn't know what she was doing, but it was exciting for her to tell you something that she knew that you didn't."

Katie remained sitting on the stump. Quietly, she whispered, "I'm sorry, Ty, I know I should have trusted you, but---." Her face was buried in her arms, while she began to cry once again.

Reaching down, he brought her to her feet. Taking her into his arms, he asked, "But what?"

"When Marie told me what she had heard, my mind flashed back to the day that Becca was married. You were on the hill overlooking the Good Hope Church. I heard you crying out, 'Becca, Becca, I love you.' Even now, whenever Becca comes into a room where you are, I sense that a light blush comes over your face. It has always made me question your love for her. I'm sorry that I questioned your fidelity. I love you, Ty Taggat, and I don't want anything to come between us." She buried her face into his chest.

Ty blushed. He confided to Katie. "I am aware of my face getting warm when Becca comes into my presence, but I had hoped that it wouldn't show. However, it isn't Becca that triggers this response, but it is the perfume that she wears. She still uses the same perfume that she used when we first started dating in college. Even in church, I try to sit as far away as I can to prevent getting a whiff of it."

Katie looked up into her husband's eyes, she said, "Well, Mr. Taggat, that is good to know. I think that perhaps, I need to visit Becca, and wish her well on her pregnancy." I think a nice vial of perfume might be the perfect gift for an expectant mother. Picking up her daughter, she said, "I will carry Kylee, and you can bring the wagon. I think that I might find some pie and coffee for us. There is something about the shedding of tears that seems to whet the appetite."

After they had their pie and coffee, Katie put Kylee in her playpen. Katie picked up the little black journal and she began to read more about the life of Meagan Moran.

Three days later, Katie paid a visit to Becca Kurtz. She knocked on the door and silently prayed for wisdom. They were not close friends, but they were neighbors. I do remember that Emilee, Ty's first wife had been a close friend of Becca when she was teaching at the Good Hope School. Becca was faithful in visiting Emilee in the last days of her terminal illness. I would usually serve coffee and cookies when she came, but I never entered in much on their visiting with one another. Now that I think about those times, I guess that the three loves of Ty's life were gathered at the table at one time. How strange, considering how shy Ty was with women. Now I understand what Agur wrote in Proverbs 30:18, 19—There be three things which are too wonderful for me, yea, four which I know not: The way of an eagle in the air; the way of a serpent upon a rock; the way of a ship in the midst of the sea; and the way of a man with a maid.

Becca opened the door, somewhat surprised that Katie was calling on her. "Come in, come in. My goodness, you and Kylee are a welcome sight."

Katie entered the foyer and handed a wrapped gift to Becca. "I understand that congratulations are in order. I am happy to hear of your pregnancy. I have brought a small gift. I remember that sometimes pregnancy can be a bit overwhelming at times."

She hugged Katie, and said, "Did Tylor tell you that we are hoping for a girl? Please sit down. If you don't mind, I will open this gift now. I was feeling a bit blue, but this visit was just what I needed." She started to remove the pink bow from the white box.

"Yes, Ty told me that you and Harry wanted a girl. I would have come sooner, but Ty thought it best to wait until we heard of your good news via the Summit County grapevine. Marie came home from school and gave us the good news." Katie sat down while Becca opened the gift of a bottle of perfume.

Touching the open bottle of perfume to her wrist, Becca took a slow sniff. A smile came over her face. "Katie, this was thoughtful of you to bring this to me. I love the fragrance. I have wanted to find a different perfume, but could never find one that I liked. Do you realize that I have used the same fragrance since high school? It was a graduation gift, and I never changed in all these years." She laughed as she placed a bit behind each ear. "I'll test it on Harry this evening to see if he notices the difference. Thank you, Katie." Getting up, she asked, "Do you have time for some tea and cookies. I imagine that Kylee would like a cookie. It has been so long since we had a baby in the family, I will need to be retrained on the ways of motherhood."

"Tea and cookies will be fine." Katie smiled, while she continued her conversation. "Don't worry about being retrained. I am sure that the ways of motherhood will return all too swiftly. I was ushered into motherhood even before I had Kylee and I survived."

"Yes, you have. I am amazed that it has only been a little over a year ago that Emilee returned. I see that the twins seem to have fit into your family quite well. I was glad that I could spend time with her before her death. When she taught school here, we became close friends. Do you hear from her sister Marilee?"

"Not often," answered Katie. "She sent gifts for

the children at Christmas, as well as for their birthday. She talks about coming out for a vacation, but other than those occasions, we don't hear much."

After a time, Katie and Kylee returned home. She liked to be home when the children returned from school.

Two days later, Becca called Katie, "Thank you for the perfume. Harry commented about it as soon as he came through the door. You made a good choice. Thanks again. Bye."

The following Sunday, the Taggat family was driving home from church, when Ty remarked, "Did Becca get a new hairdo, or what? There was something different about her, but I don't know what it was."

Katie quickly looked out the side window to keep from laughing. She replied. "I believe you are right. I noticed it too, but was unsure just what it was that seemed different." Katie thought to herself, what I noticed was the absence of Ty blushing. The change of perfume was a good choice. Ty's mother commented once that she liked to maneuver and manipulate as she worked her plan. She compared it to playing chess, except that you didn't have to set up the board. Yes, the gift of perfume has worked wonders. Isn't it great when a plan comes to fruition?

Now that the children were back in school, Katie returned to spend more time on her novel; The Ghosts of the Teasdale Cemetery.

Will Meagan find life,
As mother and wife?
Will Meagan find joy,
As she raises her boy?
An idea comes to mind
So Katie must now find
The Ghosts of the Teasdale Cemetery

CHAPTER 7
THE SECOND BABY

Meagan was not afforded any help with the caring of the household duties. Not having any children in the home previously, Big Tim saw no need of seeking out someone to come into the home to assist in the cooking and cleaning. Nor did Megan expect it. She had seen that the Irish tenant farmer's wife had taken little time off following the birth of a child. The noble English ladies were different. They were afforded the luxury of a minimum of seven days of bed rest. At the same time, they had the assistance of a nurse to care for the baby.

It was Francine that gave Meagan the greatest concern. She continued to refer to Meagan as Lila. Tim ignored the situation and Meagan had ceased to correct her. It had come to a point that Meagan questioned the sanity of the woman, but feared bringing this to Tim's attention. The first three days after the birth of Conan, she showed little interest in him. On the fourth day, Meagan, in an exhaustive state, had placed Conan in his cradle after dinner. She had gone to her bed to take a nap. The singing of Francine had awakened her. Sitting up in bed, she saw that Francine was rocking Conan. She was singing a lullaby to him. Meagan was consoled. Francine tenderly cradled Conan in her arms. Her first thought was that perhaps her son might have a calming effect upon her. Each day, she would encourage the elderly lady to rock her son. However, Meagan made an effort to be the one to take Conan from the cradle and place him in Francine's arms.

Conan was almost two weeks old, when Lord Bellingham had informed Big Tim that he would be returning to Parliament the next morning. He wanted to have a coach and driver available. The driver would remain in London, because he planned to return in a week.

The next morning, Big Tim went to the stable to harness the horses. After a time, he returned to the thatched home. Somewhat out of breath, he told Meagan, "The driver hurt his hand this morning and is unable to drive the coach. Pack me some clothes. I will be going to London. I will return in about a week. The injured driver will have to look after the stable in my absence. You have enough wood in the shed. Make do with what food supplies you have."

Meagan did as he had requested. He left, not saying anything further.

The next morning, Meagan stepped outside to fill the water bucket. When she entered the house, Francine was holding the baby at arm's length and wailing out, "Lila, you have brought a curse upon this house! The baby must die! The baby must die!"

Setting the bucket to the floor, Meagan went to her son. She snatched the crying baby out of the arms of the woman. Holding Conan, she asked, "Mrs. Moran, what is the matter, what is the matter?"

"He is cursed! His hand is like the wing of a bat. He must die, or we will all be cursed! Why did you come back Lila, why did you come back? I thought you were dead." Meagan now knew that Francine had discovered the deformity of her son's hand.

Holding her son to her bosom, Meagan fled out the door. She heard Francine continue to wail and proclaim the curse placed upon the family. After a time, it was quiet. Meagan opened the door and peered into the room. She saw that the deranged woman was seated in her rocker, humming a lullaby. Fear entered into Meagan's heart, counting the days before Big Tim's return. She now knew, Conan cannot be left alone, for the woman is unstable.

Neither is he safe in the cradle, where he might be taken up in a moment. Climbing the ladder to the loft, she placed Conan in the middle of the bed. Uncertain if Francine was able to climb the ladder, she pulled it down and laid it on the floor. Going to the wood shed, she found a small wooden box that had been used to store small pieces of wood for starting the fire. It was large enough to be a bed for her son. Turning it over, she rapped on the bottom with a small log, dislodging the accumulated dirt. Getting a bucket of soap and water, she scrubbed it and placed it upside down to dry.

Waiting for the wooden box to dry, Meagan kept herself busy in the house. She had determined that she could no longer sleep in the same bed with Francine. That left the bed in the loft, with Conan sleeping close by in the improvised crib. She was now questioning if Francine was actually blind, or was her vision so impaired that she could fake total blindness. It seemed that she had taken an unusual interest in Meagan preparing the crib. After the box had dried, Meagan fitted blankets in the bottom to make her son comfortable.

That night, Meagan was able to get her first night of uninterrupted sleep, since she had married Tim. Except for that pleasurable time while her son nursed, she did not have to endure Francine mumbling in her sleep, or crowding her in the bed. Things were fine until the second day that Conan was in the loft. He had cried out, and Francine went to the cradle. Not finding him, she began to wail uncontrollably, calling out, "Where is my baby, where is my baby?"

Meagan was upset, and Conan would not stop crying. Francine continued to wail in not being able to find her baby. In an effort to quiet things down, Meagan brought Conan to Francine. "Mrs. Moran, come and sit in your rocker and you can rock the baby." She placed him in her arms and said, "Why don't you sing him a lullaby. He enjoys your singing to him while you rock. Be careful now, and not rock too fast."

With the motion of the rocker and the soft lullaby, Conan was quieted. He was content to sleep and Francine was happy to hold him after she ceased the rocking and singing. Only Meagan was busy while she began her plan. Searching through the pile of wood stacked in the corner of the room near the fireplace, she found the ideal log. It was about the right weight, along with the length that she deemed appropriate. The girth she could adjust by wrapping the small blanket around it. Once reaching the right size, she began to sew the blanket edges together. With the sewn blanket secure, she then used her hands to mold and smooth out the rough edges. Satisfied with her project, she placed it in the cradle. Taking one of Conan's wet diapers, she gently rubbed it over the blanket. She looked down into the cradle and smiled. "Now, Francine has her own baby! Please God, please make this work!"

She went to Francine to take her son. Meagan went to take him out of her arms, and Francine cried out, "No, no! Don't take my baby!"

"But, I need to change him. Can't you smell him?" Francine ducked her head and smelled Conan. She nodded her head, and handed him to Meagan. After she had changed him, she placed him in his box in the loft. Picking up the blanket covered log from the cradle, she brought it to Francine. After she placed it in Francine's outstretched arms, she asked, "What is your baby's name?"

She smiled, and smelled the baby before answering, "His name is Timmy." She then began to rock once again. In the meantime, she started to hum a lullaby.

For two days, Meagan was able to deceive Francine. Whenever she would take 'Timmy' out of the cradle, she would smell him. Each morning, Meagan would lightly rub it with Conan's diaper. It was now to the point that Francine was a model companion. She spent much of her time rocking in her rocker and singing. The morning of the third day, the weather changed. Meagan awakened to an overcast, dreary morning.

Francine appeared to be affected by the weather. She was agitated and quite demanding of Meagan. This worsened after the rain started. At first in a gentle manner, but her demeanor worsened as the rain increased. When it came time for her to go to bed for the night, she refused to put 'Timmy' in the cradle. She cried out, "No, no, no! I want Timmy to sleep with me. I will not go to bed unless he is by my side." Meagan decided that there certainly could be no harm. It wasn't as if she was sleeping with a real baby that she could smother.

Meagan got her settled in bed. The house was a bit cool, so she put more wood on the fire in hope that it would not get too cool through the night. Meagan lay in her bed in the loft. She could hear the wind and rain increasing. She prayed to God before she dropped off to sleep, expecting that Conan would awaken her in the night so that he might nurse.

As expected, Conan did awaken, but after nursing, his mother returned him to his crib. She saw that the wood in the fireplace had burnt down, but the embers were still giving sufficient light to the room. It was then that she saw Francine cross the room, with 'Timmy' cradled in her arms. She approached the hearth and cried out while she held the blanket covered log over her head. "He is cursed! His hand is like the wing of a bat! He must die, or we will all be cursed! He is the one that brought the curse of the wind and the rain upon us all!" Meagan thought that she might hurl 'him' into the fire, but instead, she held it to her bosom. She ran out into the storm, not bothering to close the door.

Meagan climbed down from the loft. Going out the door, she expected to find Francine close by, wanting to return to the shelter and warmth of the house. She cried out, "Francine, come back. Francine, come back." There was no response. Wet and cold, she returned to the house, closing the door behind her. Though shocked by what she had witnessed, she sought the warmth of the hearth. She added additional wood to the fire. She stood before the fire and removed her nightgown, shocked at what she had witnessed. She listened for the return of Francine, but heard nothing. After she had warmed herself sufficiently, she returned to her bed, but not to her sleep.

At first light, Meagan wrapped Conan in a warm blanket and went out to look for Francine. The rain had ceased, but it had erased all signs of any footprints which Francine might have left. When she came to the road that went by their house, she turned toward Loxnard.

It was more of a struggle than she had anticipated. The road was wet and difficult to walk on because of the ruts that still held the water from the violent rain. Meagan tried to be careful to avoid falling in the mud, but her clothing was wet and mud spattered almost to her knees. She saw the village of Loxnard come into view when she came over the knoll in the road. A few of the citizens were beginning to make their way in the early morning. Stopping at the house of the vicar, she knocked on the door. Vicar Bentley opened the door, unsure of whom this mud covered woman was that was sitting on the bench close by. He saw that she was holding a small child. He recognized that it was Meagan. "Dear woman, why are you here so early in the morn?"

"Sir, it is Francine. She went out into the night and I don't know where she is. Mr. Moran has gone to London with Lord Bellingham and I have no one to help me find her."

"But why would she go out into such a vicious storm?" he asked.

"I don't know, sir, but I was awake when I saw her walking about the room. There was enough light from the hearth. I had been up with my child and had not yet gone back to sleep. She screamed out before going out into the storm. I got up and went out. I called for her, but she did not heed my call, nor return to the warmth of the house. It was still raining heavily and the wind was blowing. I did not go far, but returned to be with my son. At first light, I went looking for her, but there was no trace of her foot prints. That is when I gathered up my son and came for help. It will probably be another two days before Mr. Moran returns. Please, can you help me find her before he returns?" She was careful not to mention anything about the curse that had bothered Francine.

The vicar's wife Marta came to the door. Meagan gave a shiver to ward off the chill of the morning. Marta exclaimed, "Come inside, my dear child. You look chilled to the bone."

Meagan shook her head, "I am sorry, Mrs. Bentley, but my shoes and clothing are muddy from my walk from home. I should return. Mrs. Moran may have come home by now." She struggled to her feet, prepared to begin her return journey.

"Nonsense, girl, come in by the fire and I will fix you something to warm your soul. Here, let me take Little Tim and sit by the fire." She got a chair for Meagan before she took the baby and laid him in one of the larger chairs. She went to her cupboard and brought out a china cup, filling it from the teapot that rested near the center of the table.

Meagan took a sip of the tea, savoring the warmth that it provided. Mrs. Bentley had placed two biscuits on a small plate and moved the butter and honey close by, indicating to Meagan to help herself. She had devoured the biscuits and Mrs. Bentley refilled her cup. After a time, the chill left her and she stood up to leave. Reaching for her son, she said, "Thank you for the hospitality. I need to return. I expect Francine will come back to the house. Despite being blind, she has a sense of direction about her."

The Vicar said, "I will organize some of the men to search for her. We will stop at your house to see if she has returned. If not, then we will fan out in search of her. Thank you for coming. I know it has not been easy caring for her, especially with Big Tim gone for such a long time."

Meagan started her return trip. It was no easier than it had been before, but she avoided falling as she had earlier. She opened the door, expecting to find Francine in her rocking chair humming a lullaby, but she was not there! She stirred up the fire and changed her clothes. By the time that she had tended to her son, the vicar and four other men arrived at the house in a farm wagon, pulled by one horse.

Not finding Francine at home, they began their search. Meagan kept busy with her son, unsure of what the men might find. Mid-morning, they returned. It was a solemn group that came to the house. Vicar Bentley told Meagan, "We found her in the same pond that had claimed Lila. It seems rather ironic that each would die at the same location. I will look in the wood shed for some planks to lay her out in the house."

He returned with two logs and two planks to form a low table on which to lay Francine. The men carried her in and placed her on the planks. Meagan was shocked and fearful, as they laid out the dead woman. Her clothes were soaked, and her long gray hair was tangled. Meagan had never seen a dead person. Even she had been denied the opportunity to view the body of Lady Bellingham at the time of her death. And now, there is a dead woman in my house! Seeing her shock, Vicar Bentley comforted her. He said, "We will return to Loxnard and I will bring Marta and another woman to help you clean and dress her for burial. I will also bring the coffin for her to be placed in for viewing. We will wait for Big Tim to return before we have the funeral. She will remain in the home until the day of the funeral. We will leave now, but will return after the noon meal. I am sorry that you have to go through this without your husband being here."

He went to the door and Meagan asked, "Sir, could you go to the Bellingham estate to tell them what has happened? I would do so, but Lord Bellingham has forbidden me to set foot on the estate. Perhaps they could send someone, so that Mr. Moran can return home." The men stepped into the wagon and they left for the Bellingham estate prior to returning to Loxnard.

Meagan didn't move from her chair near the fire. Rarely did she take her eyes off of Francine. It was as if she expected her to rise up from her bed of planks. Finally, she went into the bedroom to gather clean clothing for the burial. Marta Bentley and Mrs. Cooke came to the door. Meagan greeted them and Marta began to instruct Meagan and Mrs. Cooke what she expected of them. Meagan took the soiled garments and put them to soak, while the other two washed the body. Once the body was dried off, it took the three of them to get her dressed and laid in the coffin. The man that had brought the ladies from Loxnard removed the planks to allow the coffin to rest on the logs. Marta told Meagan, "As soon as Big Tim returns home have him come see the vicar regarding the burial."

They prepared to leave and Meagan asked, "Aren't

you going to take the coffin back to Loxnard?"

Marta replied, "No, it is customary for the body to remain in the home until the day of the burial. Good bye, Meagan."

After the women left, Meagan could no longer bear seeing Francine in the coffin. She wrapped Conan in his blanket and went outside, not knowing where she would go, but she knew that she had to get away from the morbid sight of the coffin. She began to walk across the meadow, when she was drawn to an area where a small cluster of late blooming flowers were showing forth their yellow petals. She sat down on a stump, but Conan was beginning to be restless. She realized that it had been sometime since she had fed him, being involved with the preparation of the body. While he was nursing, Meagan listened to the birds singing in the trees. Evidently, they were enthralled with the warm afternoon after the severe weather of the previous night. She placed Conan on her shoulder to relieve him of his last burp, when a brown and yellow butterfly lit on his head, but only for a moment. It then fluttered to Meagan's brow before returning to the nectar of the yellow blossoms. Meagan laughed. She exclaimed, "Oh, Grace, you have come to tell me that all is well, yes, all is well."

Meagan continued on her journey. She was drawn to the pond that had claimed the life of Francine. She had been there one other time, when she had come to see where Lila had died. Looking down into the pond, she saw the burlap wrapped log had been pushed into the mud near the edge of the water. Had Francine come here that she might escape 'the curse?' In the end, it had brought about her death. But why, why did she come to the pond? Did it have any significance to the death of Lila?

Clutching her son, Meagan returned to her humble home. Conan was still sleeping when she placed him in the cradle. After she had stirred the coals in the fireplace, she added more wood to the fire. Moving the caldron of water over the flame, she waited for the water to heat, so that she might fix herself a cup of tea. Meagan had not eaten anything since the tea and biscuits that Martha Bentley had prepared for her earlier in the day. While setting out the cup and sauce, she pondered what else she might eat. She had no appetite after the events of the morning, and she questioned if she would be able to eat anything in the presence of the coffin in the room. She went into the bedroom and found a large quilt that she draped over the coffin. Now she was at peace!

Midmorning the next day, Tim Moran returned from London. When he entered the house, he saw the coffin. Removing the quilt, he looked in at his mother. In a rather stoic manner, he asked, "Meagan, what happened?"

She went to him and touched his arm. She said, "In the middle of the night, during a vicious storm, she went out into the dark. I went out, but could not find her. The next morning, I went to the vicar to report her missing. Later they found her. She was in the same pond that had claimed the life of Lila. I am sorry, Mr. Moran, I am real sorry."

> *The lady is quiet, the lady in the room*
> *A shadow of doubt, a shadow gloom*
> *The question of why, the question of death*
> *Left unanswered, with her last breath*
> *An idea comes to mind*
> *So Katie must now find*
> *The Ghosts of the Teasdale Cemetery*

CHAPTER 8
THE BURIAL

Big Tim walked to Loxnard to confer with the vicar regarding his mother's burial. It was near noon when he returned to the cottage. He entered the cottage and Meagan came to him. "Mr. Moran, I have prepared your dinner. It will only be a few moments for me to dish it up for you. I imagine that you are hungry." He nodded, but said nothing.

He sat down at the table. After he blessed the food, he began to eat. Midway through the meal, he looked up at Meagan and said, "I talked with the vicar. I will get the two wheeled cart after I finish here and I will take the coffin to the church for burial. He has arranged for the community to be present for a service at three o'clock this afternoon. If you are planning to attend the service, be ready when I return from the stable." With those few words, he turned his attention to finishing his meal.

"I will be ready, Mr. Moran. Is your mother to be buried next to your father?" He nodded his head and he took the last bite of the beef stew that Meagan had prepared. Pushing back from the table, he placed his hat on his head and left the room.

Meagan was ready when she heard the cart approach the cottage. Her first thought was how the two of them would be able to get the coffin out of the cottage and into the cart. That thought was answered when Big Tim secured a rope around the coffin and drug it outside. Reaching his arms around the coffin, he hoisted it into the cart, securing it with the rope that he used to drag it out of the cottage. Meagan held Conan in her arms. Big Tim helped her into the front of the cart. The trip to Loxnard was a quiet trip, except for the squeaking of the cart.

Neither one spoke on the trip to Loxnard.

The burial ceremony was a simple affair with about forty villagers in attendance. Francine Moran was buried next to her husband in the family plot in the cemetery adjacent to the church. There was still room for one more grave, next to where Lila was buried. The men replaced the dirt in the grave. The women had prepared something akin to an afternoon tea. Meagan had observed her first Protestant funeral. The return home from Loxnard was much like the trip into Loxnard with only the squeaking of the cart interrupting the silence.

Big Tim remained aloof and withdrawn, rarely speaking to Meagan unless it was a matter of necessity. Each night after their supper, he would read from the Bible for a time before going to the loft to retire for the night. And likewise, Meagan would feed Conan before she too went to her bed. It was now to the point that she missed the humming of the lullaby and the random talk of Francine. Just anything to break the unending silence!

It was the first of December and a fine day indeed. Meagan had washed the bed linen after breakfast. While it was drying on the line, she decided that she would wrap Conan in his heavier blanket and they would go for a walk in the woods. She started walking, not having any destination in mind. A short time later, a doe and her half grown fawn ran across the path in front of her. Meagan continued along a path, when she came to a large stump. Conan was fussing among his blanket, so she thought to stop in order to take a brief rest before returning home. He was now six weeks old and was beginning to display his personality, when he looked into his mother's eyes. He responded to her voice. It was one way of breaking the silence in the home. She began to pray and as she wept before God, she asked, "Oh God, show me your way.

I fear that I cannot endure the silence of the home and being ignored by my husband. Show me your way!" She continued to weep, her face buried in her son's blanket. She heard the rustling of the leaves nearby and looked up. Grace Bellingham was standing by her side!

The beautiful little girl shouted, "Miss Farley, I found you, I found you!"

Meagan reached out to her. "Oh, Grace, indeed, you have found me. But, I am married now and you may call me Mrs. Moran. Also, I have a little boy." She pulled the blanket from Conan's face. She said, "This is Conan. He is almost two months old."

Grace peered in at the baby. She said, "Look, he is sucking on his fingers."

Meagan reached down to take the two fingers of his left hand out of his mouth. They were the two that were joined together. She replied, "Sometimes when he gets hungry, he begins to suck on his fingers. Most children when they are young like to suck on their finger or thumb. I remember you would suck on your thumb when I first started taking care of you. You don't do that anymore, do you?"

Grace shook her head and looked at Conan with interest. "But, Miss Farley, he has his fingers stuck together. Is that what happens when he sucks them at the same time?"

Their conversation was interrupted when a breathless young lady came to them. "Grace Bellingham, don't run away from me ever again. You could get lost in among the trees."

Grace said, "But I was trying to catch the deer. I think that they are faster than me."

Meagan said, "Yes, they are. We saw the doe and her fawn, but Conan and I had to rest, as indeed, they were too fast." Reaching out, she said, "I am Mrs. Moran. My son Conan and I stopped here to rest, when Grace surprised us. I fear that in looking for the deer, I may have strayed onto the Bellingham Estate. I have no intention of trespassing."

Taking Meagan's hand, the young lady said, "I am Miss Carlyle. I came to the estate to care for Grace when Lord Bellingham and Lady Bellingham were married. No, you were not trespassing. We passed the boundary marker a short ways back. This girl is certainly a handful. Mrs. Moran, you do have a handsome son with the black hair and dark eyes." Taking Grace's hand, she said, "Grace, it is nearing time for the noon meal, so we need to return to the manor before someone starts to look for us. Goodbye, Mrs. Moran."

Before they went out of sight, Grace turned and waved at Meagan and Conan. Meagan returned the wave.

Meagan continued to sit on the stump, while she prayed to God. "Thank you, Father. You have brought Grace back into my life and I have had the opportunity to meet Miss Carlyle, her caretaker. You have given me new hope. Tonight, Mr. Moran and I will talk."

Meagan bundled the blanket around Conan. She left the comfort of the tree stump. She now began to formulate her plan for the evening. She did not hurry home for the noon meal. Her husband had taken a lunch with him when he left that morning. Drawing near to their cottage, she checked the snares that she had set in order to catch a hare to eat. Last summer, they had certainly eaten enough of her garden that she felt compelled to reduce the population a bit before another season. One of the snares had a hare in it, so she took Conan into the home and placed him in his cradle. Returning to the snare, she caught the young hare and prepared it for the basis of a stew for their supper. She had planned to use the vegetables in the root cellar to add to the stew. Along with the bread and cheese, she planned to make a small cake, topped with a sweet sauce. Tonight was to be a special night!

Meagan stirred up the fire. During the time the large caldron of water was begin to heat up, she took the opportunity to make up her bed with the fresh washed linen that she had brought in from the clothes line. She purposely neglected to make up the bed in the loft. She set the stew to simmering and prepared to take her bath. While she was bathing, she remembered that she had brought with her a small vial of the perfume that she had used while she was at the Bellingham manor. The aroma of the stew and the cake will be sufficient to get us through the supper hour, but the perfume is what she was counting on to get them through the evening. After her bath, she dried her hair and gave it a thorough brushing to restore the sheen to the dark ringlets.

The hour approached for the return of Big Tim. Meagan began to have some doubts about her plans for the evening. She had set the table, when she remembered that Tim had slippers that he would occasionally wear after a hard day at the stable. She heard him opening the door.

He entered and stopped short. He turned his head from side to side. "What smells so good? I hope that is my supper I smell."

Meagan came to him with his slippers in her hand. "Yes, that is your supper. I do hope that is as good as it smells. I have been enjoying it all afternoon. I have brought your slippers, so if you will let me put them on for you, you can rest. It will be a few more moments before it is ready." He sat down in his chair near the fire; the one that he sat in each evening to he read his Bible. She took each foot and put the slippers on his feet. "Tell me, Tim, how was your day?"

He sighed before he replied, "Busy." Meagan took that as a clue that he didn't have much to say about his day.

Meagan dished up the stew. The steam rose up from the edge of the bowls. They folded their hands and Tim asked a short blessing on the food. Meagan reached out and touched his left hand and asked, "Tim, do you think that sometimes I could ask the blessing on the food?"

Startled, his spoon stopped just short of his lips. "No, as head of the house, I will ask the blessing. Why would you ever think that you could do such a thing?"

"If you trust me to prepare the food, surely you could trust me to ask the blessing. At that point, I would certainly not be able to do it any harm, nor would I want to, for I will be eating it as well." Meagan gave him a wry smile.

Meagan had no intent of pressing the matter any further. She certainly did not want to cause any dissension that would interrupt her plan for the evening. Changing the subject, she continued, "I took Conan for some fresh air today, and we saw a doe and her fawn in the woods. Would Lord Bellingham permit you to kill a deer so that we might have some fresh meat? It would certainly be nice to supplement our diet of the hares that I have been able to snare." Tim was beginning to think that this woman with her endless ideas was getting on his nerves. Usually she sits in silence.

He answered her. "The Lords and the gentry of this nation frown upon the taking of any wild game by the commoners, whether they are employees of the estate, or are simply poachers. The wild game is for their pleasure only."

Meagan bowed her head and was intent upon eating her stew. *I am not about to tell him that I had seen Lord Bellingham's daughter Grace this morning. I am sure*

*that Lord Bellingham had informed him that I was not
to trespass upon the estate. That is why I had asked Miss
Carlyle if I was on the estate this morning.* The supper was
finished in silence.

Tim got up from the table and took his chair by the
fireplace. When he reached for his Bible, Meagan said, "If
you will wait a moment, I have some cake with a sweet
sauce, which I thought might go well with your tea. I will
serve it up before you start with your Bible reading."

"That sounds like a good idea. I do enjoy something
sweet. I will wait. I presume that you will be joining me as
well." She nodded, but the nod was interrupted by Conan
when he cried out. Her first thought was, *what is that boy
doing, trying to sabotage my plan for the evening?* Picking
him up from his cradle, she placed him on Tim's lap, with
Conan's feet resting on Tim's stomach.

She smiled at Tim and said, "Here, you can
entertain him for a moment. I sense that he is hungry. I will
start heating the water for the tea and then take him from
you, so that he can nurse. By the time that he is fed, the
water will be hot. He likes to be talked to. Just tell him how
handsome he is, but don't let him roll off of your lap." Tim
sat motionless. He was shocked at having Conan in his lap.
He said nothing, counting the moments before Meagan's
return. Meagan thought, *all right Tim, you married me so
that I might give you children, here is the first one and may
there be many more!*

She returned and taking Conan, she purposely sat
across from Tim, while she allowed him to nurse. Tim
was somewhat embarrassed, but was unable to divert his
attention from the nursing child and mother. After being
fed, the child dropped off to sleep and was returned to his
cradle.

Meagan brought the saucers with the cake and the

tea to a small table near the chairs by the fireplace. After she set them down, she spoke with uncertainty. "Tim, each evening, you sit here before the fire and read your Bible. May I join you, so that you might read to me?"

Tim was hesitant as he mulled over her request. "Well, I suppose I could, but I wasn't sure how interested you were in the Bible. I thought that at times when Vicar Bentley was preaching, your mind was off thinking of other things."

"I admit that sometimes it is difficult to follow along in his thinking. If I could read, I would be able to follow along as he reads the scripture. Tim, would you teach me to read."

Meagan had never seen Tim so belligerent. Immediately he answered her! "No, no! Absolutely not! As head of this house, I forbid you to even consider such a thing. If you have a question about the scripture, I will give you the answer, but you are not going to learn to read."

"Who taught you to read?"

He answered her, "Usually, the vicar of the church instructs the boys, that is, if the parents are agreeable to pay him. Oftentimes, that is what sustains the vicar. My tutor was Samuel Alexander. I started when I was seven. By the time I was twelve, I was old enough and big enough to start working in the stable of the Bellingham estate. I followed in my father's footsteps. Vicar Bentley has about ten or twelve boys that he tutors. If the parents are fortunate to have sufficient funds, their sons will continue to be tutored until such time that they go off for further education."

"What about Conan?" Meagan asked. "Do you think that he will be able to go to school?"

"I am not sure. You see, Lord Bellingham's father provided the funds for my education until such time that I could go to work in the stables." Tim paused, before continuing. "I rather doubt that William Bellingham will do the same for Conan. It appears that he does not hold you in very high regard. He told me at the time that we were married, that he did not want you anywhere on the estate. When you and I have a son, he may provide for his education, but not for Conan." *Tim saw that Meagan did not like what he had told her, but that is how things stood. There is no need of her getting her hopes up for her son. He is destined to be a stable hand.*

Meagan understood what Tim was trying to tell her, but she had other things on her mind before approaching the education of her son.

Nothing more was said regarding Conan's education. Tim read aloud from his Bible. Meagan enjoyed listening to the sound of his voice. Tonight was the most that they had conversed since their marriage.

After Tim closed the Bible, he commented, "Meagan, I see that you have failed to make up my bed in the loft. I am ready to go to bed at this time. If you will make it up, I will get the fire ready for the night."

"Mr. Moran," she replied. "There is room in my bed for you. I have fulfilled the time following the birth of my son. You married me that I might give you children. I see no need of making the bed in the loft until such time that we have children to put up there. I am going to bed, and I await you to join me in the wedding bed."

Meagan thought, *I believe that was well spoken. Now to add a touch of perfume, and remember what Charlotte, the French courtesan would do at this time.*

Earlier that evening, things were not going so well at the manor of Lord Bellingham. The family was gathered around the dining table that evening. Grace twisted in her chair. She told her father, "Papa, guess who I saw today! I saw Miss Farley, and she had a baby with her. She said his name was, was---." She turned to Miss Carlyle and asked, "What did she say was her baby's name?"

"Grace," she said. "His name was Conan, but that was not Miss Farley. You are mistaken. She said that her name was Mrs. Moran."

Grace was not to be denied. "I know who I saw! She said it was her baby. I saw him sucking his fingers, and when I saw that two of them had been stuck together, I asked her if that is what happens when a baby puts two of them in their mouth at once. That was Miss Farley."

Lord Bellingham interrupted their conversation. He turned to Miss Carlyle. He spoke with an angry tone of voice. "You are both right. She is one and the same person. However, where were you when you saw her? I have forbidden her to be anywhere on the estate. Also, when we placed Grace in your care, I ordered you not to have any contact with Miss Farley."

The young caretaker's face was ashen when she saw how angry Lord Bellingham had become at the news of Mrs. Moran. "Grace had run ahead of me. She was chasing after a doe and her fawn. She went to Mrs. Moran and talked with her before I could catch up with her. Mrs. Moran specifically asked if she was on the estate. She said that she did not want to be guilty of trespassing. I had remarked that in trying to find Grace, I had passed the marker establishing the boundary of the estate. I am sorry, Lord Bellingham, but I did not know that she was the former Miss Farley. I saw that Grace was happy to see her, but I thought it was because of the baby. Her baby is quite handsome, with the black hair and dark eyes. Also, I did observe the two fingers on the left hand that were joined."

Lord Bellingham turned to his wife. With anger in his voice, he said, "Lady Virginia, as soon as you find someone to replace Miss Carlyle as Grace's caretaker, you may send her back to your father's estate. Miss Carlyle, you are excused from the table and please take Grace with you. I have heard enough from the two of you for one evening."

While Miss Carlyle climbed the stairs to take Grace to her room, she reflected on the events of the day. *Well, it isn't all bad. I will return to being an upstairs maid, but I will be back at the estate where I had left the love of my life!*

Lord Bellingham had thoughts of his own. *I fear that I have not heard the last of that Irish wench. It would have been best if I had put her out on the streets of London!*

All people through this far flung land
Shall know this child with the crippled hand
Some see this as a curse upon this child
But can it be on one so sweet, so mild
An idea comes to mind
So Katie must now find
The Ghosts of the Teasdale Cemetery

CHAPTER 9
THE BOY CONAN

Conan Moran was a healthy baby; a healthy baby that grew into a healthy boy. At an early age, he acquainted himself with the outdoors and the woodland that surrounded the thatched cottage. He would accompany his mother into the woods to gather wood for the heating and cooking for the home. He learned to set the snares to catch the hares that frequented the garden. Meagan warned him to not venture into the woodlands of the Bellingham Estate, nor to set any snares on the Bellingham property. There were times that he would travel the road to meet his father at the stables. He would then walk home with his father most evenings. It was at the stable that he first met Grace. She would come several times each week to ride her pony, Gypsy. Conan was never allowed to ride Gypsy, but he was always willing to care for the pony when she returned from her ride. He would brush the pony, talking to it, while he gave the pony a rub down.

When she rode her pony; Grace was usually accompanied by her father. If not him, then the young lady that looked after her might ride with her. Otherwise, Big Tim would ride with her. The summer that Conan turned four, was when he began to frequent the stable. Grace was four years older, but she was glad to befriend the child of her former nanny. Conan was a clever lad. He learned to get on Gypsy when she was tied in the stall. As soon as he heard anyone enter the stable, he would slide off of her back and resume brushing the pony.

Conan had taken an interest in whittling and wood carving, so on his sixth birthday, he was given a knife. He began to carve small animals, such as cats and dogs,

and occasionally a bird or fish. He would give them to his
parents and the friends that he made as the family attended
the small church in Loxnard. The knife he used for other
things. From time to time, he would observe the game birds
that would feed along the road when he traveled to and fro
to the stable. He sensed that if he could snare a hare, he
could also snare a pheasant. Most of the game birds were
on the preserve of the Bellingham Estate and he knew that
Geofrey Hoke kept a sharp eye out for poachers. Meagan
had warned him to not even catch the hares anywhere
near the estate. Lord Bellingham dealt rather harshly
with poachers. Conan felt uneasy in the presence of Lord
Bellingham. He had a tendency to ignore Conan, as if he
didn't exist. It was because of this, that Conan began to
plan his first attempt at snaring a pheasant. With a bit of
grain and his snare box, he set the trap just inside of the
Bellingham game preserve. It was three days before he
caught his first pheasant. It was a young bird that was old
enough to have the tail feathers and plumage of a fine
cockerel. Wearing gloves, he grasped the bird about the
neck and legs before killing it. He was careful to not disturb
the grass and leaves. He bled the fowl before leaving the
brush. Taking his snare box with him, he started for home.
With his home within sight, he plucked the bird, removing
the innards, the head and the feet. Tucking the dressed bird
under his arm, he stopped at the woodshed and placed it
on a shelf near the back of the shed. He left the snare box
nearby, and picked up a small shovel and went back to
where he had cleaned the bird. Digging a deep hole, he
scooped in the feet, the innards and the feathers. He was
tempted to keep the tail feathers, but knew that he must
hide all of the evidence of the bird having existed.

He returned to the shed with the shovel, where he
picked up the bird and went into the house. His mother was

tending the fire. When she turned to greet him, she saw what he had brought her. In fear, she clasped her bosom. She cried out, "Conan, what have you done?"

He calmly replied, "Mother, I have brought you a young pheasant. I was tired of eating the hares that I have been catching in my snare box. Tonight we will eat well." He placed the bird on the table.

Meagan sat down at the table. She beckoned to her son, "Come and join me. We must consider what you have done." After he sat down, she began to question him. "Tell me Conan, where did you get this fine bird?" The boy was fearful of the question, so he said nothing as he looked into the far corner of the home, avoiding his mother's eyes.

"Conan, look at the bird and then look at me and answer the question."

In a defiant manner, he said to his mother, "I set a snare at the edge of the estate. Lord Bellingham has lots of pheasants. Besides, he doesn't talk to me. If he wants me to do something, he tells Father, 'Tell Conan to do this, or have Conan go here or there.' He rarely even looks at me, so how will he know that I poached one of his pheasants?"

"It doesn't make any difference if he knows or not, but I know and God knows, and you certainly cannot forget what you have done. What did you do with the feathers, feet and the insides? All these things are a witness to what you have done."

He said, "I buried them, so nobody will know."

It was then that his mother asked, "Are you sure? Unless you buried them quite deep, the first fox or dog that comes along will dig them up, and then others will know that someone has been poaching on the estate. Do you realize that if it was determined that you have been poaching, Mr. Moran could lose his position as stable master? And all of this would be because of one young pheasant. I realize that it was a challenge for you to snare a pheasant, but what do you think we should do about that beautiful bird?"

Conan quickly responded, "I could bury it, and bury it deep."

"I suppose that we could do that, but why don't we bake it. It is certainly too fine of a bird to waste in such a manner. Mr. Moran won't be home for dinner and if we start to bake it now, it will be ready to eat early this afternoon. Does that sound all right with you?"

Conan nodded his head, but uncertain if his mother was making the right decision.

Upon his agreement, she said, "Go fetch some more firewood and I will prepare the bird for baking. In the meantime, I will fix us a bite to eat. It will take a while for the bird to bake."

Early in the afternoon, Meagan took the young pheasant out of the pot and laid it on a cloth that was on the table. Conan admired the golden brown of the breast of the bird. The aroma had filled the room for some time. He was excited. He anticipated tasting a pheasant for the first time. However, his mother wrapped the bird in the cloth and placed it in a wicker basket. She beckoned her son, and said, "I will get my bonnet and we will go see Mr. Geofrey Hoke, the Gamekeeper of the Bellingham Estate."

Conan stopped and asked, "Why are we going to see Mr. Hoke? He is mean."

"Whether he is mean or not, you need to explain to him as to why we have this pheasant in our possession. You have brought sin to our home. We cannot bury it, and we certainly cannot eat it. Therefore, as Mr. Hoke is the gamekeeper, we must return it to him. It will then be his responsibility what he does with the bird. It will also be his responsibility what he does with you because of your killing one of Lord Bellingham's pheasants. Come along now. You might be thinking what you will say to Mr. Hoke. I will be with you when you talk with him. I know that this is not easy for you, but the quicker we take care of this, the quicker the burden of sin will be lifted from your soul." Meagan took her hand and put it on his shoulder. She kept it there until they approached the path leading to the gamekeeper's home.

Drawing near to the house, they saw that he was out by the dog kennels. The hounds began to bark while they approached the house. A sharp command from Mr. Hoke silenced them. Conan and his mother went to the man.

Conan was fearful while he stood before Mr. Hoke. His voice quivered when he began to speak. "Sir, I have done wrong by poaching on the estate. I snared a young pheasant and killed it."

Looking down at the young lad, he asked, "Why did you come to tell me about this?"

Conan turned his gaze to his mother, uncertain of what he should do. She nodded. He said, "My mother told me that I had brought sin upon our house, and upon myself for what I have done. As gamekeeper of the estate, I am returning the bird to you."

"You seem rather young to be poaching. How old are you, and what is your name?"

"Sir, my name is Timothy Conan Moran, but my mother calls me Conan, and I am almost seven years old. This is my mother. My father is the stable master. He doesn't know what I have done."

Geofrey Hoke gave Conan a stern look before he spoke. "I have been watching you, but I thought that you were too young to be poaching, since I never found your trap. What did you do with this bird?"

Conan reached into the basket and handed it to the

gamekeeper. It was still wrapped in the cloth. Mr. Hoke removed the cloth. He could feel its warmth. The dogs caught a whiff of its aroma, and began to bark again. He silenced them. He looked at the golden brown of the skin of the bird. Turning his gaze to Conan, he asked, "Have you ever tasted pheasant?" Conan shook his head. Mr. Hoke then asked Meagan, "And you, Mrs. Moran?"

She nodded her head, and said, "Yes. For a time I was the upstairs maid at the estate. I have tasted pheasant. I must tell you Mr. Hoke, I have been forbidden by Lord Bellingham to set foot on his estate. However, I thought it needful to bring Conan to you." Mr. Hoke nodded. He remembered seeing her in times past when she accompanied Lord Bellingham's daughter Grace, when they walked in the park.

Mr. Hoke removed a knife from a sheath on his belt. He said, "It is time that Conan tastes what he has been poaching. Let us sit on this tree stump and I will cut up this bird." After he sliced into the bird, he handed Conan and Meagan, each a portion of the breast. He then cut a slice for himself. Conan was uncertain of what he was supposed to do. Mr. Hoke took a bite and nodded to him. Conan took a bite of the still warm golden breast and smiled.

Mr. Hoke continued. "Young man, you have been blessed with a mother that has taught you integrity. Don't forget it." He then turned to the mother. "Mrs. Moran, with your permission, I would like to have Conan spend part of his time helping me with the dogs. There may be times that he could help me when we conduct hunts here on the estate. On those occasions, the attendants have an opportunity to share in the game. He will still need to spend time at the stables, but I see no reason that he cannot do both. Now, let us finish off this bird while it is still warm."

Mother and son prepared to return home. Conan

said, "Thank you, Mama. I am sorry that I poached the bird. I think it probably tasted better after we did the right thing. I feel better about it now. But Mama, what will we do if the dogs dig up the feet and the feathers?"

"It doesn't matter. You have confessed your sin and Mr. Hoke has forgiven you."

He was quiet for a time, but his mother sensed that he had more to say to her. Finally, he asked, "Mama, can I go to the classes that the vicar has to teach the boys to read and write?"

"Conan," she replied, "let me see what I can do. That is how the vicar earns his money. The congregation is not able to pay him enough unless he teaches those classes. I will talk with your father. Keep in mind, you are already committed to work in the stable, and now Mr. Hoke wants you to help him."

Conan thought a moment before he replied. "Mama, if I have a choice, I would rather work less time at the stable. But, I do want to learn to read."

That night after Conan had gone to bed, Meagan asked, "Mr. Moran, Conan is desirous of going to school, would we have enough to pay for his classes? You realize that he is quite bright and eager to learn." She feared what his answer would be.

He answered her rather sharply. He said, "Meagan, it is out of the question. We are barely able to eke out a living as it is. We have discussed this earlier, so just forget it."

"Mr. Moran, may I speak with the vicar to see if he has any solution in regard to paying for Conan's tuition?"

Tim Moran was hesitant in answering. "You can try, but from what I hear, he is firm in what he expects to receive. When he first came to Loxnard, he reduced the rate for one family. Then the other parents expected a fee reduction. Since that time, he has treated everyone the same." He picked up his Bible to read, considering that the matter was closed.

The next day, while Conan was helping his father at the stables, Meagan walked to Loxnard to visit with Vicar Bentley. She saw that he was sitting on a bench in the front of the church. She approached and he looked up from his book and greeted her. "Good morning, Mrs. Moran. What brings you here on this fine morning?" He stood up and said, "Before you answer my question, I believe Marta would have some tea and scones ready at about this time. It will be a while before my first students will arrive, so let us go to the sitting room."

They entered the house and Meagan saw that Marta was preparing a tray for them. After they sat down, the vicar once again asked Meagan the purpose of her journey. Meagan took a sip of tea before approaching the subject of Conan's education. She said, "Conan is desirous of learning to read and write. However, Mr. Moran informs me that we are not able to afford the tuition at the current rate. Do you see any solution to this problem? You realize that Conan is a bright child. I am sure that he would do well."

The vicar was quick to answer. He said, "I quite agree that Conan is bright. However, my class of boys at that age is full, so there is no benefit in us considering a rate reduction at this time."

Meagan sensed that she had come up against a stone wall, principally because she had no money for Conan's education. However, she wasn't finished just yet. "Vicar Bentley, let me pose this question to you. If I could come up with an anonymous benefactor, would you be able to find a spot in the class for Conan?"

The vicar almost choked on his tea at Meagan's question. Composing himself, he replied, "Yes, Mrs.

Moran, I do believe that I would be able to accommodate him in our class."

Meagan stood up to leave. She said, "Very well, I will see what I can do. Good day." She left the manse, knowing what she must do next.

Two days later, the opportunity arose for Meagan to put her plan into action. Big Tim left early Monday morning with the carriage to take Lady Anne to her parents' estate for a two night stay.

Monday night, Meagan took Conan with her, making their way to the estate of Lord Bellingham. She had waited in the shadows until she was sure that most of the servants had retired for the night. She left Conan on the backside of the large tree, away from the manor. She warned him not to leave under any circumstance. After pulling the hood of her coat close to her face, she rapped on the door with her closed fist. After a pause, she rapped again. Just as she was prepared to rap the third time, the door squeaked as it opened. She recognized the butler holding the candle, but she did not declare herself. He asked, "What is it?"

"I have come to see Lord Bellingham. I have a message for him."

Holding out his hand, he said, "The hour is rather late. I will take the message to him."

"No, the message is not written." With that, he opened the door wider and motioned for Meagan to come in. She shook her head and said, "No, I will wait here at the door." He closed the door and left Meagan standing outside.

The door began to squeak again as it slowly opened. Meagan saw Lord Bellingham in the candlelight. He was beginning to gray. Also, he had put on more weight. The past seven years had not been kind to him. He demanded, "Who are you, and what do you want?"

She tossed the hood back off of her head. With a toss of her head, she said, "I am Meagan, and I have come to ask you to pay for your son's schooling with Vicar Bentley."

He was startled at her beauty. She had been beautiful at sixteen, but now that she had matured, she had become more beautiful. He reached out and drew her to him. It was then that he kissed her. He hissed at her, "I have no son! I told you to stay away!"

She was frightened and speechless until she saw the white gloves on his hands. Her memory flashed back to the time that she had seen his left hand with its scars and fiery red color. She drew in a breath to answer him. "I know why you wear the white gloves. I have seen the scars and the coloring of your left hand, the result of an apparent botched operation to separate your fingers. I am sure that you are aware that Conan was born with the same two fingers joined together. I would hope, though you refuse to claim paternity of him, that you would desire a better future for him than that of a stable boy. Your secret is safe with me, but in return, I expect you to pay the vicar so that Conan can begin his education. Good night."

Once again he reached out to her. "Spend the night with me, Meagan. Lady Anne is away. Spend the night with me! At least you owe me that much."

Twisting out of his grip she said, "I am a married woman and my son is waiting for me behind that large tree. I have given you my promise of silence, but keep in mind, I am an Irish wench."

Gripping the edge of the door, his final words were, "I will pay the vicar, but this is the last that I will help the lad."

Two days later, Meagan walked with Conan to start his first day of school. Previously, she had gone to where she kept her coins that she had received when she was exiled from the Bellingham estate. Taking one of the coins, she put it in her apron pocket. When they arrived at Loxnard, they stopped at a small shop in the middle of town. It was there that she bought her son a black journal. When he learned to print, he printed his name in large letters in his journal; TIMOTHY CONAN MORAN Octobre 13, 1857. He would go to school in the morning, but his afternoons were spent at the stable, as well as with Geofrey Hoke and the dogs.

Each evening, Meagan would quiz and review with Conan what he had learned from the vicar. She studied how he had formed his letters and the sound of each letter, and the letters became words. Big Tim was unaware that Meagan was learning to read. As time progressed, she took every opportunity to read from Mr. Moran's Bible, reviewing what she had heard of the Sunday sermon.

The solemn word
Which she had heard
Brought saving joy
To mother and boy
An idea comes to mind
So Katie must now find
The Ghosts of the Teasdale Cemetery

CHAPTER 10
CONAN, MORE THAN A BOY, BUT NOT A MAN

Conan was living life to the fullest! He saw that he had the best of three worlds, and with this he worshipped three heroes. Each morning that there was to be school, Conan would run to Loxnard with his black journal tucked under his arm, striving to be the first student at school. It would be so that he could begin his questions to ask of the vicar in his quest for knowledge. His mother had pointed to him the Book of Proverbs, Chapter 9, and verse 10-- 'The fear of the Lord is the beginning of wisdom: and the knowledge of the holy is understanding.' So it was, Vicar Bentley, a servant of God, became one of Conan's heroes.

Geofrey Hokes, the gamekeeper of the Bellingham estate was a man that was feared in the community, for he was looked upon as a man of authority. But after Conan came to know him and began to work alongside of him, he recognized the gentle side of the man. This was first brought out when he shared the pheasant with Conan and Meagan when Conan had admitted poaching on the estate. Mr. Hokes, as Conan always addressed him, taught him about the animal kingdom that roamed the estate, as well as the flowers and trees that provided shelter for the birds. Conan liked to carve various objects, so Mr. Hokes suggested which trees would provide the best material for carving the images of the animals and birds. One rainy afternoon, Mr. Hokes had invited Conan into his home for afternoon tea. It was a time that would alter Conan's life for the next twenty years. That afternoon, Mr. Hokes introduced Conan to the game of chess. It was here, during their afternoon tea, they would match wits with one another. But it also provided Conan with another project.

"Mr. Hokes," he said, "I believe that I would like to carve my own chess set. What wood should I use?"

"Well now, I would suggest that for the present that you consider a light colored wood that would represent the white side. Keep in mind that the lighter colored wood is more prevalent. It may take a while to find a darker wood to represent the black side. Probably it would be best to use a hardwood, like an oak, so that it would last for years."

Conan was excited. He said, "I will start looking for some of the larger branches, when I walk through the woods. I am not sure how big I will make it, but I will probably start carving the pawns until I get used to the wood."

Geofrey Hokes got up from his chair and opened the lower door of the cabinet next to the bookcase. Reaching in, he pulled out a wooden box and handed it to Conan. "Here, Conan," he said, "this is my first chess set. I am giving it to you, so that you can use it as a pattern as to size and shape." He returned to his chair and continued, "Keep in mind, it took you a while to learn the game of chess, so it will take you much longer to carve your set. Patience is a virtue in learning and playing the game. You will experience the need of patience before you have finished carving the set. May I make a suggestion? I would suggest that you practice at first, using a soft wood. It will be easier to work with. Then as you progress in your carving, you can begin using a hardwood. This set which I have given to you was one that my father gave to me. I have cherished it. He was a true artisan in the trade of woodworking, a master in his own right. Study them as you play the game, so that your hands get the feel of the weight and symmetry of each piece. Learn from the master! I have no one to pass it on to, so I have found that you are worthy to receive it. Now tell me Conan, how many individual pieces are in a set?"

Conan pondered a moment. "Sir, that would be thirty-two. There are sixteen to a side. Thank you, Mr. Hokes. I will always remember you and this gift." Now the lad had found his second hero, a man of authority.

Big Tim Moran was a quiet man. Meagan had queried Lord Bellingham at the time that she considered marrying Mr. Moran. She had asked if he was a gentle man. He had assured her that Tim was a gentle man, and he was right. Tim had married Meagan, with the thought that she would give him children, but after a time it became apparent that Conan would be the only child in the home. It became Tim's desire that Conan should learn the skills that would prepare him to assume the position of stable master when Tim is too old to do the job. Conan had found his third hero, a man in the family.

Conan learned that it was not easy to have three heroes in his life. For as they each mentored young Moran, they also desired more and more of his time. Vicar Bentley had him six mornings each week. His afternoons were divided in working at the stable or the kennel. However, the evenings were spent on his studies. He enjoyed spending the evening hours with his mother. She would quiz him about what he had learned. It was a review for him to confirm what he had learned, but he sensed that his mother was learning along with him as well. After a time, Conan encouraged his mother and father to learn the game of chess. It afforded the opportunity for Conan and Tim to develop a closer relationship with one another.

It was the afternoons that he spent with Geofrey Hokes that Conan looked forward to. They always included one game of chess. Mr. Hokes would also inspect the pawns that Conan was carving from the soft wood. There were times that Conan, in his haste, was not as careful as Mr. Hokes thought that he should be. If he determined that it was inferior and could not be corrected, he threw it into the fire. After completing eight pawns from the soft wood, Mr. Hokes said, "Conan, it is now time for you to begin working with the hardwood. I sense that you have a desire to try your hand at carving the queen, but since it is the most difficult, save it until your last piece of the first set. I still want to inspect each piece. I know that you are capable of excellence."

Of his three heroes, Conan found that his father was the most exacting. Perhaps, it was because the horses were the most unpredictable. The year that Conan was ten, Big Tim had him spending more time working with the horses and less time grooming them and mucking out the stalls. The latter duties were assigned to Ian Butler, a twelve year old from a neighboring farm. Conan learned to drive a single horse pulling the cart and later a team hitched to the carriage. He was developing upper body strength, but was still not strong enough to handle a four horse team. It was the riding horses that he enjoyed the most. Now that he was no longer mucking out the stalls, his afternoons were spent exercising the horses kept in the stable.

Not only were the horses unpredictable, but so was Grace, the fourteen year old daughter of Lord Bellingham. With her blonde hair and cheery personality, she would be considered as quite attractive. However, once that she was mounted on a horse, she seemed to have no thought for the moment. Lord Bellingham insisted that she was not to ride alone. Her attendant, Helene Hawthorne refused to ride with her, feigning that she was frightened of horses. Big Tim sensed that it was Grace that frightened her. Lord Bellingham would ride with her when he was at the estate, but for those times that Parliament was in session, then Big Tim would ride with her. He would allow her to ride her horse Pansy at a trot, but never was she to allow the horse to run, despite her pleading.

On a sunny afternoon in late fall, Grace came to the stable accompanied by Helene Hawthorne. Conan was repairing a strap on the harness when Grace smiled and said, "Conan, I would like to go for a ride this afternoon."

"Unless Miss Hawthorne will go, there is no one to ride with you. Father has left with the coach to take Lady Anne into Loxnard."

"Well then," she replied, "I guess that leaves you to ride with me. You do know how to ride, don't you?"

Conan was quick to respond, perhaps too quick. Grace took note of his anxiety. "Of course I know how to ride. I am a good rider."

"I am sure that you are, so I will feel safe with you riding with me. Now go saddle Pansy and we will get started before it gets any later."

Conan shook his head. "Father has not given me permission to go riding with you. It will be late when he returns, so you will have to postpone your ride until tomorrow. Sorry."

"Oh, Conan," she begged. "Please saddle Pansy. I will just ride around here close. That way you can keep an eye on me. Nothing is going to happen to me." She laughed, "Conan, if I give you a kiss, will you saddle Pansy for me? It is only for a little while." Helene Hawthorne laughed at Conan's embarrassment of Grace's plea.

He blushed, and said, "No, I won't saddle Pansy for a kiss. Quit pestering me."

Grace was having too much fun to quit now. "Conan, I will promise not to kiss you if you saddle Pansy. See, we have compromised, so go ahead and bring Pansy to me."

Conan tossed the leather strap aside and went and saddled Pansy. Bringing the horse to Grace, he handed her the reins. "Are you happy now?"

He helped her mount the horse. She laughed, "Only if you join me."

She walked the horse a few steps and then kicking her in the side Pansy started to trot. Making a big loop out into the nearby meadow, she came back around and shouted, "This is too much like being on a merry-go-round. I will see you later." She then kicked the horse into an easy lope.

Conan tried to run after her, but he saw that was useless. Running back to the stable, he saddled the first horse he came to, a tall black gelding named Luke. Leading the horse outside, he saw that Grace was at the edge of the meadow. He swung into the saddle. Luke wasn't his horse of choice. Now he wished that he had been more selective. However, he knew that he was fast if he let him run. He saw that Grace was going over a slight rise in the path and was out of sight. He neared where he had last seen her, and he saw that she had stopped and was waiting for him. He was angry, but as a boy of ten, he thought it best not to say too much to her. "I think that we should go back. You have had your fun, so let's go back. I won't say anything to Father about this, if you don't say anything to your father as well."

"All right, but Conan, it was fun to have the wind blow in my face and feel my hair flying back over my shoulders. I like to ride fast, but I know that my horse is much faster than yours, so you don't know what I am talking about. Live a little, Conan, live a little!"

"I know what you are talking about. Luke is plenty fast, but Father doesn't want me to run him. He isn't that young anymore."

"Excuses, excuses." Grace laughed, "I think that you are afraid of falling off, but I understand, since you are a little boy. Go ahead and I will catch up with you. We will go home, but I get to pick the path that we will take. Now go on, but don't look back."

Luke plodded along in a lazy manner. Conan heard Grace coming behind him. It sounded as if Pansy was running fast. He looked over his shoulder and saw that Grace was almost upon him with her riding crop held high. When she came by Luke, she struck him on the rump. She yelled at Conan, "The last one to the stable is a silly goose."

The excitement of the horse running by him, and the whack on the rump, caused Luke to bolt forward, determined to catch the fleeing horse. With the sudden lunge, Conan almost was thrown from the horse. He reached forward and grabbed a bit of the horse's mane to secure his seat in the saddle. Pulling back on the reins, he tried to slow the horse, but Luke bowed his neck and plunged forward, determined to make a race of it. The young rider was at the mercy of the horse's will. Conan saw that Luke was drawing closer to Pansy, but as he looked ahead, fear entered into his heart. Grace was headed for a stone wall. It wasn't very high, but Conan was uncertain if either horse was capable of jumping it. Pansy approached the wall and she cleared it with ease. Conan gave a sigh of relief. He thought, *now if Luke will accept the challenge and not refuse to jump, everything might be all right.*

He felt the horse lift his feet to begin the jump. It was a feeling of exhilaration as he soared over the wall. He heard the scraping of a hoof on the stones. Luke's head went to the ground, jerking the reins out of Conan's hands. He knew that he was headed for a fall, as well as the horse. Now his fear was that the horse might roll on him. Conan landed on his stomach and slid along on the grass. He was trying to catch his breath without much success, but he was able to sit up. The horse had struggled in getting up and was standing with his head hanging low. One front foot was positioned to where he was not putting any weight on it.

Grace had looked back to see how Conan was taking the jump when she saw him fall to the ground. She came back to see if he was all right. She asked, "Are you hurt?"

Conan shook his head, determined that he would not give her the satisfaction of seeing him cry, even though he was unsure if he would ever be able draw another breath. He looked at Luke, but was not sure that he wanted to. It would have certainly been easier to have died on the spot rather than face his father. Getting to his feet, he went to Luke to assess the damage. The horse was trembling. He allowed the boy to run his hand over the leg and down to the hoof. There was no evidence of any broken bones, so he assumed that the horse had suffered a strain when his feet hit the ground. He reached out and gathered the reins in his right hand. He brushed the grass and dirt from his clothes. He began to lead the horse back to the stable, while it hobbled along.

Grace walked her horse alongside, not saying anything for a few minutes. "Conan, I am sorry. This was my entire fault. I get tired of being coddled, and I knew that I could manipulate you by running off." Then she began to laugh. "That was the greatest of fun as Pansy seemed to float over the wall. I am sorry that Luke was hurt, but Father can always buy another horse. Besides that, you don't seem to have been hurt very much. You are a bit dirty, but that will wash off." She paused a moment. Another thought came into her mind. "I will go on ahead, since you are taking way too long. I will tie Pansy outside and you can take care of her when you get there. Bye, Conan, and thanks for a fun afternoon." She started her horse to trotting. It was only a few minutes and she was out of sight.

Conan had unsaddled Pansy and had begun to rub her down when his father entered the stable. His first question was, "Why does Pansy look as if she had been run hard? She is coated with sweat from head to toe." He saw Luke in the next stall. He continued, "And Luke is coated with dirt as well. What went on while I was gone? Help me unhitch the horses from the coach, and then I will need some answers from you. It appears that you are not in a very talkative mood at this time."

After the horses had been fed and groomed, Conan took his father into the stall to look at Luke. "What happened here? He has quite a deep scratch on the front of his leg?"

"He went over a stone wall, and then fell. He can't put any weight on that leg."

"Were you on him when this happened?" His father asked. Conan nodded. "I presume that you took a fall as well?" Conan nodded again. "Why and how did all of this take place?" Conan shrugged his shoulders and shook his head.

Big Tim grabbed his son by the shoulders. He looked him in the eye. "Conan," he said, "until this horse is healed up and sound, your responsibilities in this stable will be to doctor this horse morning and night. Also, you will be taking over the cleaning of the stalls and grooming of the horses that Ian Butler has been doing. Ian is now my assistant!"

A week later, Helene Hawthorne had an opportunity to confide to Big Tim what had taken place on that fateful afternoon. "Mr. Moran, Conan never had a chance with Grace. No one, not even her father can escape her manipulations when she sets her mind to it."

"Miss Hawthorne, I sensed as much, but Conan

needs to stand firm. He is learning his lesson now to save himself for another day. Thank you, Miss Hawthorne. Your secret is safe with me."

But Conan had more lessons to learn, but these would be under the tutelage of Mr. Hokes. Conan was developing a keen sense of nature. It was amazing that with his deformed hand, he was able to utter bird calls that were so real that the birds would return his call. Mr. Hokes was getting up in years, so that Conan was Mr. Hokes' legs in patrolling the estate. He was also spending more time working with the dogs at the time of the hunting of the fox and the fowl. It was the early fall, just before Conan was to turn fourteen that was a turning point in his life. He was on his way home and he cut through some brush and he discovered a snare that had been set by a would-be poacher. He thought that he knew who had set it, but he would watch it to determine if he was right. He went out early the next morning to see if there was a pheasant in the box, but there was none. He waited a few minutes in the cover that he had chosen. After a time, he saw a lad approach the box. It was Phil Hamilton, a classmate of his in the vicar's school. Seeing that the snare was empty, he returned the way that he had come. Conan then went to the snare box. He pulled the stakes up and tucked the box under his arm. He took it with him when he went to school. Handing the box to Phil, he said, "Phil, I work with Mr. Hokes, the Game Keeper for Lord Bellingham. I would suggest that you do your poaching somewhere else. Mr. Hokes doesn't miss much, and neither do I."

Phil laughed, "I thought that since we are classmates that you would overlook a minor indiscretion. What are friends for, if they don't look out for one another?"

"I have helped you out this time with a warning.

You still have your box, so maybe you need to be content with snaring hares around the village. I have a responsibility to my employer, as well as to my friends. I have fulfilled my responsibility to you, so don't put me in a position to fulfill my responsibility to Lord Bellingham." Phil had nothing more to say.

Ten days later, Mr. Hokes caught Phil Hamilton with a pheasant in his snare. He released the pheasant and smashed the snare box. Phil had to pay a fine, and was cautioned that if he was caught another time the fine would double.

The next day after school, Phil and his brother Graham stopped Conan on his way home. Phil accused Conan, "You told that old man what we were doing! He never would have found us if you hadn't said anything to him."

"It was you that I talked to. I warned you that he doesn't miss much. I have been watching for you. I assumed that you would ignore my warning, but it was he that found the evidence." Conan turned to resume his walk home. That was when the two brothers set upon him with their vicious attack.

They left him on the road with these final words. "If you come this way tomorrow, we will do the same thing to you, and the day after. Stay out of our village!"

Conan arrived at home. Meagan was troubled at what she saw. Going to her son, she said, "Come into the house and let me see what I can do."

Conan shook his head. He replied, "I will be all right. It isn't as bad as it might appear. There was a little fracas after school and I got the worst of it."

"Who did this and why? Does Vicar Bentley know about this? After we have had our dinner, I will go see him about how he is handling his students."

Conan shook his head. "Mama, I will handle it. It won't do any good for the vicar to intervene. Then the culprits will be after me all the more."

"Culprits," she exclaimed. "Do you mean to tell me that there was more than one person that did this?"

He nodded his head. "Let me try it one more day. If I come home beat up like this tomorrow, then you can see what you can do, but I can't let them put fear into my heart."

Conan worked at the stable that afternoon. Big Tim looked at him and asked, "Is everything all right Son, or do I need to go see the vicar."

"No Father, it was a testing of the wills and I will be all right. These bruises will soon heal." No more was said about the subject that afternoon.

The next morning, Conan was purposely the last student to sit at his desk. Phil and Graham had been jokingly exchanging glances at one another when they observed the empty desk. They were gloating that they had seen the last of Conan Moran, at least in the classroom. When Conan took his seat, Vicar Bentley looked up from his desk and remarked, "Conan, you are cutting it mighty close. I was ready to mark you absent. Next time, get here a few minutes earlier."

"Yes Sir," he replied and ducked his head.

At the end of the morning session, Conan had purposely left his black journal at his desk. Stepping out into the sunshine, he saw the Hamilton brothers were waiting for him on the road in front of the church. Conan cut through the cemetery. He hollered, "Catch me if you can." They took up the challenge and followed him around the village, but never quite getting close enough to get their hands on him. The more they chased him, the madder they became. He continued his taunts of how they couldn't catch him. Phil tired first, but Graham was sure that he could catch Conan, as he got closer and closer. Graham gave one surge of energy, only to come short of getting Conan in his grasp. When Conan saw that he was bent over with his hands on his knees, he turned on Graham and began to flail him in the same manner that he had been flailed the day before. The tired lad was defenseless against the blows that rained upon him. Collapsing on the ground, he called out, "Stop, I have had enough!"

In the meantime, Phil continued to plod along, intent upon coming to the defense of his brother. He drew near, so Conan went out to meet him and handed him a beating similar to that which his brother had received. Leaving the brothers, tired and beaten, Conan went back to the church to get his black journal. The Hamilton brothers never bothered him again.

Grace Bellingham was now eighteen and was as pretty as any young lady in the area. Naturally, she had plenty of suitors, but it appeared that Carlton Thornwood was to be her choice. Most often, if Grace had need of a carriage, she would ask that Conan be her driver. If for some reason that she had either Ian or Big Tim drive her, they were impatient if she kept them waiting, for whatever reason it might be. Conan always had a piece of wood with him, so he was content to carve what might come to mind. Sometimes he would be working on a chess piece, but if he was content to be more casual, it might be a bird, a fish or a small animal. If it was the latter, he would usually give it to Grace.

On this particular fall day, Grace had requested that Conan was to bring the carriage to the manor before noon. She and Carlton were going on a picnic by the lake on the estate. Conan had chosen the pair of black geldings to pull the carriage. He liked them because they were spirited,

and displayed a bit of elegance while they trotted with
their heads held high. Grace would let Conan know ahead
of time if he was to be dressed proper for the occasion.
Today was one of those days. He had arrived early, but
had not started any of his carvings while he waited for
Grace. He did not want any of the wood shavings either
in the buggy or on the driveway. Conan was careful to not
reveal his displeasure when Grace came out of the manor,
accompanied by Carlton. He was carrying two picnic
baskets, one larger than the other. He thought that Carlton
was rather arrogant and brusque at times; not only with
Conan, but with Grace as well. Grace was holding a small
black puppy in one arm and a flowered parasol in the other.
She said, "Good morning, Conan. See my new puppy. He
is a Scottish Terrier, so I call him Scottie." He didn't say
anything, but nodded his acknowledgment of her greeting.

After helping the couple into the carriage, Conan
turned to Grace and asked, "Where would you like to go
this morning?" He always asked, because sometimes, she
would change her destination at the last minute. He noted
that she was cuddled close to Carlton. Evidently this day
was to be a special occasion. Perhaps, this was the day of
her engagement.

"We will go to the lake. Don't you remember me
telling you that we would go to the lake? Sometimes I think
that you are so busy with school and working with Mr.
Hokes and the stable, that you don't know where you are
going half the time. Maybe you have a girl friend. Is that
right?" She laughed at her last remark.

Conan blushed, "No, Miss Grace, no girl friend. I
asked that I might confirm where you wanted me to take
you. The lake it will be." He cracked the whip, and the
horses stepped out at a brisk trot.

Arriving near the lake, Grace touched Conan's

shoulder. She told him, "Here is a good place for you to stop the carriage."

He stopped the horses near a tree. When he got out, he remarked, "I will tie the horses here and then I will help you with your baskets." By the time that Conan had finished tying the horses, Carlton had helped Grace to the ground. Conan picked up the two baskets, following the couple while they walked around a clump of shrubs. Carlton was carrying a blanket for them to sit on. Grace turned to see if Conan was following. "Oh," she said, "the smaller basket is for you. I packed a lunch for you. We may be here most of the afternoon."

Returning the smaller basket to the buggy, he remarked, "Thank you. This is the first time that you have done that. I do appreciate it."

When they neared the picnic site, Conan set the basket to the ground. "Is there anything else? If not, I will return to the carriage and wait until I hear from you."

Grace laughed. She handed Scottie to him. "Would you mind taking Scottie with you? I don't know what I was thinking when I brought him along. There is a leash on the seat of the carriage if you need to keep him from running away. He can help keep you company."

Conan struggled with the puppy. He yelped and wiggled, wanting to be with Grace. Even as he returned to the carriage, Scottie continued to whine. Conan opened the picnic basket and began to feed the puppy little bits of his lunch. After a time, the whining ceased and Scottie went to sleep on Conan's lap. Conan placed him on a mat on the floor behind the front seat. After he finished his lunch, he got out his knife and began to carve a replica of the little Scottie pup. He anticipated that he would be here most of the afternoon, so he was extra careful with the detail of his carving. While he was intent on his carving, things were not going well with the young lovers.

What she anticipated was a romantic afternoon. In fact, she thought that she and Carlton were to the point in their relationship that he was soon to propose to her. His sister had secretly confided in Grace that he would be asking her in the very near future. She had arranged to come here by the lake as the ideal romantic setting for his proposal. What she did not know that the previous evening he had been drinking and playing cards with some of his friends. When he came to the Bellingham estate that morning he was not feeling well. Also, he was embittered that he had lost rather heavily at the card table. After they ate their lunch, Carlton lay back on the blanket and said, "I am going to take a little nap."

Grace snapped back at him and angrily replied, "And what am I going to do while you are taking your nap?"

"For one thing you can shut up for a while. You haven't shut up long enough to hardly breathe since I showed up at the manor this morning. Don't you get tired of talking?" He rolled over and turned his back to her. His last words to her were, "Go to the lake and let me rest." She picked up her parasol and stomped toward the lake.

Conan anticipated that they would be late getting back to the manor, so he unhitched the team of geldings and took them to the edge of the lake so that they could drink. He was returning to the carriage, when he and Grace crossed paths. He saw that she had been crying, so he inquired, "What causes the shedding of tears on such a fine day?"

"Oh, Conan, Carlton and I had words. He is sleeping now. I wanted everything to be perfect today, but nothing is going right."

Conan said, "Well, my basket lunch was perfect.

I am sure that his was as well. Thank you for the lunch, Grace."

"See, you thanked me. He never said one word about the lunch. Nor did he say anything about the new dress that I bought especially for today. Tell me Conan, am I that ugly? You never commented about my new dress either."

"Miss Grace, I noticed your dress, but Mama has taught me my place in society. It would have been inappropriate of me to say anything about your dress. You see, I am only a stable boy."

"Oh Conan, I don't see you that way! I think of you more as a younger brother that I never had. Sometimes, I sense that you are not comfortable when I tease you. You take things too serious."

"And you don't? This thing with Mr. Thornwood sounds pretty serious to me, but sometimes I don't understand about girls and boys." She started to leave when she said, "Conan, can you make the birds sing?"

"If there are any birds around, I can usually get them to answer my call. Why do you ask?"

"When I get to where Carlton is, will you start your bird calls for me? Maybe it will be enough to awaken him. I trust that he will be in a better mood."

He nodded his head. Giving her a grin, he started back with the horses. Conan chuckled to himself. He knew which bird he was going to imitate. After he secured the horses to a tree, he made sure that he was out of sight of the young lovers before he began his first imitation of a magpie. He paused between each bird call. After the third call, he saw a pair of magpies seek sanctuary in the tree near Carlton and Grace before returning their raucous chatter. Grace had closed her parasol. She sat near Carlton, waiting for the birds to awaken him. Suddenly he sat up

115

from his nap, angry at being awakened. He snarled, "Why can't those foolish birds go someplace else with their endless prattle." He grabbed the parasol and flung it at the birds. Hitting the trunk of the tree, the shattered handle fell to the ground.

Grace ran to the tree and picked up her parasol. She screamed at Carlton, "Aunt Anne bought that parasol for me in London. You in your tantrum have destroyed it." Reaching down, she began to pick up the remnants of the picnic lunch. "If you want a ride home, you can help me gather up these things. We are going home. I have had enough of your insolence for one day. I might as well have come out here by myself, as come with you."

"Sure," he said. "You would like to come out here with that scrawny little stable hand! I will buy you another parasol, if it will make you happy." He grabbed her wrist and pulled her to him. "I came out here to discuss with you about asking your father for your hand in marriage, but now I am having second thoughts." She struggled to free his grip on her wrist. He continued, "I sense that you knew what I had in mind. It seemed convenient for your companion, Miss Hawthorne to have a headache today and could not accompany us. Evidently this was planned. You didn't have any lunch packed for her as you did the stable boy. He is only fourteen years old, so it is easy to manipulate him, but it is different with me."

He pulled her close to him and forced a kiss upon her lips. She struggled. She hissed, "Let me go! You are hurting me!" He continued to hold her close. He saw the fear in her eyes as she feared that he would force another kiss upon her lips. "Let me go, or I will call for Conan!"

Carlton tightened his grip on her and laughed, "And, what will that little boy do to me? Do you think that he will beat me up? I don't think so. He will keep his mouth shut, just as you will, if you have any hope of marrying me!"

He started to kiss her again, when she shouted, "Help me Conan, help me!"

Conan was doing the last bit of carving of the wooden dog when he heard her cry for help. He set it and his knife aside on the seat of the phaeton carriage and ran to her aid. When he came around the thicket, he saw that she was struggling to get free from Carlton. Running toward the couple, Conan called out, "Let her go!"

"Make me, stable boy, make me," he replied. Conan darted close to the couple as if he was going to attack Carlton, but he avoided his outstretched hands after he released Grace. Conan was not going to let Carlton get him in his grasp. He knew that this man was ten years his senior, and he was an angry young man. Conan remembered the strategy that he had used against the Hamilton brothers; it was to stay close but avoid being caught.

Conan said, "I will go hitch the horses to the carriage and take the two of you home. I have no intention of being involved in any quarrel the two of you might have." He began to walk toward the carriage.

Carlton ran after him, shouting, "You became involved the moment that you shouted at me to 'let her go.' You have a smart mouth on you, and I am the one to teach you a lesson."

Conan's first thought was to defend himself with the buggy whip. But he knew that he was not to do harm to anyone of the ruling class, so he ran past the carriage. Carlton saw the knife on the seat. He picked it up and shouted, "I have your knife. Now how tough are you?"

Conan was unsure if Carlton intended to use the knife, or just threaten him, but he was aware that now he was too close for comfort. He began to run back to where the couple had eaten their lunch, thinking that Grace might calm him down. He was surprised at how fast Carlton closed the gap between them. By darting from time to time, he could keep him at his distance. Conan ran past a large tree, but he tripped on an exposed tree root. He tumbled to the ground and he tried to get to his feet. Carlton could not stop, but stumbled over Conan. He fell in a heap at the feet of Grace. Conan was on his feet and began to run once again when Grace called out. "Wait, Conan, wait. I think that he is hurt. He is not getting up."

Conan suspected a trick, but he went back to where Carlton was laying face down. He was groaning, but made no effort to get up. Conan rolled him to his side. Grace screamed. It was then that he too saw the small knife was lodged in his stomach, and the blood was seeping from the wound. Grace fell to her knees, and caressed the wounded man's head. She said, "Conan, what will we do, what will we do? I don't know what to do, but we can't just leave him here." Carlton's eyes were closed. His moaning frightened Grace and Conan.

Conan grabbed a cloth napkin from the lunch basket. He removed the knife and pressed the napkin where the knife had entered the stomach. He looked to Grace and whispered, "This is all that I know, but it will help slow the flow of blood. I will get the horses and we will take him back to the manor. I am sorry, Grace, I am sorry."

"It was an accident. It wasn't your fault. I will stay with him, so please hurry."

Conan untied the horses from the tree and hitched them to the carriage. He drove the horses near to where Carlton was lying on the ground, but the horses were agitated by the smell of the fresh blood. The horse nearest to the tree was the gentler of the two, so he tied him to the tree. Grace said, "Carlton, we are going to help you to your feet. Try to stand up. Because we are not strong enough, we cannot lift you into the carriage. We will help, but we need to get you back to the manor as quick as we can." It was a struggle for each one, but they finally managed to lay him on a blanket on the floor of the carriage. Grace held the reins of the horses while Conan untied the horse from the tree. Getting into the carriage, she then tried to comfort Carlton as they made their way home. Conan kept the Scottie pup at his feet, but his greatest concern was to hurry the horses along without making the ride home too rough. Neither Grace nor Conan said anything to one another on the way to the manor.

The carriage neared the Bellingham manor and Grace screamed out for help. The staff responded and was able to put Carlton in a spare bedroom. One servant was dispatched to go for the doctor, while another delivered a message to the Thornwood Estate.

Big Tim Moran had taken Lady Anne to Loxnard in the Landau carriage, so they did not return to the manor until after the doctor had arrived to tend to Carlton. After backing the carriage into the carriage barn, he saw that Conan was scrubbing the floor of the Phaeton carriage. When he saw his father, he ran to him. He began to sob. He told him what had happened. "Father, it was awful. I didn't know what to do. I meant him no harm, but I feared for the safety of Grace. Do you think that Carlton will die?"

The father took his son into his arms to comfort him. He said, "I don't know Son, but I won't let anything happen to you. I am sure that you did everything that you could, but time will tell, time will tell." Had Conan been able to see the fear in the heart of his father, he would have seen that Big Tim was unsure of the promise that he had made to his son. He knew that the gentry of England had little regard for the life of a stable hand.

The next morning, Grace came to the stable to let Big Tim and Conan know the condition of Carlton. His parents were staying at the manor. Other relatives came from time to time to find out if there was any change in his recovery. The third day after the incident, Meagan was out in the forest gathering fire wood when Grace called to her from a thicket of small trees. "Mrs. Moran, over here."

Meagan went to see who called her. Grace motioned to her from the thicket. "Mrs. Moran, I don't want anyone to see us, so come among the trees." Meagan drew near and she saw that Grace had been crying.

"What is it? How is Carlton?" Meagan feared that the news was not good, and was the purpose for Grace's visit.

Grace shook her head. She began to sob. "The doctor does not expect him to last through the night. He is in a lot of pain." Grasping Meagan's hands she had trouble speaking. "I fear for Conan. I know that this was not Conan's fault. But once that Carlton is dead and buried, I have learned that the Thornwood family will seek justice. Can he go back to your family in Ireland? His days in England are over."

Meagan shook her head. "I have no family left in Ireland. Everyone but me immigrated to America at the time of the famine. I have lost all contact with my family. Go now, and I will pray for my son and for a plan to keep him safe. There is a storm starting to come in this evening. Thank you for coming to me with this information. From this moment, Conan is in the hands of God. Goodbye, Grace." Meagan left the seclusion of the thicket. While she made her way home, she began to pray and formulate a plan for the safety of her son.

The chill of the late afternoon caused Meagan to

shiver when she entered the cottage. Stirring up the fire, she began to prepare for the departure of her son. She packed what clothes she could get into a small bundle, all the while praying for Conan. When Tim and Conan came to the cottage, she had the evening meal prepared, but she did not eat with them. Instead, she said, "Go ahead and eat your supper. I have an errand to run before the storm blows in." Not waiting for a response, she put on her coat and went out into the darkness. She was familiar with the path. She made her way to the Bellingham manor, rehearsing what she would say when she arrived.

She arrived at the manor and pulled the hood of her coat over her head to shield her face. Her heart was pounding. She rapped on the door with her closed fist. She remembered the last time that she had come in the night to make a request of Lord Bellingham. And more so, she remembered his parting words when he told her not to come back requesting anything more for Conan. After a pause, she rapped again. Preparing to rap the third time, the door squeaked open. She recognized the butler holding the candle, but she did not declare herself. He asked, "What is it?"

"I have come to see Lord Bellingham. I have a message for him."

Holding out his hand, he said, "The hour is rather late. I will take the message to him."

"No, the message is not written." With that, he opened the door wider and motioned for Meagan to come in. She shook her head and said, "No, I will wait here at the door." He closed the door and left Meagan standing outside.

The door began to squeak once again. It slowly opened. Meagan saw Lord Bellingham in the candlelight. It had been seven years since she had last seen him at this very door, and under similar circumstances. At that time she had requested that he fund the schooling for Conan. He demanded, "Who are you, and what do you want?"

She reached up and pushed the hood back off of her head. Looking into those fierce black eyes, she said, "I am Meagan. Once again I am here beseeching you to show mercy to your son, Conan. An informant has revealed to me that young Thornwood is near death. I also learned that the family intends to seek revenge after he is dead and buried."

He interrupted, "I have no son! I was kind to you once, but I informed you that was to be the last time. I cannot help you in this matter. Go home and leave me alone." He started to close the door, but Meagan moved forward to wedge her body in the doorway.

"You know that Conan risked his life for Grace. Had Carlton caught up with Conan, it could have easily been Conan on his death bed instead of Carlton. Now he has to flee his home to save his own life. You have connections to help him escape. Only you can save him. Surely you can do that much for what he has done for your daughter."

Meagan said no more, but waited for his answer. In the moments of silence, she prayed within her heart for her son.

Lord Bellingham sighed. "All right, have it your way. Tell Big Tim to have two of the fastest horses saddled and ready at the stable by ten o'clock tonight. After the clouds pass by, Conan and I will leave and will travel while it is moonlight. Say your goodbyes. This may well be the last that you will see of him." He started to close the door. He said, "And may this be the last time that I see you, you Irish Wench. You have been nothing but trouble in my life!"

Meagan reached down and took the two white gloved hands and brought them to her lips and kissed them. "Thank you, Lord Bellingham, thank you." She turned from the doorway and was gone into the darkness of the night.

Arriving at the cottage, she told her family of the plans for Conan's escape. "I will pack some food for you to share with Lord Bellingham. Also, I have packed a few clothes secured in a shirt. Is there anything that you want to take with you? Keep in mind that you will need to travel light."

Conan said, "I want to take my black journal, the oilskin pouch, my knife and the short length of the oak stick. I may want to do some carving while I am away."

Meagan said, "Come into my bedroom and I will see to your packing." After they entered the bedroom, Meagan turned and closed the door. She reached under the mattress and pulled out a belt. Handing it to Conan, she hugged him and whispered to him as the tears rolled down her cheeks. "In this belt are the coins that I received when I left the Bellingham manor when I married your father. They are all there except for the coin that I used to buy your journal on the first day of school. May God be with you my son, may God be with you." She kissed him goodbye. He left the bedroom. Picking up his few possessions, he went with his father. Pausing at the door, he looked back at his mother, wondering when he might see her again.

Arriving at the stable, the two men hurried to saddle the horses while they waited for Lord Bellingham. He arrived at the stable at the same time that the clouds rolled back, exhibiting a full moon. No one said anything, but Tim put his arm around his son. He helped him into the saddle. Tim turned to go home. He heard the horses running down the road. A light was still burning in the cottage when he arrived. Meagan met him at the door. She clasped him and begged, "Hold me Mr. Moran, hold me."

At first light, Conan recognized that they were making their way into a shipyard. They stopped at a large vessel, which Conan presumed to be a merchant ship. Lord Bellingham dismounted and handing the reins of his horse to Conan, he said, "You may get off of your horse now. Stay with the horses until I return."

Conan used the time to stretch his legs. He took note of the lettering on the bow of the ship. It was the HMS Bold Pelican. After about ten minutes, Lord Bellingham shouted to him, "Find a place to tie the horses and come aboard."

Finding a large crate, he secured both horses and made his way up the gangplank. He noticed a gentle sway to the ship despite it being moored. He was greeted by a man in his mid-forties. He noticed that he had a slight limp and a scar on his left jaw. He said, "I am George Cochran, the first mate. We will start you as a cabin boy until such time that you begin to develop more muscle to be a part of the deck crew. You will answer to Captain Twain and me." He called to a deck hand, "Porter, show young Conan to his quarters. We will set sail at high tide, just before the sun sets in the west. Say your goodbyes. It will be sometime before we see this port again."

He followed Porter below. With a nod of his head, he indicated a bunk for Conan to put his gear on. He slapped an iron on Conan's ankle. The chain affixed to the iron was attached to the bunk. Conan protested, "What is this all about?"

"Captain's orders. All new crewmen are chained once they are hired. You will be released as soon as we reach deep water. He doesn't want anyone jumping ship."

While this was going on, Lord Bellingham was having his own conversation with the first mate. He handed him a small leather pouch. "There are thirty silver coins in that pouch. I trust that it will be sufficient for you to see that the lad will not have an opportunity to reach dry land, whether it is England or any other port you might visit. I would be happy for him to spend the rest of his life on this ship, or any other ship, but not dry land. Spare his life, but just don't disappoint me."

The first mate grasped the pouch and nodded that he understood what he was to do. Lord Bellingham returned to where the horses were tied, looking forward to a leisurely ride home after he had rested through the day before his night of debauchery.

Already, Conan was beginning to feel the pangs of home sickness. His thoughts were of his mother. He lay back to rest on his bunk. When might he see his mother again?

It was then that Conan began to formulate his plan for freedom. He was now away from the threats of the family of Carlton Thornwood. Pulling his small knife from its sheaf, he reached for the straight tree limb that he had brought with him. On the flattened base, he delicately carved the name of the ship; HMS Bold Pelican. This was to be the first of the sixteen pawns that he would send to his mother from the ends of the earth. They would be a message of his love to her.

Avast, my lad, avast!
The die has been cast, my son, the die has been cast!
Forget the past, Conan, forget the past!
The sea at last, my boy, the sea at last!
An idea comes to mind
So Katie must now find
The ghosts of the Teasdale cemetery

CHAPTER 11
THE VISITATION

Ty Taggat entered the ranch house through the back door, expecting to smell the aroma of supper cooking, but there was nothing. His first thought was that perhaps this had been such a miserable day of working cattle that the only odor he could recognize was that of wet cows. A late November drizzle had settled in right after dinner. Despite wearing his yellow slicker, it had not prevented him from getting wet. Not that he was soaked, but he was wet and cold. Leaving his wet outer garment in the back porch, he removed his boots that were soaked. Putting on slippers, he stepped into the warmth of the kitchen. He spotted that there was still some coffee in the pot from the noon meal, so he began to warm it up. He called out, "Anybody home?" He was answered by a muffled reply that came from the living room.

Going to the doorway, the room was almost dark because of the lateness of the day. In the dim light, he saw Katie in the rocking chair, with Kylee nestled in her arms. "Kylee and I have been rocking. She seems to have a fever. Martin and Marie are each in their own room, doing their math homework. I tried to help them, but no one could agree to the solution of their problems, including me. I separated them so I could experience some peace and quiet." She then began to sob. Ty went to her.

"Come now Katie, it can't be that bad. I will help the kids after supper, and—."

Katie interrupted him, "But it is! Besides all that, I finished a chapter in the book that I am writing. It is so depressing, I'm not sure that I can continue, Why, oh why did I ever start such a task?" She then continued to sob, her body shaking so that she stopped rocking.

"Katie, let me get out of these wet clothes. I will fix this family a 'cowboy bachelor's supper.' Then I will help the twins with their math. After that, I will encourage the author to start writing fiction where everything turns out all right. It will be where the heroine marries a handsome cowboy and has a house full of obedient children." He laughed after giving Katie a kiss on the cheek.

Ty returned to the living room, with Martin and Marie. He told them, "Tonight we are going to help your mother by fixing supper. Keep in mind, any grumbling about my cooking, and you will be the cook for the week. Martin, choose a potato for each one of us and an extra one for the pot. Also wash them real good. We are going to slice them with the skins on. Also, open up two cans of peas and put in a bowl. I will fix the steak, if Marie will see to the setting of the table. All right, now get to work."

Things were going well until there was a knock at the front door. Katie hollered to Ty, "Honey, would you get it?"

Ty turned to Martin, "Check to see who is at the door. It is probably one of the men."

After a time, Martin returned. "Dad, he said that he wanted to see the man of the house. Dad, he looks kind of old and he is driving a real old car. He is waiting outside."

Ty turned the burners off of the stove. He went to see who the visitor was at this time of night. When he stepped outside, he said, "Come inside, as it is a bit cool." He noticed that the man was not dressed for the chilly weather and was shivering slightly from the cold. He offered his left hand, and said, "I am Ty Taggat. What can I do for you?"

The man offered a weak handshake, perhaps from shaking Ty's left hand. He observed the deformed right hand. He asked, "Does Katie O'Neal live here?"

"Why yes, she is now my wife. O'Neal was her maiden name. Why do you ask, and who are you?"

"I am Sam O'Neal. She is my daughter. I would like to see her."

"Mister, she has never said anything about her father. Come into the foyer where it is warm, and I will speak with her. This will be quite a shock to her. I'm not sure how she will respond to this news." Sam O'Neal followed Ty into the foyer. Ty motioned to the small bench for him to sit on. "I will be back, but I am not sure how long this will take." Sam nodded and sat on the edge of the bench while he fumbled with his cap.

Ty left, still unsure how to approach Katie with the news of her father's visit. Nor did he have any inkling as how she would accept the news.

When Ty returned to the living room, Katie asked, "Who was at the door?"

Ty didn't immediately respond to her question, but he squatted down before her, and taking her hand, he whispered, "Katie, this may come as a shock to you, but there is a man in the foyer that says he is your father, Sam O'Neal. He wants to see you. I told him that I would discuss this with you. It is your decision."

"No Ty, this involves you as much as me. We are family. This is rather sudden, but we will approach it together. You have met him. What is your first impression of the man?"

Ty laughed, "Well, my first thought was to invite him to eat with us. I can usually get a feel for someone if I have shared a meal with that person. Our cuisine this evening isn't the best, but if he likes my cooking, how bad could he be."

"That is what I love about you Ty. You can usually

see the humor in each situation, no matter how serious or complex it might be. I remember Lionel Whitman telling about when you had your fingers severed, that you asked if that meant that you wouldn't have to milk your mother's cows anymore. I know very little about my father. I was two when my parents were divorced. I do recall when I asked my mother if she loved Nick when he had asked her to marry him. She responded, what did love have to do with their marrying? She was madly in love with her first two husbands, but they both had made her miserable. You saw him. Do you think that he might like your cooking?"

Ty nodded, "He looked like he could use a good hot meal on a night like this. This might be enough to satisfy his curiosity about you. I will ask him to eat with us. If you want, we can have everything ready when you make your grand entry."

Katie nodded. Getting up from her rocking chair, she took Kylee with her.

Sam stood up when Ty returned to the foyer. "Katie is busy at the present. Our daughter Kylee is a bit under the weather. However, we would like you to eat supper with us, which will soon be ready. Katie was tending to Kylee this evening, so I volunteered to make supper. It will be plain and simple. The best news is that it is about ready if you care to join us in the kitchen."

Ty took note that Sam was quick to accept the invitation. "I will leave my coat and cap here on the bench." He stood up and removed his coat. His cap was a light weight flat cap. Ty noted that his clothes were clean but well worn. He had taken note earlier when they shook hands that his hand was calloused, indicating that he was a working man.

Ty asked, "Do you need to wash up before we eat?"
He shook his head, "No, I am fine."

They entered the kitchen and Ty introduced his children. "Sam, these are our children, Martin and Marie. They are ten years old, and since they share the same birthday, we refer to them as our twins. Martin and Marie, this is our guest for the evening, Sam O'Neal. All right, kids, let's get this meal on the table. Sam, you may sit here. The rest of us know where we sit."

The children and Ty were only a few minutes getting the food ready. Ty nodded to Marie, "Please tell your mother that we are ready to eat."

Marie returned to the table and Kylee and Katie followed her. Ty was still standing as he introduced his family. "Sam, this is my wife Katie and our almost four year old daughter Kylee. Katie, this is Sam O'Neal." Sam had stood up as Katie entered the room.Ty had strategically placed Sam at the opposite end of the table, so that they did not have the need of shaking hands. They acknowledged one another with the nod of their head. After everyone was seated, Ty turned to their guest. "Sam, at each meal we thank the Lord for our food and His goodness for the day. As we unite in prayer, we clasp the hand of the person next to us, so do not be alarmed if you find a child gripping your hand." Ty bowed his head to pray. "Father, as we come together this day, I thank you for this food and the sustenance that it provides so that we might do your will. I thank you for Sam this evening, and it is my desire that as a family, we might honor you by accepting him as our guest. In so doing, that we might also rejoice in your Son, the Lord Jesus Christ. Amen."

Things were going well at the table. Everyone was engaged in passing the food and filling their plate. Martin and Marie filled the void in any conversation with the events of the day at school. Martin spoke up, "Dad, when I was to pick out the potatoes, why did you say, 'get a potato for everyone and one for the pot?' We had enough for everyone and the bowl is empty. How did you know that we needed that extra potato?"

Ty set his fork on the table alongside of his plate. When Katie saw him do that, she knew that he had something rather profound to share. He looked up and smiled before he spoke. "Well, there are two possible reasons, so you may choose the most logical. The first is that knowing what a great cook that I am, everyone would want more of my fine food. The second is that God knew that we were to have a guest and he put it into my heart to have you get another potato for the pot. Which do you choose?"

"Dad, I have never heard you use that phrase before, so I think that God had you say those words. Your potatoes were good, but I am not sure that they were that good. I like the way that Momma cooks better." The family laughed at his remarks, nodding their head in agreement.

"Good choice Martin, good choice. God directs us in the little things in life as well as the big things of life." Ty turned to their guest. "Sam, where do you call home, and what is your vocation?"

Sam and Katie had been eyeing one another through the evening, but avoiding eye contact when their eyes met. Katie noticed that Sam was uncomfortable with Ty's question.

"I have been residing in Indiana, but I am on my way to Oregon. I am an illustrator, but when things are slow, I do resolve to menial labor to meet my physical needs."

"That is interesting," replied Ty. "What kind of illustrations do you do?"

"I will be working for a newspaper, so I may do political cartoons, as well as portrait illustrations in a closed courtroom scene. If things are slow, I will do pencil portraits at county fairs and carnivals. I have been doing this since I was about Martin's age."

Katie interrupted the conversation. "Martin and Marie, you may have your dessert and then I want you to clear off the table. Stack the dishes and I will do them later. Then you will need to get back to your math homework. I want it finished before bedtime. I will put Kylee to bed." Turning to Ty, she said, "You can come with me and read her a short story while I give her the medicine the doctor prescribed earlier. Sam. it won't take us long, so don't run off. We will be back and have some pie and coffee for our dessert." She picked up Kylee and started for the bedroom. Ty went to the backdoor and looked out to check the weather before he went to Kylee's room.

As soon as he came into the bedroom, Katie closed the door. She said, "Now is the time to determine what we are going to do with that man out there." She began to get Kylee ready for bed.

Ty was shocked. "What do you mean, about that man? That man happens to be your father. Is it your intention to send him down the road as quick as he came?"

"He has waited thirty-five years to come to see me. Should I wait as long to send him down the road? What do you think that we should do?"

Ty reached out to her before speaking. "I sense that you are carrying a hurt that has lain dormant for years. I don't know why he has waited all these years to come to you, but I sense that God does. He has sent him to you and me. I looked out to check the weather. It is starting to snow. I don't feel comfortable sending him back to Summit City to seek lodging for the night. Looking at the age of his car, I can imagine that the tires are probably not that good. Also, he certainly isn't dressed for a Sandhill's snowstorm.

We have the guest lodge next door, so what do you say that we offer him lodging for the night? That will give us a little more time to sort things out." He turned to his daughter and he exclaimed, "Look, already one problem is solved. Kylee has dropped off to sleep while we have been discussing the problem. Perhaps over pie and coffee we can learn a lot more about this man."

Katie reached out to Ty to hug him. "I'm sorry to be so hasty in judging the man. I was robbed of a father through an early divorce. Unfortunately, Derk was never a father to me, even as Tag was not a father to you. Thank you for being considerate. Also, I want to thank you for being a father to our own children as well. Let's go see if the coffee is hot."

When they returned to the kitchen, the twins were finishing the stacking of the dishes. Katie said, "Thank you. I will check with you before going to bed." She began serving the pie, while Ty filled the coffee mugs. He set out the sugar bowl and the creamer. Only Ty added cream to his coffee.

Katie took a sip of her coffee. She set the mug down, and looked at Sam and asked, "Why?"

Sam replied, "What do you mean, why?"

Katie was unaware that she had raised her voice as she blurted out, "Why have you waited until now to seek me out. I have been waiting since I was two years old for you to come to me!" Ty sensed the anger in her voice, and this was not going as he had hoped.

Sam pointed his fork toward Katie. "There are some things that you don't need to know. I have come to you, and I see that you have done quite well without me. That is enough for me." He started to get up from the table. "Thank you for the meal. I will get on down the road and out of your life."

Katie responded in haste. "I think that might be a good idea."

"Please," begged Ty. "Sam, please stay and finish your pie and coffee and hear me out. I don't know what you expected when you came here tonight, but this is not going well. If you leave here it will leave a void in all of our lives that in all probability needs to be answered. Besides that, in good conscience, as a guest in our home, I cannot have you go out into the dark of the night. I looked out earlier, and the light rain has turned into snow. It would not be good for you to venture out. The roads would be unfamiliar to you, and you could easily get lost. This is a big country. We have a guest lodge next door, so we are able to put you up for the night. Breakfast is at seven in the morning. If you want to stay after that for a while, or go down the road, that is your option. However, you are not leaving here tonight."

Sam and Katie each had a startled look on their face. Ty stood up and said, "Anyone for more coffee?"

After they finished their dessert, Ty offered, "Sam, I will help you with the things from your car and get you settled for the night." When they stepped out on the porch, Ty remarked, "It looks like we have accumulated about three inches and still snowing."

They entered the guest lodge. Sam commented, "This is nice. Ty, I'm sorry about how I acted earlier this evening. When I left Indiana, I was excited about seeing Katie. I assumed that she would be glad to see me. I guess that I had forgotten that she was only two when Darla and I separated. I didn't know that she was married. The fellow at the gas station never said anything different when he directed me to the 99 Ranch."

"How about Darla, have you kept in touch with her?"

Sam shook his head. "No. It was kind of a bitter

divorce. After thirty-five years, I probably wouldn't even recognize her or want to for that matter." Shaking Ty's left hand he said, "Thanks. I will see you in the morning."

When Ty went to their bedroom, Katie was asleep.

Ty was up early the next morning and had the coffee going when Katie entered the kitchen. She asked, "How is the coffee this morning?"

He replied, "I made it according to your formula, with just a pinch of grounds added for the pot, but it will be hot." He laughed. They had a running battle about the strength of the coffee. The first one to the kitchen made the coffee to their liking. "I checked the snow level, and we probably have five inches of snow, but it has quit snowing. I caught the school closings on the radio. They will have school, but the buses will run two hours late. I need to go into town, so I will take the twins with me. That way, they won't miss any classes. That will make Marie happy, but not Martin." He shrugged his shoulders. He said, "I guess you can't make everyone happy. This will leave you and Sam alone to sort things out between the both of you. Don't give me that look Katie. I am not abandoning you, but I intend to do a bit of research on my own. Don't let Sam leave, at least not until the roads have been plowed. Try to encourage him to stay for dinner. That way, he will have some insight as to what kind of a cook I married. Now, what's for breakfast?" He replied before she could answer him. "I think I hear him coming in the back door now."

Ty greeted him as he came into the kitchen. "Morning, Sam. Well, I see you survived my cooking. This morning will be the real test. Katie prepares the breakfasts here. I will take the twins into town. The buses aren't running until later."

"Thank you for the accommodations, as I slept well. Will the snow hinder me from leaving this morning? I should be on my way as soon as possible. They are looking for me to start work as soon as I get to Oregon."

"It would be best if you waited until after dinner. The county will plow the roads by noon. I noticed that your tires don't have a lot of tread, so it would be best to wait a while. I should be back around nine. We can get you back on the road this afternoon, if you have a mind to leave." Sam nodded, but seemed rather noncommittal in the matter.

After Ty had left the twins off at the school, he drove to Nick's café. He entered the café and was greeted by the bell that rang when he opened the door. Going to the counter, he saw that most of the morning crowd had already left. Nick came to him and asked, "Coffee this morning?" Ty nodded and reached for the creamer. "You are out and about rather early this morning. What can we do for you? You seem rather deep in thought"

"When I came through the door, the bell did its little tinkling sound as it always does. Is that the same bell that was here when you bought this café from Maude?"

Nick nodded, "The same bell. I believe that I have replaced about everything in the café at least once, but the bell continues to announce everyone when they enter or leave. It must be one of those bells with a lifetime guarantee. Things must be a bit slow at the 99 Ranch if you are hearing bells ringing."

"I guess you are right. The day that I retire, I will come in here and count the number of times that the bell rings each day and then try to figure out when it was first installed. Then you could have a contest to see who guesses the closest to the number of times it has rang. In the meantime, is Darla busy? She and I need to have a visit."

"I'll get her. She is probably ready for a break." Nick went into the kitchen. Ty took his coffee with him and went to a table to the back of the dining area.

With coffee in hand, Darla approached the table. Sitting down, she gave a sigh of relief. "Thank you for rescuing me from cleaning the pots and pans. What is on your mind this morning that brings you to town this time of day? Oh sure, you thought that I needed help, so you drove into town to help me."

Ty ignored her remarks. "Darla, we had a visitor last night." Darla didn't say anything, waiting for Ty to continue the conversation. "It was Sam O'Neal." Darla spilled some of her coffee before regaining her composure. "What can you tell me about the man? He is still at the ranch. I am hoping that he and Katie are conversing at this time. Things were quite tense for a time last night. He stayed all night. I wouldn't let him leave during the snowstorm. Katie was upset that he had waited thirty-five years to come see her. Katie needs some answers and I am presuming that you know most of them. Sam wouldn't say anything, but he seemed in a better mood this morning, A good place is to start at the beginning, and here I am."

Darla folded her hands on the table. She began, "Sam was a charmer. I first met him at a dance in Turnersville, Indiana. I had graduated from high school, and a carload of us girls went to the dance. He was the lead singer and he played the banjo. Oh, how he could play that banjo! He would come alive as he strummed that instrument. Sam was somewhat older than me, but despite our age difference, we soon married. We had been married just under a year when Katie was born. Sam loved me and his daughter, but he wasn't cut out to be a family man. The banjo and the band was his life. Unfortunately it was his life, but not his livelihood. It didn't bring in enough money to provide for a family. My family never approved of Sam, particularly my mother. When Katie was two months old, I got a secretarial job and mother took care of her. I missed being with my daughter, but Sam had no concept of money." Darla paused. She brought the coffee mug to her lips. She continued, "He was multitalented, as he could draw. He got a job as an illustrator with a newspaper. He could charm people while he would draw the caricatures of individuals while riding the bus to work. However, he never took anything serious. He had somewhat of a drinking problem and he liked to party. It also concerned me that he was too popular with the women at the dances. Unfortunately, I couldn't be with him at night at the dances and at home with my daughter. My mother encouraged me to file for divorce. I think that Sam realized that we were both unhappy, despite being in love. Sam agreed that I would have full custody, but he insisted that Katie was to retain the O'Neal name. He had visitation rights, but after a time, he saw that it was too painful for Katie, even at two years of age to see him come and then go. He agreed to child support, little as it was, but he was faithful in meeting his obligation right up to the time that Katie was eighteen. That is the story of Sam O'Neal."

"Did you ever tell Katie much about her father?"

"No, not really. She never asked, and there wasn't much that I knew about his family. He sent his child support money through the court system, so we had no contact. Later, I met Derk. After we married, we left Turnersville. While there, we would occasionally run into Sam. I think it bothered Derk. He never said anything, but after a time we moved and over time, we ended up in Summit City. I guess I should ask how he is, but I have pretty much written him out of my life."

Ty drained the last of his coffee. After he stood up, he reached in his shirt pocket and pulled out a dollar bill. Throwing it on the table, he said, "Thanks for the coffee and the information." He opened the door. Once again the bell tinkling as he went out.

Nearing the Good Hope Church, he met the snow plow clearing the road. The sun was trying to make its appearance, indicating that it was to be a crisp clear day. He entered the back door and he could hear Katie's laughter, which was a good indication of how her morning went.

Going into the kitchen, he saw that she was sitting at the kitchen table by herself. She was leafing through what appeared to be some sort of a scrapbook. He asked, "What is so funny? Where is everyone?"

Katie looked up and replied, "I put Kylee down for a nap. Poppa was a bit under the weather, so he took two aspirin and is lying down in the guest lodge. He brought out this scrapbook. I have been looking through it. It is absolutely amazing what he has compiled over the years." She closed the book and said, "I could heat some coffee for you. Harry Kurtz wanted you to call him when you have a free moment. Incidentally, what did Mother have to tell you? Was she surprised at Poppa's visit?"

"Evidently things went well this morning if you are calling him Poppa."

"Yes, it did. Each of us apologized and Poppa shared with me the purpose of his visit. We are the only family that he has. He has no siblings, and he never remarried after he and Mother divorced. I asked if I could call him Poppa. Did you know that all the time that I was growing up, I didn't have a dad? My brothers had a dad, but I only had Derk. He never permitted me to call him anything else but Derk. When I think back, my coming to this ranch to care for your mother was when I first experienced what it was like to have a father. It may seem strange, but Tag was like a father to me. Our father-daughter relationship was never sordid as the community imagined. Tag was never angry towards me until it came time for me to stop enabling him in his alcoholism and to prohibit him from coming to my home. I thought that I was protecting him in providing a safe place for his drinking. In essence, I was robbing your mother of his companionship. That is in the past. Now I have a dad." She smiled, as she continued. "Ty, you have avoided my question as to your visit with my mother. That was the purpose of your trip to town this morning, wasn't it?"

Ty laughed, "I can't keep anything from you. Yes, I wanted to see what Darla had to say. She said that he was a charmer. I think that she was swept off her feet. I sense that her mother pressed her into filing for the divorce. Evidently, Sam had trouble supporting a family, because music was his life."

"Yes, yes. I remember now. He played a banjo. How is it possible at that young age that I would remember the banjo? I would dance around when he played it. Go on, what else did she have to say?"

"He faithfully paid child support until you were eighteen. He had visitation rights, but it bothered him that you would be upset when he had to leave after each visit. I suppose in your childlike mind you thought that your parents were getting back together. About that time, your mother married Derk and they left Turnersville."

Katie wiped a tear from her cheek. When she brushed against Ty, he reached out and took her in his arms. He held her. She whispered, "Oh Ty, to think that in my resentment and anger, I wanted him to leave. It was you that kept him from leaving. Had he left, I would have missed so much. Now I am dreading the moment that he decides to leave for Oregon. I know that he must go, but I savor each moment that he is here. Thank you for being the peacemaker last night."

Ty laughed, giving her a squeeze. "Remember the

night that Emily came to the ranch with the twins. I was all for letting her leave, but you intervened and would not excuse either of us from the table. Sometimes, cooler heads do prevail." He was bringing the coffee to the table, when he heard the back door open. "Come in Sam, we are having pie and coffee. I need to get down to the feedlot, but I never pass up a slice of Katie's pie. How were your accommodations last night?"

Sam sat down at the table and responded. "They were terrific. I didn't realize how tired I was last night. Thanks for stopping me from heading out in the snowstorm. I had planned to leave as soon as the roads were clear, but if you don't mind, I would like to stay one more night. I guess the travel was a bit hard on me yesterday."

Katie put her hands on his shoulders. "Oh Poppa, that will be great. I will fix you a typical Sandhills supper, with the feminine touch. What you had last night was a bachelor's supper. It was sufficient, but tonight you will see why cowboys marry. Poppa, don't be in a hurry to leave." She brought the pie to the table. "Poppa, do you still play the banjo? I was telling Ty, that I recall you playing the banjo, and I would dance. Is that right, or am I imagining things?"

"Do you remember that? You were my greatest fan. It seemed that you never wanted me to stop. Yes, I still play. If you would like, I will bring my banjo into the house and let it warm up. Then tonight after the evening meal, I will play for you and the family."

"That would be great Poppa, that would be great! Of all the instruments, what made you choose the banjo?"

"Oh, it wasn't my choice. Grandma Tully made the choice for me. She came to live with us, shortly after I was born. Actually, she was my great grandmother, but we always called her Grandma Tully. She was widowed.

Grandpa Cullen had died fairly young, and she moved in with my grandparents Dylan and Heather O'Neal. We all lived in the Bronx on the same block. I have all of this in my scrapbook that I showed you this morning. Grandma Tully was like a family heirloom. She was passed from one generation to another. She was eighty-four when she came to live with us. When I was old enough to understand the order of things, I would ask my mother if Grandma Tully was going to live with me when I got married. Before Mother could answer, Grandma would say, 'Of course I will. I will even help you choose the right bride.' Unfortunately, on her way to church, Grandma missed the top step of our front stoop and died at the age of ninety-four. I was ten at the time. I thought my life had come to an end."

Sam didn't speak for a few moments, apparently lost in his thoughts. Neither did Ty or Katie say anything. Then he continued. "When I was six, I wanted to be a drummer. I would bang on anything, keeping time with the beat. Grandma Tully went to her trunk. In her trunk were her life possessions, which had followed her from one generation to another. She brought out a small banjo and handing it to me she said, 'if you want to make noise, be a drummer, but if you want to make music this is what you play. Your Grandpa Cullen brought this from Ireland when we came to America. I was a girl of twelve when we met on the ship, *The Spirit of Spring.* I knew right then that he was the man that I would marry. Sam, learn the banjo and you will never be without friends.' So, I learned to play the banjo."

Ty looked over at Katie. He was frightened at the look on her face, while the tears flowed down her cheeks. "Katie," he exclaimed, "why are you weeping?"

She shook her head. "Poppa, was Grandma Tully's

maiden name Farley?"

He thought a moment before answering. "Yes, I do believe it was. I could verify that by looking it up in the family genealogy in the scrapbook. Why do you ask?"

"This has been an answer to my prayers. Ty, the tears that I shed have been tears of joy. Poppa, I have been writing from an old journal that we found in a desk here at the ranch. In it tells about Meagan Farley that was left behind in Ireland when she had the measles. The rest of the family migrated to America on a ship named *The Spirit of Spring.* Her sister's name was Tully. Last night I was so despondent that I was unsure if I could continue with the story. Now I understand why God brought you to me at this time. This has given me new hope while I continue to write the history of this ranch."

Sam was hesitant. He turned to his daughter, "Katie, I have noticed that you and Ty speak often about God with such reverence. And yet, you speak of God in a casual manner, as if He is a part of your everyday life."

"But he is! It is so natural for us, now that we are drawn to the Trinity; that is God the Father, Jesus Christ the Son and the Holy Spirit. I view God as the creator, not only of the mountains and the seas, but he is the creator of each of us as individuals. Just as each mountain is different, each member of the human race is different because he created us that way. Because he created us, he takes a special interest in us."

Sam interrupted her, "I am not sure that he takes a special interest in me. He might you, but not me."

Katie reached out to touch his hand. "Oh Poppa, what brought about the urge to come to me at this time? Why didn't you seek me out when I turned eighteen? Even our first meeting did not go well. I am ashamed that my anger and my hurt feelings last night was intent upon having you leave. But God intervened when Ty came forward as the peacemaker. Ty has a special verse in Jeremiah 10: 23—'O Lord, I know that the way of man is not in himself. It is not in man that walketh to direct his steps.' Had either one of us held on to our own stubborn will we would have parted, but we would have missed the blessings which we are experiencing here and now. God isn't forcing us, but He is providing the opportunity that we might have joy. Jesus said, 'I come that you might have joy, and that your joy might be full.' He came that we might have joy in Him; that joy is in the salvation that he provided to each of us through his shed blood. In His salvation, it brings us to be at peace with God. It gets even better. When Jesus left this earth, he promised that he would send one to comfort us, the Holy Spirit. As we allow the Holy Spirit to dwell within us, we can show forth God through our deeds and actions."

Sam shook his head in unbelief. "I don't know Katie, I don't know. I could never understand why God let Grandma Tully die, or die by falling down the steps. Why couldn't she have died in her sleep?"

"Poppa, I don't pretend to understand why God does what he does, but He can do these things because he is God. Even now, the thought of her death has brought this conversation and how God can be real in your life."

Sam laughed. "Katie, God knows a lot more about me than you do. He wouldn't want an old sinner like me."

She reached out and grasped his hand. "But Poppa, he does, he does. He wants us so much that he sent his son, Jesus Christ to the cross so that we can come to God. He sent his son for me and for you. He sent his son for young sinners and old sinners. In the book of Romans 3: 23 it tells the world 'The wages of sin is death, but the gift of God is eternal life through Jesus Christ, his son.' It is up to you to receive this gift."

Shaking his head, he said, "I don't know, Katie, I just don't know."

"Last night you heard about the extra potato. Was it a coincidence, or was it God working through the Holy Spirit to prompt Ty to ask for another potato? This is a little thing, but I fear that Mr. Coincidence gets a lot more credit than he deserves. Whatever you might think, I am rejoicing that you are in our home. I am looking forward to hearing you play the banjo tonight. I love you, Poppa." Wiping at her tears, Katie left the kitchen. She went to her bedroom to pray for this fragile man that had unexpectedly entered her life once again.

That night was a joyous occasion in the Taggat household. Katie had prepared the kind of supper that the 99 Ranch was famous for. It was the same menu that is fed to the branding crew each spring. Ty's mother, Laura started the tradition the year that Ty was a baby when she prepared Swiss steak at the first branding dinner.

After supper, everyone gathered in the living room to hear Sam entertain the family with his banjo music. Katie laughed when she said, "Poppa, it is just as I remembered it. It is certainly a gift."

Martin was fascinated with the banjo. "Grandpa, do you think that you could teach me to play the banjo?"

"I could teach you if you had a banjo and if you would be willing to practice. In among my possessions, few as they may be, I have the banjo that I learned to play on. It belonged to my great-grandfather. I will give it to you, with the understanding that it is never to be sold. It is a family heirloom, to be passed on from generation to generation." He went to the guest lodge and brought out the banjo that he had learned to play on as a boy of six. That night, Martin had his first lesson.

The next morning at breakfast, Sam said to the Martin and Marie, "Children, I will be leaving after breakfast on my way to Oregon. I have enjoyed my visit, but I will be gone when you return home this afternoon." They hugged him before leaving the house to go to school.

Katie reached out to him and touched his hand. "But Poppa, can't you stay another day or two?"

Getting up from the table, he shook his head. "No Katie, I need to get to my job." But he didn't get to his feet, but sank back on his chair. She saw that his eyes were glazed and the color had left his face.

"What is it Poppa? What is it?"

He shook his head. "I don't know. I guess that I got up too quick. I'll sit here a moment. I'll be fine."

Touching his brow, Katie said, "Just sit there a moment. I'll be back and take your blood pressure. Don't get up."

She went to the hall closet and brought out her medical bag. When she returned, Sam was resting his head in his arms on the kitchen table. She had him sit up and attached the blood pressure cup to his arm. Removing it from his arm, she put her hand on his shoulder. "Poppa, let me take you to Summit City. Dr. Mockett needs to take a look at you. If he says it is alright for you to travel, I will let you go. But, I do want you to see the doctor." Katie sensed that she had made the right decision when Sam nodded his head.

After dinner, Katie, Kylee and Sam went to Summit City. Dr. Mockett examined Sam thoroughly. Later, the doctor met with Sam and Katie. "Sam, you are a very sick man. Not only that, but you are in a rundown condition. You are an adult, but I would discourage you from traveling. Certainly, you should not be going that far alone. Katie tells me that you have a job waiting for you in Oregon."

Sam sensed that the doctor had more to say, but

he stopped him. "Doctor, I would prefer that I talk to you alone." Katie was shocked, but left the room after a nod of the head from the doctor.

Katie left and Sam began. "I need to leave, even if the trip kills me. I have very little money. I can't expect Katie and her family to take me in at this time. I haven't seen Katie since she was two years old. It wouldn't be right, so I will take my chance going to my next job. I have money to pay you, but I will leave the Sandhills in the morning. It would have been best if I had bypassed Summit City."

Sam got up out of his chair. Dr. Mockett put up his hand to stop him. "Sam, let me tell you something about your daughter and Ty. I know them, and it wouldn't make any difference it you were a total stranger, they would offer the same hospitality. Katie will be brokenhearted to have you leave now. She knows how sick you are. That is why you are sitting in my office now. Give her an opportunity to help you. I will write your employer a letter indicating your need to have your health restored before you start work. You left Katie when she was two, so don't leave her now. How about it Sam, give me a shot at getting you on your feet?" Sam was silent, but nodded his head and sat back down.

Doctor Mockett opened the door and invited Katie back into the room. With his back turned to Sam, he gave her a wink. "Katie, I am going to write a prescription for your father. I have other instructions to follow as well. He needs a little more time to get on his feet before heading west. Come back in a week." He shook Sam's hand and left the room.

Katie stopped at the pharmacy for the medication. Sam insisted that he would pay for it. Katie said, "Poppa, because I help at the hospital from time to time, the pharmacy gives me a discount. We can keep track and then when you are ready to leave, we can settle up." He nodded his head in agreement, but was silent during the trip home.

This was the beginning of Sam's return to good health, or at least, it was supposed to be. Katie would encourage him to take his medicine and get some exercise each day. One morning in mid December, she went to his room to gather the bedding and his dirty clothes. There on the nightstand was a half empty bottle of whiskey and a shot glass. Ty had left early to go to the feedlot. Katie and Sam had established a routine each morning of having coffee and going through his scrapbook, explaining to Katie the details of each page. This morning, Katie was hesitant in her approach. Taking his hand, she began, "Poppa, I found your bottle. I don't think that it is one of Dr. Mockett's medicines that he prescribed."

Jerking his hand free, he looked surprised. "Oh Katie, I guess that I was a bit careless this morning and didn't hide it in the closet. I will be more careful next time."

"Poppa, this is difficult for me. My husband is very adamant about the presence of liquor here on the ranch."

Before she could say anything more, Sam interrupted her. "Katie my dear, you don't understand. I am Irish, and all my life, I have had a wee nip of the finest Irish whiskey every morning before my feet hit the cold, cold floor. It's just who we are and who I am. Leaving the bottle out won't happen again." He paused for a moment. He had a childish grin before he continued. "Katie, I believe there is a verse in the Bible that says something about a little wine for the stomach."

Katie responded, "Yes Poppa, I am familiar with that verse. It is I Timothy 5:23--Drink no longer water, but use a little wine for thy stomach's sake and thine often infirmities."

Katie dropped the subject, but the next time that she was in Summit City, she went to see Dr. Mockett. She explained to the doctor her conversation with her father. "Doctor, what should I do? I am caught between obedience to my husband and the health and welfare of my father?"

The doctor smiled and nodded his head. "Katie, how you handle this with Ty is not my problem. I am sure that you will solve that after I have given you my advice concerning Sam. I will be blunt with you; your father is not going to recover his health. He is as well as he is ever going to get. He has lived his three score and ten as depicted in the bible. If I can get a person that far, I think that I have done well. No matter what I might say, Sam is not going to give up his Irish whiskey. He is an adult and you are not his mother. He doesn't have a whole lot to live for, so don't take away what little joy he has. I would suggest that he delay taking his medication until the noon meal, so that it might be more effective. I sense that perhaps that shot of whiskey first thing in the morning is his tonic for the day. I can see that eating at your table has prolonged the inevitable. His color is better and he is gaining some weight. Keep him active, maybe a few chores around the ranch would help. Marty told me that his grandfather is teaching him to play the banjo. That is good. Now, anymore questions?"

Katie shook her head and went to the waiting area to get the children. Mulling over the conversation with the doctor was perplexing. It wasn't the advice that she wanted, but she could see the merit in his reasoning. When and how I tell Ty is what I fear now.

About once a month, Sam would drive his car to Summit City in the afternoon. Katie sensed that it was probably to replenish his supply of Irish whiskey.

The middle of January, Ty went to Lincoln to attend a convention of the feedlot operators. Sometimes, Katie would go with him, but this time she opted to stay at home. It was while Ty was gone that Sam said, "Katie, I am going to town this afternoon. It might be late when I get back, so I will eat in town." She said nothing, but noticed that he took his banjo with him.

Katie was putting Kylee to bed when the phone rang. After her usual greeting, she was surprised that it was the sheriff, Johnny Morgan. "Katie, is Ty there?"

"No, he went to Lincoln, and won't be back until tomorrow night. Is there a problem?"

"Yes, Katie, there is. It is your father. He is at the Corner Bar, playing his banjo and singing to the customers. Man, that guy can sing. Unfortunately, the more he sings the more drinks they buy him. It doesn't seem to bother his singing, but I don't want him behind the wheel of that old car when he decides to go home. Can you get one of the hands to come and drive him home? Maybe you can talk him into going home."

"I will get Jack Canon to come with me. I'm sorry. Thanks for letting me know."

Jack's wife Janet stayed with the children, while she and Jack went to get Sam. Entering the door, she could hear him singing the songs of the old country in the fashion of an Irish tenor. She waited until he finished his song. He then leaned against the bar, his banjo at his feet. Katie went to him, "Poppa, I am sorry to bother you, but I need you at home. I brought Jack with me to drive your car, so that you could ride with me."

"Sure Katie, I can go with you." Looking around, he said, "Where's my banjo? I think that I have lost my banjo. Where's Ty? Why didn't he come with you? Katie, they liked my singing. Next time, Marty can come and sing and play with me. He is good Katie, Marty can play real good."

She replied, "Poppa, Ty isn't home, that is why you need to come with me." She picked up his banjo. Walking past the bartender, she said, "Casey Collins, you will hear from me tomorrow. This is shameful to let him get in this shape."

The next morning, Sam could not, or would not get out of bed. Katie brought him a large glass of orange juice. Propping him up so that he could drink the juice, she said, "Sam, we can't have a repeat of last night."

He interrupted her, "I thought you were calling me Poppa. Why the change?"

"Last night was a far cry from 'a little wine for the stomach's sake.' Last night was more like Ephesians 5:18 which says, 'And be not drunk with wine, wherein is excess; but be filled with the Spirit.' Dr. Mockett has been doctoring you, and I have been feeding you for three months. We have been making a change in your life, and you have destroyed it all in one night. You can't even get out of bed this morning."

"But Katie, they liked my singing and playing. They kept buying me drinks. The more I sang, the more they bought for me. I couldn't be rude. Last night, I was on top."

"Poppa, I know that you like to sing and I know that you like your Irish whiskey, but last night was more than a wee nip. I called Casey, the owner of the Corner Bar this morning. He wants you back next Friday night. Poppa, you need an agent. You can't be singing and playing your banjo for drinks. Starting today, I am your agent. Casey has agreed not to sell any alcohol to be consumed by you. He isn't paying you anything, but you will work for tips. I will set up a milk bucket for your money. That way, the patrons will avoid seeming cheap by throwing in paper money instead of coins that will clang. I have cautioned

Casey. If you have any alcohol, that will be the end of your singing. You can always go to the other bar in town with your banjo."

Sam laughed, "Katie, you are a clever girl."

Next Friday night, Sam went to town with his banjo and a milk bucket. Katie called Sheriff Morgan and told him what she had done. She asked, "Johnny, when you make your rounds, could you check on my father? I don't want him drinking. He can sing without all that alcohol. Casey knows that I mean business."

Katie stayed up until Sam returned home. It was after 1:00 a.m. He came in with his banjo in one hand and the milk bucket in the other. He was elated, but she saw that something was different about him. It was his flat cap; it was gone. He was wearing a cowboy hat, a white Stetson! "Poppa, where did you get that hat? It is a nice one."

Sam laughed. "Katie, you won't believe this, but when I started singing the Irish tunes, they began requesting cowboy songs. I sang 'Home on the Range,' and then one fellow requested 'Strawberry Roan.' I had never heard of it, but I told him, if I had the music, I would give it a try. Usually, if they will sing a few bars, I can pick up on the melody. He came back later with the sheet music and lyrics and this hat. He told me, 'Irish, we can't have you singing cowboy songs with that pancake on your head. Here's a cowboy hat for you. I can't keep it on my head with all this wind. Give me that pancake. I can pull it over my ears.' The Strawberry Roan must have at least seven stanzas. It is their favorite, so I will have to practice it this week."

Sam's agent kept him busy. Katie had him booked at civic organizations, birthdays and anniversaries. He would play in the afternoons at some of the brandings, always wearing his white hat. Often he was joined by his young apprentice, Marty. Katie noticed that from time to time, her mother would be in the crowd, but she was never aware that her parents spoke to one another.

In late May, Sam told Katie, "Don't book any more brandings for me. After the 99 Ranch branding tomorrow, I will be leaving for Oregon. It has been fun, but I need to move on."

Katie was saddened. She and her father had many talks about spiritual things, but he always acknowledged that she was special in the eyes of God, but he was not. It grieved her, but she would continue to pray for him, even as Laura had prayed for Tag. She reached out and gripped his hands. She said, "Poppa, may I pray for you? This could be the last time that we will be together." He nodded his head. She began, "Father, I thank you for these days that Poppa has been in our family. I thank you for the comfort that you have given me in my writing, as I learned about Grandma Tully."

Sam interrupted her prayers as he cried out, "Stop it, stop it! Don't talk about Grandma Tully! It was my fault that she died. I was supposed to sweep the snow off of the front stoop. She slipped on the icy surface and fell down the steps. I blamed God for letting her die, but it was really my fault. That is why I am too great of a sinner. God doesn't want me because of my sin."

Katie reached out to him, "Poppa, you have carried this burden too long. You were a ten year old boy when this happened. God forgives you, I forgive you, and if Grandma Tully was here today, she would forgive you. Now is the time that your sins can be washed away by the blood of Jesus Christ, so that you may be at peace with God." Sam nodded and a smile crept across his face.

"Thank you Katie. Now I understand why I made this trip. Not only did I get to see my daughter and her family, but now I have finally found peace." He stood up and said, "Tonight, after the family has gone to bed, could I have a few moments of your time, just you and me?"

Katie nodded and wiped the tears of joy from her eyes. She went to her bedroom that she might pray a prayer of thanksgiving for her father's salvation.

After the children were in bed, Katie said to Ty, "Poppa and I will say our goodbyes tonight. He plans to leave early tomorrow morning. He was appreciative of you buying new tires for his car. Go ahead and go to bed. I am not sure how long I will be. His leaving will make a big void in our life, but I sense that he is anxious to leave. I don't think he is prone to stay too long in any one place."

Katie rapped on the door of his room and entered. He had what appeared to be a special kind of chocolate candy and a hot drink waiting for her. He came to her and motioned to a chair.

"Katie, please sit down. I have made a special drink for you this evening. If you are tired and stressed out, it is a good relaxant. Think of your father when you drink of it. I have left the recipe on the counter." She took a chair near the small table at the edge of the room. He handed her a mug that was filled with steaming hot liquid, topped off with heavy cream. She took a cautious sip and sampling the sweetness, she gave a nod of her head, indicating her approval. She nibbled a bit on the chocolate, sensing that her father had more to say to her. Sitting down on a chair nearby, he took her hands in his. "Katie, I want to thank you and your family for the hospitality that you have shown to me. I am sorry to leave you, but I think that it is best this way. You enjoyed the scrapbook so much, that I want you to have it. It is a part of your heritage. I sense that I don't have long in this world, but I don't want to be a burden to you in my last days. You made me feel welcome in your home, and it was you that made me accepted in this tiny community. It is best that I leave on a high note. Thank you for introducing me to Jesus Christ. Now I am at peace with God."

Katie drank the last of the liquid in the mug. Setting it aside, she felt a warmth come over. She stood to leave. Bending down, she gave Sam a kiss on the cheek. "Good night Poppa."

Leaving the room, she feared that she would have a sleepless night, knowing that he would be leaving in the morning. She was surprised that as soon as she brought the covers to her chin, it seemed that she drifted off to sleep immediately.

The next morning, she looked out and saw that he had not yet left. When everyone had come to the kitchen, she went to his room to let him know that breakfast was ready. Not getting any response from her knock, she went in to awaken him. He was dressed and laying on his bed, but he was not going to Oregon. The shot glass was on the night stand, but the bottle of whiskey was not. Evidently, he had his wee nip earlier and had done something with the bottle. Katie glanced at the recipe that he had left behind. She saw the title of the recipe, "Irish Coffee" scrawled on the flap of an envelope. Inside was the recipe scrawled in Sam's handwriting. Looking over the list of ingredients, Katie saw that one of those was one and a half ounces of Irish whiskey per serving. She laughed. She remembered the time that they had bantered back and forth about strong drink. Sam had the last word, but she did sleep well last night.

Two days later, Sam lay in the casket. His hands held the white hat that he had cherished. Pastor Roth spoke to the large crowd that had gathered that day. He commented, "Sam O'Neal was only in this community a short while, but he blessed all of us with his music. Whether he was playing the tunes of Ireland, the cowboy songs of the west, or the gospel music of the church, he united us with his rich Irish tenor voice and his melodious banjo. We will miss him." He was buried in the Teasdale Cemetery. While the casket was being lowered into the grave, Marty Taggat played his grandfather's banjo and with a quivering voice he sang the cowboy song, "I'm Heading for the Last Roundup."

I'm heading for the last roundup
Gonna saddle old paint for the last time and ride
So long old pal, its time your tears were dried
I'm heading for the last roundup
Git along little doggie, git along, git along
Git along little doggie, git along, git along
I'm heading for the last roundup

CHAPTER 12
THE JOURNEY

The motion of the ship, coupled by the pungent smell of the harbor was enough to unsettle his stomach. Conan was unsure of what was expected of him, but he had an uneasy feeling that his life was about to change drastically. He had nothing to eat since early that morning. He and Lord Willingham had stopped to stretch their legs at the time the sun was appearing on the eastern horizon. It was then that they shared the food that Meagan had prepared. Still chained to his bunk, he decided to while away the time by beginning to carve the first of the pawns that he hoped to send to his mother. He feared that he would be unable write to her. But, it was his prayer that he could assure her of his well being if she received a pawn from time to time.

He had carefully formed the rough outline of the first of the pawns when he heard the anchor being raised. They were preparing to set sail. He could hear the orders being shouted for the crew to raise the sails in preparation of leaving the harbor. Conan could feel the motion of the ship. He was unable to look out, but the rocking motion ceased and the ship began to glide. After a time, Porter came to the quarters and released the crewmen and allowed them to go on the deck. There they met Captain Twain. He was a small man with very little hair on his head, but he had a full black beard. There was an air of arrogance about him that put fear into the heart of Conan. He sensed that it would be difficult to please him.

The first mate Cochran pulled him to the side and

explained that he would be awakened at the ringing of
eight bells to go to the galley to help the cook prepare the
breakfast for the crew. Conan later learned that it would
be 4:00 a.m. He also learned that eight bells meant it was
either four, eight or twelve o'clock whether it was day or
night. For each thirty minutes after those times, it would
be signified by one bell. Conan was to have the breakfast
served to the captain's quarters at the second bell, or five
in the morning. Cochran said, "Trego has been serving as
cabin boy. He will work with you one day, and then you
will be on your own. Pay close attention. He is Portuguese,
so he is difficult to understand." He paused before he
continued. Then he shook his head. "I will not say anything
further, but Trego will explain to you what you can expect
from Captain Twain. Do not be late. Do not be lazy!"

Conan did not sleep well that night. He could hear
the faint ringing of each bell through the night. The next
morning, he was the first one in the galley, except for the
ship's cook. Upon his arrival, he was put to work. At the
second bell, he was sought out by a young man with a
gold ring in his right ear. In a crude form of English, he
began to bark out instructions. The only thing Conan could
understand was, "Hurry, hurry, hurry." Conan took the tray
and followed him up the stairs to the captain's quarters.
They stood back by the door while Captain Twain ate
his breakfast. With their arms at their side, they stood at
attention. Trego nodded with his head toward a small rack
where a thin rod was lodged. Conan thought that he wanted
him to fetch it for him. Conan moved toward it, but Trego
suddenly shook his head.

After Captain Twain had finished eating, he
motioned for them to take away the tray. He said, "Conan,
come back after you have returned the tray to the galley. I
will go over what I expect from you." Conan nodded and

left with Trego.

Conan was unsure why he couldn't have stayed and let Trego return the tray. He asked, "What were you trying to tell me about the rod on the rack?"

In his broken English, Trego tried to explain. "First day, he use rod on new boy. Every time. Raise shirt and get three stripes across back. Make boy be afraid. Captain calls it a caning." He lifted his shirt and turned away from Conan. He saw three welts on Trego's back.

He asked Trego, "How long have you been a cabin boy?"

He raised two fingers, "Two years. Now I will be crewman. You go to captain."

Conan gave him the tray and returned to the captain's cabin, prepared to receive his punishment. He rapped on the door. The captain asked. "Who is it?"

"Sir, it is Conan. I am reporting as ordered, Sir."

"Come in."

Conan entered and stood at attention. The captain rose up out of his chair. He said, "Conan, I expect respect from all crew members, of which you are one of them. I don't require you to salute, but you will be expected to address me as Captain Twain, or Sir. Is that understood?"

Conan nodded and said, "Yes, sir."

Captain Twain had more to say to him. "Conan, you will be under orders of the cook in the galley. There is a red flag in the galley. If that flag drops, it means that I want you here at once. There is one other thing. I want you to remove your shirt and grab that pole at the foot of the stairs. I want to demonstrate what the penalty is for disobeying my orders. Do you understand?"

"Yes, Sir. I would be disappointed if I was not shown what the penalty is to be." He removed his shirt and placed his fingers around the pole. He gritted his teeth, prepared to receive the first blow. He heard the captain walk over to the rack, and in a matter of moments, he felt the first slash of the rod. It felt as if his back was on fire.

Awaiting the next blow to his back, he heard the rod being replaced on the rack. The captain remarked, "Normally, I would strike you three times, which is my usual punishment. However, since you expected it, I will reserve the other two slashes with the cane for the times when you have offended me. Put your shirt back on. You are dismissed."

Conan put his shirt back on. He said, "Thank you, Sir, for your mercy. I will leave now."

He returned to the galley where he was met by Trego. He asked, "Did you feel the cane?" Conan nodded. Trego showed him a small tin of a foul smelling salve. "Here, let me put some on your back. This will take some of the fire out of it and help it to scar over." Conan turned his back to him and pulled his shirt out of his trousers. Trego exclaimed, "What, only one?" He rubbed it with the salve, which soothed the wound.

Conan nodded. "I told him that I expected to receive the penalty. He struck me once, but cautioned that the next time I would receive the other two slashes with the cane. Thank you for the warning. It made it much easier to be prepared for the caning."

Though he missed his parents and those he worked with on the estate, he knew that it would do no good to dwell on it. He was assured that his mother was praying for him, so that was covered. He was confined to the ship, so now he must learn to cope and make the best of it. The first three days had been what one would call smooth sailing. In what moments that he had free, he availed himself of the opportunity to acquaint himself with the innards of the ship. The hold was packed with goods that would be exchanged for other goods, or gold or silver. It was always a matter of commerce, and the destination would change as the demand for merchandise changed.

By chance, Conan came upon a small area referred to as the carpenter's shop. It had a small array of lumber for the repair of the ship. Included was an area for the repair of the sails. It was here that he met Nathan Eton, the ship carpenter. As they conversed, Conan noticed a box with odd and end pieces of wood. Conan asked, "Do you have any scrap pieces of wood? In my spare time, I like to carve animals and birds. Sometime, I would like to carve a person's face and head."

"You mean a bust, you know, the head and neck down to the shoulders?"

"Yes, yes. Is that what you call it? I did not know."

Nathan replied, "Yes, that is it, but that would take a lot of carving. That box over there is my scrap box. Anything in there, you can have.

"Do you have any dark wood? I brought an oak branch with me, but I am looking for some small dark wood like a walnut. I am carving a chess set. I have enough light colored wood, but nothing to make the dark chess pieces."

Nathan thought a moment. "Down in the bottom of that box may be some pieces of walnut spindle. The Captain gets angry sometimes and knocks out a spindle or two in his staircase. I usually don't clean the box out until we are at the end of a voyage, so don't think that you have to store it at your bunk. In fact, if you have free time, come down and work here. If I have a big repair project, you can help me instead of being in the galley. I will tell the first mate to send you here if I need additional help."

"Thanks, Nathan. I will search through the box and see what I can use. Then I need to get back to the galley."

163

Conan found a piece of wood. He knew what he was going to carve. This was a part of his long range plan. At the beginning of each month he would carve one light colored pawn and one dark colored pawn. After that, it was pick and choose. He had already started on the light colored pawn. He had found enough walnut in the scrap box for his eight dark colored pawns.

By the second week on the water, Conan was beginning to enjoy the sea life. Also, by now he was able to understand Trego a little bit better. Other than the pawns, Trego and Nathan were the first on board to receive Conan's carvings. Trego received a pelican that stood three inches high. Nathan's was a seagull. After the crew had seen what he could do, they clamored to be the next one to have one of the carvings. They offered money for the next creation. Conan said, "No, I will not take money from my fellow crewmen, but you may draw lots. The winner can choose what I am to carve within reason. Once you have a carving, you will no longer be in the lottery. Is that fair enough?"

They all agreed. Someone asked, "What about the captain and first mate? Will they be first in line, or do they have to be in the lottery?"

Conan asked, "What do you men see as fair? You choose, and I will abide by your decision. What say you?"

To a man, they said, "Lottery!"

Conan said, "Agreed." He looked over the men. "I say that the cook has a pot big enough to hold the names. He will hold the lottery tomorrow at eight bells. Not everyone is here, so inform others to put their name in the pot, including the captain and first mate if they so desire. Trego has his prize, so he will draw the next name."

By the time that the ship had reached Portugal, the second name had been drawn, but the carving had not been completed. Prego wanted to take Conan with him to visit his family, but the first mate had forbidden Conan to leave the ship. In fact, all the time that the ship was in port, Conan was chained to his bunk. He was released when they were in open water. Conan had received permission from the captain to send a package to his mother on the ship in port that was returning to England.

Conan was never sure where they were going, or where they had been. He did know that whenever they were in port, he would be chained to his bunk. He prayed often, but he sensed that God had forgotten him, for his prayers were never answered. One day, Conan requested to speak with the first mate. "Why am I restricted to quarters when we are in port? Also, you have not allowed me to send mail to my mother. You have permitted me to send the chess pawns. However, you confiscated the first ones because they had the name of the ship inscribed on the underside. When is this ship returning to England so that I might go home?"

"Young man, you need to face the reality that you may never go home. At this time, you are a fugitive from the authorities. The man that you stabbed is dead. Most of the ports that we enter are a part of the British Commonwealth. Should you leave the ship, you would be arrested immediately. The man that brought you to me knew this would happen to you. His instructions were that you are never to set foot again in England. Nor are you to leave this ship. The HMS Bold Pelican is your own private little prison. You will leave it only when it sinks. If you wish to continue sending your family those funny little chess men, that is fine with me, but send no correspondence or fancy code. There is only one man in England that knows where you are, and he is not telling anyone. Now go back to work."

Conan went back to work, but he also began to form a plan. His plan was to bring about his release. He continued his duties as cabin boy, but he carved every spare moment that he had. The more he carved, the more the crew clamored for his work. The captain and first mate did not have their name drawn. This disturbed Conan, but he was unsure of how to handle the situation. With fifty men, it was a slow process. The first year he had carved six, and the following year it was seven. It was nearing the end of the third year and the news was that the HMS Bold Pelican would be returning to England. Conan was planning to make his escape when they returned home. His plan was to find his mother and the two of them would flee to Ireland. He feared that his father was deceased by this time, but his mother was still young. We will see, we will see. In the meantime, he continued to carve, but he had a secret project that he only worked on when he was alone. He had found a secluded spot to hide his work when he was out of the carpenter shop.

There was discontent among the men when they learned that they were not going directly to England, but would stop at a port on the west coast of Africa to meet another ship. The delay was to cost them six weeks time. Added to this, the winds had not been favorable, so they were delayed further.

After breakfast, Conan was called to the quarters of Captain Twain. There he met with the captain and First Mate Cochran. "Conan," the captain began. "First Mate Cochran and I are unhappy how you are handling the lottery. I want my name drawn next and Cochran's after that. See that it is done." He turned to the side, considering that it was settled. "Dismissed. You may leave now."

Conan was standing at attention. "Sir, it is not as simple as that. I do not handle the lottery drawing.

166

Everyone agreed to a man that you and the first mate would be included, but would take your chance of when your name might be drawn. Keep in mind. Each time there is a drawing, your chances of winning are greater than the time before."

The captain was angry. "Are you refusing to co-operate?"

Looking straight ahead, Conan replied. "No, Sir, but I cannot change the rules."

"If that is the case, then you will no longer be permitted to send anymore of your funny little chess men to England. Now you will have more time to carve, and carve you will, or be flogged for insubordination."

Conan looked at Captain Twain. "Sir, I accept your refusal to allow me to send my chess men to England. I do not care to have them drowned at sea. I accept the offer of flogging, but I would ask that it be limited to two lashes with the whip. It seems that you still owe me two lashes when I started as cabin boy. I ask that these be administered on deck in front of the crew. I appreciate more time to carve, but I cannot change the rules. Sir, may I point out that it is the little things in life that move people. I sense that I will be on this ship a long time. So, if you are patient, your name will be drawn. I have no way of knowing if the lottery is fixed, or if God is teaching you patience, but your name will be drawn. Don't incite a mutiny among the crew because of your impatience."

At eight bells in the afternoon, the crew met on deck. The captain pronounced judgment upon Conan, and he received the two lashes administered by a crewman. Once again, Trego was present to soothe his wounds with the foul smelling ointment to his back. The whip was more severe than the cane. Perhaps it was because it was used twice. The one thing that was a discouragement to Conan, he had sent all of the chess pieces to his mother, except for the queens. He had realized that they would require the most work and patience to complete, so he had left them until last. What would his mother think when she did not receive the last two pieces of the set? Then he remembered his plan. He would make his escape when they tied up in London. He did not know how it would happen, but he trusted God to reveal it to him.

On the deck of the ship
Came the sting of the whip
His fate has been planned
To return to the land
An idea comes to mind
So Katie must now find
The Ghosts of Teasdale Cemetery

CHAPTER 13
THE HMS BOLD PELICAN

Meagan Moran added another stick to the small flame under the boiling pot of soup. She looked over to where her husband, Big Tim sat in his rocker. She reminisced of how it was when she came to this home almost twenty years ago. Mr. Moran, as she always called him, had been a tower of strength. Not much had changed in the cottage. Over the years, Meagan had set a small table in front of the window by the door. On it was a chess board with each of the pieces in place, as if one was ready to begin a match. The chess board had been placed upon a white lace doily. On close examination, one could detect the detail and craftsmanship of each piece. However, it soon became obvious that the two queens were missing, awaiting their places. Meagan had started the ritual of the chess board upon the arrival of the first two pawns. One was of oak, and the second, a fine walnut. It had been six months since the kings had arrived. This had been the longest interval since the beginning.

Meagan ladled the soup into a bowl and went to her husband. She placed a cloth around his neck and tucked it under his chin. She began to spoon the soup into his mouth. From time to time, she wiped his lips. He asked, "Has Conan come home from the stables?"

This was a ritual each day, and she would reply, "Not yet, Mr. Moran, not yet?"

Then he would respond and say, "He is a good boy. Meagan, you have been a good wife."

Meagan would remove the cloth and pat his hand. "Thank you, Mr. Moran. I love you." Meagan set the bowl to the side when she heard a knock at the door. She opened

169

the door and recognized one of the stable hands. She was not sure of his name, but she invited him in. "Is there something that I can help you with?"

He replied, "Yes, Lord Bellingham wanted Big Tim to come to the stable today. He needs someone to take him to London."

She went over to her husband. She touched his arm and said something to him. He did not respond. She returned to the stable hand and told him, "No, he won't be going to the stable today."

The young man touched his cap and said, "Thank you, Mrs. Moran."

Meagan went to where her shawl was hanging on a peg. Putting her shawl over her shoulders, she closed the door and made her way to Loxnard to see the vicar. It was regarding the burial of Mr. Moran, for today he took his last breath. She would bury her husband by his first wife, Lila. There was only one plot. She had no thought as to where she would be buried. Perhaps the Lord shall return and I will be taken up in the Rapture.

It was a simple ceremony, but it was fitting, for Tim Moran was a simple man. He had served the gentry of the Bellingham estate from the time he was twelve years old until he died at age seventy. He had attended the church at Loxnard all of his life. The residents of Loxnard came and paid their respects and saw that he had a fitting burial. One resident came from the Bellingham estate. A driver had brought Lady Grace Bellingham in a carriage. He remained with the horses during the funeral. After the service and burial, the community had put together a lunch of tea and crumpets, so that the mourners might socialize. Grace went to Meagan. "I am sorry that he is gone. Big Tim was always so gracious and kind. I will miss him. But Meagan, what about you? What will you do?"

"I will be fine. We saved a bit of money over the years. Thank you for your concern."

Grace was not convinced that she would be fine. She was aware how stingy her father had been with the help. "Meagan, since Lady Anne has died, I have a lot of social responsibilities connected with the estate. I would dearly like your help. You are aware that I will be getting married in four months. We will have six months together and then Major Abbott will be going to India for a tour of duty with his brigade. When you have time, come and see me." She reached out and patted Meagan's hand.

Meagan brought her handkerchief to her eyes to wipe away the tears. "Grace, you have always been so dear to me. Unfortunately, your father and I have had some harsh words over the years, and it would be better that I not accept your offer. However, come and see me whenever you can. Thank you Lady Grace, for coming today." Meagan turned, and ran into the church, bringing an end to their conversation. Grace was unsure what Meagan meant about the harsh words between her father and her.

That night, Meagan wept for her son. "Now that I am alone, Lord, please send my son home to comfort me."

****

Conan Moran had been training for his escape from the first day that he had set foot on the HMS Bold Pelican. When he had been chained to his bunk, he sensed that he was a prisoner. It was confirmed each time the ship entered a foreign port. He was always chained. Someday, I will be able to slip away, and I must be able to swim. When the crew was allowed to dive off the deck and swim around the ship, he would swim around and around the ship. He was the first one in and the last one out. He would challenge others to a race, so he knew that if he could get free in the water, he had a chance of escaping. Now he knew that

London was his opportunity. He would not wait until they reached the port, but would make his attempt in open water, even if it meant swimming a long distance.

Not only did Conan have a plan, but the first mate Cochran also had a plan. He feared that Conan would try to escape when the ship docked at London. The crew was to have a thirty day leave while the ship was being repaired and restocked. He could not leave him on the ship for that time, but he was unsure how he was going to handle it. It then came to him when they were moored in the bay on the western coast of Africa. He had become acquainted with a man called Slater, the first mate of the ship Dark Lady. In comparing their schedules, they would both be in the same port on the coast of Portugal in sixty days. Two days later, in the middle of the night, a row boat from the Dark Lady tied up at the Bold Pelican. They roused Conan out of his bunk and took him back to the Dark Lady. Nobody on the Bold Pelican knew what happened to Conan. Sixty days later they made the switch, and Conan was back with his original crew. In his absence, another had been appointed as cabin boy. He was a youth of fifteen. Conan learned that he too had received the customary caning.

Conan knew now that he was not going to be able to make his escape to England. Where would be his next choice? He was now one of the many crewmen. He relished the change of duties, for now he had the opportunity to strengthen his body even more. His favorite duty was being in the crow's nest. It afforded him the solitude to think and to plan. He had seen that the cunningness of first mate Cochran required all the resources he could muster if he was to leave this ship alive. Now he had included prayer in his time of solitude. Only by divine guidance and the will of God was he to escape.

Sometimes in the early dawn or the late dusk, he would entertain himself in the crow's nest by imitating the noise of the sea gulls, or the warbling of various song birds. He would place the left hand with the joined fingers to his lips, and wrap the right hand around it. The crew would look around, trying to catch a glimpse of the birds. He taught some of the bird calls to Trego, so they would answer back and forth.

Conan had altered his plan. If he couldn't go to England, he would go to Ireland or America. His mother often spoke of her family migrating to New York City. There were other opportunities to escape, but he did not want to go to a non-English speaking country, nor one of an unfamiliar culture. He was fearful that he would not survive.

Once again, it was time to return to England. Conan had been on the Bold Pelican for almost seven years. He had marked the date of his twenty-first birthday. This was to be the year of his escape. He mused to himself. Wouldn't it be ironic if I could escape before the captain or first mate had their name drawn for one of my carvings?

****

Near the village of Loxnard and the town of Cotswold, there was sadness at the Bellingham Estate. Lord William Bellingham was dying after a lingering illness. His daughter Grace had been faithful in nursing him in his last days. Her husband, Major Abbott had returned from India two months before his death. While Grace ministered to her father, Major Abbott had availed himself of the opportunity to get reacquainted with their two children, Virginia and John. Virginia had been one year old and John less than a month when he had left for his second tour of duty in India.

In the last month of his life, Grace would ask her father about various events. She asked about his parents and his siblings. He responded quite well. She then turned to the time that Carlton Thornwood had died. She asked, "Do you remember Carlton Thornwood?"

"Oh yes," he said. "I remember Carlton. I thought

that the two of you might marry. Whatever happened to young Thornwood?"

"He died when he accidently stumbled and stabbed himself."

"That's right. I recall that they thought our stable master's son was at fault. Let me see, his name was Conan. That Irish wench would give him an Irish name. That woman was trouble, always wanting me to do something for that son of hers. I was going to send her to the streets of London when Big Tim said that he would marry her. She was always trouble."

"Did you take Conan to London before Carlton died?"

"Yes, as I said, she always wanted me to do something for her son. She was afraid that the Carlton family was going to harm him. We rode all night to get him away from Cotswold."

Grace asked, "Father, where did you take him?"

"I took him where they would never find him. I put him on a ship in London. Who knows where he is today? He certainly isn't in Cotswold, and that Irish wench hasn't bothered me since."

"What ship did you put him on? Do you remember the name of the ship?"

He laughed a scornful laugh. "I even remember the captain. It was Captain Twain. The name of the ship was--." He paused and a strange look came upon his face. He shook his head and stammered. "I, I can't remember the ship. I just can't remember the ship. Grace, who were we talking about? Oh yes, it was that bothersome Irish wench. She has not been back for a long time. I told her to never come to the manor again."

Two weeks later, Lord Bellingham was dying with Grace at his bedside. He turned to his daughter and gripped her hand. He said, "Grace, I remember, I remember. The name of the ship was the HMS Bold Pelican." He then released her hand. Lord Bellingham was dead.

Two days later, Lord Bellingham was buried in the family cemetery on the estate. Meagan Moran had walked to the cemetery for the service. It was one of those unusually warm days that England experienced in the month of August. After the service, Meagan had stopped to rest on one of the benches placed in among the trees. She was admiring one of the floral gardens, and pondering the events of the day. Earlier, when she had walked past the casket, she saw the white gloved hands folded on his chest.

Grace came to sit beside her. She reached out and took Meagan's hands in hers. "Meagan," she said, "now that Father is gone, would you consider coming into my home? Major Abbott will be returning next month to India to rejoin his regiment. I dearly desire your companionship. I cherish the moments as a child when you cared for me. I would like John and Virginia to be under your care and tutelage. I don't know what happened between you and Father, but that is past. It is time for you to return to Bellingham. Will you do that for me?"

Meagan was weeping, and could not answer, but she nodded her head. A weak smile came to her face.

"I take that as a yes," exclaimed Grace. "We will get you moved whenever you wish. I have some news about Conan. Just before Father died, he remembered the ship that he put Conan on. It is the HMS Bold Pelican. Earlier he had told me the Captain's name was Twain. We will be able to do some research and perhaps find out where he is." Meagan's tears had dried and a smile was on her face. She gripped Grace's hands.

In the days that followed, Meagan left her thatched roof cottage and returned to the Bellingham estate to serve as a nanny to John and Virginia. Grace had sought the services of her husband's friend in London to monitor the coming and going of the vessel, HMS Bold Pelican.

In the meantime, Conan was aware that the time for their vessel to return to England was imminent. He had reckoned that the ship returned every four years. It had been almost eight years since he had seen his mother. Should he fail to escape this time, it would be another four years. He must not fail! Surely, enough time had passed since the death of Carleton that he would not easily be recognized and arrested. Then he and his mother could escape to Ireland. If his plan failed, it could mean another four years of captivity.

Conan had planned to have completed his carving for each member of the crew by the time that they arrived in London. It was now time to draw again. There were only three whose names had not been drawn; Captain Twain, First Mate Cochran and the cabin boy. The chief cook brought out the same pot that had been used since the beginning. He held it high enough that a person could not look in at the time of drawing. The last person to have their name drawn was the one to draw the name of the next person to receive a carving of their choice. The crewman reached in and pulled out a slip of paper. The cook took the slip and read, "Tommy Wills, our cabin boy." The crew cheered and Tommy beamed with joy.

Captain Twain yelled out. "This is not right! Let me see if my name is in the pot."

The cook handed the pot to the Captain. He reached in and read the names on the two remaining slips of paper. They were of the first mate and the captain. Satisfied, he returned the pot to the cook and stormed out.

Three weeks later, the scene was reenacted once again. This time, Tommy Wills drew out the name of First

Mate Cochran. The cook let the captain look into the pot. His name was there. Once again he stormed out. Conan asked the first mate what carving he desired. He said, "I would like a mermaid." Conan nodded his head. It was a bit more than he had expected to carve, but he would complete it before they reached London.

The ship was one day away from London when Conan presented the carving of the mermaid to First Mate Cochran. It was the largest of any of the carvings that he had made. She had been carved out of a wood of light color. She was sitting on a small rock.

First Mate Cochran drew the last paper out of the pot. The cook read the name, "Captain Twain."

He said, "It is about time! How are you going to carve out anything in one day, unless it is a little bird?"

Before he had an opportunity to register any further complaint, Conan replied, "Sir, in anticipation of something like this, I have made something of my own choosing for you. I will go, if all of you will be patient." He went to the carpenter shop and returned with his carving. It was covered with a white cloth and stood about twelve inches high. He placed it before the captain. He motioned for him to unveil it.

Removing the cloth he revealed a bust carved in a dark walnut wood that gleamed under the light in the galley. Turning it around, he saw that it was his likeness. Those near him were awestruck. It was the first time that they had ever heard him laugh. He caressed the bald head of the bust and his fingers brushed over the facial features. The beard had been finely chiseled. He lifted it high for all to see. There were no words of praise for the sculptor. He uttered, "It is about time!" He left the group and went to his quarters. He placed the bust on his desk that he might observe it with only a tilt of his head.

After the captain was gone, Conan went to the cook. He laughed and then asked, "I know that you rigged the lottery drawing, but how did you do it?"

"It was easy. I always had the two names in my hand. After a name was drawn, I would drop them back in the pot. It was always my intent that they would be last."

The next morning, Conan was awakened when he felt the cold iron clasped around his ankle. First Mate Cochran was by his bunk. He chuckled and remarked, "Your little scheme did not work. There is no way that you are getting off of this ship a free man."

****

Lady Grace Abbott had received word from her husband's friend in London that the HMS Bold Pelican would reach London the end of the month. It would be docking at the South West India Dock. He was able to see the crew manifest, but Conan Moran was not on it. He assured her not to be alarmed. Many times they were incomplete, or members of the crew took on another name if they were running from the authorities. Grace and Meagan went to London to await the arrival of the HMS Bold Pelican. Each day, they went to the South West India Dock where the ships were moored, preparing to load or unload. On the morning of the seventh day, they saw the ship that they were looking for. They saw an officer at the railing. Grace called out, "Are you Captain Twain? We need to talk with Captain Twain."

He waved and shouted back, "I am Captain Twain. Come over to the gang plank and I will visit with you."

The ladies went to meet the captain. He came down the gang plank and was waiting for them on the wharf. Grace introduced herself. "I am Lady Abbott and this is my friend, Mrs. Moran. We are from Cotswold. We have come here to meet Mrs. Moran's son, Conan. He shipped out on your ship eight years ago as a cabin boy. He was fourteen at the time. It has been over four years since we have heard anything from him. Is he a part of your crew?"

The captain was quite endearing. "Lady Abbott, the name does not sound familiar. However, I have had a number of cabin boys over the years. Usually the young lads do not remain cabin boys for very long. As they mature, they soon become seamen. Would the young lad be running away from home and sought to go to sea? Let me get the manifest of the crew and you may look it over. Sometimes, members of our crew use an alias if they have run away from home, or running from the authorities. We will see if you recognize any of the names. I would have you come aboard, but we are busy unlading the cargo. We got in at dawn this morning, so we started right away. I will be right back."

He departed up the gang plank. "Lady Grace," said Meagan, "what do you think? Is he being honest with us?"

"I am not sure. We will know more after looking over the manifest," replied Grace.

The captain returned and had another seaman with him. He said, "Ladies, I have brought First Mate Cochran with me. Perhaps he will be able to answer your questions. Here is the crew manifest. Please look it over."

He handed it to Lady Abbott. They looked it over, but said nothing. Meagan pointed her finger to one name. She said, "Tim Loxnard. Where is he?"

The first mate looked surprised. "I thought you were looking for a Conan Moran. Why, Tim Loxnard?"

Meagan answered, "My son's first name is Timothy, but he went by Conan which is his middle name. We lived near the village of Loxnard. Is my son here?"

The captain interrupted. "Mr. Cochran, do you remember this man? I cannot seem to recall him."

"Sure, he was the one that liked to go to the crow's nest." He turned to the ladies. "Most seaman do not like being that high, but Tim would volunteer every time. He was with the group of seamen that left early this morning. We only needed twenty men in the hold this morning. The rest received their pay and headed home. He will probably be there when you return."

"Now I remember him," stated the Captain. He started up the gang plank. "Does that answer your questions? When you see him, remind him that he needs to be here by the fifteenth of next month if he is going with us again. I will save him a spot until then, but we ship out three days later with a full crew, with or without him." Touching the visor of his cap, he said, "Good day, ladies."

Lady Grace replied, "Thank you, Captain. Evidently we were overly anxious to see him. We will leave now."

Walking back to their inn, Meagan remarked, "Did it seem that they wanted to be rid of us? They were nice enough, but I am not sure that they were sincere."

Grace replied, "You could be right. Shall we find a place where we can purchase a cup of tea and something to eat? I fear that I did not eat enough so early in the morning. Here is a gift shop with sidewalk tables."

Meagan said, "I will look at some of their merchandise. Go ahead and order tea for me, but nothing else. Perhaps I can find something for John and Virginia."

Meagan returned to the table before the tea was served. She was excited. "Lady Grace, I found a wooden dog. The clerk said that a seaman had been in the shop as soon as it opened and traded the carving for food. It looks like something that Conan might have carved. She could not describe him, except that he was young and had dark hair. Oh, Lady Grace, for some reason or other, I sense his presence even now. Do you really think that he might be on his way home?"

Grace reached out to Meagan. "Here is the tea and crumpets. Let us partake of these first. We shall return to the inn. The coachman can ready our carriage and we will return to Cotswold. Perhaps we may find him making his way home. This could be the answer to our many prayers. Should he return to your cottage, I am sure that he will ask around in order to locate you."

The two ladies were unaware that the long stone building they walked by on their way to the gift shop housed a young seaman. Conan Moran was praying for his deliverance. Early this morning, he had been brought to Port London Maritime Detention Center. He was uncertain when he would be free, but he was asking God to set him free. He was so close to Loxnard. He had hoped that the gifts to the first mate and captain would be such that they would set him free. He sensed that they were billing the shipping company for his services. He had received nothing more than a few articles of clothing in the past eight years.

Right now, these men were gloating how they had duped the mother into thinking that her son was making his way home. Captain Twain said, "That was close. Fortunately, you got Conan off the ship early enough to the Detention Center. He can sit there until we are ready to sail again. I have bribed the guards to not let anyone get close to him. Did you notice that I set the sailing date so that we will be at sea if they come back another time?"

CHAPTER 14
ONE MORE TRY

First thing each morning, Conan Moran would scratch a mark on the wall. Twice each day he would receive food. Every other day the slop bucket was emptied. Conversation between guards and him was kept to a minimum. Conan didn't understand it, but he was not bitter toward God. He viewed his incarceration as a time of fasting and prayer. Some days he ate nothing. At one time, he went three days without eating; only taking a bit of water. He recited scripture verses that he had committed to memory. He was amazed how the Lord had renewed his mind. He sang hymns and practiced his bird calls. After a time, he was able to have the birds of his voice sing the simpler songs.

One morning, he scratched the mark on the wall. He knew that it was the thirtieth day. He began his prayers, beseeching God to free him. He stopped, and then he said, "God, I sense that as Jesus was in the wilderness for forty days, that is how many days I will be in this cell. I will continue to make a mark on the wall, but I will no longer pray for my release." Ten days later he heard the click of the key in the lock. Once again, he was returned to the HMS Bold Pelican. No one said anything. Everyone assumed that he had visited his family and had returned to the sea.

Three days after the HMS Bold Pelican went to sea, two ladies from Cotswold were standing on the wharf of the South West India Dock. They were disappointed. They had been duped by Captain Twain!

The ship returned to Portugal and began to make stops along the western coast of Africa. Word spread among the crew that they would be crossing the southern portion of the Atlantic Ocean. They would stop at some ports in South America, making their way to Havana, Cuba. Evidently Cuban cigars were to be sought for the aristocrats of England.

Rumors would abound as to the next port to be entered. After Cuba, Conan had heard that there last port before returning to England would be Galveston along the coast of Texas. The intent was to fill the hold with bales of cotton for the clothing mills of England. Conan was excited when he learned that Texas was a part of America. Yes, America where my mother's family had gone to. Now I know that I will escape when we get to port. When the HMS Bold Pelican leaves Texas, I will not be on it. I may be dead, but I will no longer be at sea. Once again, he planned his escape.

Before he was chained to his bunk, Conan had been helping Nathan repair the anchor chain. Two days later, he was back to where they had repaired the anchor. He noticed that a file which they had been using was wedged under a brace. Nathan was always cautious of accounting for his tools. Conan made a mental note of its location. This may be a part of my plan. That night he retrieved the file and hid it near his bunk. The next night, he was chained to his bunk. The following morning, the ship entered the Port of Houston. Later that morning, Conan learned that it would be three days before they could start loading the vessel. The first mate had given shore leave to the crew. Four men and an officer had to remain with the ship at all times. They had taken two large row boats and one dinghy to take the crew ashore. The dinghy was used to rotate four men and an officer every twelve hours to look after the ship. Conan bided his time. He knew that the first watch would be alert. However, when the second watch returned from the shore, they would be suffering the aftermath of a night of carousing. A long period of sea travel was an encouragement to engage in excessive debauchery.

Conan waited until the second watch returned to the ship. It was stifling hot in the quarters, so the men slept on the deck. Conan used the file to cut through a link of the chain. He was unable to do anything about removing the metal shackle on his ankle. Once he was free, he replaced the file in the carpenter shop. He went to the captain's quarters and removed the bust of the captain which sat on his desk. He stopped by the first mate's room and took the carving of the mermaid from the shelf above his bunk. Returning to the carpenter shop, he worked feverishly to alter the two carvings. When he was finished, he returned them and covered each item with a cloth. He went to his bunk and slipped the severed link into place, so it would appear that nothing had been done to the chain. Now, he had to await his opportunity to steal away in the dinghy. He set aside his oilskin pouch. It was large enough to hold the black journal that he had brought from home. At the bottom of it, he had placed two short dowels. One was oak, the other was walnut. He slipped over his head, the thong holding a leather pouch. This held the coins that his mother had given him when he left home. They would provide for him, once he reached shore.

The only time any of the crew came to his bunk was when they brought rations to him each morning and night. He would remove the connecting link and he could go about the ship as long as he stayed out of sight. He was unable to steal away with the dinghy. As soon as the seamen returned from the shore, the others jumped into the boat and left the ship. Now, his only means of escape was to swim. He feared that it was further than he would be able to endure. It had been more than two years since he had been in the water. He also knew that it was his only hope.

He deemed that death was nobler than captivity. He had one more day before making his escape.

That evening, he looked out in the distance. He saw the three boats returning to the ship. Something has happened to cut short their shore leave. He realized that tonight was when he must make his escape, but he would wait for the tide to help take him to shore. He needed to hide before the entire crew arrived. He went back to his bunk for his oilskin pouch. He fashioned a short rope to make a sling, so that he could hang it over his shoulder. Going back on deck, he climbed the mast and hid in the crow's nest before the crew was close enough to spot him. He crouched down to avoid being seen. Now that they were in the harbor, no one would be needed as a lookout. When they rang eight bells at the midnight hour he would make his escape.

Eight bells rang out. The crew was preparing to go to their bunks for the night in preparation for the loading of the ship on the morrow. Two days of revelry had exhausted them. The evening calm was pierced with a scream. It was the Captain Twain. "I know who is responsible for this. Go find him and I will have him hung from the yardarm!" He held aloft his bust. It was now the bust of the head of an ugly rat. He yelled out once more. "I will give five silver coins to the man that finds him."

First Mate Cochran ran to his quarters. He returned with what had once been a lovely mermaid. It was now an ape with a potbelly, but still with the fins.

After thoroughly searching the ship, the crew went to their bunks. Everyone assumed that Conan had left the vessel. At midnight, Conan heard the eight bells. He crept along the deck and crawled over the railing. All the ropes had been secured, so there was no way for him to go hand over hand down the hull of the boat. There wasn't much cargo in the hold. Therefore, the ship was riding high in the water. Conan knew that he had to drop some distance into the water. He wanted to avoid making a loud splash that might awaken anyone on the deck. He climbed over the railing and began to ease himself down the hull. He released his grip on the rail. He expected to plunge into the water, but he dropped about a foot and his head was snapped around, slamming into the side of the ship. The thong that held the leather coin pouch had caught on a projection of the hull. He hung there, unable to get loose. He reached for his knife with one hand while he grasped the thong with the other hand. When he cut the leather thong, it slid through his clenched fist. The pouch and the coins fell into the ocean! Conan dropped into the water and began to make his way to the shore. First light was beginning to appear on the horizon when he reached the beach. Conan presumed that New York City was to the north, so north he would go. His first stop in America was a cemetery.

Conan was spent, so he curled up near a large headstone. He felt the heat still emanating from the granite in the early morning. He slept about four hours and awakened hungry, but had no food. He deemed that during the day, the safest place for him to be was the cemetery. He anticipated that if he traveled at night he would be safer. It would also be easier to find food in the fields and orchards. He was drawn to the inscription on the small headstone near the large one that he had slept by last night. There was an angel chiseled into the stone, and the inscription, "I will be your guardian angel." He looked at the name and the dates on the stone. He was amazed. This little boy died when he was two years old. Most fascinating was that he was born the same day that Conan had been born. He had been dead for over twenty years.

Conan left the cemetery early in the evening. He wanted to get out of the city and his purpose was to travel north. He had watched the stars the many nights that he had been in the crow's nest. He was aware of the position of the stars. He was pleased that he had found an apple orchard. The apples relieved his hunger pangs, but walking barefoot was difficult. He soaked his feet in each stream that he came to. The metal shackle was painful, but he had worked a part of his pant leg to keep the metal from chafing his ankle. After two weeks, his feet became toughened up. He was getting tired of apples, but it was better than being hungry.

The further he traveled, he experienced less humidity. Late one evening, he came to the edge of a town. It wasn't large, but neither was it as small as many of the towns he had encountered. It had a sign at the edge of town. It read, 'Welcome to Tipton, Texas.' Immediately, he was disheartened. He had hoped that he had left Texas and was getting near to New York City. He saw the storm clouds gathering in the west. He thought he might seek shelter under a bridge, but no stream was near the town. Large drops of rain and hail began to pelt him. He sought shelter in a building built with rough sawn boards. He eased through a side door. It was dark. He immediately knew that it was a shelter for horses. He could smell the horses, but he also inhaled the smell of the hay. He was chilled, but he sought the comfort and warmth of new hay. It was his first night of uninterrupted sleep since leaving the HMS Bold Pelican.

He was awakened by the whinny of a horse. Next, he heard two men talking outside. It was now light enough for him to look around him. Conan heard the large double doors on the rollers being opened. He stepped into a box stall to avoid being seen. The structure was similar to a jail cell. There was a horse in the stall and he lunged at Conan with his teeth bared. Conan wrapped his arms about the horse's neck and spoke softly to him. The first man said something to the other, but Conan could not understand what he said. The other man opened the door of the box stall. Conan rushed by the men and out the double doors. He started running down the street. One of the men yelled at him. "Hey Fella, you forgot your saddlebag." Conan turned. He saw that the man was holding his oilskin pouch over his head.

Conan turned back. He considered the consequences, but he could not go on without his oilskin pouch. He returned to where the two men were standing outside of the stable. He did not want to do battle with either one, but he did want his pouch. The eldest of the two was over six feet tall and all muscle. His hair was black with a touch of gray at the temples. The younger man was a replica of his elder. Conan held out his hand and asked. "May I have my oilskin pouch? I slept in your stable last night, but I did no harm. I have no money, but I will work if you think that I owe you for the nights lodging."

The younger man spoke up. Conan thought him to be about the same age as he. "Dad, this fella isn't from around here. See how he is dressed, and he talks funny. What do you think?"

"I don't know. Young man, what is your name?" Conan was silent. He was uncertain if he should answer the question. The older man repeated the question. "Mister, if we are to carry on a conversation, I need to know your name. What is it?"

His mind was a blank. Suddenly the tombstone with the inscription, 'I will be your guardian angel' loomed into his mind. He remembered the name of the child that was born the same day as he. "My name is Elmer, Elmer Ray

Teasdale."

The older man stuck out his hand. "Now I know why you sounded funny. I sensed that you grew up in an English family. I don't know what we are, except we are Texans. We probably sound strange to you. I am Harvey, and this is my son George. We own this livery stable." They each shook hands with Elmer.

Elmer looked at the sign over the double doors. It read 'Taggat and Son.' He replied, "Then, you are the Taggats, I presume."

"That's right. We are the Taggats. I have two more questions for you. I see that you are carrying a chunk of iron on your ankle. Are you running from the Texas authorities? The other question is, do you want a job? If you answer no to the first and yes to the second, we are in business."

Elmer Teasdale said, "No Sir, I am not running from the Texas authorities. I sense that if I say yes to the second question, you will help me be rid of that chunk of iron and you will feed me before I start working for you. If so, we have a deal. After we know one another better, I may tell you about my ankle bracelet. I have been living on apples and field corn for over two weeks. I am hungry."

"One more question. What do you know about horses? Can you drive harness horses?"

Elmer nodded. "I can drive two, four and six horse hitches. I can ride and I know how to shovel manure."

"You are hired. I will pay you five dollars a week. You and George will work every other Sunday. You will live and eat with us." He turned to his son. "George, take him down to the blacksmith shop and have that iron taken off. Tell Charlie to never mind why. I have it covered. Then take him home and Mother will feed him. I will stop at the house and tell her to fix him a good breakfast. She will need to look through some of your clothes that you have outgrown. Elmer, expect her to want you to bathe before you are fed. That is a start for now." He paused for a moment and then added. "After all that, you can go to the barber for a shave and a haircut. Mother will give you the money. Also Elmer, get a razor at the barbershop and have him show you how to use it. I want to see what you look like under all that hair." He tossed the oilskin pouch to him and went to the stable.

Mrs.Taggat was as he imagined she would be. She was a petite red head and in her mid-forties. He thought her to be pretty. There was a tin bathtub partially filled with hot water waiting for him on the back porch when he returned from the blacksmith. It was a relief to be shed of the metal cuff on his ankle. She introduced herself. She said, "I am Alma Taggat, but Harvey prefers that you address me as Mrs. Taggat. I will leave you, but scrub your hair and beard real good. I will be back with more hot water. Take your time. I sense that it has been some time since you had a hot bath. Enjoy the soak. I have laid out clothes for you. If you don't mind, I will burn the rags that you were wearing."

She left, giving him privacy. The water was hot, but it helped soothe the sore ankle. Later, Mrs.Taggat announced that she was entering the porch with more hot water. Pouring the water into the tub, she saw the scars on his back. She gasped. She asked, "Who put the scars on your back? Was it the same man to put the iron on your ankle?"

Elmer nodded, "The same man. The first scar was when I was fourteen with a caning rod. I had just met him. The other two scars were for disobedience. I was flogged with a whip. Perhaps at a later time I will reveal the circumstances with you."

"I understand," she said. "Here, let me wash your

191

back. I will be careful with the welts."

After she finished, she asked, "Is there anything you need? If not, I will let you dress and then I will cook you some breakfast. Try on the clothes to see what will fit. I have also set out some old shoes. You can't go around barefooted and work among the horses. "

"No, nothing more is needed. Thank you for washing my back. You were quite careful. When I am dressed, I will empty the water. Just tell me where you want it."

She laughed. "In Texas, we either have too much water, or too little. Now we have too little. There is a flower bed just out the back door. That is a good place to pour the water. You can use that bucket by the door to dip it out."

He found clothes to wear. They were a bit baggy, but they felt comfortable. The shoes were a different matter. He rarely wore shoes on the ship. If the weather was chilly, rubber boots were available. The socks helped to cushion his feet in the shoes. He dumped the water in the flowerbed. He was amazed at how much dirt was in the water. He saw that there was a nail on the outside of the porch where the tub hung, so he hung it up. He could smell food being prepared. Now he realized how hungry he was. He entered the kitchen and Mrs. Taggat motioned for him to sit down.

She commented, "My, you do look good. The clothes are a bit baggy, but after two weeks of my cooking you will begin to fill them out. Now, let me tell you what I have for you to eat. I need for you to tell me how much. I have fried eggs, bacon and cornbread with butter and sorghum. I will warm up the coffee."

"Ma'am, fix me a normal breakfast like you would fix for your men. I am hungry, but I do not want to overeat. I sense that you will have sufficient for me again at eight bells."

"Eight bells! What do you mean?"

"I am sorry. That is a nautical term. I should have said twelve noon."

"Then you were on a ship?"

Elmer nodded. "For more than ten years. I started as a cabin boy. When I matured, I was a deckhand."

She asked, "Where were you from?"

"It is best that I not tell you. However, I can tell you where I am headed. I was on my way to New York City. Am I close to where it is?"

She shook her head. "No, it is a long way off. I think it might be a couple thousand miles away."

"What do you mean a couple thousand? I do not understand a couple." Elmer was confused.

Mrs. Taggat laughed. "I am sorry. Couple means two, like man and wife is a couple. When I said couple thousand, I mean two thousand miles." By this time, she set the first of the breakfast before him.

Elmer looked down at his food. He adjusted the plate and straightened his utensils. Mrs. Taggat looked at him. She saw the tears on his cheeks. She reached out to touch his shoulder. "Is anything wrong?"

He shook his head. He tried to speak, but could not. He stammered a few words. "This is l-l-like Mama--." He stopped. "I must thank God, but I am too overwhelmed. Can you tell him for me?" He wiped his eyes with his shirt sleeve.

"Yes, I will thank him for you." Her hand was still on his shoulder. She began, "Heavenly Father, I thank you for this food, and for this young man that is going to eat it. I sense that he has endured much hardship. I thank you that you have brought him to us, and that we might be a friend to Elmer. We ask this in your Son's name. The Son, that endured the cross for us. Amen." She patted his shoulder.

193

He reached up with his left hand and gripped her hand. At that time she saw the second and third fingers that were joined. He picked up his knife and fork and began to eat in silence. He ate everything that she had cooked for him. He had only a sip of the coffee, but nothing more.

CHAPTER 15
TEXAS IS MY HOME

Elmer liked the way his face looked and felt after he had his first shave. In the years that he had been on the ship, he had his hair and beard trimmed occasionally, but never shaved. He remembered how the seamen would tease him at the time of his first whiskers coming in during his adolescent years. Elmer was diligent in shaving every morning. George and his father Harvey were prone to let their whiskers grow for two or three days before shaving. Alma took notice and began to chide the men in her family. She would say, "Why can't the two of you shave each day like Elmer. See how nice he looks." Elmer remembered how white his face had been after his first shave. The Texas sun had put a tan on his face.

George would usually respond to his mother's comments. "Yes, he does look nice, but it doesn't do him much good. When you are busy shoveling horse manure, there is no benefit in looking clean shaven. Maybe it is a little easier to wash your face." Then he would laugh.

After he had worked for the Taggats about a month, Elmer asked Harvey, "What is the story on the horse you call Dragon? The Sundays that George works, he will clean all of the stalls except for Dragon's. I don't mind cleaning it, even if it is a little extra work, but is there something that I should know?"

Harvey nodded. "Dragon is the reason I offered you a job. The morning I opened that box stall and saw you with your arms around his neck, I knew that you were different. Nobody has been able to touch him until that morning. Maybe he smells fear, but it takes two men to do anything with him. I haven't said anything to you. I wanted to see how he would respond to you. I bought him at a horse auction about fifty miles north of here. I liked what I saw. He wasn't broke to the halter. In fact, I don't think he had a rope on him until the day that I bought him. He has a lot of action. I thought as a stallion, he could sire a number of colts that would bring some big bucks. It took George and me two hard days to get him home. He is no good to me the way he is. Unless he changes, I might as well destroy him before he hurts somebody. That is the story of Dragon. Incidentally, we came up with the name for him on the way home."

Elmer asked, "What do you want me to do? He has not caused me any problems. I let him out in the alleyway to clean his stall. I wondered why we had to carry drinking water to him. He goes back in his stall after I have cleaned it."

Harvey asked, "Do you think you can work with him, so that he won't harm anyone else?"

Elmer nodded. "Give me two weeks, but I won't do anything else during that time. The only time I leave him is at meal time. I will sleep out here. Find me a few covers that you don't mind getting a little hay and straw on them. Agreed?"

Harvey hesitated. "When do you start?"

"I will bring the covers with me right after supper. We begin tonight. I will clean his stall each day. I don't want anybody to get near him during these two weeks. Starting tomorrow, I will have my meals in the back porch." Elmer started to leave, but then he came back. "I would like to have a new leather halter and a new saddle blanket. I don't want either of them to have been on another horse before." Once again he started to leave. With the wave of his hand, he said, "I will take them to the stable tonight after I have had my supper." After supper that night, Elmer took the halter, the saddle blanket and the blankets for sleeping. Slung over his shoulder was his oilskin pouch.

The next morning, Elmer opened the stable door so that Dragon could go into the round corral. He took a wooden stool and set it in the middle of the corral. He placed the saddle blanket on it. He sat down on the blanket and began to carefully whittle on a small piece of wood. He had the halter hanging around his own neck. Dragon ran around and around the corral, experiencing his newfound freedom. Other times he would buck and kick up his heels. Elmer began to whistle softly. It had the sound of a mourning dove, cooing in the distance. At no time did he look at the horse. At midmorning he went into the stable. After he had quenched his thirst, he filled the water bucket and set it in the middle of the corral, about ten feet from his stool. He went back to his whittling and whistling; the same mourning dove tune, over and over again. The horse recognized his water bucket and he could smell the water. He ventured closer and closer. He stuck his nose in the bucket, but suddenly darted away. His nose caught the edge of the bucket, spilling the water. He was frightened and ran away, kicking up his heels. He went to the outer perimeter of the corral and stopped and looked back. Elmer got up and went for another bucket of water. The next time, Dragon drank out of the bucket. When he was finished, he looked up at Elmer.

Every day was a work in progress. By the third day, he had the halter on the horse. Some days, Dragon would stand, staring at Elmer while he whittled and whistled. The day that he came up behind Elmer and nudged him on the back, Elmer knew that they were friends. That was when he began to curry and brush him. He loved being brushed. It provided an opportunity to handle his feet and legs. While he was brushing him, he had attached a rope to the halter. He tied the rope to the snubbing post. The snubbing post was a large post that was firmly planted in the center of the corral. Usually, animals were roped and the rope was wrapped around the post to hold them. Sometimes, if there wasn't enough wraps around the post, the rope would slip around the post. Over the years, the post would acquire a smooth finish from the rope sliding around the post. Dragon had pulled back, but he learned that he couldn't escape. While Dragon was standing still, Elmer fitted the blanket to his back with a surcingle to hold it in place. Elmer foresaw one problem. He wanted to get on the horse but Dragon was taller than most horses. Also, he had never been on a horse that bucked seriously. He remembered going over the rock wall on the horse called Luke. He was ten at the time, and it was not a good experience. A sudden thought came into his mind. *I have tamed the horse, George can train him! He is always bragging what a good rider he is, well we will see. It has been over ten years since I was on a horse.*

Each morning, Harvey and George would look through a knothole of the stable wall to see how Elmer was progressing. At first they would chuckle, seeing Elmer sitting in the hot sun, whittling and whistling. They had wagered as to how long Elmer would stay with the training. George bet that he wouldn't last a week, while Harvey said he will last a week, but will give it up before the end of the second week. Only Alma had confidence in Elmer. She was sure that he would complete the two weeks.

That evening, after supper, Elmer asked George, "I have a favor to ask of you. I have tamed Dragon, or at least the two of us get along well enough. It has been eleven days. The next step is for him to be gentle around others. Will you help me tomorrow?"

George laughed, "Does that mean I have to sit in the hot sun and whittle and whistle?"

Elmer nodded. "I suppose that Mrs. Taggat has a parasol that I could hold over you to keep the sun off. If this works like I think it will, you could have the finest saddle horse in Texas. I have tamed the horse, but you can train him. Right now, he needs to be comfortable with you. Also, you need to be assured that he isn't going to tear your head off. That is what I want to accomplish in the next three days. What do you think?"

"If you think it can be done, count me in. I will see you in the morning."

The next morning, there were two stools in the corral. Also a saddle and a hackamore had been placed nearby. After Dragon was turned into the corral, the two men entered and sat down on the stools. Dragon did his usual running and kicking up in the air while he circled the corral. After a time, he came to the two men. He looked at George. He sniffed the air, and backed off and made another lap before returning to confront the men. This time he nudged Elmer. Elmer got up and began to curry him. The horse looked back at George and stomped his foot and wrung his tail. Elmer nodded to George and handed him the brush. Elmer began to whistle the tune of the mourning dove. George brushed while Elmer curried the mane and tail of Dragon. They each made a point to circle the horse several times. Each time, Dragon would smell them.

Elmer nodded to his companion. "Do you think it is time to try the saddle on him?"

"I don't know," he replied. "He is a lot of horse. Is he as tame as you would have me believe?" He peered at the horse. "Let's wait until after dinner to saddle him. Maybe he and I need to get better acquainted. Are you sure you don't want to get on him first? You have put in ten days whistling to him. It would be a shame for me to ride him first."

"All right, you help me saddle him. I will get on him to prove to you that he is gentle. However, it will be up to you to train him."

The two men sat back down on their stools. Elmer brought out his knife and began to carve on a piece of walnut. George asked, "What are you carving? From the knothole in the stable, it looked like you were just whittling?"

Elmer handed him the carving. "I was doing some serious whittling for it to take shape. Now I am doing the final shaping and putting in the detail. Tell me, what is it that I have been whittling?"

He shook his head. "I have no idea. Maybe it is a tower of some kind. What is it?" He handed it back to Elmer.

Elmer answered, "It is a game piece. In a game of chess, it is referred to as the queen. The detail that I am working on is to form a sort of a crown. It is probably the most difficult to carve. I take it that the game of chess is unfamiliar to you." He removed a fleck of wood. "The game of chess is played on a checker board. It is believed to have originated in India in the seventh century. At that time it was called Chaturanga. It is a game of strategy between two people. I will carve another queen out of light oak. When completed, I will send them to my mother." He was silent for a moment. He looked off into the distance, but George sought not to interfere in his thoughts.

After dinner, the two men went back to the corral. They had left the saddle and blanket by the two stools. They saw that Dragon had slobbered on the saddle, which they deemed to be a good thing.

Dragon came to the two men. Elmer put his arm around his neck and fitted the hackamore on the horse's head. He nodded to George. While Elmer rubbed the neck of the horse, George placed the blanket on his back and then the saddle. He was careful when he tightened the cinch. When finished, he stepped back for Elmer to get on.

Elmer said, "Come up by his head. I don't want him taking off while I try to get on. I really don't like putting my foot into the stirrups with these big shoes. He is taller than I like. I am going to set this stool so I can step on it and pull myself into the saddle." He set the stool like he wanted. He stepped on it with his right foot. Then he put his left foot in the stirrup and throwing the right foot over the cantle of the saddle. Sitting down in the seat of the saddle, he moved his right foot into the stirrup. He put only the toe into the stirrup, not wanting to be in too deep.

Dragon did not move. He looked around to see what was on his back. George took the hackamore reins and led the horse once around the corral. Coming back to where they had started, Elmer nodded to George. "This is far enough. Now it is your turn. I would suggest that you remove the spurs until he is used to you. He likes you. He is your horse from now on. I have tamed him, now you can train him." He got off of Dragon and began to gather up the stools and the water bucket. He emptied the bucket out and put the comb and brush in it. "I think that I will go take a bath and see you at supper time."

At supper that night, George told his parents about Dragon. "I was wrong. I didn't think that Elmer could tame that horse. Can you imagine if he would whistle that mourning dove tune to the girls, they would come flocking to him." Elmer blushed with embarrassment.

Harvey laughed and shook his head. "I don't know if it was the whistling or the whittling that brought that horse around. At times, I thought that Elmer was crazier than the horse."

Alma spoke up. "Elmer, I was the only that had

faith in you. George didn't think you would last a week, and Harvey thought you might get into the second week before you gave up. I think that the two of you owe that boy a pair of boots. Elmer, tomorrow morning, you go down to Johnnie the boot maker and order a pair of boots. Tell him that Harvey and George will be down to settle up with him. Make sure that they are a good pair and that they fit. I can see that the old pair of shoes of George's that you are wearing are too tight. Ten years of running bare footed on a ship deck wasn't very good for your feet."

Harvey exclaimed, "Mother, you are certainly generous with my money. He didn't do a lick of work for two weeks. He sat on a stool and whittled the whole time. We had to do his work for him. He should buy each of us a pair of boots."

"Harvey, that is ridiculous. Because you have complained, I think that he deserves two pair of boots. One is for work, and the other is for dress when he whistles for the ladies. He saved you a lot of money. You were so frightened of that horse that you were going to destroy him. I know how much you paid for him. It was more than you told me. If I hear one more complaint out of you, I may have you throw in a saddle for good measure."

George said, "Dad, just forget it. I will give you what you have invested in that horse, including a pair of boots. He will be a money maker. You and Elmer can do the work now that I will be spending my time training him." Elmer didn't respond to his remark about doing the work and Harvey did not respond on his offer to buy Dragon.

After he got the two pair of boots, Elmer thought it would be better if he moved out of the Taggat's home. Harvey treated him as if he was a hired man, which he was. However, it was different with Mrs. Taggat. She treated him like a son. He thought it might be because she was aware of the abuse that he had endured since he was fourteen. Elmer sensed that George was jealous of the attention that he had to share with one who was a hired hand. Her coercing the second pair of boots from Harvey may have been a bit too much. Elmer was careful not to wear the dress boots when he was in the home.

One Monday morning, Elmer remarked to Harvey, "I am getting on my feet financially now, so I thought it might be better if I found a place of my own. I appreciate everything you have done for me, but it might be better if I move on."

Harvey was shocked! "You mean to say that you aren't happy here?"

"No, no. It isn't anything like that. You said that you hired me to tame Dragon. I have him gentled down, so that is done. I am not sure that I am carrying my share of the workload. Maybe it is time for me to be on the road. My intent is to make my way to New York City."

Harvey was angry. He pulled the hat off of his head and slammed it to the ground. "What is with you young whippersnappers? George wants to take cattle on north to start a ranch, and now you want to go to New York. I don't know what got into the both of you. Both of you are plumb loco."

"I'm sorry, Harvey. I didn't know that George was planning to leave. He never said anything to me. I thought maybe he was unhappy with me. If it was over the boot deal, I will sure pay for the boots."

"No, it isn't that. He is upset over the banker and his two daughters. You are certainly aware that each Sunday, Jacob Conrad, his wife and two daughters rent our carriage and driver to drive them to church. George is sweet on Elizabeth. He thinks that the Sunday that you drive, you are trying to cut him out."

Elmer shook his head. "That is not true. Yes, I am taken with her beauty. But, I am making five dollars a week. There is no way that I can be interested at that rate. I am not complaining about my wages, but I have to face reality. Sometimes she acts giddy around me. I know that she is flirting with me, but there is nothing I can do about it. Look what happens in this town. By the time a girl turns sixteen, she is wooed pretty heavy. Most of the girls get married by that time, but not to young men. It is usually to someone thirty or older; unless his dad or the girl's dad has some money. If I wasn't going to New York City, I would hang around this town and make my play for Elizabeth. Or, I could wait for the bratty one that is thirteen. That would give me three years to save my money. As ugly and skinny as she is, he might give me a job at the bank just to be rid of her. That is, if I could stand her that long. My mother would remark about the English royalty. She said, those who marry for money usually earn it. On second thought, it is probably better if I pass on the younger one." Harvey had nothing more to say. He shook his head and went to his office.

Elmer remembered the first encounter he had with banker's younger daughter. She had stopped by the livery stable to remind him that her father wanted the carriage for the next day. She asked, "Hey Mister, are you an Englishman? People say that you are from England because your name is Elmer Teasdale."

He replied, "What is your first name? I understand that your last name is Conrad. You could be Scottish. Are you from Scotland?"

"I don't think so. I'm from Texas. You still didn't tell me where you are from."

He grinned. *I may have a bit of fun with this girl.* "Well, Miss Conrad, I might be from Texas with an English name. Or I might be from Great Britain. In fact, your ancestors might be from Great Britain also."

"Why do you tell me that we may be from Great Britain? I thought you were from England."

Elmer responded. "England, Scotland and Wales make up the total area referred to as Great Britain. It is a large island and the people are referred to as British. Now, I have told you my first name, but you have not disclosed your first name. What is it?"

"I don't like my name and I am not going to tell you. You will just laugh at it. I don't like your name, so I will call you Brit, because you are from Great Britain."

Elmer nodded. "I have to call you something, so I will name you Turk. Have you ever seen a turkey egg?" She shook her head. He continued, "A turkey egg is larger than a hen egg. The shell is a soft tan with freckles all over it. Because you have freckles on your face, you look like a turkey egg. That is why I will call you Turk." She was angry and left in a huff.

The next day, Harvey stopped to talk with Elmer while he was cleaning out a stall. He said, "I was thinking about our conversation yesterday. George will be happy to know that you are not giving him a hard run for his money with Elizabeth. He is thinking like you. If he could make some serious money, he would feel better about his chances with that girl." Harvey was quiet for a moment. He leaned up against the corral fence and looked off into the horizon. "Elmer, if you will stick around here and help George trail a herd of breeding stock into Wyoming or Nebraska, I will pay your way to New York. When you get to Cheyenne, there is a rail line that will take you all the way in less than a week. There is one condition. My brother has a ranch about seven miles out of town. You go out there and he will teach you everything to know about the ranching business.

I sense that you two boys know very little about cows. You are good with horses, but not cows. Think about it. Here is your opportunity to get Elizabeth Conrad out of your mind and still learn about cows."

Elmer grinned and nodded his head. "I will take it. There is nothing better than picking up a little knowledge about life. I may even like being a cowboy."

"There is one condition. Don't tell George what I am doing. He will learn in his own time."

The next day, Harvey and Elmer went out to the Harold Taggat ranch. Since Elmer didn't have a horse, they took the buckboard to carry what belongings that he had accumulated. He had bought a saddle from Harvey for eight dollars. George tried unsuccessfully to feign sorrow at Elmer leaving town. Now he would have Elizabeth all to himself. In fact, now he would drive the carriage each Sunday.

Mrs. Taggat was the one most displeased at his departure. Elmer had been carving a statue of Dragon in the evenings. While Harvey slept in his chair, she and Elmer would visit about what went on in the community. He had been faithful in attending the church that she went to. He would go on Sunday evenings. Harvey usually had something for him to do around the livery stable during the day on Sundays. The last night that he was there, he gave her the miniature replica of Dragon. He had carved it out of a chunk of a black walnut tree. It was the most difficult carving he had made; even more so than the bust of Captain Twain.

From the very beginning, Elmer took to the life on the Circle H Ranch. The story of Dragon had preceded him, so they presumed him to be the authority on horsemanship. Consequently, because of this and the fact that he was the youngest of the five ranch hands, he was given the responsibility of dealing with any unruly horses. One thing that he recognized was that he learned from the horses while working the cattle. Every day was a learning process for him. He was becoming proficient with the rope and the doctoring of sick cattle. At night, he wrote in his journal of his experiences of the day.

He continued to burnish the two remaining chess pieces that he carried in his oilskin pouch. They were now ready to mail. He was uncertain if he should include any correspondence in the package. To be on the safe side, he decided not to, should the wrong people intercept the package. He had not written anything in his previous mailings. The first mate of the HMS Bold Pelican had picked up on his subtle message of putting the name of the ship on the underside of the first chess pieces. No one will recognize his name, but with the receipt of the last game pieces, it will convey to his mother that he is still alive and living in Texas. He was presuming that she had received all of the previous carvings.

It was a fine day in June that Elmer rode to Tipton. It was a Saturday afternoon, and Harold had sent him to town to pick up the mail. It provided an opportunity for Elmer to mail his package to his mother. He had planned to spend the night with Harvey and Alma. Perhaps he would linger long enough to go to church with Mrs. Taggat the next day. He looked forward to having Sunday dinner with them. The cook at the Circle H cooked plenty of food, but it didn't have the woman's touch.

At church the next morning, he saw Elizabeth. She came to him and asked, "When are you coming back to work at the livery stable? You are a better driver than that awful George Taggat. You would think that I wasn't even a passenger in the carriage. I can't tease him like I did you."

Elmer blushed. He said, "I think my livery stable

days are over, but I did want to see you. Next time that I come back to town, I will borrow a buggy from Harley and take you to church. Then you won't have to depend upon George."

She giggled. "Good. I will see you then. Goodbye."

He tipped his hat and said, "Goodbye." He thought, *I wonder if she saw that I wore my new boots. She certainly has blossomed since I last saw her. If she gets any prettier, I may forget about going with George on his trail drive to the north.* He returned to the Circle H Ranch, thinking about Elizabeth all the way home.

CHAPTER 16
THE PAIR OF QUEENS

At the Bellingham Estate, Lady Grace was looking out the upstairs bedroom window when she turned to her maid. "Anna, would you please pack my bags, but only enough for three days. I am going to London to purchase an entirely new wardrobe. It has been more than a year since the death of Major Abbott. I have become dreadfully bored of wearing black. Why must a woman subject herself to being morbid for an entire year upon the death of her husband? Surely it isn't some Act of Parliament that demands a year of mourning. Major Abbott spent so little time with me during our marriage. I have spent more time in mourning than I did in his company during our marriage. If I would look back through my diary, I know that he was home less than a year in total. At the time of our marriage, we were together for six months before he was sent back to his regiment in India. I did not see him again for another four years. This last time he was here for four months."

She went back to the window again. She continued, "I was always concerned about his safety, being in the army and such. He would assure me that he did not have any worries of danger. Once he had moved up in rank, he would have a better posting and the family would be able to join him. He could have resigned from the Lancers and spent his remaining years here on the estate. But, he truly loved being in the military." She began to weep softly. "Little did we think that he would be killed in a railway accident?"

Lady Grace dried her tears. "Anna, I would like you to accompany me. Meagan will be going with me as well. Plan to be gone about ten days. We will leave next Monday morning for London and return home the following Tuesday. It will mean that we will spend the night going and coming at the inn near Cotswold. I will arrange for the carriage with the stable master."

After a week of shopping and eating at an elegant café each evening, the three ladies returned to the Bellingham Estate. Lady Grace was no longer dressed in black. Meagan sensed that her Lady would not remain single for very long.

It was almost a ritual with Meagan. She would walk to the post office each Thursday morning to ask if she had any mail. In the many years since her son had left, she had received thirty parcels, but no correspondence. Each parcel had contained one chess piece. She had received nothing in the last four years, but each trip to the post office offered her hope. Today was different. Today she received a package from Tipton, Texas without a return address. She knew nothing of the whereabouts of Tipton, Texas. She decided not to open it, but would wait until she could discuss this with Lady Grace.

Meagan returned to the estate. She waited until it was time for their afternoon tea. She brought out the package and set it at the table. She said, "Lady Grace, this package was waiting at the post office. I did not recognize the name or the place. Should I even open it?"

Lady Grace picked it up and looked it over. "It has your name on it. If it doesn't belong to you, you can certainly take it back. Yes, go ahead and open it. I am curious."

Meagan was quite careful in opening the package. It seemed to Lady Grace that Meagan expected to return the package to the post office. Meagan pulled the cotton to the side that was at the top of the box. She looked in. She gave a stifled sob. She exclaimed, "The queens have come home. The set is complete." She showed them to Lady Grace. She then took them to their respective places at the chess board.

"Conan is alive, but who sent this to me?"

Lady Grace spoke right up, "Meagan, I am presuming that Conan wanted to let you know that he is alive. He may have sent the chess pieces from another address, not knowing if he is wanted by the authorities. The Thornwood family made a lot of brash talk while Carlton lay dying. After the funeral, once they learned that Conan was gone, the talk subsided. I don't believe that they ever filed a formal complaint."

"But we cannot be sure, My Lady. Evidently, Conan is unsure as well, or he would have written something." She twisted the handkerchief between her fingers. "Oh, if I only knew that he is all right."

Lady Grace went to Meagan. "I have an idea. I will confer with the family barrister to see if he has any thoughts on how we might find Conan. I will write a letter to him first thing in the morning. Don't worry, we will find Conan."

"I am sorry to put you to all this trouble and expense. I have a bit of money. It is yours for all the trouble in locating him."

"Don't worry about the money. All of this stemmed from the trouble with Carlton Thornwood. Conan was my protector. Carlton was so angry that day, even I feared for my life. I owe that much to Conan."

Ten days later, a letter was delivered to the Bellingham estate. The barrister, Sir Thomas Collier informed Lady Grace that the transatlantic cable was back in service. Therefore he had been able to retain the services of the Pinkerton Detective Agency to investigate the person of Conan Moran. He would be in touch as soon they were able to complete their investigation. He expected to have the results in sixty to ninety days.

Lady Grace and Meagan began to count off the

days. It was day eighty-one that they received the news. The report read as follows: Regarding the whereabouts of Timothy Conan Moran, we are sorry to report that we were unable to determine his whereabouts. You must realize that Texas is a very large state. We centered our investigation in the rural town of Tipton. At no time did we encounter a white male in his mid-twenties with the deformed hand which you had described. Nor did anyone have any knowledge of such an individual by the name of Timothy Conan Moran. The details of the report will follow at a later date.

Meagan was saddened, but she tried to accept the news with a positive attitude. "One thing I am assured of is that he is alive. The queens verify his existence. Whether he wants to be found or not is another matter. Apparently he has left the ship. What was the name of that vessel? For some reason Captain Twain didn't want us to know that he was on board." She shook her head and muttered, "I just don't know, I just don't know." She began to weep.

Lady Grace went to her. "Meagan, I know that you are disappointed, but maybe there is something in the detailed report that will give us hope. We have gone too far to give up hope now. The name of the vessel was the HMS Bold Pelican. I will have my friend check out the whereabouts of that ship. Remind me tomorrow to send him a letter. I think that he is still in London." Meagan nodded and dried her tears.

Two weeks later, Lady Grace received a letter from her friend. He reported that the HMS Bold Pelican left the Galveston area, heavily loaded with cotton. Its destination was the South West India Dock on the Thames River near London. It appeared that it may have encountered a heavy storm and was destroyed. Debris washed up on the coast of France indicated that it was the HMS Bold Pelican.

Evidently there were no survivors. I am sorry for this news.

Lady Grace determined she would not share the contents of the letter with Meagan. She would at least wait until she had the detailed report from the Pinkerton Agency.

Upon the receipt of the detailed report from the Pinkerton Agency, Lady Grace decided to share it with Meagan during their afternoon tea. It was a warm afternoon, and they were seated at a small table on the lawn in the shade of the trees. It was as follows:

Dear Lady Grace Abbott:

Our agent went to the town of Tipton, Texas to investigate the disappearance of Timothy Conan Moran. At the time of his leaving his home near Cotswold, England, he was a lad of fourteen. It has now been almost another thirteen years. The only distinguishing feature which we had to go on was that the second and third fingers of his left hand were grown together since birth. Tipton, Texas is a town of about five hundred people, so a newcomer to the town would be newsworthy. Because of the reputation of our agency in being diligent in any investigation, the community was rather reluctant to be free with any information. In the past year, there was one man in his mid-twenties that we investigated thoroughly. His name was Elmer Ray Teasdale. He first appeared at the blacksmith shop to have a metal ankle restraint removed. The blacksmith was unfamiliar with the type of restraint. It was not anything used in Texas, so we ruled out him running from the Texas authorities. The blacksmith said that Elmer had a heavy black beard and long hair. A local livery stable owner had vouched for him. He lived with that family for a short time, but then he left town and no one knew of his whereabouts. The owner of the stable and his son denied of having any knowledge of the deformity of his

213

hand. All the witnesses that were questioned were cautious,
but forthright in their answers. They commented that
after he had shaved and had a hair cut that he was rather
handsome. There was one exception. The wife of the stable
owner, Mrs. Alma Taggat may have been hiding something.
She is an attractive red head in her mid-forties. It may have
been romance or she may have known something about the
stranger. She made the comment that he shaved every day.
After that comment, I particularly noticed that her husband
was usually unshaven for two or three days at a time. She
liked her new boarder. Maybe she liked him too well.

We will keep the name of Elmer Ray Teasdale in
our files. If we hear of anything significant, we will let you
know at once.

Sincerely, Ted H. Rowe.

Lady Grace left the letter in her lap. Meagan stared
into her hands. They were folded on her lap, clutching her
handkerchief. She said nothing, but the tears slid down
her cheeks. She reached up and wiped the tears away. She
looked up and said, "I think now is the time for us to accept
that he is alive. That is enough for me." She started to get
up. Lady Grace reached out to stop her.

"Meagan, I think now is the time to pay Alma
Taggat a visit!"

Meagan was adamant. "Good heavens, Grace! Give
it up! We can't be chasing every whim that comes along.
As a child, you would chase a squirrel for what seemed like
hours but never catching it. Just give it up, Grace!" Grace
was shocked. It was the first time that Meagan had not
addressed her by her title.

Grace fell to her knees and put her head in
Meagan's lap. "Meagan, you scolded me as you did
when I was a child." She looked up. "What about chasing
butterflies? There is a butterfly on your head!" She reached

up and it flew away for both of them to see. "Did you ever tell Conan the story of the butterfly? When you left me to marry Mr. Moran, you said you would tell me a story that I would never forget. Though we couldn't be together in the body, you would come to me in the form of a butterfly. Conan has come to us today! See, I never forgot the butterfly story." She got back on her feet. "Meagan, Conan has invited us to Tipton, Texas. I will see to ocean transportation on one of those new steamships."

CHAPTER 17
TIPTON, TEXAS

Two very tired and dusty ladies got off the afternoon stage in Tipton. They were hot and thirsty, but first they had to look about their luggage. The elder of the two stepped into the stage station. She asked the manager, "Where is a suitable inn for two ladies? We are planning to spend a few days in Tipton, and we desire accommodations. Then too, once we locate an inn, there is the matter of our luggage."

He replied, "There is the Tipton House. It is the only hotel in town. It is two blocks to the west of here. Most people that come off the stage don't have that much luggage." He looked out the window. "There is George Taggat now. He usually meets the stage, but seems to be running behind. Let me get him." He stepped out of the station and waved to George.

Meagan followed him out. She whispered to Lady Grace. "That is George Taggat. Do you think that is Alma's husband? He does need a shave, so he sure fits the description."

"I'm not sure, but he doesn't look that old. Maybe we can find out."

George brought his carriage close to where they were standing. He tipped his hat and asked, "Are you the two ladies that need a ride to the Tipton House?"

Lady Grace responded, "Yes, we do and our luggage as well. We could have walked, but our luggage is a bit excessive."

He said, "I see what you mean. Most people don't own that many clothes let alone traveling with them. Say, where are you ladies from? You talk different than we do. I suppose you think the same about us."

"We are from Cotswold, England. It is not far from

London," replied Grace.

"What are you doing way out here?"

Grace stammered a bit before answering George. "We are, uh, we are looking at investments. We may want to buy some land. A great number of English and Scottish investors are interested in the ranching industry. We are thinking to do the same."

He scratched the whiskers on his chin. "Well," he said, "I don't know but I think that most of the investing is much further north where they have more open range, but you could be right." By this time, he had the luggage loaded and the women in the carriage.

When they came to the Tipton House, he took their luggage inside. Lady Grace asked, "How much do I owe you for your work?"

He said, "I reckon a half dollar should be sufficient."

She pulled a coin from her purse. She had a puzzled look on her face. "I know so little about your money. Is this sufficient?"

"Ma'am, that is too much. That is a dollar."

She handed it to him, and with a flip of her hand, she said, "Oh, keep it. You have been most helpful. One other thing, do you know of a lady that would wash out some of our clothing? We have been traveling for some time and are running short on clean clothes."

George nodded his head. "My mother would. Sometimes she does washing for others."

"That is great. Now where does your mother live?"

He pointed up the street. "It is the third house. It is the one with the white picket fence."

"And her name is what?"

"She is Alma, Alma Taggat. Just like mine. Do you want her to stop by for your clothing?"

"No," said Grace. "We will stop by her house at four this afternoon. That will give us some time to freshen up. Thank you, George. You have been very kind." The women entered the Tipton House.

When they were alone, Meagan said, "But Lady Grace, I could have washed out our things. Why pay another for what I can do?"

"I know you can, but this will get us in the house of Alma Taggat. We will engage her in her own home. George will stop by and tell her to expect us. Perhaps she will have tea for us. I sense that if Conan was here, she will recognize our English accent. We are close, ever so close. I can sense it Meagan, I can sense it."

After a brief nap, the two ladies went to the Taggat home. Meagan had the suitcase of dirty clothes. She rapped on the door. Alma came to the door. "Good afternoon ladies. I am Alma Taggat and I have been expecting you."

Meagan said, "I am Mrs. Meagan Moran. This is Lady Grace Abbott. I have brought the clothes in the valise."

"Come in. You may set the clothes by the stand. I have taken the liberty of making tea for you. This way, we can visit a bit. I also have milk and sugar cubes. I have heard the British enjoy sugar and milk in their tea."

Lady Grace answered, "Tea will be fine. Our schedule is so mixed up, we don't know if it is afternoon tea or morning tea. My I certainly enjoy your kitchen. And thank you for agreeing to do our laundry."

"That is nothing. I don't do that much, but George is always looking for ways to be helpful to others. Sometimes, he will volunteer my services." She picked up the tea tray. "Let us go into the parlor. It is cooler there." After her guests were seated, Alma poured the tea. She was handing a cup to Meagan, when Meagan took her eyes off of the cup and dropped it and its contents on the front of her dress. Mrs. Taggat said, "Oh, how clumsy of me. I am sorry."

Meagan jumped up. She shook her head, "No, it isn't your fault. I wasn't paying attention."

"I will get a cloth from the kitchen and be right back." After she left, Meagan picked up her cup. She pointed to a sculpture of a horse sitting on top of a buffet. It stood about twelve inches high and had a sheen to it that had caught her eye. Grace nodded.

Alma returned from the kitchen with a dish towel. She apologized, "I guess we could have used our napkins to sop up the tea. I will be more careful next time."

Meagan walked over to the sculpture. "I saw this sculpture and took my eyes off of my cup." She ran her fingers over the horse. "I first thought it was bronze metal, but now I see that it is wood. Is that a mahogany? What exquisite craftsmanship. Is something like that available locally?"

"It is one of a kind. A friend of the family gave that to me. He had carved it while he was staying with us."

Meagan turned to confront Alma Taggat. "Would the name of that friend happen to be Elmer Ray Teasdale?"

Now it was Alma's turn to juggle her cup and saucer. She set it down. "I believe it is time for you ladies to leave my home. The visit is over now. You may take your laundry with you. Evidently, the Pinkerton's did not get their information right the first time, so they used a more subtle approach. Good day, ladies."

Lady Grace spoke up. "The Pinkerton agency was satisfied that the townspeople were telling the truth about not knowing a man with a deformed hand. They were not sure about Mrs. Alma Taggat. When did you see the deformed hand? I first saw it when he was a few weeks old. Mrs. Moran saw it the day of his birth. We have come all the way from England to find her son. We need to see Elmer Ray Teasdale and find out why he was in Tipton, Texas."

"The first day that he was here, I saw the whip marks on his back. I fed him and he said something about how his mother would feed him. He was in such awe, that he asked me to thank God for the food. He began to weep. I was standing behind him and put my hands on his shoulder. After I had finished praying, he reached up and touched my hand. It was then that I saw the two fingers as one. No one else in town knows about them. I never told anyone. I know where he is. I will tell him that you are in town. If he wants to see you, then I will arrange a meeting, but I don't trust the Pinkerton agency."

"That is fine," said Meagan. "Now, may we finish with the tea? Tell my son, the queens made it home. Now it is time for him to come home."

After the ladies had their tea and prepared to leave, Mrs. Taggat said, "I will be in touch with Elmer and let you know what he wants to do. Leave the laundry. I will get to it in the morning."

That night, at the time that the moon was making its appearance in the eastern sky, Harvey and Alma were making their way out of town in a light buggy. Alma wanted to make sure that no one was following them. After an hour of travel, they came to the Circle H Ranch. They stopped at the ranch house. Harvey went to his brother. "Harold, Alma and I have some business with Elmer. Is it all right if we go have a talk with him?"

"Sure. He is at the bunkhouse. He might be in bed. We worked him pretty hard today."

"Thanks. We won't keep him up very long, but something has come up. Alma couldn't wait until he came to town."

Harvey drove the buggy to the bunkhouse. He went in and saw that Elmer was sitting on the edge of his bunk, whittling on a block of wood. Elmer looked up. Harvey gave a toss of his head aside, indicating that he wanted to see him outside. He pulled on his boots and went with him. He saw Alma in the buggy and waved to her. They walked to the buggy. Alma said, "Elmer, I had a visit today from two ladies. The older lady said, 'Tell my son the queens made it home. Now it is time for him to come home.' That is all she said."

He nodded. "Mama. How did she look?"

"She looked tired, but I would say that she looked relieved."

"You said that there were two ladies. Who was other lady?"

"Your mother introduced her as Lady Grace Abbott. She is probably about thirty years old and very pretty." Elmer nodded. Alma continued, "They want to meet with you. I said that I would talk with you. Evidently they had hired the Pinkerton Agency after you had sent them a package. I guess that I was the only one aware that your two fingers were together. I thought the Pinkerton detective was looking for you as a result of the ankle restraint. I can arrange for you to get a glimpse of them. That way you can make sure that they are not working for the Pinkerton Agency. I never told them where you were. We were careful not to be followed tonight. The decision is yours. Do you want to see them?"

"Of course I do. I'm sorry. That sounded rather brusque. I understand your caution. Can you take them for a ride in the carriage tomorrow afternoon? Have them meet you in the stable. I will be in the hay mow where they won't be able to see me. Oh, Lord, I pray that this is right." He turned and went back to the bunkhouse where he experienced a sleepless night.

The next day, the cook at the Circle H fixed an early dinner for Elmer. He saddled his horse and rode the seven miles to Tipton with great anticipation. It was noon when he stabled his horse at the Taggat & Son Livery Stable. He removed the saddle from his horse and rubbed him down. He crawled up the ladder to the hay mow and laid back, waiting for the women to enter. He relaxed and dozed off. He heard the women below. George had not yet entered the barn to harness the horses. He peered over the edge. They were walking toward the office when he got a glimpse of his mother. He gasped. Though her hair had grayed some, he saw that she was as beautiful as the night that he left home. His next thought, but what about Father? He saw Lady Grace. She was eighteen when he went to sea. He let them continue to the office. He crawled down from the mow and brushed aside what hay that had clung to his clothes. He had remembered to wear his best boots.

He opened the door. All eyes were turned to him. He reached out to his mother. "Mama, Mama," was all that he could say.

She took him in her arms, "My Son, My Son. I love you."

After she released him, Grace came to him. She hugged him. She then looked him in the eye. "What a handsome man you are. I never did get to thank you for what you meant to me. It was worth the trip."

He went to Mrs. Taggat. "Thank you, for bringing us together. You have been kind to me in so many ways. Now I think that you promised these ladies a ride around the town. I will go and harness the horses and we will be on our way."

Meagan rode up front with her son. Mrs. Taggat and Lady Grace were in the rear. Mrs. Taggat explained a number of things while they drove around town. Meagan asked, "Now that we have been reunited, what name do you wish to go by?"

He was startled by her question. He delayed answering, so that she would not misunderstand his decision. "Mother, in Texas I am known as Elmer Ray Teasdale. I feared being Conan Moran because it was a link to my past. When I waded ashore after my escape from the Bold Pelican, I was a free man and I was a new man."

"But, how did you come up with that name? It seems to be a rather unusual name."

"Once I reached land, I was trying to get as far as I could from the coast. I was unsure if my captors on the ship would come looking for me. I hid in cemeteries by day and moved about at night. I awoke one morning and I looked down at a headstone. The inscription was, 'I will be your guardian angel.' The child had died at two years of age. However, his birth date was the same as mine. He was buried alongside his parents. When Harvey Taggat asked what my name was, I remembered the name on the headstone. It was Elmer Ray Teasdale. I have gone by Elmer ever since. That same day, the shackle was removed from my ankle."

Meagan was quiet for a while. He then asked, "What about Father? You haven't said anything about him."

"He died like he lived. He died quietly in his rocker about six years after you left. I remained in the home. Three years ago, Lord Bellingham died. After his death, Lady Grace asked me to come to the manor and assist her in the rearing of the children. Her husband, Major Abbott died in India as a result of a railroad accident. She has been most helpful in my search for you. She realizes the misfortune which you have endured has been as a result of your coming to her aid. This reunion has been a healing for all of us."

There was a time that neither of them spoke. The only noise was the jingle of the harness chains and the clomping of the feet of the horses on the cobblestone street. Meagan asked, "Elmer. See, I used your new name. Elmer, will you be returning to England with us when we go?"

"Probably not. At this point, other than you, England does not hold much promise for me. I enjoy the West. I have been working on a ranch run by Harvey's brother. I am learning a lot about cattle, and I have always liked horses. George Taggat is planning to establish a ranch in the Wyoming or Nebraska Territory. He is taking a herd north within thirty days. I hope to be going with him and possibly be his ranch foreman. At least, that is what his father has planned for me. His father is financing the operation, so he has a lot to say in the decision making." His mother did not say anything, only watching the movement of the horses.

"That is not what I wanted to hear," she said, "but I understand. It is a consolation to me to know that you are alive and well. I want you to be happy. I am well provided by Lady Grace. We enjoy one another's company. However, I sense that she will soon marry. She does not like being a widow. She certainly is too young to be a widow. Her two children, John and Virginia are lovely children. She may be disappointed to hear that you are not planning to return with us."

Elmer stopped the horses. He turned around and said to the ladies in the rear. "I think it may be time for you ladies to rest and have tea at the Tipton House. Perhaps the horses could stand a bit of a rest as well."

After they had been served, Alma laughed, "This is something. Here is a real live cowboy having afternoon tea with the ladies. If only your cowboy friends could see you now."

"They wouldn't laugh. They would be envious, seeing that I am having tea with three lovely ladies."

Alma said, "Now I understand. You really do like tea. I noticed that you rarely drank much of my coffee. You would drink water, but very little coffee. I never understood until now."

"We drank a lot of tea on the vessel, being British of course. Coffee was a new experience for me. I don't say I don't like it, but I much prefer tea. I must say, I do like the beef. Also, I miss the pheasant of the Bellingham Estate. Mama, perhaps the best pheasant that I ever had was the first bite there with Geofrey Hoke. I had admitted my sin for poaching the bird. I was then able to eat, knowing that I had been forgiven. Then too, I couldn't omit that fine breakfast that Mrs. Taggat made for me my first day in Tipton. I hadn't had a home cooked meal since I left Loxnard on that stormy night." Alma blushed at the recognition.

"Before I forget, Elmer, I have made up the bed in your old room. You can stay with us. Feel free to come and go. I know you have a great deal of catching up with your family."

Meagan touched Elmer's hand. "Son, if you don't mind, I have had enough sightseeing for the day. I will go to my room and rest. Thank you for an enjoyable afternoon. I will see you at the evening meal."

Lady Grace nodded her head. "I believe that is an excellent idea. Thank you, Mrs. Taggat for arranging our afternoon."

Mrs. Taggat said, "I will walk home from here. Thank you for the tea. Goodbye."

Elmer went to where the horses had been tethered. He returned to the stable with the horses and carriage. He put the horses in the stall, and when he came out of the stable, there was George. He said, "Well, well, if it isn't our famous celebrity. Did you just return from your parade?"

Elmer blushed. "No, there was nothing like that. Your mother and I were giving my mother and Lady Grace a tour of the town. We had afternoon tea at the Tipton House. They were a bit tired, so each of the ladies went their own way, including your mother." Elmer sensed, by George's demeanor that he was unhappy with him. "Is something bothering you George, or am I misinterpreting your sarcasm?"

"Oh, you have noticed have you. That is good. Evidently, now I am doing something right. When are you planning to return to England? It won't be any too soon enough for me."

"I have no intention of returning to England. I was looking forward to going north with you on the cattle drive."

Before Elmer could say anything more, George butted in and shouted, "That is not going to happen! I know, Dad talked to you about going, but he isn't the one to ramrod this drive. I need people that I can trust."

"Are you saying that I am untrustworthy?"

"When it comes to women, you are about as untrustworthy as anyone could be. After you moved out of our house and went to the ranch is when you changed. The next thing that I knew, you had started courting Elizabeth Conrad."

Elmer laughed, trying to cool off the situation. "Maybe it is Elizabeth that is not to be trusted. She gave me the indication that I was a person of interest. Perhaps, you should marry her and take her on the cattle drive. Surely you aren't going to leave me here with Elizabeth while you go north to Nebraska or Wyoming."

"Elizabeth said that she was not getting married until she turned eighteen. That will be the middle of April next year."

"That makes it real simple," said Elmer. "Let us make an agreement that we will have a chaperone present whenever either one of us are in the company of Elizabeth. On the fifteenth day of April next year, the three of us will meet here in Tipton. At that time, Elizabeth will make her choice."

"I will agree to that," said George. He offered his hand and they each shook hands with one another.

Elmer warned George. "You better do your heavy courting now, because I will be courting her all winter long. Think about it when the snow is deep and the wind is blowing."

"Sorry, Elmer, but by then, she will only be thinking of me and the middle of April."

They left the stable and headed for the Taggat residence, expecting that Mrs. Taggat would have supper waiting for them. The bitter words between them had been forgotten.

CHAPTER 18
GOODBYE FAIR LADIES

Elmer took advantage of sitting at the dining table of Mrs. Taggat and eating of her fine culinary creations. Not that they were fancy, but they were good. Good is what he liked. After supper, he went to the Tipton House. Meagan and Grace had finished their evening meal and looked forward to him coming to them. They were waiting on the veranda, enjoying the serenity of the evening. There was very little traffic on the streets. Most of the residents of Tipton were still at the supper table.

Elmer saw the ladies on the veranda, so he decided to have a bit of fun with them. He began to imitate the song of a chickadee. He saw that they began to look around. They apparently asked a gentleman on the veranda about the birds. He began to look as well. When he got closer, Elmer was laughing. Meagan said to the others, "Forget about looking for the birds. My son is having a bit of fun with us. It is he with his bird calls." She stopped. "Listen, he did get them to answer him."

Grace said, "I guess that I forgot that he could do that with his hands and his mouth. It was the call of a magpie that infuriated Carlton so that day." She stopped. She was sorry for remembering that fatal day.

He greeted the ladies. "Did you get a good rest? What would you like to do this evening? It is pleasant. We could go to the park across the street."

Meagan said, "You two go along. I am going to walk to Mrs. Taggat's and get our clean clothes that she washed. I may visit a bit with her and then I have some mending to do before we return home. It seems that we just arrived here, but already, I am getting a bit homesick for England." She walked down the steps on her way to Alma

229

Taggat's house.

Lady Grace and Elmer sat on the veranda for a time, talking about some of the things of their youth. They walked across the street to the park. They walked the few paths and as dusk was beginning to set in, they stopped to sit at a bench across from Tipton House. Meagan had returned and was out on the veranda, mending and sorting clothes. Mostly, she was keeping her eye on her son and Grace.

Grace started the conversation. "Your mother tells me that you are not going back to England. She told me that you will be going north with a trail herd. Is this what you want, or is it a way of avoiding the inevitable?"

"It is what I wanted. I thought I was going with George until this afternoon. He is not allowing me to go with him, despite the wishes of his father." He then changed the subject. "What did you mean about avoiding the inevitable?"

She stood up and turned from him. She looked across the park. Slowly she turned back to him and said, "The inevitable is that I love you. Return to England and marry me. Your dream is shattered of going north with a bunch of cows. I have heard of how demanding it is on a trail drive. Haven't you had enough of adventure for one lifetime? Marry me and you can experience a life of ease. You have paid your price to humanity. I love you, Elmer, or whatever you wish to be called, I love you."

He jumped to his feet and took her in his arms and kissed her. It was the first time that he had ever kissed a woman, other than his mother. He liked it and he kissed her a second time. Suddenly, he realized what he had done. He released her and stepped back. "I am sorry Lady Grace. I should not have done that. I forgot my place in society."

She reached forward and clutched his arm. "But, I

want you to forget about society. I want to be free to marry whomever I choose. We can be happy together."

"I can't return to England. There are too many memories. Too many people would remember me as the stable master's son."

"Forget about England. My family has a chateau in southern France. We could live out the rest of our days in luxury away from the gossip. Your mother could go with us, as well as my children. We could have more children. Think about it Elmer, think about it. I love you." She waited for his answer. There was none, so she bid him goodnight.

She ran across the street and up the steps of the veranda, into the Tipton House. She didn't see Meagan standing on the veranda, hidden in the shadows.

Elmer watched Grace enter the Tipton House. He walked up the street until he came to the livery stable. He went in and saddled his horse. After the bitter words between his friend George and himself, he thought it best if he didn't spend the night at the Taggat house.

It was a long ride to the ranch. It was a ride that gave him the opportunity to rethink what had taken place between he and Grace. Lying in his bunk that night, he could not erase the image of Grace in his arms. Next, he rehearsed the words that he had with George. Then he would remember the words of Grace confessing her love. Exhausted, sleep finally came to him.

He wasn't the only one to have a sleepless night. Meagan was shocked and heartbroken over what she had witnessed that evening. She was uncertain what to do, but she knew that she needed guidance from God. She continued to pray until she dropped off to sleep.

Lady Grace was elated. She had confessed her love to Elmer. Now she must convince him to marry her. She could invent him as being some nobleman that had been exiled to America. Perhaps, it could be for some frivolous indiscretion and now he was returning to England as her husband. She had a restful sleep.

The next morning, Elmer awakened. He remembered that he had promised his mother and Lady Grace that he would show them the cattle ranch where he worked. He saddled his horse and rode into Tipton. He went to the livery stable and harnessed the horse that would pull the buggy. Elmer wanted to visit with Harvey Taggat regarding the words that he and George had with one another yesterday. He sensed that Harvey had heard from George, and he was purposely avoiding him. Evidently he had not been able to convince George to take Elmer with him on the trail drive.

He drove to the Tipton House and the two ladies were sitting on the veranda with a picnic basket nearby. Lady Grace made sure that she was in place to sit in front with Elmer. Meagan was seated in the back with the picnic basket.

On the trip out to the Circle H Ranch, Grace seemed to be full of chatter. Meagan was sullen, and Elmer mostly nodded his head. When they pulled into the ranch headquarters, Grace remarked, "Where are the trees and the lawn? This is nothing like I imagined. The buildings are constructed of weathered wood. It is rather stark. How can we have a picnic in these surroundings?"

Elmer was apologetic. "Lady Grace, this is a cattle ranch. Nothing is here for show. There are times in Texas that it is dry, and there are times that it is wet. This happens to be one of those dry times. Rarely will you find a ranch that possesses the splendor of the estates of England. This is a fairly new country as compared to the centuries of inhabitation of England. Don't worry about your picnic. I know of a secluded spot with a small stream and a big oak tree."

They traveled a short distance and encountered some of the cattle grazing in among the brush. "Stop the buggy," said Grace. "What are those things?"

Elmer stopped the horses. He explained, "Those are Texas Longhorns. In England, you have your Shorthorn cattle, we have our own breed of cattle. They can be any color and any size, but they are distinctive. I know that they cannot compare to the English breeds of beef cattle such as the Shorthorns, the Herefords, or the Aberdeen Angus, but they are tough. They have to be to survive in Texas. Just like the men, they have to be tough."

"And, what about the women?" she asked.

He replied, "The women don't have to be, but they are naturally beautiful."

She laughed. "My, aren't you the charmer."

"I think that I need to bring that topic of conversation to a close. Our picnic destination is just ahead by that tree." When they arrived near the tree he stopped the buggy. He stepped down to help the ladies to the ground.

Grace said, "It is no park, but it will do. If we sit close together, we can share the shade. I am sorry, Elmer. I am not being sarcastic, but trying to bring a little cheer to our outing. Meagan, you have been unusually quiet this morning. Are you all right?"

"Yes, yes, Lady Grace. I am fine."

"I don't want you to get too tired. When we go back, you can ride up front with your son. Then I can daydream about what it would be like to be a rancher's wife here in Texas, or maybe anywhere in the west." She paused before turning the conversation to Elmer. She asked, "Elmer, do you ever dream about how you would go about establishing a ranch?"

"Sure I do, much of the time."

"Then tell me about it."

"The headquarters of the ranch would be near
a stream with year round water. The trees nearby are
cottonwood that would provide shade in the summertime
and an ample nesting area for the birds. The house is of
either logs or painted wood. In this house, is a wife, the
mother of my children. The ranch headquarters would be
surrounded by the finest of prairie grass, as far as the eye
could see. I would populate the ranch with five hundred
Texas Longhorn heifers brought up from this state. I would
obtain breeding bulls from the English bloodlines that we
talked about earlier. I might even try my hand at raising fine
saddle horses on the ranch. This is my prayer for me and
the family that I am to have."

"But you won't be going with George Taggat," said
Grace.

"It is very unlikely that I will be going with
George," he said. "However, I have peace that God will
bless me, how I do not know. On our return to England the
last time, I had planned my escape, only to be foiled at the
last moment. I was shut up in solitaire confinement. During
that time I fasted and prayed, assured that I would be taken
out after forty days. The Lord provided another plan for
my escape, and it was successful. Here I am today, but God
knows where I will be tomorrow, and the day after that, and
on and on."

"Your mother and I went to the South West India
Dock to look for you. We knew that the HMS Bold Pelican
was to tie up there. We talked with Captain Twain and
he assured us that you were probably on your way home.
We went back two days before the ship was to return to
the seas, but it had already disembarked. He deliberately

deceived us. Once again, four years later I learned that the ship was on its way home from the Galveston Port and sank." She turned to Meagan. "I never told you. I feared that you would give up hope of finding your son."

Elmer asked, "Did any of them survive?"

She shook her head, "Apparently not. They only knew that the ship had sunk because the debris had washed up on the coast of France. Had you not escaped, you would have perished."

Elmer was stunned by the news. He had friends on that vessel, but now they are gone. That news had taken the life out of the party. They gathered up the remains of the picnic lunch and started back to Tipton.

When they went by the ranch house on their return, Grace asked, "What about the rancher's wife? What is she like, and how does she endure being isolated out here?"

"There is no rancher's wife. There is no semblance of a woman's touch. She died ten years ago. They had no children. Don't ask me how she died. She just died." That quelled any further conversation on the ride back to Tipton.

Upon their arrival at Tipton House, Elmer helped Lady Grace to the ground. Meagan said, "I will ride to the stable with Elmer and then walk back. I presume that we are eating together this evening here at the Tipton House. Elmer, set the basket on the veranda and I will take care of it later." Lady Grace never commented on Meagan's decision to go with Elmer, but went into the hotel, leaving the basket where he had placed it.

Elmer turned the buggy around to go to the stable. "What is it, Mother? What do you want?"

"Find a shady place to park. I have some questions to ask of you."

He pulled into a side street. He stopped the horse under a bur oak tree and wrapped the lines around the buggy whip stand. He turned to face his mother and folded his arms. "Mother, your demeanor indicates that I have displeased you. What has upset you so? You have scarcely said two words the whole trip."

"Last night, the scene in the park is what has upset me. I saw you kiss her. In fact, I saw you kiss her twice. Have you no decency or respect for the ruling class of England? I can understand how the two of you might have fallen in love with one another, but that does not make it right."

"Mother, she has asked me to marry her. She understands the consequences of my not wanting to return to England. She has offered to move to southern France where the family has a chateau. We could take the children and you with us. Then we could live out our life in seclusion from British society. We would expect to have more children and be one big happy family. Is that so bad?"

"What about your dream of staying here in America and building up a ranch? What about that?"

"Mother, it is a dream. I have no money. Most dreams never come true." He stopped, unsure of what he might say next. "Evidently, the only alternative I have is to marry Lady Grace and go to southern France." He shrugged his shoulders, evidence of despair.

"Her dream of marrying you is the one dream that cannot come true."

"Why not, Mama, why not?"

"Son, what I am about to tell you is something that I intended to take to the grave with me. Don't think ill of me about what I am going to reveal to you. Grace is your sister. In reality, she is your half-sister." Meagan stopped at the look of unbelief on her son's face. "I came to the Bellingham Estate when I was sixteen. You have heard me say that my family went to America. I could not go because

I had contacted the measles. I cared for Grace before and after her mother had died. Soon after Lady Virginia died, Lord Bellingham forced me to submit to his pleasure. It continued until he married Lady Anne. I had no choice. I was the upstairs maid. I was also the daughter of an Irish tenant farmer. I had seen what poverty and starvation had done to the weak and poor in Ireland. I was vulnerable, since I had no protector."

Elmer stammered when he interrupted her. "But what, what about Father?"

"At the time Lord Bellingham was to marry Lady Anne, he wanted me out of his life and away from the manor. I had the choice of being dumped on the streets of London, or marry Big Tim. Big Tim was aware that I was pregnant, but he was unaware that Lord Bellingham was the father of the child I was carrying. He wanted a wife that would give him children, so we were married in the village of Loxnard. Unfortunately we were unable to have other children." Meagan paused to regain her thoughts. *This was becoming more difficult than she imagined it would be.* "You probably remember that Lord Bellingham always wore the white gloves. One night when he was with me, he fell into a deep sleep. I pulled the gloves off of his hands. That is when I saw that the fingers had been damaged in a botched operation to separate the second and third fingers of the left hand. After you were born, he became aware that your fingers were like those of his. When I wanted him to pay the vicar for your education, I reminded him that he was buying my silence. The same thing occurred when you were fleeing for your life. Little did I think that he would condemn you to a lifetime at sea? Now you know why you cannot marry Lady Grace."

"What will I do Mother, what will I do? I can't tell Lady Grace what you have told me. It would devastate her to hear this about her father."

"I don't know, Son. I have carried the burden long enough. It is now your turn. Don't delay the separation. We each need to get on with our lives. We came to find out if you were alive. I am sorry that it has come to this, but this is what life is all about. I will get out and walk back to the Tipton House." She reached across and kissed his cheek. She stepped out of the buggy and started on her way. She came to the corner. She looked back. He was still sitting in the buggy.

Elmer continued to sit in the buggy. He felt drained of all energy. He was unable to vent his anger toward Lord Bellingham, though that was what his mind desired. Yet, his body failed to respond. He was unable to comprehend how a man, despite his lustful greed, could treat his own flesh and blood as he had treated me. He had shunned me as stable boy, and he had deserted me to be destined to a life at sea. Was it me, or was it that he hated my mother because she reminded him of his degradation in forcing her to submit to him.

The horse stomped his feet to rid his legs of the flies that were biting him. This brought Elmer's mind back to realize that he was still sitting on the buggy seat under the bur oak tree. He returned to the stable and took care of the buggy horse. He was not up to facing Lady Grace this evening. He saddled his horse and returned to the Circle H Ranch. After a restless night he came to a solution to his problem.

CHAPTER 19
A ROYAL PARTNERSHIP

The next morning after breakfast, Elmer met with Harold Taggat. "Mr. Taggat, I am quitting, so I would like to draw my pay."

"I'm sorry to hear that you are leaving. I don't have enough money with me to pay for your time. I am going into Tipton this morning. I will have the money this evening. Is that all right?"

Elmer shook his head. "Would you trade a horse for what you owe me? I don't want to waste any more time than I have to."

Harold nodded, "Is that sorrel horse you call Red worth the trade? If it is, then we have a deal. Elmer, you are a good hand. What are you planning to do?"

"I plan to get on with a trail drive heading north. I have seen enough of Texas. I have a letter that needs to go to a lady in Tipton. I would count it a favor if you could give it to Mrs. Meagan Moran. She is staying at the Tipton House." He gave him the letter and offered his hand to Harold. "Mr. Taggat, I appreciate you teaching me about ranching. You have been a real gentleman."

Elmer saddled the sorrel horse and tied his gear behind the cantle of the saddle. He pointed the horse north and touched the spurs to him. He knew of one herd that had come through the area three days ago. They were running shorthanded, so he figured that he could sign on as soon as he caught up with them.

Elmer rode north for about an hour. He stopped his horse to give him a breather. He got off the horse and stretched his legs. He was ready to resume his ride. He put his hand on the saddle horn and then he stopped. He rested his forehead on the seat of the saddle. He cried out, "Oh

God, give me wisdom, give me strength." After a brief time, he raised his head and stepped up on his horse. He turned the horse around and started heading south; south to Tipton, Texas.

He rode the horse hard. Red was covered with sweat when they came to the edge of town. He walked his horse to let him cool down. He looked down the street and saw Harold Taggat leave the Tipton House. He peered in the sky, looking to the south. It was near noon by his calculation. He feared that his mother had already read the letter. Elmer entered the hotel. He walked by the dining room and saw his mother and Grace at a table. They had not been served, so he went to the wash room to get rid of the dust that he had accumulated in his speedy ride. After he had finished, he went in and nodded to the two ladies.

Meagan spoke first. "We have been expecting you, so we have not yet ordered." She motioned to the waitress. Elmer looked down and saw his letter setting at the edge of her tableware. It had not been opened. He wanted to reach out and grab it. Perhaps when Mother prays over the food, I can get it while her head is bowed. He decided that was not a good idea!

They each gave their order to the young lady and sampled their water. Meagan reached down and handed him the letter. There was a twinkle in her eye as she spoke. "I thought you might soon show up, so there is no need of me reading it. I will give it back to you. The front desk clerk said that Harold Taggat had left it earlier." Elmer nodded. He sensed that she knew what was in the letter. He had been too cowardly to say anything to Lady Grace.

After they had finished eating, they lingered over a late cup of tea. Meagan gave her son a meaningful look, but he shook it off. Perspiration beaded his forehead. He needed to tell Lady Grace he would not marry her, but he couldn't do it now. I will put it off until our afternoon tea. Maybe when I ride Red to the livery stable, he will buck me off and I will die. That will be better than telling her. That thought gave him courage. He spoke up, "I will take care of my horse and then we can meet for afternoon tea." He got up and left in a hurry. He missed the glare that his mother gave him.

He got on Red, but he had ridden him so hard that there was no buck in him. He unsaddled him at the livery stable and rubbed him down. He fed him grain and checked the hay in the bunk. He left the stall and gave Red a final pat on the rump. He looked up and there was George. He said, "I just saw Harold and he told me that you headed north to sign on with the Hackens trail herd. That was quick. Did you get fired already?"

"No, I had some unfinished business to take care of before I left."

"Yeah, I suppose like Elizabeth Conrad. You just don't give up."

"I don't give up as long as I am winning the race, especially when Elizabeth is the prize." *I won't give him any further information,* thought Elmer.

Elmer went to the park across from the Tipton House and sat down at a bench. Since he didn't get killed by his horse, he needed to rehearse what he was going to say to Grace. Nothing would come to mind, but the thought that she was his sister had shocked him. It continued to loom in his mind. He glanced and saw his mother waving at him. He looked up at the sun and saw that indeed it was time for afternoon tea. He went across the street to the Tipton House.

The ladies were sitting at the table and the tea had been poured. Lady Grace reached out and touched his hand. "Elmer, I have good news for you. This past week has meant so much to me, and it has been an eye opener for me. I am looking forward to our return to England and the beginning of life anew." Elmer could not look at her. He continually stirred the tea in his cup. "Elmer, do you remember when you were a stable boy in my father's stable? Sad to say, but my impetuous behavior got you into a lot of trouble. I can still see you after the horse called Luke fell while going over the stone wall. It was all because of me and the desire to see how fast Daisy could run. Then too, the events of the day of Carlton's death brought about by Carlton and me arguing. I got you involved in that as well. I am sorry Elmer, but I have tried to coerce you into marrying me and moving to southern France. I noted your reluctance, but still you would not deny my wishes. When you were as young as ten, I sensed our kinship, almost like a brother and sister. It was when you shared your dream of building a ranch in the west that I realized that not all dreams need to be about me." He had nothing to say, but Meagan noted the relief he expressed.

Now it was Meagan's turn. "Son, Lady Grace and I will soon return to England. This is your opportunity to share what you want. If you want to return with us, she has assured me that you have employment on the Estate. If you want, you and I can return to Ireland, but I am unsure what would be in store for us there. Or, you can remain in America. Do not think that you have to be with me. God has been so gracious to restore us to one another. I can live with the thought that you are alive and safe. Best of all, you are in God's hands. It is your choice."

He nodded his head. "Thank you for finding me. Once I was free, I never wanted to experience the loss of my freedom again. I will remain in Tipton until you leave. Then I will go north to seek my fortune."

The two ladies looked at one another. Meagan

nodded. Lady Grace said, "I liked your dream, but it seemed more of a plan than a dream. I liked it so much that I wanted to know if you would consider taking on a partner. Father left me well off financially. I would finance your plan if I could be assured that you would run the operation. The big cost would be the start up. For my financing, I would ask for one-half of the profits for the first twenty years. At that time, you would receive one-half of the assets and I would continue to share in the profits. I talked with the local banker, Mr. Conrad. He assured me that he could have money transferred into his bank within ten days after we reached Houston. He thought that I should transfer five thousand British pounds. Once you were established wherever you are going, then it would be best to do your banking locally. Mr. Conrad has observed you since you first came to Tipton. He saw that you were a hard working man that has taken to the ways of the West. I know that this is rather fast, but think about it and let us know in the morning." She dropped her napkin on the table. "I will leave mother and son to discuss these matters." She got out of her chair and went to her room.

Elmer was dumbfounded at what he had heard. He looked at his mother. "Why didn't you open the letter and read it?"

"I didn't need to. I knew that you were running. I didn't know how far, but I knew that you would return. Your father and I instilled character and courage from the day that you were born. You didn't disappoint me today. What is your decision?"

"When I had ridden my horse as far as I could go, I laid my head on my saddle and beseeched God to help me and to give me strength. That is when I returned to Tipton. That which Lady Grace has offered is of the Lord. I will remain in America, even though I desire to spend the rest of my days with you. I love you, Mama, I love you."

She kissed him. "I love you. I will go now to pack. We will be leaving in the morning for Houston. I will see you at supper tonight."

Elmer stopped at Mrs. Taggats before going to the stable. He asked her, "Mrs. Taggat, I need a place to sleep for the next two weeks. Could I rent my old room?"

"Of course you can, but I won't charge you rent. Harold was here earlier and said that you were trying to catch up with a trail herd. If you have changed your mind, why don't you stay in Tipton and help Harvey at the livery stable. With George leaving, he needs a good hand."

"No, I think that two weeks is as long as I will be in town, but thanks for the offer. Is George at the livery stable this afternoon? I need to visit with him."

"Yes, he is there. Since he got the notion to go north he hasn't been much help. I think that he is trying to get in as much courting with the banker's daughter as he can before he leaves."

Elmer found George cleaning out a stall. He asked, "How are you getting along putting things together for your trail drive?"

"I need to get a few more horses. We plan to leave in two weeks. Why do you ask?"

"I have taken on a partner. We are putting together a herd of five hundred bred heifers. I wondered if I could throw in with you. We would have more cowboys, but only need one chuck wagon. Both of us could save some money."

George threw his manure fork to the floor. "No, no, no! How many times do I have to tell you that I don't want anything to do with you? It wouldn't work. We have a different outlook on life. You would want to stop and whittle and give bird calls to those cattle. Who is your partner anyway? You had to borrow a shirt and pants from me when you came to town. Now you have a herd of cattle. I don't understand it, I just don't understand it."

"That is fine, George, that is fine. I won't ask again. Oh, so you don't get upset, I have my room back at your home until I go north with my trail herd." He took his gear with him, so that he might get cleaned up to spend the last evening meal with his mother and Lady Grace.

The next morning he saw the ladies off on the morning stage. He promised his mother that he would write as soon as he established a post office address. At the same time, he would send Lady Grace a progress report.

CHAPTER 20
HEAD 'EM UP, AND MOVE 'EM OUT

The same morning, he went to the bank and met with Mr. Conrad to go over what his timelines were for money requirements. After he left the bank, he heard someone call his name. He turned to see who it was, and in doing so, he bumped into a young lady.

She fell to the ground. He tried to help her up, but she escaped his grasp. She called out, "Keep your hands off of me, Brit. Why don't you look where you are going?" It was Elizabeth's sister.

"I'm sorry, Turk. If you would grow a little, I could see you."

Elizabeth Conrad came running to him. "Is my sister bothering you? I called out to remind you that I will see you in church on Sunday. I will have to ride with my family in the carriage, but you can sit with me in church. That way, I can keep you and my sister apart. I don't know what it is, but I don't think she likes you. She always refers to you as 'Brit.' How did she ever come up with that name?"

"She is all right. I try to ignore her, and I sense that is what infuriates her. I will see you Sunday. Once George Taggat leaves town with his trail herd, I hope to see more of you. Goodbye."

Elmer went to his horse. He saw Turk walking on the board walk near the General Store. He rode by her and he tipped his hat and said, "Good day, Miss Turk." Then he laughed. After he got by her, she stepped off the board walk and found a clump of dirt. She threw it, hitting his horse on the rump. Red made three jumps before he could get him under control.

She called out, "Good day, Mr. Brit." Then she

laughed.

Elmer rode out to the Circle H Ranch. It was noon when he arrived, so he went to the cook shack. Harold was there. He always ate dinner with the men. Elmer sat beside him. He said, "Harold, I need your advice. I am taking a trail herd to the north in about three weeks. Can you help me determine everything that I will need?"

He nodded. "How many head are you taking?"

"I want to take five hundred bred heifers, and a few steers for trading stock. Where can I find that many heifers? I would prefer all one brand."

"Have you put together a crew?" Elmer shook his head. "What is your financing like? I have that many heifers, but I need to be sure that I get paid for them. Last week you were working for wages, and now you are buying a herd."

"I have the financing. You can check with the banker in Tipton. Will you help me put all of this together?"

He nodded, "But I would like to add another five hundred head of three year old steers to the herd. I can't ride that much anymore, but I would like to go along as the cook. I have the chuck wagon. As dry as it has been, I am afraid I will be short of grass here. If I could get rid of a thousand head, it would help a lot. That would leave me with the cows and calves. The men that I have now could handle those without much supervision."

"How do you figure to handle the expenses? Also, how many men do we need, and how many horses will we need to buy? I need some pretty solid figures to take to the bank, so I don't run out of funds."

Harold leaned back on the bench and stretched his legs. "I thought we could split the expenses in half. We each will have the same number of cattle. You will handle the drive and I will handle the chuck wagon. This was your idea, so you are in charge. I think that we should have ten men to start the drive. We might lose one or two to being homesick, but we would still have enough. My cattle aren't that wild, so they could handle them. I will furnish the horses. I have enough, and I figure that they will be worth more after we have ridden them most of the summer." He paused a moment before he continued. "Elmer, you might reconsider taking them heifers up north. They are bred to start calving in mid-February. We start calving early in the season here to avoid the screw worms. You won't have that problem, but you might have a few snowstorms in February and March. I will save a spot in the wagon to pack some winter clothes. Some of the men may want to stay on with you, which might be a good idea."

Elmer nodded that he understood Harold's thinking. "The weather is a risk that I will have to live with if I want to make my mark in the land. I like your thinking on sharing responsibilities. George has been counting on going north for some time. Because of this, I think he deserves to go first. We should give him at least three days head start. Is that all right with you?"

Harold laughed. "Normally, I would prefer to leave first. The grass will be fresher. Your decision is a gentlemanly thing to do. I rather doubt that George would do the same for you, but as I said, you are in charge. I will go into Tipton and talk with the banker. I will find out when George is planning to leave. Then I can start putting together a crew. My cattle are branded, but it might be well to put your own brand on the heifers. We can do that a few days before we leave. It will also let us see how our horses will respond to not being ridden for a while."

Harold came back that afternoon, accompanied by a young man riding a mule. Harold got Elmer alone and told him, "This fellow with the mule tried to sign up with

George, but he turned him down. You gave me the job of putting the crew together, but I would feel better if you passed judgment on this one. He wants to be a cowboy, but I am not sure how much good he might be. I could use him to help me, but he insists on being a cowboy. His name is Gomer Stumpf. He says that the 'p' in his last name is silent."

Elmer nodded his head and went to where Gomer was sitting on his mule. "Gomer, I am Elmer Teasdale." They shook hands. "Harold says that you want to be a cowboy. There are three things that you will need to do if you want to go with this herd. We can't have a mule. The first time that he brayed early in the morning, we would have a stampede on our hands. Take him back to the livery stable and trade him to Harvey for a saddle. Mule or no mule, you can't be riding bareback. I will furnish the horses. The third thing is, you can't ride hard and fast wearing those plow shoes. Stop at the undertaker's and buy a good pair of secondhand boots. He has a number to choose from. Cowboys may die with their boots on, but they bury them in their stocking feet. Two dollars will buy you a decent pair. If you can do those three things, then I can use you. I will give you a horse to lead back to Tipton. Say good bye to the mule, get you a saddle and a pair of boots and come back and I will put you to work. I pay fifteen dollars a month, payable at the end of the drive. Take the first horse inside the barn door." He waited for Gomer's response.

Gomer said, "I'll be back this afternoon." He turned the mule toward the barn. Elmer went back to where the men were branding cattle.

The next day, Harold came back from Tipton with the news that George was leaving a week from Monday. The Sunday before George left, he and Elmer were both at the Conrad home for dinner. Neither one was going to let the other get the better of him in paying court to Elizabeth Conrad. They left together, vowing to meet again next April when Elizabeth would make her choice.

Thursday was the day that Harold and Elmer started their drive. Once it was started, Elmer chose to drive their cattle parallel to the route that George took, so that they would have fresh grass. At noon, Elmer asked Harold, "Could you arrange to get ahead of us in the middle of the afternoon, so that you could start a small fire to warm up some coffee for the men. This first day it would give them a chance to stretch and also the cattle could graze as they moved along. I would be happy with a spot of tea at that time as well."

Harold laughed, "George warned me that you would do something like that. I thought he was funning me, but you are serious, aren't you?"

Elmer nodded. "I'll send Gomer to give you a hand. It will give him an opportunity to look at his boots. He said the undertaker had eight pair to choose from." Elmer started to leave, but then he turned back. "See how it works. If it doesn't work we can always stop the afternoon tea time." Then he laughed and got on his horse to join the rest of the crew.

On Sunday, Elmer said, "Let's not push the cattle real hard. Let them graze and get a chance to fill up. This is the Lord's Day. We are on schedule."

On the third Sunday, Elmer sensed that Harold was not happy with the slower pace on Sunday, and especially heating up coffee and hot water for tea in the middle of the afternoon. After the noon meal, Elmer asked, "Harold, are things going all right? You haven't had much to say the last few days."

"Elmer, I haven't said much because I have been

biting my tongue. That's why. If we don't get a move on these cattle, we will be wintering in Kansas. I'll bet that George is a week ahead of us instead of three days." Elmer saw that the men were picking up on their conversation.

"I will have Gomer break camp and you and I will inspect the trail that George is taking. I will have Claude saddle a horse for you, and we will take a ride. I will be back in less than an hour." He rode back to the herd to tell Claude to catch and saddle a horse for Harold. Also, to keep the herd pointed north while they grazed.

Harold and Elmer were silent. They rode west to intersect where the other herd had been. After a time, Elmer got off his horse to inspect the cattle droppings. He remarked, "Three or four days old. Harold, how many of your steers do you expect to lose on this drive? That is, die or drift away from the herd?"

"Maybe twenty. It depends if you have a stampede or not."

"We haven't had any die, and I doubt if any have drifted off. Our men are doing a good job of keeping watch over them. We have more cattle in the herd than when we started." Elmer sensed the doubt in Harold's eyes at his statement. He continued. "We have gathered eight of George's heifers and a young bull. Two of the heifers were lame, but have recovered. George has been pushing his herd. At one time they were five days ahead of us, but it is telling on their cattle. When we get to Dodge City, I want your steers to have gained while on the trail. Tomorrow, I will saddle Red and see how close we are to them. Let's go back." Neither one said anything for a while. Finally Elmer said, "Harold, I want you to be content with how I am running this drive. If you would rather ramrod the drive, that is fine. I will do the cooking, but I can't have you second guessing me in front of the men." That put an end to their conversation for the rest of the ride.

The next morning Elmer saddled Red and headed north to overtake the Taggat trail herd. The morning of the second day, he spotted the herd. He didn't approach, but observed them through his binoculars. He saw that their chuck wagon had apparently broken an axle, and it was delaying them. He had seen enough. He turned back to return to his own herd.

Late that afternoon, he had stopped to water his horse from a small stream in a narrow arroyo. He was startled by a band of Indians coming down the path from the bank above. His first inclination was to make a run for it, but deemed it unwise. He lifted his arm in a gesture of welcoming them. While the chief of the tribe came to him, Elmer saw that it was mostly women and children that made up the band. They looked tired and hungry. The chief gave a sign of peace and spoke in broken English. "I am Chief Two Feathers. Do you have food? There are no buffalo for my people to kill and eat. The children are starving." The warriors of the group said nothing, but stared at this lone man with the fine sorrel horse.

Elmer was struck by his own words when he answered the chief. "I have food, but not here. One day's ride to the south and I will give you food." He gestured with his left hand the direction the ride would be. "I have a trail herd coming this way."

The chief grabbed his hand and said, "You are a man of nine fingers." He had observed how the second and third fingers of the left hand were joined. Elmer nodded. Some of the warriors looked at the hand.

Elmer told the chief, "I will go now to bring the food to you." He started to mount his horse.

One of the braves reached out and grabbed the reins out of Elmer's hand. "No, you wait here. Let the food come to you. If you speak truth, food will be here tomorrow. If you don't speak truth, then you will die." The brave appeared to be the son of the chief.

The chief nodded his head. "We will make camp here. We will wait." Elmer unsaddled Red and let them take his horse. They took his rifle and pistol, but left his bedroll. The chief said, "My son Gray Horse is young. He thinks I am weak, because I trust you. I saw in your eyes that you are a man that means what he says. Tomorrow we will have food. Sleep well. No one will harm you."

Mid-morning the next day, the herd appeared on the horizon. Elmer took Chief Two Feathers, his son Gray Horse and ten braves to meet the herd. Elmer took the chief and his son to the chuck wagon to meet Harold. He said, "I have promised them food. The people are starving. I will give them four steers. That will be two from you and two from me. I will reimburse you for the two steers when we get to Dodge City. I am giving them twelve heifers from my herd and the bull from the Taggat herd. That will be a start for them to begin raising cattle. Get a fire started and we will put a brand on them. Is that agreeable with you?"

Harold nodded. "It is if it will keep them from trying to steal from us."

Elmer explained to the chief what he was going to do. He said, "I will give you four steers for your people to eat. That is the food I promised to you." He held up four fingers. "I will give you twelve heifers and one bull." He showed fingers on his right hand until he had displayed twelve. "They will have calves next year. Soon you will have many cattle. I will give you a paper saying that they are your cattle. My men will brand the cattle. Your brand will be like a tepee. It will have two bars crossed at the top. Watch over your cattle and you will not starve."

Chief Two Feathers took his lance and tapped Elmer

on the right shoulder. "Today I will make you a chief of my tribe. You shall be called Chief Nine Fingers."

After the cattle had been branded, two of the cowboys helped them start their cattle to where the tribe had camped last night.

The next day, the Teasdale trail herd caught up with George Taggat and his crew. Elmer had the herd veer to the right and pass around them. He was taking the herd to Dodge City to sell the steers. They waved to the cowboys in the distance, but did not stop.

The trail to Dodge City was uneventful. Before they got to Dodge City, they began to separate the herd. The steers had a chance to get filled up before they took them into town. Harold found a buyer and sold all but two of the steers. Elmer bought them so that he would have meat for his crew when they wintered in Nebraska.

After the steers were sold, Elmer asked, "Harold, are you going with us to Nebraska?"

He shook his head, "No, I think that I will head back to Tipton."

"I was hoping that you would go with us the rest of the way. Will you sell me the chuck wagon, horses and harness, along with the horses that we have been riding? I don't have that much money with me, but I can give you a draft on the bank at Tipton. I need my cash to stock up on supplies for the rest of the trip." Elmer waited for a response from him. He then asked, "Do you know if anyone else will be going back with you?"

"Chub might go with me. I think he is getting lonesome for his wife. I will need a horse and at least one pack horse. I would like to have someone to ride with me. That is a mighty long ride without any company. I will get back with you in the morning."

It was starting to rain when the men came for

255

breakfast. Harold handed Elmer a slip of paper with some figures on it. He said, "Check the figures. I tried to be reasonable on each item. Chub and Whitney are going with me, so we will need five horses. Chub and Whitney will need to be paid. Then I figured what the others have coming. If you don't want that many horses to go the rest of the way, take your pick and I will sell the rest here at Dodge. I didn't charge for the two steers you gave to the Indians and the two you are taking with the herd. You deserve a bonus for being the ramrod."

Elmer looked it over. "It looks good to me. I will make out the draft. Give me a bill of sale for the horses and the two steers. Put on it that I own the wagon. As soon as you get your gear together and pick your horses, we will head for Nebraska. Thanks Harold. I will see you in the spring. I have a bride to claim in Tipton."

Elmer started the herd north to the Republican River. Now he was looking for landmarks that would direct him to the crossing used by earlier trail herds. Taking the steers to Dodge City cost him some time, but it was part of the agreement with Harold Taggat. With a smaller herd, they were easier to handle and they were making better time without putting a stress on the cattle.

About every day they experienced afternoon rains. Some were severe. Midmorning thunderheads would begin to build up in the west and roll in during the supper hour. Homer Stumpf had taken over the cooking after Harold left. He wasn't the best of cooks, but no one complained for fear that they would have their turn at cooking. Elmer rode ahead each day to see what was coming up. On one of the afternoons the sky was clear, so it appeared they would not encounter any rain. Off in the distance he saw a herd near a river. He presumed it to be the Republican in southern Nebraska. It looked like they were preparing to cross. He stopped his horse and pulled out his binoculars. At first glance it looked like it might be the Taggat herd. Then he spotted a familiar horse. George was riding Dragon; the horse that Elmer had tamed. George must have talked Harvey out of the horse. The cattle were in the water, but from where Elmer was, it did not look like it was an easy crossing. That is what he feared. He was uncertain how much water had been dumped upstream with all of the rains. He looked again, and they were crossing with the chuck wagon. Then he saw it swing around and turn over on its side. He could see the driver jump clear of the wagon. A cowboy threw him a rope, but the water was so swift that he had been swept out of reach of the rope. The horses were still hitched to the running gear, but with them harnessed together, he saw one of them flounder and he then pulled his mate down into the muddy water and they drowned.

Elmer turned his horse toward the river. When he got there, part of the crew was searching downstream for the cook that had been driving the chuck wagon. He sensed that he had not survived. George rode up to him and Elmer saw the look of defeat on his face. He shook his head and said, "Too much water, way too much water. We lost our chuck wagon and I doubt that Spike Gurney made it. I don't think that he was a swimmer. I should have stayed in Texas. How far back is your herd?"

Elmer nodded. "We are about a day behind you. I have a pack rigging back at camp. Send a man with me and I can get enough supplies and cooking utensils to sustain you until we catch up with you. If we leave now, he can be back here toward evening. That will give you time to think through your next step. If you want, we can throw the two herds together and run with one chuck wagon, but it is up to you."

"I'll send Carter with you," he replied. "I could send a horse to use for a pack horse, but I guess that you would make better time without." He paused before asking. "You would take me in after I refused to let you join the herd out of Tipton?"

Elmer nodded. "Sure, and I am thinking if the situation was reversed, you would do the same for me." George didn't declare himself, but rode off.

Elmer and Carter rode hard toward the Teasdale herd. Gomer fed Carter and Elmer helped put together the pack. They had an extra coffee pot and two cast iron pots that he sent along with enough supplies to last them until they caught up with the Taggat herd. Elmer knew that it would be near sundown before Carter got back, but that would give them grub for a day. Elmer cautioned him, "Do not to try crossing the river with the pack horse. Have them set up camp on this side of the river. It means that the crew will have to ford the river in order to eat, but we can't afford to lose any more supplies or cooking ware. We should be there tomorrow afternoon. Good luck!" Carter waved goodbye and took off at a trot.

The next afternoon, Elmer and his crew arrived at the river, but the Taggat herd was gone! Elmer rode upstream for about a mile, but there was no evidence that they had set up camp. Tom Catcher rode downstream. He came back with the news that he had found the packhorse washed up on the river bank. It still had the pack tied on its back. Elmer sent Tom and Harry Potts back downstream to salvage what gear they could. The rest of the crew let the cattle graze while Elmer rode further upstream to determine if the river might be decreasing its flow. It had not rained for three days and it seemed to Elmer the river was not as high as when he first saw it the day that the Taggat herd had lost their chuck wagon.

Elmer returned late that evening. Before going
to the chuck wagon, he went to the river. The moon was
appearing on the horizon and Elmer stepped down from his
horse. For a time he watched the moon cast its reflection
on the water. His mind was brought back to a time that he
watched this same moon from the heights of the crow's
nest on the HMS Bold Pelican. He had prayed for guidance
and safety in planning his escape. He removed his hat
and began to pray. "Oh Lord, I come to you this night for
guidance. That night I prayed it was for me, but tonight I
have the safety of my crew in my hand. Not only my crew,
but I sense that I need to be seeing about my friend, George
Taggat and his crew. I have witnessed the power of the
oceans and the rivers, but I have also witnessed your power
in my life. Give me wisdom and safety for those I am
responsible for as my employees. I ask these things in the
name of my Savior, Jesus Christ. Amen.

The next morning he called the men together. He
said, "Men, we can't afford to lose our chuck wagon. This
morning we will start to build a raft. If the weather holds
while we are building it, the water will begin to drop. Three
days from now we will cross the river. Two men will stay
with the herd and the rest of us will build the raft. Let's get
to work!"

At the close of the second day, the raft was finished.
Elmer was pleased with the effort that the men put in on
building it. It was held together by rope. By nightfall, they
had the raft secured in shallow water. They pulled the
wagon on the raft and removed the wheels and the tongue
and secured them to the side of the wagon. The harness was
put inside.

At first light they had breakfast and moved the herd
across the river. Elmer noted that it was an easier crossing
than the Taggat herd experienced. One man stayed with

the herd which was content to be on fresh grass. The rest
of the crew forded the river and changed mounts before
cutting the raft lose. Elmer wanted his men to have fresh
mounts for crossing with the wagon. He also encouraged
them to use their strongest horses because their ropes
would be tied to the raft to help slow the current from
taking it downstream. He cautioned them to dally the rope
around the saddle horn so it could be released if they had
any problem. Elmer had fashioned a long pole which he
had marked in five foot increments so he could measure the
depth of the water. He was going to ride on the raft and use
the pole if needed to navigate the crossing. After witnessing
the destruction of the Taggat chuck wagon, Elmer did not
want to put any of his men in more danger than necessary.
He knew that if he ended up in the river, he was the
strongest swimmer.

He nodded to Tom Catcher to loosen the rope from
the tree and toss it on the raft. He used the pole to push off
into deeper water. He was amazed at how well the wagon
rode. The water was deep, but not particularly fast. The raft
had drifted downstream, but only about a fourth mile in the
crossing. When the raft reached the shore, the men gave a
big shout!

It was a little before noon when the team of horses
pulled the wagon off of the raft. Elmer left the raft tied
to a tree. Perhaps someone else might be able to use it.
Gomer fixed a quick noon meal for the crew. While he
was preparing the meal, Elmer returned to the river. It
was there that he prayed. "Father, I thank you for the safe
crossing of the river. Only by your guidance did we make
it this morning. Amen." After the short rations at noon, they
made five miles that day, leaving the Republican River to
challenge the next herd.

The next morning, Elmer rode north in search of

the Taggat herd. Mid-afternoon he caught sight of them by looking through his binoculars. Something was wrong. Elmer saw only three riders with the herd. He hurried to catch up with them, but he didn't see George with the herd. He recognized Carter and rode up to him. "What has happened here? Where is George and what has happened to the rest of the crew?"

Carter shook his head. "I told George the last words of caution you gave me when I left your camp. He insisted that the supplies needed to be on the other side of the river with the herd. I begged him to wait for you, or at least lighten the load for the pack animal. He was obsessed with staying ahead of you. I knew that the pack horse was carrying a heavy load. Once he was swept off his feet, he was gone. When the crew saw that the supplies were gone, half of them quit the herd and headed north after they had collected their wages. It came to the point that they forced George to pay them when they drew their guns on him. I was afraid that they might kill him."

Elmer nodded and asked, "Where is George?"

"I have him laying in the shade of a tree. He is suffering from dysentery and is delusional at times. He is in bad shape. I'm not sure that he will make it."

"Take me to him. Don't let the herd go any further until we get here with our chuck wagon. It took us two days to cross the Republican. What have you been doing for grub?"

Carter shrugged, "We have been living off the land the best that we can. We have shot a couple of rabbits, and we did get into a bevy of sage hens. The men that left took our guns, but left them a couple hundred yards away from us. We only have water when we come to a stream. The crew that left took our canteens."

They came to George asleep under the tree. At first

261

glance, Elmer thought that he was dead. He stirred when he heard them talking. Elmer got off his horse and brought his canteen with him. He said, "Here George, you need to get some liquid into you."

George tried to get up by clutching the tree. He refused the water and tried to yell at Elmer, but only a faint sound revealed the anger in his voice. "Get out of here! Don't think that you can get away with my herd! I know what you are up to! Carter, get him away from here!" He stumbled and fell to the ground. He tried to crawl to where he had been resting.

Elmer backed off. He handed the canteen to Carter. "See that he drinks some water. I will go back for our chuck wagon and hurry as fast as I can. Two of you can kill one of your heifers and have her butchered out by the time that we get here. You fellas will have steak tonight, but we need to get George started on broth to get him on the road to recovery. Get some wood gathered up for us. I should be here before dark." He got on his horse and started off at a gallop.

The sun had disappeared on the western horizon when Gomer and Elmer pulled up with the chuck wagon near the tree where Elmer had last seen George. Hanging in a nearby tree was a beef carcass. A small fire was burning close by. The two men began to pull pots and pans from the back of the wagon. Carter rode up and greeted the men. Elmer asked, "How is George? I didn't want to disturb him. My presence seemed to anger him, but I do want to help in his recovery." Carter didn't say anything, but shrugged his shoulders, a sign of defeat etched on his face. Elmer continued, "Our herd will be here in about an hour. I think it best that we not mingle the herds until morning. I can spare a couple men to help with the night herding." Elmer paused when he realized what he was doing. "Carter, I am sorry. It may appear that I am taking over. However, I see there is no other alternative until such time that George is able to function. If you are not happy with what I am doing, then we will be on our way at first light."

"No, no. You are doing fine. After George took sick, I was hoping that you would catch up with us. When you didn't show up, I feared that you had passed by us. How did you escape crossing the Republican?"

"We spent two days building a raft for the chuck wagon. With three days of no rain, the river was easier to cross." Elmer paused. He knew that he needed some answers before they went any further. "Carter, if we are to blend the herds, there needs to be some ground rules established. I will be the boss until such time that we split up and each go their own way. I know that George doesn't approve of how I do things, but that is how it will be. I will see that your herd is delivered to where you want to go. After we get deep into Nebraska, I will be loading our wagon with supplies to carry us through the winter. George will need to figure out what he wants to do. Tom Catcher has been up here before. He has an insight of what I want in regard to establishing my ranch headquarters. We will be going there as soon as the herd is split up. I was surprised at the hostility George exhibited toward me. His parents, Harvey and Alma took me under their wing when I drifted into Tipton. I feel a sense of responsibility toward George because of their hospitality. Because of that, I waited for three days to let him go ahead of us. His Uncle Harold wanted us to go first."

Carter shook his head, "I don't know what is between you two, but he has been bitter most of the trip. Though we started three days ahead of you, he has been afraid that you would catch us. He drove the cattle hard and the men harder, but it seemed that we could not break away from you. He would send me out each morning to check on your progress. If I told him that you were closing the gap, he would be furious. If he couldn't see your dust, then I would give him a glowing report of how we were surging ahead. He liked it when I would report that your herd shut down in the afternoon for coffee."

Elmer laughed, "I think all of this is because of Elizabeth Conrad, the banker's daughter. We are to meet in Tipton next April, and Elizabeth is to choose one of us for her husband. Incidentally, does George know where he is going to settle?"

He looked down and nodded. "Tucker Bare told him about a place in the Sandhills near a trading post. Since we don't have a wagon just now to haul in supplies, we can get them from the trading post. There is a preacher that was a circuit rider for a number of years in that area. His name is John Madden. He married an Indian girl from the Omaha tribe, so then he decided to settle down. That is when he opened a trading post on the Dismal River." Had Carter been looking up, he would have seen the shock on Elmer's face. That is where Tom Catcher suggested Elmer establish his ranch headquarters!

The next morning, Elmer met with Carter. "How is George doing? Did you have an opportunity to discuss with him the possibility of combining the herds?"

"I think that he is better. That is, if being cantankerous is any indication of getting well. I told him that there is no way that we can continue without a chuck wagon. He is worried that you will gouge him on the price of feeding our crew."

"What does he want from me? Is he short of money? Tell him that he can pay me whatever it is worth to him at any time that he has the money. Either you or he needs to come to a decision. I am taking my herd and my chuck wagon right after breakfast. If he is too sick to ride his horse, then he better be on the wagon seat when Gomer is leaving." Elmer threw the contents of his cup on the ground. "I have offered him help, but I won't beg. Make up your mind!"

He went to his horse and tightened the cinch. He had his foot in the stirrup when Carter said, "We are going with you!"

The first two hours on the trail, Elmer had the cowboys move the cattle at a rapid pace. With the blended herd, there was the threat of establishing the pecking order among the cattle. Elmer didn't give them the opportunity to fight one another.

That night after supper, Elmer told Carter, "Tom and I are going to look over our maps to establish our route. You need to be there, and if George wants to show up, that is fine. We need to take the herd to your destination first."

Carter was at the meeting, but George was not. The three men picked their route. It was certain that they had to cross the Platte River. Tom was sure that there was a toll bridge where they could cross with the chuck wagon, but the cattle would need to swim. Elmer knew that when they crossed the Platte, the chuck wagon would be heavily loaded with supplies for the coming winter.

They arrived at the Madden Trading Post on the second day of September. They spent the next two days sorting cattle. Before leaving the area, Elmer went to meet John Madden at his trading post. He observed that it was well stocked. Two women were clerking for him. He saw that the older woman was probably his wife. The other woman was in her late teens or early twenties and quite pretty. He perceived that she was John's daughter by his Indian wife. Carter had said that John did not tolerate any misbehavior of any of the men around his daughter. Elmer had to remind himself that he had a bride waiting for him in Tipton. The following day, Elmer and his crew headed east along the Dismal River. Carter came to them and said, "Thanks Elmer, for all that you have done for us. I will talk with George about making it right with you. Without your help, I do believe that he would have died. Come back and see us." They shook hands.

Elmer was saddened that George did not bid him farewell. He and Tom rode side by side for an hour before either one said anything. Finally, Tom said, "You saw the spot that I had chosen for you?" Elmer nodded. Tom continued, "Tucker Bare was with me when we came through there two years ago. I had no idea that he had taken a liking to it. You know, we could have left them behind."

Elmer nodded. "You know and I know that would not have been right. We need to be gone from George for now. When he comes to his senses, he will do that which is right. In the mean time, I have confidence that God has a place for us. I don't know where, but we will recognize it as being God's will. By tomorrow night we will be gone from George's range and we can begin the Teasdale Ranch." He turned his horse to the side of the herd to bring back a heifer that had strayed too far from the herd.

Late afternoon the next day, Elmer trotted his horse over to where Tom was riding point. "Tom," he said and pointing to the northeast, "that is where we will stop and make camp. See the top of those trees behind that hill? Those are Cottonwoods. The explorer John C. Fremont had discovered that wherever you encountered cottonwood trees you would find water. That is where the headquarters will be for the ranch." When they arrived at the top of the hill, they sat on their horses and looked down into a valley where the Dismal River wound its way into a horseshoe shape before flowing on to the east.

When Elmer had purchased the winter supplies, he had also purchased a tent that would house eight men. He had acquired folding cots at the same time. Tom and Elmer rode the area surrounding the ranch headquarters to get familiar with where the cattle would be grazing. A week later, Elmer rode out to find the nearest land office so that he might file a claim where he planned to build. He returned with three loads of lumber that he had bought. He hired a freight company to deliver the lumber. At the same time, he became friends with a Norwegian carpenter. Luther Eiklan had come west with his bride to find a homestead. His wife had died before they arrived at their destination. After the death of his wife, Luther had lost all interest in homesteading, so Elmer had encouraged him to come to the Teasdale Ranch to help build the first structure, a bunkhouse. When one building was finished, Elmer had plans for the next one.

It had been a good winter and the cattle had done well. On the twentieth day of March, Elmer headed south on the horse called Red. He took with him a pack horse, and he left for Tipton, Texas. He had thought about inviting George to ride along with him, but then George might want to ride back to the Sandhills with him when Elmer brought his bride.

It was a pleasant ride for Elmer. It gave him an opportunity to plan for the future. The winter had its fair share of snow, but it also had warm days when the snow would melt and the men could work on the construction. He was satisfied that about everything had been built except for the house. He wanted Elizabeth to have an input on its construction. He had forewarned the cook that he and Elizabeth would be living in the quarters of the cook shack until the house was built.

On Friday, the fourteenth day of April, Elmer

stopped at the Taggat Livery Stable. He was greeted by a young man. He said, "I would like to leave my two horses for a few days. Is Harvey Taggat here this afternoon?"

"No, he and Mrs.Taggat took the buggy and drove out to see his brother, Harold. Is there something that I can help you with?"

Elmer shook his head. "No, just give my horses a good measure of grain and a rub down. I will be staying at the Tipton House." He paused a moment, and then asked, "Has George Taggat ridden in today? I am supposed to meet him here tomorrow."

The young man shook his head. "No, I haven't seen him."

Elmer took what things he needed from the pack and left the stable. He went to the Tipton House and signed the register for a room and requested water for a bath. That evening, he had steak for supper. He remembered how nice it was to sit down to a meal surrounded by the fine things of life. The last meal he had here was with his mother and Lady Grace. He slept until eight and had a late breakfast. After a light noon meal, he dressed in his best clothes and boots and went to the Conrad house. He had not seen anything of George.

At one o'clock he knocked on the door. The door opened, and it was not who he wanted to see. There stood Turk! Or, at least he thought it was Turk. She didn't seem to be quite the same skinny, freckled face girl that he remembered. He stuttered, "I-I-Is Elizabeth here?"

She was shocked at the sight of this man that seemed to enjoy taunting her. She ran out of the room and Elmer could hear her calling, "Father, Father, he's here."

Jacob Conrad came to the door. He offered his hand, "Come in, Elmer, come in. Let us go into the study. Would you care for something to drink? Coffee perhaps?"

Elmer shook his head. "No Sir. I came to see Elizabeth. She, George Taggat and I were to meet this day and Elizabeth was to choose one of us to be her husband. I don't know where George is, but I am here, and I would like to ask for your daughter's hand in marriage."

Jacob Conrad's face turned red. "You see Elmer, this is rather awkward. I was unaware of this strange pact that the three of you might have had. Elizabeth never confided in us that she was going to make a choice on this date. Two months after you left, Elizabeth married Thomas Butler, an attorney from Meyers, Texas. That is where they are living at the present. I am terribly sorry. I know that you must have traveled a great number of miles, anticipating that she would be waiting for you."

"Tell me, Mr. Conrad, is she happy?"

"Yes, I would say that she is happy."

"That is good," said Elmer. "Married people should be happy. I will leave now, and my apologies for interrupting your day." He stood up and shook Mr. Conrad's hand and left the house.

He walked down the street, not knowing where he was going. He was aghast at what he had just experienced. Before he came to the end of the block, his thoughts were interrupted by this voice from behind a tree. "Hey Brit, are you serious about getting married?"

"Yes, I am. I rode over one thousand miles the last twenty-five days, expecting that Elizabeth would make a choice between George Taggat and me."

"Don't feel bad. It could have been worse."

"What do you mean, it could have been worse?"

"Well, she could have been here, and said yes!" She laughed, "Now you can marry me. I would make you a better wife than she would."

"But, I don't even know your name. I couldn't go

through life, calling you Turk."

"If I told you my name, does that mean you would marry me?"

"You surely can't be serious. This has been a huge let down to hear that Elizabeth has married. Not only that, but you think it is funny and you are laughing at my misfortune."

"See, wouldn't I make a great companion. In times of adversity, I could bring cheer into your life."

Elmer replied, "I don't know if that would happen. You still haven't told me your name."

She blushed, "It is Viola."

He took her hand. "Hmm," he said. "That is a beautiful name. It is much better than Turk. Turk would be fine for a dog, but never for a beautiful girl like you. Are you old enough to be married? I am not sure that your parents would consent to your marrying a cowboy like me." He paused, "Viola. I like that name. If I recall, it is a dainty flower. It befits you quite well." Still holding her hand, he said, "Viola, with your permission, I will call on your parents this evening to ask for your hand in marriage. If it is not to be, I will know their decision when I look upon your face. I will respect their decision. Good bye, Viola."

She said, "Wait, Brit. I am almost seventeen, but I have not sparked any interest in the young men of Tipton. I have overheard my parents talking, and there fear is that I will be an old maid. They still see me as the spindly legged, gawky girl of the early teens. I assure you, they will be glad to see me marry a handsome fellow like you. At least, they will have beautiful grandchildren." She laughed and stood on her tiptoes. She kissed him on the cheek. "Seven o'clock is a good time. Good bye, Brit."

CHAPTER 21
WEDDED BLISS

Elmer walked back to the center of town. He stopped at the barber shop to get a shave and his hair cut. There was a young lad that put a shine on his boots. He had some time to kill, so he walked the short distance to the Taggat residence. He knocked on the door and Alma opened the screen door. "My goodness, look who is here! I can't believe it. What are you doing in Tipton? Are you here to stay?" She started setting out cups and saucers. "Here, let me fix you a cup of tea, or have you taking a liking to coffee?"

"Tea will be fine. No, there is nothing to my moving back to Texas. I am here to meet with a gentleman, so thought that I would stop in to see my favorite people here in Tipton. What do you hear from George? I haven't seen him since we made it to the Sandhills of Nebraska. I expected to see him here. The last time I saw him, he indicated that he might be down here the middle of April. We had a good winter, and things were looking good for this spring. I stopped at the livery stable yesterday and the young man said that you went out to Harold's. How is he doing?"

"He is doing fine. He was happy with the selling of his steers in Dodge City. We laughed when he told us about you stopping the trail drive for afternoon tea. He did say that apparently his steers enjoyed the break in the afternoon since they put on weight during the drive. Here is your tea, just like before." He took a sip of the tea and gave a nod of approval.

He was taking another sip when Alma said, "Speaking of George, did you know that he was married? He married the daughter of the couple that runs the trading post." Elmer choked on the tea, and it took a bit of coughing before he could say anything. She asked, "Did you happen to see her? He did say that was where the cattle were sorted and you moved on to the east. It was nice that he could help you after his Uncle Harold left you at Dodge City."

Elmer nodded and said, "Yes, I did see John Madden's daughter. She was a beautiful young lady with dark hair and eyes. I am surprised that George didn't come back to Tipton to marry Elizabeth Conrad. I thought he was rather smitten over her beauty."

"He was, but when he saw John Madden's daughter, he was bent on marrying the girl closer to home. Speaking of marrying, when are you going to make the plunge?"

"I don't know, but when I find the right lady, I will probably marry. I should be going. I will probably see Harvey before I go back to the Sandhills. Say, does Harvey still have that mule he got from the Tennessee boy that went with us? Tell him I need a good pack animal, and I imagine Gomer would be glad to be reacquainted with his animal friend. I will see you later. Bye." He left, pondering what he heard about George getting married. Evidently, George didn't know that Elizabeth had married the attorney, or he would have sent Carter to let me know. It would have saved me a long trip. But then, I would have missed seeing Viola. On his walk back to the Tipton House, he stopped under the burr oak tree nearby. He started to quietly pray, "Lord, you have led me in so many ways during my life. Is this your leading, or am I running ahead of you and not seeking your council? Give me a sign Lord, give me a sign. Amen."

Elmer stopped at the desk of the hotel for his key. The clerk handed him a note. He opened it and he read, 'Mr. Conrad and I wish to extend an invitation to you to sup with us at our evening meal at six p.m. this evening.'

It was signed by Mrs. Jacob Conrad. Elmer saw that his petition for a sign had been granted by this note.

Elmer was prompt, arriving at the fine home at six o'clock. He knocked on the door, and Mrs. Conrad answered the door. "Good evening, Mr. Teasdale. Welcome to our home. Let me take your hat, and follow me into the dining room. We are ready to eat. Hattie has prepared our supper this evening, and she will be serving us."

Elmer cringed. That is not a good sign. Lord, does this mean that Viola cannot cook? Has she been coddled by a live-in cook and servant?

Mr. Conrad was seated at the head of the table and Mrs. Conrad at the foot. Elmer was seated across from Viola. She gave him a weak smile after he had been seated. Mr. Conrad said, "I will ask the blessing on the food." He began to pray and Elmer peeked across at Viola. With her head bowed, she peered up at him and gave him a quizzical look. Her eyebrows were raised and she gave a slight shrug. *So much for knowing their decision by the look on her face.* Elmer didn't remember when Mr. Conrad ceased praying, but he was brought back to reality when he was handed the meat platter.

Mrs. Conrad and Viola said very little during the meal, but Elmer and Jacob Conrad kept the conversation going while Elmer related the events of the trail drive. After dessert, they were having a final cup of coffee or tea. Elmer was unsure how he was going to steer the conversation to matters of matrimony. He looked across at Viola. She saw the beads of perspiration on his brow. She thought, *oh dear, Brit is on the verge of fleeing! I must act now or I never will marry.* She spoke up. "Father, Mr. Teasdale has something to ask you."

Jacob turned to Elmer. "What is it?" Elmer was silent. After a short pause he said, "Come, come my good man, it can't be that bad."

Elmer looked across at Viola. She gave him a
meaningful look. He cleared his throat and said, "Mr. and
Mrs. Conrad, I have come to ask for your daughter's hand
in marriage. I find she is a most pleasant young lady and I
desire to take her as my wife." The pounding of his heart
indicated to him that he could start breathing again. He
looked across at Viola. She nodded her head and gave him
a smile of approval. He didn't see the smile, but he did see
her blue eyes, beaming with joy.

Mrs. Conrad got up and went to Viola and hugged
her. Mrs. Conrad said, "But Jacob, our daughter is so
young. Do you think she should marry just yet?" Viola
did not see it, but Elmer saw her nod of approval to her
husband and the little smile on her face.

Jacob turned to his daughter. "Viola, is this your
desire, or is it a passing fancy of yours? How well do you
know this man? I have done business with him and find him
quite capable, but do you love him? I fear that you hardly
know him, or am I wrong about your knowing him?"

"Father, Mr. Teasdale and I have encountered one
another a number of times since his coming to Tipton.
I have assured him that I will make him happy. If he is
happy, he will do right by me."

"Very well. If that is your desire, then your mother
and I will agree to this marriage."

"Thank you, Father and Mother for giving your
blessing on this marriage." She went around the table and
hugged Elmer. She whispered in his ear, "See, that wasn't
so difficult to do. I love you Elmer Teasdale."

So the die had been cast, and a flurry of activities
was to take place in the next week. Elmer wanted to leave
Tipton in seven days. They had a long trip ahead of them
and he needed to be back at the ranch in time for the first

branding.

The next morning, Elmer had breakfast at the Conrad residence. He wanted to take Viola to Johnnie, the boot maker. She needed to be fitted before she began her wedding plans. This would give Johnnie time to work on the boots. After the measuring for the boots he took her back to her home. He needed to visit with Harvey to buy a horse for Viola.

He walked by the Taggat home, and Alma was weeding in the flower garden. She waved to him and invited him in for tea. After he sat down, she said, "Elmer, now that you are getting married to Viola Conrad, why don't you move into your old room until your return to the Sandhills? That way we can visit with you."

"Whoa, Alma. That was fast. I only asked her last night at supper. How did you learn of it so soon? I took her to Johnnie's to get her fitted for boots this morning. I thought he had a little smirk on his face, like he knew our secret."

Alma laughed. "You have a lot to learn about Viola Conrad. I would say that she is the town favorite. Evidently she let you get back to the Tipton House before she made her declaration."

He grinned. "I am almost afraid to ask. What was her declaration?"

Alma giggled. "Viola stood out by the front gate and yelled, 'Hear ye, hear ye, citizens of Tipton. This is Viola Conrad and I am getting married one week from today to Elmer Teasdale. You are invited to the wedding at the First Baptist Church at two o'clock in the afternoon.' Yippee!"

Elmer shook his head, "I am not surprised, I am not surprised. What did you mean about her being the town favorite?"

275

"Ever since Elizabeth was born, Mrs. Conrad has doted on Elizabeth. Viola grew up living in the shadow of her sister and everyone in town was aware of it. Viola roamed the town almost as soon as she could run. She was a friend to everyone. Keep in mind, Elmer, you got the pick of the litter when you chose Viola." He nodded.

Elmer got up from the table. He said, "I guess I will go get my things and accept your offer of the room. Then I will go see Harvey."

After checking out of the Tipton House, Elmer went to the livery stable. He took his horse for a ride to keep him in shape for the return home. Afterwards, he bought the mule that Gomer had owned and a horse for Viola to ride. He bought a saddle and another pack rigging. After they had finished dickering with one another, Harvey got real serious. He said, "Elmer, I am going to ask you some tough questions. You may not want to answer them, but I expect you to be forthright with me. I need to know what George is up to now that he has reached his destination. My brother Harold told me a few things, but he didn't go all the way into Nebraska."

"Harvey, let it go. I have no interest in telling you what went on between George and me. We have each gone our own way and it is over."

"It is certainly over for Spike Gurney. You were there when he got killed. What happened?"

"Harvey, it all started before we even left Tipton. George and I were each sweet on Elizabeth Conrad. We, including Elizabeth had agreed that we would meet the middle of April to decide which one she would choose. From that time forward there was a barrier between us. After I decided that I was not returning to England with my mother, I tried to hire on with George, but he refused. Even after I had my own herd, there was tension between the two herds. Harold wanted to leave ahead of George, but I put a stop to that notion. I figured if George came up with the idea first we would wait three days before we left. All the way north, Harold thought we were falling behind. I had to take him on a scouting trip to where he could see George's herd. Likewise, George feared that we were going to catch him, or bypass him. Carter had to take him to show him where we were." Elmer stopped.

"Go on, go on. I know that there is more. You haven't said anything about Spike Gurney," insisted Harvey.

Elmer nodded. "We veered off toward Dodge City so that Harold could sell his steers. I was disappointed that he was anxious to return home, but I could understand. We settled up with the crew, as we each agreed to stand half of the expenses. Some of the men wanted to return home. I bought the chuck wagon and the horses that belonged to Harold. Now that our herd was smaller, we made better time. Earlier, we never did push the herd hard because I wanted the steers to be fleshy when we arrived at Dodge City. I was scouting ahead when I saw George's herd cross the Republican River. For some reason, I was not looking forward to crossing that river. We had encountered rain about every day. I saw with my binoculars his herd crossing, and I sensed that it was difficult. The chuck wagon hadn't got very far into the stream when the current tipped it over, and Spike went over the side. The team thrashed around in the water. One horse was tangled up and went under, pulling his teammate with him. The cowboys went downstream, searching for Spike, but they never found him."

Harvey shook his head, "That is what I needed to know about Spike. He was a close friend of mine. I begged him to go with George. I knew that George needed help to make it a success. I am glad George is married. Is she a good woman?"

"Yes, I would say that she is. George made a wise decision in settling where he did. If it will make you feel any better about his decision, that was my first choice. However, I am happy where I am." Elmer was content to drop the conversation concerning his and George's relationship.

Elmer spent his days preparing for the return trip. He had the horses shod, and he bought what supplies that they might need. He had also purchased a small tent. He reminded Viola there was a limit to how much the mule might be able to carry.

The day of the wedding, Elmer moved back into the Tipton House. He had the same room that he occupied earlier. He told Viola that he had reserved the honeymoon suite. She was pleased. She did not want to sleep under the same roof as her parents on her wedding night.

The day of the wedding was a typical spring day. The flowers were in bloom and the birds were singing. A large crowd had come to the First Baptist Church to see Viola married to Elmer. He didn't realize how beautiful she was until he saw her walking down the aisle with her father. Her strawberry blond hair glistened. She still had just a touch of freckles across the bridge of her nose, but they were not noticeable because of the smile on her face. Her blue eyes sparkled when she looked at Elmer. He reached out and took her hand.

The reception was held on the front lawn of the Conrad residence. They were visiting with some of the guests, and Viola said, "Oh, look Brit! A butterfly lit on your head. Oh my, it has flown away."

He laughed and replied, "It has come back and is now on your head. It is Mother! She has come to give her blessing on our marriage."

"What do you mean, your mother?"

"She would tell me when I was little, that when we were separated from one another, if a butterfly lit on your head that the other person has come to visit you."

"That is interesting. I will have to remember that."

"On our way home, I will have to tell you the whole story. She first told it to Lady Grace when mother was her nanny. It actually involves a big toad and a beautiful caterpillar. I have been amazed at the number of times that a butterfly has lit on my head."

She hugged his arm, "Brit, you are funny. I think that life with you will be fun. I love you, Brit Teasdale." She stopped and then looked up at him. "Do you mind me calling you Brit? It just seems so natural, but I will change if you want."

"It is fine with me, but I prefer to call you Viola."

"That is fine with me. Oh, Brit, I do want to make you happy!"

"You say that you want to make me happy, and you have this day by being my bride." He paused for a moment, and with a smile on his face, he said to his bride, "There is an old Irish proverb that says if a man wants to be happy for a day, he should get drunk. If he wants to be happy for three days, he should marry. But, if he wants to be happy for a season, he should plant a garden."

"You have some funny ideas. I said that I do want to make you happy, and I will. But I trust that I will make you happy for more than three days. The garden will only make the man happy as long as it is growing, but I want to make you happy as long as the both of us shall live." He squeezed her hand and gave her a smile.

Suddenly she said, "I know what I will do. I will revise that old Irish proverb. My version will be, 'if a man wants to be happy for a day, he should get drunk. If he wants to be happy for three days, he should plant a garden. But, if he wants to be happy for a season, he should marry.' Since it is April, spring shall be the first season in which I shall make you happy. When summer begins, I will start over making you happy. The same will happen with fall and winter. Each season I will make you happy!"

Elmer teased her and asked, "Does that mean after you have gone through the seasons you will see that you no longer need to make me happy?"

"Absolutely not! Just as a garden is planted each spring, I will renew my efforts to make you happy each season of each year, year after year." She stood on her tip toes and kissed his cheek.

They remained at the Conrad home until dusk. He whispered to Viola, "We should return to our room at the Tipton House. Tell your mother that we will eat breakfast there, but then we will come here for the noon meal. After that, we will set out for the Sandhills. A half day travel the first day will be a plenty for you." She nodded to him.

Later they walked to the Tipton House, holding hands while Viola chattered most of the way. After he carried her over the threshold of their room, she kissed his cheek and said, "Brit, if I could have a few moments alone, I will get ready for bed. Then you can come in."

He blushed. He nodded his head and stepped out. He walked outside and went to the park across the street. After a time, he looked up and saw Viola at the window. She waved to him. He returned to the room and she said, "Good heavens, Brit! I was afraid that you might have run out on me."

"Don't worry. I kept my eye on the street, in case you tried to return home." He started to undress, when he said, "You don't need to watch me so closely." He was now down to his long underwear. He started to crawl into bed.

Viola was up in the middle of the bed on her hands and knees, her flannel nightgown covering her. "But, I do. I knew this would happen. I have heard how cowboys go to bed with their long underwear on, after having worn it all day long. I determined that would not happen in my bed." This was not going like Elmer expected it would. He started to unbutton his underwear. She continued, "I sensed this would happen. I have made you a cotton nightshirt." She reached over and pulled a white garment from his pillow. She tossed it to him. "Here, this is for you. It will be much better than your underwear." She was now sitting in the middle of the bed. Elmer took the nightshirt and held it to the front of his body. He said nothing, but thought, this is neither the time nor the place to do battle over what I wear to bed tonight. There may not be a better place, but there is a better time. This too shall pass. He removed his underwear and slipped the nightshirt over his head. He blew out the lamp and crawled into bed.

CHAPTER 22
THE TRIP HOME

Elmer awakened the next morning and looked over to his bride. She stretched, yawned and gave him a big smile. "Tell me, Brit. You have been married almost a day. Are you happy?"

He gave her a kiss and said, "Yes, Viola, I am happy."

Suddenly she rose up on one elbow and exclaimed, "Brit, what have you done with your nightshirt?"

He rose up on one elbow as well and looked at her. "It must have been about midnight when I woke up. That thing was twisted around my body and I thought it was trying to choke me. You have too many covers for me to wear that thing. I was hot and needing air, so I tossed it toward that chair by the dresser. You can give it to your father, but I am not wearing it. You don't want me wearing my underwear to bed, so that doesn't leave me much choice. I guess that is one problem solved until you come up with a better solution. The next problem is which side of the bed are you going to sleep on? You started on the right side, but ended up on the left side."

She sat up in bed and looked around. "I remember waking up and thinking that the pillow was awful hard. I gave it a toss and found a softer pillow. I slept better until you awakened me by staring at me."

"That is why I ended up with a soft pillow." Elmer chuckled, "You rolled up your nightgown and used it for a pillow." She looked down and saw that she had been sleeping on her wadded up nightgown. She grabbed the covers and wrapped them around her and stepped behind the screen. He tossed her nightgown over the screen and said, "Maybe you want to leave your flannel nightgown with your mother. Then we will start off even."

She stuck her head around the screen, "Brit, will I have to endure this kind of humor all the way to the Sandhills?"

He started getting dressed and said, "Yes, and it might even get worse."

"Promise me, Brit. Don't say anything about this to my mother."

"Be assured, nobody is going to hear about our first night together. Now I am wondering how things will go when we are sleeping under the stars." That is when she hit him in the back of the head with the hard pillow.

They went downstairs for breakfast. Because it was late, they had the dining room to themselves. Midway through the breakfast, Viola got the giggles. Elmer asked, "What is so funny?"

Between giggles, she said, "It was the nightshirt. You were like a little boy, uncertain if you should run and hide, or begin to cry. I saw that you did not like it, but was not going to make a scene." She giggled some more before she continued. "Tell me Brit, did you really wait until midnight before you took it off?" She stifled one more giggle before she was able to compose herself.

He nodded his head. "I did not want to disappoint you, but when that thing began to strangle me and shut off my air, I panicked and got out of it. I tried Viola, I really tried."

She reached across the table and patted his hand. "I know Brit, I know. I love you for it."

Right after breakfast, Elmer went for the horses and the mule. He carefully packed each critter. He had forewarned Viola that she would not be riding sidesaddle as most women did at that time. He had purchased a youth saddle from Harley, and she had tried it two days earlier, so all of the adjustments had been made. It was a warm afternoon when they bid their goodbyes to Viola's parents and left Tipton, Texas.

Elmer sensed that Viola was tiring, though she did not complain, so they made camp in the early evening. He saw that she would be a good travel companion. They established a routine that they would carry forth the rest of the trip. After watering the animals, Elmer hobbled each one and let them begin foraging. He had brought some grain, but was saving that for when the grass was scarcer. The small tent was set up, but when Viola saw the stars coming out, she wanted to sleep outside. Elmer said, "That is fine. I enjoy watching the stars at night, but each night we will set up the tent, in the event of a rain storm coming through. That is not a good time to be erecting a tent." From time to time he saw that she would grimace while moving about the camp. He asked, "Are you stiff and sore?"

She nodded, "I didn't want to complain. It is a matter of getting used to the riding."

"That is why I made this first day a short day. When you are ready for bed, I have some liniment that I will rub on you to relieve the soreness. Where is it sore?"

She laughed, "It would be easier for me to tell you where I am not sore. My ears and nose are not sore, but I think everything else is; some sorer than others. My buttocks, legs and the small of my back and shoulders are the worst. If you don't mind, I think that I am ready for bed."

"Go ahead and get ready for bed. I will join you after I have put out the rope." He got his rope from his saddle and encircled the area.

She asked, "What is that for?"

"I don't want to alarm you, but that will keep out

the snakes and spiders that come along. They don't like to cross over that manila rope." He sat in the middle of the bedroll and began to take off his boots. Viola took her nightgown and disappeared behind a tree. "Viola, where are you going? I admire that you are a modest woman. But out here, there is no need of being so modest around me. When I start rubbing the liniment on you, I will be seeing about every part of your body but your ears, and they will be covered by your nightgown after you have pulled it up over your head."

She tiptoed back to the bedroll. After she dropped all of her clothes, she stood looking into the sky and raised her arms upward. She breathed in the night air and sighed. "Ah, this is what Eve must have experienced the first night that she spent in the Garden of Eden. I love it!"

Elmer laughed and shook his head. "I'm thinking that it is a good thing I got you out of Tipton. I believe that you could be a modern day Lady Godiva of Coventry, England. Did you know that she was married to an Englishman?"

She lay down on the blanket face down and said, "Yes, I know all about Lady Godiva. Now will you start massaging me?" After he had finished massaging her with the liniment, he took her in his arms. She laid her head on his chest and they looked up at the stars. It was now dark and the moon was coming up over the horizon. She said, "Brit, thank you for the massage. I feel much better now." She watched the stars for a few minutes, and then he was aware that she was fast asleep."

At first light, Elmer was awake. He looked out at the horses, and saw that the mule was gone. He awakened Viola. "The mule is gone. I need to go look for her. Gertie may have broken loose from her hobbles." He saddled Red and was gone in a matter of minutes. Thirty minutes later, he was back with the mule. Viola was up and had started breakfast.

She asked, "What happened?"

"Oh, some mules are smart enough to hobble along and get away from the camp. She had gone about a mile away. Tonight, I will put her on a picket line. I see you have started breakfast. I will be right with you." He came back by the campfire, but Viola said very little to him. He ate his breakfast, and was drinking the last of his coffee, when he asked, "Is something wrong? You are unusually quiet this morning."

She rushed to him and put her arms around his waist. "I am sorry, Brit, but I fear that I have failed you. Last night I went to sleep in your arms and I did not make you happy. Just when I promised that I would make you happy every day."

He hugged her and said, "Vi, there are many ways to make me happy. You made me happy when you felt comfortable enough to be in my arms. I knew that you were exhausted after the first day of travel. You make me happy by just being you. You are an excellent travel companion. You are helpful, and you make me laugh. I love you."

"Brit," she exclaimed. "You called me, Vi! That is the first time! I like it! Viola is much too formal, but you may call me that when you introduce me as your wife."

They had traveled a couple hours, and Elmer asked, "How are the sore muscles this morning?"

She said, "They feel good. I was amazed at how good the massage felt. What is the name of the liniment that you used?"

"It really doesn't have a name, like a trade name. It is just liniment."

"If I was to go to a general store, what would I ask for to get that particular liniment? It did smell a bit strong, but it worked well for me."

He reached back into his saddle bag. He pulled out a flat metal tin and handed it to her. He blushed when he said, "Well, if you really need to know, you would ask for this."

She looked at it and stopped her horse. She turned to him and said, "This is Call's Horse Liniment. You mean to tell me that you used horse liniment on me?"

He nodded. "That is all that I had, and you were hurting. It did make you feel better, didn't it?"

She nodded and kicked her horse into a gallop, leaving Elmer with a smile on his face.

Elmer was glad that each day they were getting closer to home. Viola was an excellent companion. She never complained and she managed to keep the conversation going with her questions and witty remarks. Each evening before going to bed, she greeted the stars with her gesture to the sky.

After ten days on the trail they stopped in a small grove of trees for the night. Elmer remarked, "Vi, I think it would be well to prepare for rain tonight. The weather seems a bit eerie. I will dig a trench to carry any rainwater away from the tent. I think tonight will be a test to see how good our tent is about repelling the rain."

"Oh Brit, can't we start out under the stars? There is something so romantic about sleeping in the open."

"Vi, you have to trust my instinct on this one. I sense that when it hits, it will hit with a fury." He said nothing more about the matter, but went about the task of preparation. VI didn't contest his decision any further.

The storm struck about midnight with heavy rain, thunder and lightning. It didn't last long. It was a fast moving storm that left the air fresh and cool. Elmer was up at first light and went out to check on the animals and their supplies. He came back, and Viola knew that something was not right. "Brit, what is it? Did the horses run away in the storm?"

He shook his head. "No, they were hobbled. Red was hit by lightning, so we are down to one horse and two pack animals."

She went to him, "Oh, Brit. He was your favorite horse." Tears came to her eyes. "I wish now that I hadn't hit him with the clod of dirt on the street of Tipton. Can we both ride Bunny?"

"Bunny wouldn't carry both of us. I wanted you to have a smaller horse because she is easier to get off and on. Red would have handled the both of us, but not Bunny."

She asked, "Can we take the pack horse to ride the rest of the way, or at least until we can buy another horse?"

He shook his head, "No, that would mean we would have to dump some of our supplies or equipment. We need everything that we are packing. I will have to walk until we come to where we can buy a horse. We haven't met anyone since we left Tipton and we are still a week away from Dodge City."

"You mean, we will have to walk until we buy a horse. We are in this together, Brit." She gave him a hug. "I will start breakfast. Now I know why you brought some wood into our tent. At least we will start off with a good breakfast."

They sat on their blankets to eat their breakfast. Viola said, "Brit, I have been reluctant to pray for the food, but may I pray this morning?"

He nodded, and said, "Sure Vi, anytime you want to pray, that is fine with me."

She began, "Father, I thank you for our safety during the storm. We are sorry to have lost Red, because he was a good horse. I trust you Lord, to find a better horse for Brit. I saw how you brought us together, and gave me a husband to cherish. Thank you for the food this day. Amen."

"That was good, VI. Real good."

Elmer added his saddle to the load that Gertie was packing.

They took turns walking for about an hour each time. Elmer made sure that he started walking first in the morning, and took the last walk of the day.

Late afternoon of the third day, they were surprised by a small band of Indians that came out of a grove of trees and surrounded them. Elmer was walking and Viola was riding Bunny. Elmer had started walking about fifteen minutes earlier. Elmer recognized the one leading the band was Gray Horse. He was riding a sorrel stallion. The horse was not the average Indian pony. Except for the coloring, the horse was almost a duplication of George Taggat's horse, Dragon. He had probably been stolen from a ranch and been traded a number times before Gray Horse had acquired him. Fear gripped his heart when he did not see Chief Two Feathers with the band. Elmer whispered, "Vi, I know these Indians. Don't say anything. I will do the talking."

Gray Horse said, "Hey Cowboy! Where is your horse? Where is your cows? White man walks and woman rides." He laughed and the rest of the Indians joined in.

"Two moons ago, fire come out of sky and kill horse. I buy horse from you. I have money. Woman is lazy. I take her back to her Mama and Papa. She can't cook and she won't walk, so she ride and I walk."

"White man money no good. I trade horse for your woman. I don't care if she is lazy. I like color of her hair. I trade one horse for one woman. What is her name?"

"Good. I will take horse that you are riding. I like color of his hair." He turned to Viola. "Get off of horse. Her name is Viola."

She kicked out at Elmer and shouted, "No, you can't do this!"

He grabbed her and jerked her off of Bunny. "Silence, Woman! What is name of horse that you trade for woman?"

"No, no. No trade horse for woman."

"What is name of horse? Horse has name. What is his name?"

"His name is War Bonnet, but no trade."

"Where is Chief Two Feathers? I trade with him. He is chief. You are not chief. Where is Chief Two Feathers? He gave me name of Chief Nine Fingers. Chief trade with Chief."

Gray Horse said something to one of the braves. He turned his horse and rode back to the trees. Viola was still on the ground where she had fallen when Elmer jerked her off of her horse. She looked up at him, uncertain of what was taking place. When their eyes met, he gave her a slight twitch of his eye. He shouted to her, "Woman, don't look at me, you lazy wench." She looked down, frightened at his demeanor. Elmer looked to the trees and saw Chief Two Feathers approaching the group. He got off his horse to welcome Elmer. He said, "Welcome my friend, Chief Nine Fingers. Red Fox told me your red horse is dead." They went off away from the rest of the braves.

Elmer nodded, "Yes, horses come, horses go. Gray Horse wants to trade War Bonnet for my woman. Woman is lazy and bad cook. I take her back to her people." He didn't say anything more.

Chief Two Feathers said, "We have many cattle now. Sometimes we find stray cattle from trail herd. When they come to our herd, we brand right away with 'tepee brand.' That is good brand. Our young boys ride herd on cattle day and night. That was a good gift from my friend Chief Nine Fingers. You like horse called War Bonnet?" Elmer nodded. "Then horse is yours."

"What will Gray Horse say? Will he want my woman?"

"Horse is gift to my friend. Not a trade. Gray Eagle has three wives. All lazy. He not need any more lazy wives." They returned to the rest of the men. Chief Two Feathers stripped the gear from the back of War Bonnet. He handed the reins of the hackamore to Elmer. "May the gods be with you, my friend." He got on his horse and returned to the grove of trees. Gray Horse took his gear and got on behind another brave, not looking back at VI or Elmer. Elmer led War Bonnet to where VI was holding Bunny and the two pack animals.

"That went well," remarked Elmer. He pulled the saddle off of the pack that was on Gertie. He saddled War Bonnet and pulled himself into the saddle. He looked down at his wife. "VI, are you ready to continue our journey?"

"I want to go home."

"So do I, so get on Bunny and we will be on our way. We are well mounted and we have some time to make up."

"No, I want to go home to Texas. You were going to trade me to that Indian, just to get a horse that you liked. You made no effort to protect me." Elmer laughed. That infuriated her all the more. "You degraded me in front of all of those men. You jerked me off of Bunny and said that I was lazy. Not only that, but you called me a wench."

"Vi, I am sorry if I have disappointed you, but what I did here today was to protect you. A year ago I had befriended that tribe when I gave them twelve heifers, a bull and four steers. They were starving and I had made a friend of Chief Two Feathers. Gray Horse was not a friend, and he could have easily killed me and taken you as his wife today. I had cornered him into thinking that I would trade you for a horse. Not any horse, but probably the best horse he had ever seen or ridden. I was counting on my friendship with Chief Two Feathers to get us out of that jam. I did not remind him about the cattle that I had given them. They were a gift and required no retribution, just as the horse was a gift to me. He asked for nothing in return. Vi, when I saw War Bonnet, I remembered your prayers of three days ago. You asked God to get me a horse, one better than Red. I was confident that God was about to honor your request. This horse will be the very foundation of our horse herd. He will sire colts that will be worth a lot of money." Elmer straightened up in his saddle. He continued, "However, if you want to return to Tipton, that is your prerogative, but I am on my way to the Sandhills. I want you to go with me, but I will not force you to accompany me. You are married now and a mature woman. You can continue with me, or we can divide up the supplies and you take your choice of a pack animal. Then you can return to Texas, but we need to make a decision right now. What will it be?"

She grabbed his leg and said, "I'm sorry Brit for doubting you. I'm sorry. Please forgive me." Elmer bent down and kissed her. She gathered her reins and got on Bunny, ready to go to the Sandhills.

They rode in silence for about an hour. Elmer remarked, "Vi, you haven't said one word since we saddled up. This is not like you, and I sense that you are still miffed at me. Tell me, have you ever played chess, or know anything about chess?" She remained silent but shook her head. "Well, the bantering back and forth with Gray Horse was much like chess. In a chess match, each player has one piece that they must protect. It is the king, the most vulnerable of all the pieces. All of the other pieces are expendable in the process of protecting the king. In essence, you were my king, and War Bonnet was his king. He would have given me any number of horses, or perhaps the choice of any of his three wives just to have you. I ignored him and began to hammer away at his horse and his horse's name. To me, your feelings and honor was temporal and expendable if I could protect you. He feared that I was out to get his horse and he panicked. He forgot about wanting you, and abandoned all reasoning in order to protect War Bonnet. That is when I was able to bring Chief Two Feathers into the negotiations. You see, I offered to buy a horse, any horse, but no, in his greed, he wanted to take the one possession that I deemed most highly. You were the one that I deemed most highly, even above my own life. In the end he lost his most prized possession, War Bonnet. That is how a game of chess is played."

"Brit, do you think that you could teach me how to play chess? I believe I would do well in that game."

"I am sure you would, seeing how you so easily ensnared me in the game of matrimony."

They made their way to Dodge City. They spent one night there and bought a few supplies, namely Call's Horse Liniment. Vi had the luxury of a bath and sleeping in a bed. They left early the next morning. The Republican River was their next obstacle and Elmer was not looking forward to the crossing. Vi's horse, Bunny had not traveled well. She had lost considerable weight, despite feeding her extra grain. He was uncertain if she would survive the river crossing. Now he was wishing that he had traded for a better horse in Dodge City, but Vi had begged him to not trade her.

They arrived at the river in the evening. With his binoculars, Elmer looked for the raft which they had used to cross the river late last summer, but did not see it. He sensed that it might have been cut adrift or else, someone had used it to cross from the other side. While Vi was preparing the evening meal, he rode War Bonnet along the bank downstream. He found the raft tied to a tree.

The next morning he said, "Vi, I am going to cross the river with Gertie to see how difficult the crossing will be. I will leave her there and come back for the raft. You will ride Oscar and I will tie Bunny down on the raft. We will put the packs on the raft. Are you up to riding Oscar in the water?" She nodded her head, but he saw the fear in her eyes.

She asked, "Is this where Spike Gurney lost his life? I knew him quite well. He was a friendly man."

She needed some assurance. "Yes he was, but the Taggat crew rushed the crossing. There was no need of him dying. I rode the raft with the chuck wagon on it last year. I will instruct you all the way. I know that you will do well. I will cross now."

When Elmer returned, he said, "The river is down from what it was last year. The horses can wade a good distance before they have to swim. If for any reason you end up in the water, grab the tail of the horse. He will swim for the shore. We will each have a rope tied to the raft and the horses will drift along with the raft. Are you ready?" She nodded and gave him a weak grin.

He tied Bunny's feet and was able to lay her down on the raft. Vi gave a sharp sob when Bunny fell on her side. They loaded the packs on the raft. The horses pulled the raft into deeper water. They were able to ease the raft downriver, at the same time tugging it to the opposite shore. Vi commented, "Brit, that was easier than I anticipated."

"Most things are. Often times, we expect the worst. If we take our time and plan ahead, we can avoid many a pitfalls. We have the Platte River to cross, but there is a toll bridge, so we won't worry about a wet crossing. Let's get Bunny on her feet and the packs reset. In two days I plan crossing the Platte River.

Late afternoon of the second day they came to the toll bridge. Ahead of them was a small, gray-haired black man with a burro, waiting to cross. Elmer motioned to him to go an ahead. He shook his head and said, "I don't have the money for the toll. I see that you have your pack animals. If you will pay my toll, I will cook your supper tonight."

Elmer asked, "Where are you headed?"

He responded, "I am going to the Black Hills to pan for gold."

"Mister, I will pay your toll, but you will need money to live in the Black Hills before you even see any gold dust."

He smiled with a toothless grin, "Maybe you will stake me for a share of my claim?"

Elmer laughed, "You promised to cook our supper. Let me see how good of a cook you are before I stake you. We can camp on the other side of the river. Let's go. I am hungry. Incidentally, my name is Elmer Teasdale, and this is my wife, Viola."

The old man tipped his hat and replied, "I am Rufus Rains." He pointed to his burro. "His name is Bubba."

They crossed the bridge, the old man leading his burro. They found a spot and Elmer began unpacking Oscar and Gertie. Vi was looking after Bunny. Rufus said, "Your horse is ill, very ill."

Vi nodded and Elmer said, "I don't know what ails her, but she has been unhealthy most of the trip." Elmer nodded to Vi, and she started to gather wood for a fire.

"I can make her well, but you cannot ride her

tomorrow. Do you want me to make her well?"

Elmer nodded, "Do what you need to Rufus, if you can make her well."

Rufus said, "You show me what you want to eat and I will fix supper. Then we will doctor horse."

Rufus cooked supper and later Vi whispered, "Brit, he is a good cook. You said that Gomer doesn't like to cook, so maybe Rufus is the answer to your solution." Elmer nodded.

Vi said, "I will take care of the clean up if you two fellows want to doctor the horse."

"We make another pot of coffee for the horse, but strong, really, really strong. I think that she has eaten a poisonous weed, so I will purge her." Vi saw that he put an unusual amount of coffee grounds in the pot. He boiled the coffee longer than normal, and then he added something from a bottle that he had removed from his pack. After a time, he set the coffee to cool and went to his pack and removed a long necked bottle. He said, "Elmer, saddle your horse and you can snub her head to the saddle horn and we will drench her. This will get most of the liquid in her stomach. We can tie her away from the camp, but it is better for her not to be hobbled." He grinned. "Later, she will have stomach pains and there will be much squealing and stomping of feet, even much of tomorrow. That is why you cannot ride her tomorrow. Then I am going to turn in and I will cook breakfast in the morning."

Vi did not sleep well. She heard Bunny squealing and stamping her feet most of the night.

The next morning, Rufus had breakfast for them. Vi had scoured the coffee pot and gave it a thorough scrubbing the night before. She didn't want any residue of what had been given to Bunny.

After breakfast, Elmer was taking care of the

horses, preparing to be on the trail. He said, "Rufus, I won't stake you in your quest for gold, but I will offer you a job as our ranch cook. You will sleep warm this winter, and you won't have to worry about where your next meal is coming from. You can bring your burro with you. I will pay you twenty dollars a month, which is five dollars more than the cowboys get. I'll see that someone else chops your firewood. What do you say?"

"Tell me where it is and I will be there as soon as I can."

"I'll draw you a map. Take what food you will need for the trip and we will see you there. We have to go out of our way, but we will be looking for you."

Elmer and Vi left, both riding on War Bonnet. Bunny was still squealing and stomping, but much improved.

CHAPTER 23
FRIENDSHIP RENEWED

Elmer and Vi rode double. Vi kept up a continual running conversation all day. She enjoyed the opportunity of hugging her husband and talking in his ear. Tomorrow, Bunny will be able to accept the burden of a rider. It was amazing the recovery that Bunny had made.

Towards evening, they stopped at the Madden trading post. Elmer told Vi, "I am not sure how well we will be received. George was bitter toward me, why I am not sure. His mother had asked that I deliver the two parcels she gave me. We can give them to his wife, and be on our way. We will set up camp a few miles downriver and be home tomorrow evening."

Elmer retrieved the packages from the pack rigging and they entered the trading post. The lamps had been lit and it provided a pleasant atmosphere. He saw the young lady that he presumed to be George's wife. He went to her. "Excuse me, but are you Mrs. Taggat?"

"Yes I am. And you?"

"I am Elmer Teasdale, and this is my wife, Viola. We have come from Tipton, Texas and on our way home. I am a friend of George's parents, and Mrs. Taggat asked if I would deliver these packages to you." He handed her the packages. "We will be leaving now. Tell George hi for me."

He turned to leave, and she said, "Mr. Teasdale, George speaks so highly of you, he would be unhappy if I let you leave without seeing him. It is getting late, so why don't the two of you stay for supper. In fact, I am working on supper now. I help out in my father's trading post, so we have quarters here." Elmer turned to Vi for some response. She nodded her head.

"That would be gracious of you. We have ridden

double all day because we had a sick horse, so it was somewhat of a strain. I will go out and check my animals."

Viola said, "Mrs. Taggat, what can I do to help you with supper?"

"Come back with me and you can help while we visit. My name is Sand Blossom, but everyone calls me Sandi. I am puzzled. George told me that Elmer was going to Texas to marry a girl named Elizabeth. In fact George told me that if I didn't marry him, he was going to marry Elizabeth in the spring. Now we are to have our first child this fall. Oh, I am sorry. Maybe I should not have said anything about Elizabeth."

Viola laughed. "That is all right. Elizabeth is my sister, and she married soon after George and Elmer left with their trail herds. I am happy and my husband is happy."

Elmer was checking on Bunny when George came by. He looked surprised to see Elmer. He stuck out his hand and exclaimed, "Well, I declare. Elmer Teasdale, how are you?" He shook Elmer's hand and gave him a hug. "What are you doing up here? Let me run inside. I will tell Sandi to put on an extra plate, and then we can visit."

"She has already invited us to supper. I came out to check on my animals. We are on our way home, so we will go a ways before making camp."

"When you say 'we,' do you mean that you are married?" Elmer nodded. "Did you go all the way to Tipton and marry that Conrad girl?" Once again, Elmer nodded. George continued, "I hope that she wasn't too disappointed when I didn't show up to marry her."

"Oh no. She is plum happy with me. Your mother sent some things with us, and we stopped by to deliver them."

"Elmer, let me put your animals up for the night.

You can stay with us. There are some things that I need to discuss with you. Then you can leave in the morning. That will give me time to trade you out of that sorrel stallion that you have there. At first I thought it was that horse you called Red, but this is a lot more horse. Where did you get him?"

"That is a long story. Help me get my horses settled for the night and then we can visit."

When the men entered the trading post living quarters, George was astonished. "I was expecting Elizabeth. Is that really you, Viola?"

She said, "Yes, Here I am. Who did you expect?"

"I asked Elmer if he married that Conrad girl, but I wasn't expecting you. It is amazing what can happen in a year. What happened to Elizabeth?"

"She married an attorney from Meyers, Texas two months after you and Elmer left with your trail herds. Elmer didn't want to return to Nebraska empty handed, so this is what he got. I am happy, and I trust that he is happy."

Elmer spoke up, "I am more than happy. I fear that Elizabeth would not have been a good travel companion. I sense that she could be somewhat of a whiner." Vi laughed at Elmer's remarks.

After supper, George and Sandi opened their gifts from his parents. Alma had put together an album of the family history of the Taggat family and included what few photographs she had available. This was the gift to Sandi. George received a new pair of boots. Elmer remarked, "If I had known those were in the pack, I could have worn them when we were doing so much walking."

The next morning, George was helping Elmer fit the packs on the two pack animals. He said, "Elmer, I must apology for the way that I have treated you. I was wrong in not having you throw the two herds together when we left Tipton. I was jealous of the attention that Elizabeth was giving you. Carter and I had words with one another over the way I have treated you. He said that I would have probably lost the herd and may have died without your help. In the next stall is a horse to replace the pack horse that you provided for me that was lost in the river. She is a young mare to have a colt from my stallion, Dragon. What more do I owe you for the supplies and the use of your chuck wagon that you shared with me after ours was lost?"

Elmer shook his head, "George, the mare is sufficient. I did that because we are neighbors, even if we are thirty miles apart. You and your family were gracious to me when I arrived in Tipton, and I appreciated it." He paused before he continued. "I did want to ask you about combining our crews to work our cattle in the spring branding. I know that even though we each have our own range, some of the cattle drift away. I still have the chuck wagon, and I have hired a new cook. I figure that in a week to ten days we could cover the whole territory and move the strays back to where they belong."

"That sounds good to me. How about a week from today we start working your range and then finish up here with my cattle? If you furnish the chuck wagon and the cook, I will provide the supplies." They shook hands. Viola came out of the trading post and she and Elmer left for the last day of their trip home.

When they arrived at the ranch, Gomer Stumpf came out of the cook shack. He saw his mule Gertie. Gomer was excited as a kid at Christmas.

The next day, Rufus Rains came to the Dismal River and hollered for help in crossing the river. Elmer took a horse down to the river for him to ride across, so that his burro, Buddy could make the crossing. They went to the cook shack where he introduced Rufus to Gomer. He said, "Gomer, I don't want to disappoint you, but I have hired Rufus to do the cooking for the crew. Show him to a bunk in the bunkhouse. Viola and I will be using the cook quarters in the cook shack until we get a house built."

"Mr. Teasdale, I will be glad to show him around. Praise the Lord, I have cooked my last meal."

That night, the men entered the cook shack and were pleased with the aroma of the food that had been prepared. Elmer introduced Viola to the men. He said, "This is my wife, Mrs. Teasdale. You may remember her as Viola Conrad if you spent much time in Tipton. Also, we have a new cook. Come out here Rufus, and meet the crew. This is Rufus Rains. Mrs. Teasdale and I will be living in the cook quarters until our house is built. Therefore, until such time that happens, Rufus will be bunking with you in the bunk house."

Cleve Tucker jumped to his feet. "Mr. Teasdale, I will not sleep in the same room with a black man."

Elmer looked at him. "I understand your position on this, so I will offer you three options. The first is that you can draw your pay. Or, you can swallow your pride and sleep in the same room as Rufus. The last is that you can take your gear and sleep in the barn. The decision is yours." Elmer waited for his response. As an afterthought, Elmer added, "Your first priority, if you decide to stay, is to see that there is ample wood for Rufus to cook with. Keep in mind that good wood for fuel means there will be good food." After supper that night, Cleve gathered his gear and moved to the barn.

CHAPTER 24
THE FINAL CHAPTER

Katie turned to the next page of the worn black journal. She was expecting to read a continuation of the saga of the life of Elmer and Viola Teasdale. She was disappointed, because she had made an effort not to read the journal in its entirety, but bits and pieces as if she was living the entries day by day. It began: To Whom It May Concern

Today is Octobre 13, 1930, my seventy-ninth birthday. If Vi was to see this, she would criticize my spelling of the month, but I remember that is how I spelled it when I made my first entry in this journal. I apology for not keeping up with the activities of the Teasdale Ranch. Once I married Vi, life was at such a fast pace, I didn't take time to write. I remember on our wedding night, I quoted an Irish proverb that if a man wanted to be happy for a day to get drunk, to be happy for three days to get married, but to be happy for a season was to plant a garden. She insisted that by marrying her, she would make me happy for a season, year after year. She has done that and more. We have been married almost fifty years. She thinks that we should make it to sixty years, as if fifty wasn't enough. However, I sense my remaining days are numbered, and they are few. Therefore, I will write these thoughts, close the journal and put it into its hiding place for you to find. Do with it as you see fit. I have no interest in going over the details of my life with another person. What has happened, has happened.

Early in my life, I learned that things come upon a person that you have to deal with, even though you are unprepared. Three days after Vi and I returned from Texas, Gomer Stumpf drowned in the Dismal River. We were miles from anyone else, so we buried him away from the buildings. Luther Eiklan had made a casket, and the men built an enclosure, large enough to accommodate future burials. Little did we realize that the next year, we would bury our stillborn son, Timothy Conrad Teasdale. He was the second burial in the cemetery.

It was ten more years before we had a second child, a girl we called Claire Beth. We loved her dearly, but I saw in Claire what I would have had for a wife if I had married Elizabeth. Claire was not drawn to the ranch as her mother, Viola. Claire did not possess the frontier spirit. Her Grandmother Conrad had encouraged her to go east for her education and in her pursuit of a husband. She was successful in both. She is married to Charles Beaumont and they live in Boston. They have no children, so the continuity of the Teasdale Ranch is in question. I imagine that perhaps one day, the Taggats will begin to migrate to Summit County. Won't that be something if a Taggat was to have this ranch!

It is strange that of the two early settlers, George Taggat and myself, George fathered a number of sons, and they in turn fathered sons; many more sons than daughters. I often wondered where they got wives for all of those Taggat men. I sensed that in some instances, they may have married their cousins.

It was different for Vi and me. Our family consisted of those loyal workers that stayed with us, year after year. Some left when they became too old to work, going to their relatives in the last years of their life. But, some remained to live out their lives right here on the ranch. Each one of those men was as important to us, as if they were family, so let me tell you about them. I have already commented about Gomer.

Two brothers of Bohemian descent homesteaded a

mile south of our ranch. Each year they would help us with our haying during the summer. The younger of the two, Krog Brochak was cleaning his revolver and accidentally shot himself in the stomach. The doctor from Summit City came and attended him, but because of the severity of the stomach wound, he could do nothing for him. He left some laudanum to ease the pain. The older brother, Karl rode one of his farm horses to Madden to have the Catholic priest come to their dugout to conduct the last rites for his brother. When they arrived, they saw that he had shot himself, ending his suffering. Karl began to make plans to have him buried in the cemetery in Madden. The priest refused, stating that because Krog had killed himself, he would not permit him to be buried in the church cemetery. Karl came to me, and we buried Krog in the ranch cemetery. That day, I promised Karl that we would save a spot next to Krog for his burial. Twenty years later, Karl was laid to rest next to Krog. We had made arrangements that I was to purchase his homestead at the time of his death. I sent the money to his sister that lived south of Lincoln.

Luther Eiklan had the most dramatic impact on the Teasdale ranch. He died two years ago. Luther was a craftsman. He could build most anything. He supervised the construction of all the buildings and corrals on the ranch. He made his own casket and had it in his workshop three years before his death.

Probably the most interesting men that are buried here, are Cleve Tucker and Rufus Rains. Cleve had refused to sleep in the same room with Rufus, because he was black. I let Cleve sleep in the barn, but I appointed him the responsibility of keeping the wood box full to heat the bunk house and the cook shack. It didn't bother Rufus if Cleve didn't want to sleep in the same room with him. However, whenever Cleve would fill the wood box at the cook shack,

Rufus always had a piece of pie or some cookies for him. The first cold spell that winter, Cleve moved back to the bunk house. His bunk was next to the bunk that Rufus occupied. Rufus died first and Cleve told me at his funeral that I could bury him next to Rufus.

The last person I will write about was Del Tanner. Except for Luther, he had the most impact on the Teasdale Ranch of any other employee. It was eighteen years after we had established the ranch. It was early spring that Del came riding in at dusk. He was riding a grey gelding, and he had been ridden hard; too hard in fact. The ranch foreman, Tom Catcher offered him a bunk for the night and Rufus fixed him a meal of leftovers. The next morning, Tom saw that the grey horse had some age on him and needed to rest up. Del had a way about him that you couldn't help but like. We needed some help until after the cattle were branded, so Tom offered him a job. He worked about a week, and Tom was happy at how well he was working out. Del had taken a liking to a black horse we called Raven. The day after we had finished branding, Del did not show up for breakfast. He had not slept in his bunk and his gear was gone. His grey horse was still in the corral, but Raven was gone. Tom asked what I wanted to do about catching him. It had rained in the night, so there was no telling which way he might have gone. Evidently, he had traded the grey for Raven. He had also borrowed money from most of the ranch hands, so they were out too. I gave Tom what money that Del had earned and told him to divide it among the men that lost money.

Two days later, John Taggat, George Taggat's seventeen year old son rode in. He told me that his dad had recognized Del at the trading post the night before last. He remembered him from the roundup. Del had told him he was on his way back to the Teasdale Ranch. The next morning they were short one of their best horses. Del had left a black horse carrying the Teasdale brand. The horse had been ridden hard and was lame. George had sent his son to find out if Del was here. I told John about Raven being taken. He said that his dad wanted to track him down and wanted me to ride along with him. I responded that I was sorry, but I didn't have time to track him down, and I had no idea where he might have gone. John informed me that his dad said that he was going with or without me, but nobody was going to get away stealing a horse from him.

Two months later, George Taggat rode in, leading Raven with a body drooped over the saddle. He tossed the rope to me and said, "Elmer, since you didn't have the guts to run down and hang a horse thief, then you can bury him. I caught up with him in Wyoming, in a town called Rawlins. I brought him back to Madden and hanged him this morning in front of the trading post. Let this be a lesson to you and the people of Madden that nobody steals a horse from George Taggat."

I replied, "I am sorry that you felt it necessary to take a man's life for the theft of a horse. Especially since the horse was retrieved. I have often wondered when that archaic tradition of hanging a horse thief began. I thought that by now, a man could be brought to justice in a more humane way. I will see that Del receives a proper burial. Did he indicate before his death that he had anyone that could be contacted regarding his demise?"

George replied. "I didn't look for anything on his person, and I didn't ask him. If you want to, go ahead and go through his pockets. Also, I no longer care to take part in further roundups with you or your men." He spit on the ground.

The last words that I had for him were, "I am sorry that your bitterness has brought you to this decision. I have good memories of you and your family. I still think that it would be best for you to have a representative at our roundup, and I will do likewise." I reached up to shake his hand. "Goodbye George." He refused my hand, and turned his horse to leave. It grieved me deeply that twenty years of friendship could be dissolved so quickly. That is the last that I have seen of George to this day. I sense that George may have harbored some form of jealousy that was fostered when I first arrived in Tipton.

That evening, we buried Del Tanner. I found an address in his shirt pocket. The next day I wrote to his mother. I told her that I did not know her son for very long, but I saw that he was a man that knew a good horse when he saw it.

At the bottom of the last page, Elmer had signed it, *Timothy Conan Moran.* He had written, *Summit County in the State of Nebraska.* It was dated, *Octobre 13, 1930.*

Katie turned the next page and the next. The remaining pages in the journal were blank.

310

CHAPTER 25
MUSINGS BY THE AUTHOR

Katie was stunned by the abruptness of the closing entries in the journal. She was compelled to go to the Dismal River and the stump that provided her comfort and inspiration.

She began to write. As the author of the book entitled, *The Ghosts of the Teasdale Cemetery*; I have been privileged to read the journal of Timothy Conan Moran, aka Elmer Ray Teasdale. The past ten years I have taken from this journal what I considered to be the personal diary of the first thirty years of Conan's life. What was most amazing through the years of writing, I learned that he was the nephew of my great, great grandmother, Tully Farley O'Brien. It gave greater impetus for me to complete *The Ghosts of the Teasdale Cemetery*. I will include this journal along with the cemetery journal of those that have been buried on the ranch. I have made notes and references of those that have been buried since those noted in Conan's journal. The one person that remains a mystery is Ty's natural father, Tylor George Taggat. Perhaps at a later date I can get ancestral information from the *Sisters of St. Elisabeth*. This was the orphanage where he was when Hiram and Metta Taggat adopted him.

She watched the water of the Dismal River flow by. Katie began to ponder what she had learned about Conan Moran from his journal. *Not only his journey through life, but it has given me an insight into the character and integrity of a young man that endured so much at the hands of others that oppressed him. Had I not entitled this book, The Ghosts of the Teasdale Cemetery when I first read from the journal, I would have probably named it, Longsuffering at the Dismal River. I remember Galatians 5:22 and 23—*

311

But the fruit of the Spirit is love, joy, peace, longsuffering, gentleness, goodness, faith, meekness and temperance. Katie stood and looked at the large cottonwood trees that lined the river. She began to pray. "Dear God, as I stand among these trees along the Dismal River that has provided shade for me and a nesting place for the birds that sing to me, I am reminded of Psalms, chapter one, verse three. The blessed man that it speaks of is so reminiscent of Elmer Teasdale. *"And he shall be like a tree planted by the rivers of water, that bringeth forth his fruit in his season; his leaf also shall not wither; and whatsoever he doeth shall prosper."* She stopped for a moment to subdue a sob. "Father, may I show forth in my life the patience and fortitude as exhibited in Elmer's life. Amen."

Make a change here
Add a letter there
With one last look
We close the book
The pages are bound
For Katie has found
The Ghosts of the Dismal River

CHAPTER 26
IRELAND; THE LAND OF 100 COLORS OF GREEN

Katie was ecstatic! She hugged and kissed each
of the children, giving each child a word of caution and
last minute instructions. Kylee was in tears at the thought
of being without her parents for a whole month. Ty
encouraged her. "Kylee, your mother and I will have a lot
to tell you, and tons of pictures to show you when we return
next month. I am counting on you to help Mrs. Winslow.
There are the household chores as well as the looking after
the chickens and gathering the eggs. Marty will have his
hands full with seeing that the cows are milked. When
you see that the milk jug needs replenishing, remind him
that he is the one that drinks most of the milk. Take some
pictures of his football games. We plan on calling you once
a week."

Katie was holding Marie's hands. "Marie, we are
leaving Mrs. Winslow to keep the household running, but I
am counting on you to be the adult among the children. You
amaze me with your maturity. But, I also count on you to
keep those impetuous moments to a minimum. You know
what I mean, don't you?" Marie smiled and nodded her
head. Katie continued, "I want this to be a special time for
your father. We will visit where Grandma Laura grew up in
Maine. We have heard so much about the fall colors in New
England, so we will view them. And then, there is Niagara
Falls. I will spend a few days in The Big Apple with my
agent and the book publisher. It is hard for me to visualize
that my book, 'The Ghosts of the Teasdale Cemetery' will
actually be in print. I want to go to Ireland to the village
near New Bridges where my great, great grandmother Tully
Farley lived. If we have time we will retrace the journey
of Meagan Farley and view the Bellingham Estate near

Loxnard and then go to London to fly home. I love you, Marie."

"Mama," she asked, "will you go to Connecticut and see where we lived with Mother before she died?"

"No, we weren't planning to on this trip. Your home there doesn't hold any memories for your father or me. Perhaps someday there will be the opportunity for you to go to Connecticut, and even Marty could go with you. Then too, there is Marilee to visit in Washington, D.C. She would be an excellent guide to see the history of the nation's capital."

Ty wanted to talk with Marty while the two of them were carrying the luggage to the car. Marty was shy. He scraped the dirt at his feet with his boot when Ty hugged his son. He said, "Son, keep an eye out for anything unusual that goes on here. You will be seventeen in a couple months, and already I see the making of a top hand. We will be back in time for deer season, so check out their trails. It will be an opportunity for us to go bow hunting. Take care."

Marty shook his head. "Dad, I'm sorry, but I don't want to go bow hunting." Once again, the boy ducked his head and scraped the side of his boot in the sand. He looked up. "Dad, I want to get started in the purebred cattle business." He gave a sigh of relief. He had broken out of his timidity and was now able to express to his father that which he had been carrying for days. He waited for his father's response.

Ty said, "Go on. I sense that you have more to say."

"You know Mary Little Crow, don't you?"

Ty nodded, "Yes, she is the Native American lady in the sheriff's office."

"Well, really, she is only part Native American. Her father is Lakota, but her mother is Swedish. I became acquainted with her, and she tells me that her family has a ranch on the Bad River in South Dakota."

Ty interrupted, "Whoa, Son. How well have you become acquainted with her? You aren't quite seventeen, and she is all of twenty-five. I admit she is a mighty pretty gal, but you still have some growing up to do."

Marty blushed, and was having difficulty explaining to his father. "No, no, it is nothing like that. It is just cow talk. She stopped me one day for a broken tail light on my truck. I was coming home from football practice and we got to visiting. She said that her dad hasn't had much rain this summer and wanted to sell half of his cow herd. I checked on the breeding background of his cattle and it is pretty solid. He has last year's calf crop. I thought that if we bought the half of the cows that have bull calves at the side, and the bulls that are a year old, we would have a good start in the purebred Angus cattle business. What do you think, Dad?" Marty looked at his dad for any feedback.

"Is there more to this plan?" asked Ty. "You would be adding another one hundred and fifty head to our cattle inventory. That is a lot of cattle and a lot of money."

"I know it is," responded Marty. "I thought that we could buy the cows by the pound, plus so much per head for the pedigree. If we culled fifty head of our older cows, they would probably weigh enough more to pay for the purebred cows. As to the yearling bulls, we could feed them this winter and sell them in the spring for breeding bulls. We would still have fifty of the bull calves to sell the following year as breeding stock."

The father said, "Sounds good to me. Do you want to go ahead and get things rolling?"

"But Dad, you are getting ready to leave on your vacation. It can wait until you get back. You can think about it before we do anything."

Ty shook his son's hand. "Marty, I will be gone for a month. You have put a lot of thought into this. If it is as dry as you said it is, you need to act while the iron is hot. Those cows might be gone to market when I come back. We have plenty of grass, and we can sort off our cull cows when I return. I will stop at the bank when we go through town and tell Todd Holliday to set up a line of credit for you to work from. Just remember, no more than the number of cattle we talked about. Good thinking, Marty, that was good thinking." Shaking his son's hand, he said, "Son, you got the makings of a cattleman. See you in thirty days."

Katie was driving when they left the ranch on the fifteenth day of September. Ty and Katie had an agreement that she would drive so that he could look at the scenery. He would do most of the driving in heavy traffic. This worked fine until they reached the tourist information facility at the entrance to Indiana. Ty had been driving, and pulled in front of the stone structure. He turned to Katie, "Let's stop here and get some information on how to get to Turnersville. We need to stretch a bit and use the restroom."

Katie asked, "Why Turnersville?"

By the tone of her voice, he was perplexed at her attitude. "I thought that you might want to see where you lived while there. Your mother's parents are undoubtedly buried there." Katie made no effort to get out of the car. He opened the door and turned in the seat. Looking at her, he asked, "Are you coming in?"

She shook her head. "No, I have no interest in Turnersville. I have no pleasant memories of the town. Ty, sometimes it is not a good idea to sort through ones roots. Oftentimes there is nothing but skeletons that are unearthed. I appreciate your thinking of me, but I have no intention of going to Turnersville. I will go use the restroom, but I will not look at a map, or ask any questions to determine how near we are to the town." She opened the door and went inside. Ten minutes later they were pulling back on the interstate with Ty at the wheel.

Silence reigned as the miles ticked off one by one. Ty thought it best to not say anything, but he was perplexed. It was not like Katie to be so adamant. She reached across the span that had separated them. "Ty, I am sorry. It was rude of me to speak to you in such a manner. It was thoughtful of you to offer to go to Turnersville. By my refusal, I trust that this doesn't hinder our visit to White Oak, Maine. Your mother spoke so endearing of her mother, even though her mother lived for only ten years of Laura's life. I don't remember of her saying what her mother's name was. What was her name?"

Ty was relieved at the breaking of the silence. "Her name was Olivia."

"I like that name," said Katie. "Perhaps, our next daughter could be named Olivia."

Ty laughed. "Katie, are you trying to tell me something? Are we to have another child?"

Now it was Katie's turn to laugh. "No, I am not pregnant, but it is a thought. Kylee will be eleven in a few more months. Isn't it amazing that the twins have been in the home for almost eleven years? These have been good years. Ty, you have worked hard to accumulate what we have financially. It is good that we can take this time to together and relax a bit. I thought that I would never get you off that ranch!"

"Now that we have Duke Marco on board, maybe we can get away more often. Marty and I can work on the purebred aspect of the ranch and leave more of the feedlot management with Duke."

Katie was silent. Duke Marco was an enigma. He showed up at the ranch a month ago in the afternoon while she and Ty were having iced tea and cookies on the front lawn. He had been at the university when Ty was going there. He was one year ahead of Ty, but they had graduated together because Ty had finished in three years. She thought, *I had an uneasy feeling about him when I first met him. He was smooth, much too smooth. But I had not said anything to Ty. By nightfall, Ty had hired him in the number two spot of the 99 Ranch. He was divorced and had brought two teenagers to Summit City; a boy and a girl. Marty and Marie didn't say much about the newcomers, but Marie's raised eyebrows told the story. One of the men had confided in Ty two weeks later, that a woman had moved in. I don't trust him, and I don't have to like him, but I do need to pray for him.*

Katie remarked, "That was a mighty big responsibility you left in Marty's hands. How do you think he will do?"

"He will do fine. He will want to prove to me that he is capable of making decisions. Sometimes, I sense that he is a bit apprehensive, living in the shadow of his sister's exuberance for life."

"Exuberance, huh? That's a pretty big word for a Sandhills cowboy. Do you think that he is intimidated by Marie?"

"Yes, yes I do. I think you do too. I overheard you talking to her about being an adult and her impetuous decisions. Marty plans to ask Brodie to go with him and help with the driving. Brodie is older and that will work well. It will be interesting to see how Marty responds when he gets his first look at some thin cows. It has been a number of years since we have had a drought in the Sandhills. Marty will probably take his banjo and entertain Brodie while they go down the road. Maybe he can entertain the Crow family and come away with a good deal."

As an afterthought, Ty asked, "What did you mean about Marie's impetuous decisions? Am I missing something?"

"I am thinking that you are forgetting about some of the weird things she has done and also coerced her brother and sister into doing. Marty wasn't very old when she convinced him to dye his hair green for St. Patrick's Day. She used green Kool-Aid. I wasn't able to wash it out afterwards. His hair had to grow out to get rid of the color. That is when he started wearing his hair clipped short." Ty nodded and laughed.

Katie continued, "She convinced Kylee that the two of them would be vegans. I didn't think that it would last with them, so I let them experiment with it. After the first week, I came into the kitchen and discovered Marie had come from school and fixed a roast beef sandwich from the meat left over from dinner. She had two slices of cheese and a glass of milk. When I questioned her about what she was doing, she said that she was only a vegan at meal time. She was interested in how long Kylee would stay on the diet. When Kylee came in from gathering the eggs, she saw what Marie had done. She was so upset with her sister, that I wasn't sure if she was going to give her a present for her birthday. Of course, Kylee is so soft hearted that she forgave her sister after a short time."

"How about you Katie, did you do anything like that with your siblings?"

"No, by the time that my brothers came along, I was the adult. Even now, they look to me as the responsible one to go to in regard to family matters. When Derk died, so much of the getting a house and moving was placed on me. Mother was more of a leaner. Derk made all the decisions. So, when he died, Mother looked to me for guidance.

Fortunately, Nick is five years her junior. Maybe I won't have to make any decisions in that family for a while."

"I know that we try to talk things through before we make most decisions," said Ty. "I sensed that you weren't very happy with me when I quit the sheriff job to take over the feedlot at the time of the bankruptcy."

"I wasn't," replied Katie. "I was pregnant and only working part time. We had added two more mouths to feed. My biggest fear was the huge debt that you had incurred in buying all of the cattle in the feedlot. I thought, if the two sisters, Pauline and Daphne couldn't make a go of it, how could you make it work. You said their problem was greed. I was unsure if it was greed that spurred you on, or seeking satisfaction. I thought that you wanted to succeed where others had failed."

"You were probably right in your assessment. However, I had a plan. The sisters and Tub Turner did not. I had witnessed how a feedlot bankruptcy worked. Regarding Marty, he kind of blindsided me with his plan. We were ready to leave on this trip, and he presented it to me as I was putting my foot in the car. He was unsure if it had any merit, but he couldn't keep it to himself any longer. He knew that he had to share it with me, or wait a month for our return."

Ty paused while he changed lanes to pass a slow moving car. He resumed his conversation. "Marty had a plan and he was able to present it in a few sentences. You and I discussed it on the way to Summit City. We agreed that it was workable, so we were able to give the go ahead for Todd Holliday to make the funds available. Even now, I can scarcely wait to get back to see how it goes. Maybe I am too lenient with the kids and their 'exuberance,' but it is good for their development. Katie, do you realize that in all of my growing up, my father never permitted me to fulfill a plan!"

As if by divine nature, there was a sign denoting a Rest Area ahead. Ty signaled his exit and pulled the car into a parking spot. He turned off the ignition. Draping his arms on the steering wheel, he stared through the windshield, but said nothing. Finally he spoke, but there was a quiver to his voice. "Katie, don't ever let me be guilty of thwarting you or our children's ideas and goals. My father insisted that I be involved in sports when I really wanted music. I wanted to develop a herd of purebred Herefords. These I had to sell so that I might pursue my dream of a college education, which he tried to stifle. At the time of the drought, I had a plan to bring additional income to the ranch, but he vetoed it. Mama wanted me to have a pair of handmade boots to fit my feet, but he thought that I could get along with a cheaper pair off of the shelf while TJ would wear the better boots. TJ and I couldn't make a decision about cleaning the tank and putting oil in the windmill without infuriating him." Ty stopped to catch his breath.

"He was angry when he saw that it was TJ that fell off of the windmill instead of me. Had it been me, his life would have changed dramatically. As it was, had Jim McCann not stopped him, he would have killed me that day. Katie, for all he presumed to like you, no matter how much you loved me, he could not permit us to be happy." He reached across to his wife. "Oh, Katie, I love you more than life itself."

They continued to embrace. Wiping the tears from her eyes, she whispered, "Ty, let me do the driving. We will stop early tonight and dine well. There is something about a good cry that whets the appetite."

The next morning, while they ate breakfast, they began to plan the day. Ty set his fork beside his plate and looked across at Katie. She knew that it was going to be a serious conversation. "Katie, already I am having pangs of homesickness. May I make a suggestion for the balance of our itinerary?" He saw the fear in her eyes, so he quickly responded. "Be assured, I am not going to abandon you and return home. How would it be that when we leave here that we make Niagara Falls our next stop? Then we can take our time to view the fall foliage through New England with White Oak, Maine as our destination. Spend what time we need to satisfy our curiosity before we go to New York City. I am not sure how much time you need with your publisher before flying to Dublin. Spend some time in Ireland, but probably you want to spend more time at Loxnard, as that is where Meagan is probably buried. After seeing the sights of London, it will be back to New York City. Once we land in the USA, I will be ready to head for the Sandhills. I know that this is a bit reverse of what we had planned, but this way we will enjoy New England without being hurried." He picked up his fork and resumed eating his breakfast.

Holding her fork in her hand, she pointed it at him while she responded. "After yesterday's discourse on having your plans rejected by your father, how can I refute your plans for our itinerary. My first thought was that we were going to return to the Sandhills after breakfast. It is good that we have goals, but not be hurried. Ty, this is a special time. It is one of the few times that I have you all to myself. I plan to make the most of it. Who knows when something like this will happen again? I know that when we land at LaGuardia we will be going home. I miss the Sandhills as well."

And so they spent a leisurely week of touring New England. Katie's favorite time was the day they spent at Niagara Falls. She sensed that Ty, despite his fear of water, endured the day that she might be pleased with the scenic wonder. Ty found his joy in the covered bridges and the farmsteads nestled among the hills. Katie remarked, "The fall colors are beautiful, but some years, our Sandhills have colors as bright; just not as many."

To take in the nostalgia of the area, they sought the unique bed and breakfast accommodations for their lodging. White Oak, Maine gave them their first glimpse of the Atlantic Ocean. It was after dark when they found lodging on the sea shore. It was a restless night for Ty, with the pounding of the waves. It was a gray morning while they walked on the beach before breakfast. The clouds had moved in, and there was a slight bit of moisture in the air. There was a decided chill that brought shivers to them. They could see the fishing vessels going out from the harbor, bobbing in the waves and wind. Katie tugged on Ty's arm. She said, "Hey Cowboy, you are certainly quiet this morning. What are you thinking about?"

He smiled. "I probably shouldn't tell you, but I was thinking of Emilee."

Katie stopped and loosened her grip on his arm. "Why, Emilee?"

"After we left Summit City, we spent some time vacationing in California. I wanted some stability in our life, so we were traveling through Texas and Oklahoma. She knew that I was checking out the feedlots. Earlier, I had scoped the job market in Nebraska, and there was nothing open. Emilee suggested that we could go to New England. My grandfather had a fishing boat, so why couldn't I take up fishing. We had a good sum of money, so she thought that I could invest in a fishing boat. I was thinking this morning, that could be me, bobbing up and down out on the water. I would be sick for sure."

Katie shuddered, "Let's go back and have breakfast. Then we can look around town and visit the cemetery and maybe the school where your mother attended."

After breakfast, they went to the cemetery and found the headstones for his grandparents; Traynor and Olivia Martin. Ty remarked, "Olivia sounds good for a daughter, but if we have a son, are you sure you would want to call him Traynor?"

"Ty Taggat, you are beginning to sound serious about another child. Perhaps the boy could be named after my side of the family. How does Sam sound to you?"

Ty hugged her, "Sam sounds good to me. It is short and easy to spell. Did you know that my grandparents were lost at sea when a storm came up suddenly and capsized their boat? It always bothered me when a pastor would have a sermon about the resurrection of the dead, and the graves would be opened up. What about Grandpa and Grandma? What happens to them?" He stopped to ponder the question. "Mama showed me in the Bible, Revelation 20: 13."

Ty said, "Here next to my grandparents' tombstones are the graves of my great grandparents, Horace and Isabel Martin. Isn't it amazing that Mama ended up in the Sandhills. She often talked about the rocky soil here along the ocean. How she enjoyed running her fingers through the sandy soil in her garden and flowerbeds."

Katie remarked, "Since I have been working in the Teasdale cemetery, I appreciate the communities that make an endeavor to keep their burial grounds neat and clean." Taking Ty by the hand, she said, "Marie and I often pray over the graves at home after we have worked. I would like to pray for this family of yours, and now is mine." Ty nodded. She began, "Lord, we thank you for these ancestors of Ty, and our children. We thank you for the heritage that has been instilled in our lives. We rejoice until that time of the resurrection of the body. Amen."

Leaving the cemetery, Ty said, "If there is nothing more, shall we make our way to New York City?" Katie nodded. When they arrived at the gate, they turned for one last look at the headstones.

Ty was getting somewhat accustomed to the fast paced driving, but the toll roads brought laughter to him whenever they paid their toll. He said, "Each time, after we have paid our toll, it is like a herd of cattle going through a gate. The cars seem to fan out, each one trying to get ahead of the next one. That is until the next time when we are funneled through another toll gate."

Arriving in New York City, they found a hotel that was within walking distance of the publishing house. Ty walked around, sightseeing while Katie spent time with the publisher. He would visit the shops, looking for presents to take home to the children. He looked for something that would be a special gift for Katie. Each evening, Katie was physically spent from the sessions of changing and rewriting portions of her novel. Ty encouraged her to take in some of the nightlife of the city, but she would decline, saying that she was too tired. After two days, Katie said, "Ty, let's continue our journey. I can work on the cover for the book after we get home. I fear if we spend any more time here, you will be bored and go on without me. Perhaps, after our visit to Ireland and England, I will have a better insight of how the cover will look."

The next day they booked their flight to Dublin. They left in the early evening so they would be able to sleep during much of the flight. After they arrived in Dublin, Ty suggested to Katie that they find someone with an automobile to serve as a tour guide for them. Katie saw that it was a good suggestion. She sensed that Ty was a bit apprehensive about driving on the left hand side of the road. Also, it afforded both of them an opportunity to view the countryside.

After seeing the sights in Dublin, they made their way to New Bridges to see the area where Katie's ancestors, the Farleys had lived. The cottages with the thatched roofs were scattered among the neighborhoods. One evening, after they had dined, Katie said, "Isn't it amazing, because of my ancestors, I have developed an affinity for this nation. I love the Sandhills, but I could be at peace living here." She stopped a moment. "And yet, when I think of the number of people that died and had to leave their homes because of the famine, it brings sadness to my very being. I don't know, Ty, I just don't know."

Ty reached across the table and touched her hand. "I understand how you must feel. You are such a caring person. That is what has made you such a great mother and wife."

They crossed the Irish Sea on a ferry to Scotland. Ty had wanted to see the heather that grew on the mountainsides and lowlands of Scotland. One evening, he ordered roast leg of lamb, reminiscing of the night that he had dined with Emilee at the teacherage. It was just as he had remembered it.

In England, they toured London for a few days, but each of them was intent on going to Cotswold to the Bellingham Estate. Katie had corresponded with Lady Miriam Abbott and explained the purpose of her visit. They had lunch with Lord and Lady Abbott. Afterwards, they observed the portraits of the ancestors of the family. Katie was particularly taken by the portrait of Lord William Bellingham. She observed how rigid and stern he seemed to be. Lady Grace was just as she had imagined, as well as Meagan Moran. There was a sense of tranquility about each lady. Meagan had been buried in the family cemetery.

Katie and Ty thanked them for their hospitality.

Katie had promised to send them a copy of her book when it was available. After leaving the Bellingham Estate, they drove to Loxnard. It was a quaint little village, much like it might have been when Conan went to school and church. The church had withstood the years of time. When Ty and Katie walked in the church cemetery, Katie was reminded of the Teasdale cemetery.

The next day they drove to the Heathrow Airport in London and took the first available flight to New York. They arrived early in the morning, so after they had breakfast, Ty suggested, "Why don't each of us go our own way, and get completed what we need to accomplish before leaving tomorrow morning. I have one errand to take care of before we have lunch and get our hotel room. Katie, how much time do you need?"

"I will visit with my publisher. I had made an appointment to meet with her at 10:00 this morning. I had wanted to buy something for the kids, but instead, I have decided to take the girls on a shopping trip to Omaha during teacher's convention. We will have four days, and it will give them an opportunity to decide for themselves what they might want."

"What about Marty? I don't think he would want to go shopping with you, but he deserves something for staying at home."

"Why not take him to Madden to the boot shop? Now that Harley's nephew has taken over the boot making, you might see how good he is. A cowboy can always use a new pair of boots."

"Good idea. Maybe while he is there, I will have a pair made up for myself." He laughed, seeing the face that Katie made at him.

They returned home late in the afternoon on the last Monday in October. Before any of the children asked,

'What did you bring us?' Katie told them, "Girls, we had very little time to do much shopping, so I have planned a shopping spree. We will leave early Thursday morning for a total of four fun filled days in Omaha. We did buy a few things on our trip overseas, but those items are being shipped to us. Marty, Ty will take you to Madden for your first pair of handmade boots."

Ty asked, "Marty, when can I see those cows that you purchased?"

"Tomorrow afternoon I will get home early from school. We don't have football practice, as the next day is our night game. Dad, you won't believe how well they have done in the past three weeks."

"I will wait for you to show them to me. Then you can tell me how things went on your buying trip. Anything else that was great and exciting happen while we were gone?"

Marty nodded. "Dad, I don't know what happened, but Clayton Green left a week after you went on vacation. Two days later, Duke Marco brought in a feedlot foreman from western Kansas. His name is Billie Barr. That is about all that is new."

The next day, Ty and Marty rode through the cattle that Marty had purchased. Ty said, "Son, they look good. While the women are shopping, we will spend time sorting off fifty cows of our herd to make room for those cows you purchased. We should get those yearling bulls on a good feeding program for next spring sale. We also need to wean the bull calves that you purchased. I like the cattle that you bought." Ty noticed that Marty was pleased with his dad's comments.

Wednesday noon, Ty came to the house for dinner. He was quiet all through the time that he was eating. Katie asked, "What is it Ty? Except for asking the blessing on the food, you haven't said one word to me."

"Oh, Katie. I am sorry. I don't remember praying. I'm sorry."

"Is something bothering you?"

He got up from the table and took up his hat from the washing machine in the back porch. "No, no, but I need to sort through a number of things. I have saddled Tig and I will be taking a ride through the ranch. I will see you at supper time."

"Wait a minute, Cowboy. Don't I even get a kiss?" He came back and gave her a quick kiss. Katie reminded him. "Don't forget, we have a football game this evening. Marty would not be happy if you missed it."

"Yeah," was his response.

Katie had written a check for the telephone bill, so she picked it off the secretary in the hall. She looked in the mirror before going out the front door on her way to the mail box. She crossed the bridge and was sorting through the mail when a white pickup truck approached from the Good Hope Community Church. Her first thought was, *it is not a ranch truck. It is too clean, and it has a cover over the box.* She waited until it pulled alongside. The driver was careful not to create a cloud of dust. He stepped out and touched the brim of his white Stetson. "Excuse me ma'am, but is Tylor Taggat close by?"

"I'm sorry, but he left early to go riding. Is there any way that I can be of help?"

"I have come to ask permission to hunt deer on the ranch. I have hunted here the last two years with success, so thought that I would try my luck one more time."

With the wave of a hand, Katie responded, "That should be no problem. I will tell Ty that I gave you permission." She laughed, and added, "Just don't shoot any cows, or we both will be in big trouble. What is the name, so that I can tell Ty?"

"My apologies for not introducing myself." He reached out to shake her hand. "My name is Chase Adams. I have retired from the Stockgrowers Association, and I live in Lincoln."

Katie returned the handshake. "I am Mrs. Taggat. Good luck on the hunt."

"Thank you, and tell Tylor thanks as well. I will be hunting over on the east side of the ranch in case he wonders. That is where he pointed out for me to hunt the last time." He got back in his truck and backed it up to the intersection and took the county road to the east.

Katie watched as the truck crested the hill and was out of sight. What was there about Chase Adams that was so familiar? *I have seen him before, but I can't remember where. When I shook his hand, there was something about his eyes that I remember. The train! He was on the train when Laura and I went to California; also, when we returned. Those steel grey eyes never left Laura. Not that he stared at her, but she was always in his peripheral vision. He was at the hearing when Tylor was ordered to leave Summit County. The last time was at Laura's funeral.*

Katie laughed at herself. W*hy am I obsessed with that man? He said that he is retired, so he must be in his sixties. But, why was he dressed so neat, if he was going hunting? My first thoughts of the man was that he was a feed salesman or a cattle buyer; fancy boots and hat and definitely not wearing camouflage clothing.*

The afternoon was not going as Ty had planned. He had missed meeting with Duke Marco. He needed some answers as to why Clayton Green was no longer employed as the feedlot foreman. He looked up and saw that the turkey vultures were circling over where the breaks began. He turned Tig in that direction. He came over the hill and saw vultures feeding on a carcass in a swale of the terrain. He presumed that it was probably a wounded deer that had only made it that far. He rode over to the edge of the swale and the vultures took flight. The stench of the carcass would indicate that it had been dead for a couple days. He rode closer and saw that it was a horse. Tig was spooked at the sight of the dead horse. He snorted and shied away. Ty brought him under control. He dismounted and tied Tig to a tree. Ty mumbled to himself when he recognized it as being Bill. "That is one of the draft horses that we used in the hayfield. It looks like he had been tied to a tree and then shot. The hair has rubbed off when he struggled. The rope is gone. It was probably taken off after he was shot. Did someone kill him there to use as bait? But, for what? Maybe coyotes, but unlikely. Bear hunters would often kill a crow bait horse in the woods to draw bears, but we have no bears. Awe, the mystery of life. I have seen enough and smelled enough."

Ty walked back to the tree where he had tied Tig. He was thinking, *I need to get back to the house*. He reached in his shirt pocket and pulled out a jeweler's box. He opened it and glanced in at the ring with the four gems. In the center was an emerald. To the outer edge were two topaz gems and a garnet. The late afternoon sun glistened on the gems. *Tonight, when we get home from the football game, I will give Katie the ring, honoring her motherhood.* He began to slip it into his shirt pocket while he gathered the reins, preparing to mount Tig for the ride home.

At about the same time, Katie was eager to share with Ty the news from her literary agent. *Ty was so patient while I was meeting with the publisher and my agent. I have been so blessed by God, that he has given me a husband that is kind and gentle. I know that this has only been possible by the Spirit of God dwelling within Ty that has made this possible. He has suffered so much in his life, both physically and emotionally. When I reflect upon Galatians 5:22 and 23—But the fruit of the Spirit is love, joy, peace, longsuffering, gentleness, goodness, faith, temperance and meekness.* Katie tried to suppress a sob, while she wiped at her tears. *Ah, yes, the gentleness of the Holy Spirit.*

THE END

ABOUT THE AUTHOR

To the average reader, one would think that the writing of the book is the conclusion of the task. Once the manuscript has been edited and considered complete, the writer's task is finished. Not so; inside the back cover is a place to tell about the author. It started simply enough with the first book, but as each novel is written, the task becomes more difficult. Alas, there is only so much to be written about one person without writing what appears to be an autobiography. With that in mind, let me tell you what I would prefer to be doing at this early hour of the day.

The seventh book, and quite likely the last book in this series, is slowly bubbling along in my mind like a crock pot; awaiting the chef to turn up the heat. This book will be different, in that it is to be a mystery novel. The setting is the same; the 99 Ranch, the Teasdale Cemetery, the Dismal River and Summit City. All of this is neatly packaged in Summit County and the twelve hundred residents. Which one of these citizens has committed this vicious crime? This is the responsibility of the deputy sheriff, Mary Little Crow. She is a twenty five year old Native American from South Dakota. She made the initial investigation, but reveals very little to the community or the victim's family. With twenty percent of the novel written, Mary Little Crow has revealed very little to me, as the author. At this point, I am unsure of the identity of the perpetrator of this crime against a citizen of Summit City. Not only am I unsure of the perpetrator, but for what reason that person was chosen. The last time there was a murder in Summit County was 1906. This was over the dispute of the ownership of a horse. The plaintiff lost in a court battle, but prevailed in the street in front of the courthouse when he shot the defendant. He was tried and hanged two months later.

Let us turn up the heat and begin book seven of the Fruit of the Spirit series, Meekness at the Dismal River.